WHERE THE TRACKS GO

WHERE THE TRACKS GO

A PRINCIPAL'S STORY

MARK MIJUSKOVIC

WHERE THE TRACKS GO
A PRINCIPAL'S STORY

iUniverse books may be ordered through booksellers or by contacting:

iUniverse
1663 Liberty Drive
Bloomington, IN 47403
www.iuniverse.com
1-800-Authors (1-800-288-4677)

ISBN: 978-1-5320-0272-4 (sc)
ISBN: 978-1-5320-0273-1 (e)

Library of Congress Control Number: 2016914205

Print information available on the last page.

iUniverse rev. date: 10/13/2016

Cover Design by Mark Cole

Prologue

Roger Traynor was a fat black man who easily could be dismissed upon appearance, but his Harvard pedigree and his skills as an orator not only brought notice to him but also signaled to everyone that there was a new superintendent in Demming County. A fiftyish, baby-faced Buddha, Traynor rolled in with a plan and a corresponding metaphor.

"… And you can see that we need to market not only this plan but our schools and ourselves. This train theme we've got going throughout the PowerPoint presentation and the decor in this auditorium are fluff if they don't have substance. That substance must be created, molded, shaped, and configured in some way by each of you. And while your version may look and feel a little different, it goes back to the essence of needed change. This conversation is in its infancy, but we will have it again and again. So the cardboard train that is to my left beckons all aboard. It's clearly a play on my name, but more importantly, it's already moving, so you need to decide whether to get on or off. Some of you will wait for the next train, but keep in mind that I've got a three-year contract. Some of you will hop on board right away. Whether you're on board or back at the station, there will be casualties along the way. The ride will be bumpy for all of you, and some of you will derail. That's just the way it is with change."

That was three years ago, and on their drive back to school, Mark Mahovlic and Manny Hernandez were listening to a sports talk radio program but contemplating the message they had heard.

"Where do you think those tracks go, Marko?" Manny asked. They were stopped at a traffic light just a few feet behind some railroad tracks that stretched into the northern horizon. Mark didn't have an answer but began wondering the same thing. He had never seen a train on them, and he questioned their purpose.

"I don't know," he said as the light changed, and they moved forward.

"One day," Manny suggested, "we should get out and just walk those tracks to see where they end up."

As his assistant principal, right-hand man, and longtime friend, he had never seen Manny's contemplative and philosophical side. He rarely displayed worrisome emotions but opted to have a positive spin on everything, always quick to shake a hand and display a smile. Then again, this was before open season on principals and the big train that rolled into town carrying a bunch of new sheriffs, a bunch of new ideas, traveling light with the knowledge that there soon would be a bunch of new baggage for others to carry.

Growing whimsical, Mark fancied that several blocks in back of them, a bell was chiming in staccato, a red signal light was flashing, a long wooden railing was coming down, and a train was preparing to pass through. He humored himself in this manner, not unlike the character in some horror tale who attempts to find reason in the inexplicable.

He never liked mysteries or delving into the unknown, but like Manny, he had been unwittingly written into the script. He hated the sophomoric metaphor of a passing train, but because he didn't know where those tracks ended up, he couldn't get the question out of his head.

Chapter 1

RECYCLED LEADERSHIP

Dr. Alice Chandler-Lopez was almost as fond of her title as she was of the hyphen that protected her singularly unique disposition. Marriage and motherhood had not softened her as much as they'd engendered an imbalance within her. Her reputation was one where those serving under her never knew where they stood. The hyphen was a plank to be negotiated as it bridged the gap between an insufferable supervisor and somebody's wife and mother. On this day, it was the former who picked up the phone.

"So where does he get off?" she bellowed. "He's a first-year principal, and he can't even be somewhere on time to meet his direct supervisor on the first day of his job!" Her eyes opened wide, and her forehead twisted into a long exclamation point. Alice Chandler-Lopez was big on punctuation.

On the other end of the line, Dr. Pamela Gratton held the phone about six inches away from her ear. She had the title in front of her name but did not feel entitled. She too had a husband and a child but did not weld her identity into her profession and marriage. She exercised patience in all her interpersonal transactions, and with a voice of experience and humanity, she asked a simple question. "Did you ask him? Mark's not the type of person to do something like that. I'm sure there's a logical explanation."

Sometime after the doctors offered their respective opinions, Mark's phone rang while he was on the way home. It was Pam Gratton, the newly appointed associate superintendent at the district, who brought him on board to work under her in Area 6 and then several days later was promoted, leaving him in her wake to bob at the whim of his new supervisor, Alice Chandler-Lopez.

"Mark, I just got done speaking with Alice. You need to be careful around her. She says you missed a meeting with her this morning. What happened?"

"Dr. Gratton," Mark started, "I am at a loss here. I didn't miss a meeting with her. I arrived at the school an hour ahead of our appointment time, and Heffernan took me for a drive to show me the surrounding community and just talk about the school."

"So what time did you get back?" she asked.

"We were on our way back, and Hef's phone rang. It was his—I mean my—secretary calling to say that Dr. Chandler was there and wanted to know where I was. My appointment was for 8:30. It was 8:20, and we were less than two minutes from the school. Rather than wait, she left and, from what you're telling me, was upset."

"Mark, just be careful around her. She's a very difficult person. Listen—I felt you had the right to know. The last thing I want to do with this is spoil your weekend. I know you would never do anything to be rude to anyone."

This was Mark Mahovlic's welcome aboard the train. It took three years to get there, and now stopped at a traffic light, he stared out the car window, dumbfounded, feeling like taking the initiative was a form of robbery to which he had to plead guilty.

After his disheartening phone call, he arrived home to see twenty or thirty cars parked in the vicinity. His wife, Sylvia, greeted him at the door with a shot and a beer, and behind her a large group of people awaited the cue. She popped the top of the can, and everyone yelled, "Surprise!" To Mark they were all familiar and comfortable faces to help him celebrate his promotion. Manny Hernandez was there, and it made him think of the railroad tracks. Within the context of his day, this surprise was a pleasant one. He downed his shot and made a conscious effort to not flinch.

At the beginning of each school year and monthly throughout the year, principals attend their respective area meetings. The longest part of the agenda occurs when the directors clear their respective plates of things that the principals must accomplish. To usher in the first Monday of the new school year, Dr. Mitch Warner, a body double for the Michelin Man, disclosed new construction projects and their future impact on school boundaries. Dr. Alice Chandler-Lopez twisted her angry face and reminded everyone of timely teacher observations and the need to single out at least two people to put on prescription, a kind term referring to the initial process for getting rid of a teacher. Dr. Wilma Hart, she of the overbearing New York accent and elfin stature, talked at length regarding the district's reading and math initiatives and the importance of monitoring instruction, and Dr. Fred Roberts shared a few of his funny anecdotes, accrued over a lengthy career, leaving everyone wondering what he actually did for the area office and when was he finally retiring, and how was it that all these doctors ended up making people feel sick.

The directors set the table for their boss, Area 6 associate superintendent Magda Robreno. Resurrected from a demotion to a director the previous year, she found new life under Roger Traynor. Mrs. Robreno smiled between gritted teeth as she sauntered to the front of the room, almost seeming to float, and, for maximum effect, looked over the group with a pregnant pause and declared, "I'm baaaaaaaaack."

There was graduated applause and some laughter upon this announcement, and the gathering anticipated her words like flies caught in a web.

"What happened to me should never have happened to me," Robreno clarified in her decidedly Spanish accent. "That is why I brought back Dr. Warner"—who had been demoted to a principal—"because what happened to him should never have happened to him. But that is yesterday, and this is today, and we all have jobs to do."

Her choice of the present tense to refer to yesterday was something that struck Mark as rather odd, but yesterday obviously was still on her mind as she continued her speech.

"Those of you who know me know that I'm a straight shooter," Robreno said as her eyes looked upward to gather her thoughts. "You do your jobs 24-7, and we will have no problem. You wear your BlackBerrys 24-7. Sleep with them. Don't let me call you and not get an answer. Rest assured that I am not going to lose my job because you are not doing yours. Those are my terms. Those of you who don't like that can always turn in a letter of resignation. You all are replaceable. There are plenty of people out there looking for the opportunity."

Mrs. Robreno reminded the group of her more nurturing side in the form of her alter ego. "I'm like a mother bear," she went on. "Principals are like little cubs. They need to be told what to do and how to do it. Are there any questions?" The only sound to be heard was the whooshing of passing cars two floors below.

"I didn't think so," she concluded. "Have a good afternoon." And her smile once again forced its way through clenched teeth.

Seeking relief in the lobby restroom, Mark noticed a cockroach lying prostrate in the bowl. He flushed, and the roach came to life, struggling against the tide, fighting to not drown, all to no avail.

On the way to the elevator, he saw the principals gathered, talking and shaking their heads. One of them, Don Torrento, a large, bespectacled veteran principal, looked at him and said, "Welcome to Area 6." He put his arm around his shoulder, and as they walked, he asked, "Mr. Mahovlic, can I give you some friendly advice?"

"Go for it."

"The directors and Robreno"—he started laughing—"they're your supervisors; they're not your friends."

"I wouldn't have guessed that. Thanks for the advice."

"My pleasure," Torrento continued. "If you want to know the truth about things in our little world, I cannot tell a lie, and I'll give it to you straight, but you've got to promise me one thing."

"What's that?"

"Don't tell them you got it from me, because I'll deny I ever said it."

These were the days before the kids came to start the academic year. The job of a new principal is defined by an uneasiness that goes with doing anything for the first time. There is an inherent loneliness to being the one ultimately responsible for almost three thousand students and staff members. Mark had initial doubts as to whether or not he was ready for the assignment, and the mother bear's words did little to help.

Chapter 2

GETTING TO KNOW YOU

The next morning was filled with the anticipation of a full day during which most of the staff would be returning. The drive down Minneola Street, a pathway lined by palm trees and framed by farmland, became the first in a series of dichotomies that regulated the pulse of Mark's arrival on the scene.

Immediately to the north of South Demming, his school, an old man in a baseball cap walked his dog, a golden retriever in its golden years as evidenced by its whitened muzzle. As he got closer, Mark drew preliminary conclusions regarding their reliance upon each other. The old man was hunched over in such a fashion that he saw more of his feet than his surroundings. The dog was bobbing its head as it walked because it only had three legs. Here was longevity of friendship, a testimony to perseverance, and a sign of hope.

Immediately to the south of South Demming, gigantic concrete walls were propped up by metallic supports at perfect ninety-degree angles. These were promised to be the trappings of the new South Demming, scheduled for completion in two years. Even in their infancy, these walls offered an inviting atmosphere, a tribute to progress, and, once again, a sign of hope.

Farther south of South Demming, teenage boys and girls in their swimsuits took turns swinging from a rope and jumping from a low bridge overpass into a canal. Light skinned, light haired, and light eyed, they made light of their last few days of summer, filling the air with laughter and doing their best to conjure the ghost of Norman Rockwell to paint the picture of this perfect moment, in a perfect day, during a perfect time in their lives.

As a witness to all this, Mark decided that his glass was half-full and that no matter what awaited at the end of those tracks, no matter what refractory barriers he might encounter, no matter what invisible force might work against him, he could do this job. It was with self-inflicted inspiration that he opened the car door to hope and its ambassador, Joe Carrera.

"Listen," Carrera said as he extended his hand, "if it's okay with you, I think I'm just going to call you 'Magic.' This job is hard enough without having to stumble on your name. Can you live with that?"

"I'm good," Mark answered as Carrera released his considerable grip.

Athletic Director Joe Carrera was a fast talker. Gigantic, gray haired, and distinguished-looking, he used a deep voice, his commanding physical presence, and little regard for proximity to buttress his words. Even though Mark was slightly taller, he yielded space and initiated a conversation as they walked to the main building.

"Joe," he asked, "what do I have to do to fit in around here?" He had done his homework prior to his arrival to South Demming. He knew that Joe Carrera had been there twenty-seven years and was not only hugely influential over a mostly veteran staff; he also had a great deal of pull with local politicos and businesspeople.

Carrera stopped walking, and closing the gap between them, he now was almost nose to nose. "Magic, yeah Magic is going to work for me, just keep doing what you're doing now."

"What do you mean?"

"Just ask questions, watch what's going on, draw your own conclusions, but most importantly, let the people who are doing their jobs do their fucking jobs. Take me for instance," he continued. "I'm never going to do anything to embarrass you, and whatever you need, I'm going to be there to support you. I know how to do my job, and the athletic program in this school is clean and goes by the book. I've got a simple philosophy and plenty of success stories to back it up." Carrera's pause begged the question.

"So what is it?"

"In this county, and particularly in this school, athletics is the number-one dropout-prevention program."

At that moment, and almost by divine timing, a John Wayne–like older man, even in his Bermuda shorts, walked by the office, and his presence compelled Carrera to summon him.

"Hey, Don, get your ass in here. Magic, I want you to meet this guy. Don Reinhold, this is the new principal. I call him Magic because I can't pronounce his fucking last name."

"Oh, okay, great to meet you," Reinhold said, and he stuck out his thick hand, looked Mark squarely in the eyes, and provided a smile that struck him as among the most genuine he had ever seen.

"Magic, this guy is a legend in this county. Not only is he a great football coach; he's an even better human being."

Having worked in Demming County for two decades and being a sports fan, Mark knew Coach Reinhold from a distance and felt a strange kind of privilege to be meeting him in the capacity of his new principal.

"Actually, I know this guy," he said. "I follow high school sports, Coach. Everybody knows who you are, and it's a real pleasure to meet you."

"Same here," Reinhold said in his gravelly voice, "but don't listen to this guy," he pointed to Carrera. "I do what I do because it's all about the kids. Listen, let me know what you need, but right now I've got to make some phone calls trying to line up some scholarships."

"See what I mean, Magic?" Carrera said, and he slapped Reinhold hard enough on the back to leave an imprint. "What a guy!"

Waiting until Reinhold was out of earshot, Carrera turned to Mark and said, "Magic, I've got to share a great story with you. Don hates when I tell it, but it'll give you an idea of what he's all about."

"Let's hear it then," Mark agreed.

They both took a seat at the conference table, and Carrera's eyes looked upward as he began to spin his tale. "Magic, Don didn't get the best reception when he took over as football coach back in 1970. Back then, South Demming's mascot was a Confederate soldier, and the school's teams were called the Rebels. The views of the community kind of reflected that as well."

"What are you saying exactly?" Mark asked.

"Don came in at the same time that a neighboring all-black high school closed down because of declining enrollment. The kids from that school were bussed into South Demming."

"I know the times and the attitudes," Mark interrupted, "but how did this translate to Don?"

"Magic, the Rebels, like the Buccaneers, had a great football tradition, but on the first day of practice in August of Don's first year, only nine players showed up, and they were all the new black kids. Understand that the team usually had seventy or more players come out every year."

"I get the picture, so what did Don do?"

"He did the right thing, Magic, like he's done every day of his life. He didn't give a shit what the community might think of its new coach. He got the addresses of the white kids on the team, got in his truck, and drove from house to house and farm to farm, meeting the parents and the players and convincing them to do the right thing as well."

"So how did that go over?"

"He had forty show up the next day, and by the end of the week, his whole team was there."

"That's amazing!"

"Yeah, not too many people could have pulled that off. You know they plant a lot of shit on the land in this community—avocados, strawberries, onions, beans—but when they planted Don on the football field, they grew something really special."

"That's a nice way to put it," Mark said.

"You'll never find a recipe for that in a coach's manual or a playbook. Don's one of a kind, Magic. He's one of a kind."

Manny Hernandez always used to say, "Marko, you're only as good as the people you have around you." Beyond the positive initial vibes he received courtesy of Joe Carrera, Mark found himself having to be a quick study of the other members of his inherited team.

The assistant principal over curriculum, Belinda Ruiz, was thirtyish, diminutive, and unfriendly, even at this time when everyone was jockeying for position, trying to win favor or simply impress the new boss. She did not inspire confidence, and in the less than airtight office environment, Mark had overheard her conversations with the registrar, Penny Wolf, and they focused on the idea that there were problems with the master schedule.

The assistant principal over attendance, Melissa Franco, was fortyish, more than full-figured, and very friendly, even to the point of sharing some of the interpersonal dynamics of the office. "Listen," she told him. "I'm telling you this because you have the right to know. Belinda doesn't know what she's doing with the schedule, and Penny just told me the whole thing crashed, and they have to do it all over again. I have offered to help, but Belinda doesn't like me and acts like I'm invading her space when I throw my two cents in."

Melissa Franco was a highly competent, veteran assistant principal, who like others in the county was moved from a middle school in which she had flourished to a floundering high school. She was brought in to replace an assistant principal that was a personal friend of Tom Heffernan, and according to her, in his anger over this decision, Heffernan relegated Franco to a lesser role and promoted Ruiz to a position that she was unequipped to handle. This was not a smart move, but it came after his planned departure to the private school setting.

Larry Jefferson, the lone black administrator—to provide an ethnic balance—was a fortyish, agreeable individual. Mark felt like a Baptist minister when he talked with Jefferson.

"We need a presence in our hallways," he might offer.

"Uh-huh!" Jefferson would agree.

"We have to be in classrooms to monitor instruction."

"Dat's right!" Jefferson would chime in.

"Our parent community is part of the solution."

"Amen to that!" Jefferson would rejoin.

When he wasn't putting his boss on the pulpit, Jefferson had another tendency. He laughed, usually for no reason and out of nowhere, or simply to express his disagreement or discomfort.

"Oh, we done tried that, boss," he might say, and then he'd follow with, "Ahh, ha, ha, ha," and a shrill "Woooh-wee, oh Lord!" These exclamations would emit from a short, bearded individual with long fingernails who wore contact lenses that gave him cat's eyes.

Sarah Szemanski was the assistant principal over exceptional student education and school security. A fiftyish, masculine-looking woman, she sounded like a woman trying to sound like a guy when she talked. She had continuously beady eyes complemented by pursed lips that upon opening usually spilled out some negative statement that Mark already had likened to oozing lava.

"We've got to get tough with these people," was a favored remark, and it was versatile enough a beginning to work whether she was talking about students, parents, or teachers. She referred to herself as the one who carried the stick on the administrative team. Her love for instilling discipline in people would find her so absorbed in a single incident that she could stay buried in her office for an entire day. Teachers and staff members clandestinely referred to her as "The Manski," and many attributed poor morale of the staff directly to her lack of people skills.

Shortly after Carrera left the office, Wendy Akins, the guidance department chair, came by to say hello. She was a fiftyish lifer at South Demming. Like several other staff members, she had a father who taught there, she went to school there, and she had been working there for more than twenty years. Knowing this, Mark excused her overly made-up face and hair that made her look like Snoopy's bird pal, Woodstock. He figured she would be an asset and a positive team member given her history with the place.

"Welcome to our dysfunctional family," she said with a wry smile and a high-pitched voice, and without waiting for his reaction, she walked away.

On his way home, Mark drove by the new school construction site. This time, he noticed that he was identified as the principal on the marquee advertising the project. The kids were still splashing around in that canal, and the old man once again was walking the three-legged dog. Midway through the twenty-five-minute drive home, a train signal flashed, and the wooden rail came down. For lack of anything constructive to do, he counted the passing cars. There were 236 of them, pretty much the size of the faculty and staff at South Demming.

Chapter 3

THE MEXICAN CONNECTION

"Mr. Mahovlic, I'm glad you called us because we weren't going to call you," Pep Garces began with his matter-of-fact approach to their first meeting. "I'm going to be frank with you and tell you that you've walked into a snake pit."

Mark studied Garces for a moment and then asked, "What do you mean?"

"Let's go for a ride, so we can talk without interruption."

Pep Garces was the district's executive director of the Migrant Education Program. As such, he was responsible for the welfare and education of more than two hundred primarily Mexican students in the two southernmost high schools, South Demming and Hanford.

Garces's ride was a mid-1980s Chevy Astro van. It had carpeting that clearly was a do-it-yourself installation, and over the years it accumulated a mixture of scents that now only could be described as old and musty. Garces, an olive-skinned, mustached man in his early fifties, had a full head of salt-and-pepper hair and a heart full of pent-up emotions. Looking over the steering wheel that he held with his left hand at twelve o'clock, he began sharing his story, moving the right hand to conduct his words.

"Can I call you Mark?" he asked.

"Yes, of course."

"Mark, the Mexican community is in an uproar over an event that transpired at South Demming toward the end of last year."

"What is it? What happened?"

"Right before spring break, a team of school police officers arrived at South Demming during lunchtime. As you know by now, students eat in the cafeteria or the pavilion area. Led by two of your security monitors, about eight of these officers went to the pavilion area, and as your monitors pointed out certain kids, all Mexicans, those chosen, about fifteen, were lined up against the building wall and frisked for weapons or drugs in front of all the other students. They found nothing, but they succeeded in humiliating these kids. Now, I'll be the first one to tell you that some of the Mexican kids are in gangs, do drugs, and carry weapons, but there has to be another method and approach to something like this."

"That shouldn't have happened," Mark stated, and he let Pep continue, noticing for the first time the trace of a Spanish accent.

"Well, as unfair as it is to you, the Mexican community never got the audience that it was promised when we agreed to not go public with this event, and it is looking to you for a response, a sentiment, a pulse with regard to where you stand. With your permission, I want to introduce you to some key people."

"Absolutely." Mark exhaled at length to relieve the overwhelming feeling that was growing within him.

"Pedro and Maria will be happy to know that you are willing to meet with them."

They pulled into a stucco office building that housed the Mexican American Advocacy Group, a political entity formed by successful and borderline ethnocentric Mexicans. There he was introduced to Maria, who turned out to be Pep's beautiful wife, and Pedro Quiroz, a short, balding, fortyish owner of a local Mexican restaurant. Pep reviewed with them what he had shared regarding the ill-planned sting operation of the previous year and then offered the stage.

"On the way over, Mr. Mahovlic explained to me how he would have handled this situation, and I know this is of interest to you."

"First of all," Mark began, "thanks for the opportunity to meet with you and explain a little bit about my style, especially as it pertains to this situation. I'm a person who is here for the benefit of all kids. I only can tell you what I would have done in this situation."

For the next several minutes, he discussed with them the right to conduct searches upon reasonable suspicion but emphasized the aspect of not humiliating individuals during the process. He talked about privately conducting searches out of the view of others and affording those being searched with an explanation or reason for the suspicion, and then he provided them with details of a typical search.

"This is done respectfully, and students are thanked for their cooperation. The key words here are reasonable suspicion. There are times when such searches yield weapons and/or drugs. Regardless of the results, we contact parents to let them know of the search. Some end up displeased, but most understand the safety purpose behind this."

Pep Garces provided him with the opportunity to close the meeting. "Mark, we are proud people. For some time now after this event, we had contemplated going to the media, but it is not our desire to bring negative publicity to the school and take it away from its educational purpose."

"Know this about me," Mark reiterated. "I'm here for all the students, and even when they need to be disciplined, there's no need to rob them of their dignity."

"I really believe you did a great job and were sincere in there," Pep said as they went back to the van to begin the tour. "Pedro will get the word to the community that you seem to be a good man who wishes to work closely with us on behalf of our kids."

As they rode, Pep's eyes got a little glassy, and he spoke about himself. "Mark, I'm a graduate of South Demming, class of 1973. I played football there, and I wrestled. In those days, I could run the hundred in 9.5 seconds; nobody could outrun me. I really care about the welfare of the school."

They drove a few more miles and made a right turn into the Hanford Center, a housing installation for migrant families. Mark was taken aback by the living conditions there, noticing clothing drying on clotheslines in front of small rectangular dwellings with nothing to discern one from the other. Shirtless men sat in folding lounge chairs, smoking cigarettes and drinking beer. Young children under their supervision ran around the varied yards, chasing each other, rather than a ball of some sorts. A few babies in diapers and nothing more dotted the landscape and stayed within eyeshot of the smoking, drinking, shirtless men. Pep provided this visual segue before beginning his diatribe.

"What you see is all there is," he stated solemnly. "When it's not picking season, the men of this community are content to sit around, smoke, get drunk, and get into fistfights. Sometimes they break out knives, and occasionally someone gets killed. Those homes are six hundred square feet, and in some cases, you have as many as eleven family members living in one. To them and a generation or two before them, this has been enough. Most are here illegally, but the cheap labor they provide to the farming community is invaluable. While we provide them with an education, most of their children have no hope of going beyond high school because even the ones who excel in school can't avail themselves of scholarship opportunities."

They drove around the place, and Mark found no landmark to assist him in negotiating where they were in regard to the entrance, the exit, or the middle. For a moment, he felt just as lost as the souls who called this place home.

They pulled into a gas station so Pep could fill up. Mark got out with him to stretch, and Pep pointed to an apartment complex. "You see those buildings over there? Those are part of the Modesto Projects. Many of the black kids that go to South Demming live there. By day, you can drive through it, but we won't. The drug dealers and prostitutes keep vampires' hours, but it is no-man's land by night. People are shot and killed there on a regular basis."

"Unbelievable," was all Mark could think of saying.

Pep then pointed to the road. "Mark, US1 is a six-lane highway. The kids from the Hanford Center and the kids who live in Modesto have to cross this road to get to school. We have been fighting to no avail to get a bus to bring them to South Demming and its feeder schools, but they live within two miles, so their personal safety isn't considered. Over the years, no one has been hit by a car when going to school, but they get hit all the time at night, and it's just a matter of time before something happens on the way to school. Maybe as the new principal, you could try to get them a bus."

They drove several miles back to South Demming, and Pep dropped him off. They shook hands, and Mark was feeling a little bit like he had been abducted. That feeling quickly subsided as Pep's parting words washed away his selfishness, leaving a humble clarity in their wake.

"Mark, I have more than just a casual interest in Modesto and particularly the Hanford Center. You see, I grew up there."

Standing there for some time with his hands in his pockets and watching the Astro fade away, he wondered if Pep Garces ever saw the three-legged dog, and if so, what he might think of it. He wondered if as an alumnus, he might have a different view of the new South Demming. He wondered if he ever was one of those kids jumping into the canal, or if maybe the train he'd been on never bothered to stop there.

Chapter 4

NEW BEGINNINGS

"As big as you are," Angela Leon advised, "I would get in some kid's face real bad on day one just to show them you mean business." These were the words of the mentor principal assigned by the mother bear to assist with the process of becoming a principal.

Angela Leon was a veteran principal who fit the mold into which Magda Robreno wished she could pour all of her principals. In her late fifties, Leon was a short, stocky, toothy chain-smoker. Her administrative stops were characterized by high-performing schools whose students' scores on advanced placement tests yielded hundreds of thousands of discretionary dollars. During principals' meetings, Robreno lauded Leon as a fiscal genius, implying that those in schools like South Demming and Hanford needed to be more careful with their budgetary management. The reality was and always had been that money grows from the trees that frame the beautiful courtyard of Leon's relatively new, A-rated Great Palm High. The rest had to shake their trees and scramble for any dollars like little kids who hurl themselves on the floor when the piñata breaks.

For her treatment of teachers and staff, Leon also gained favor with Dr. Chandler-Lopez. During her career, she made it a point to go after a teacher or two each school year, even if it wasn't warranted. This practice generally resulted in the chosen individuals either resigning or transferring to another school. The residual effect of this was the staff members' credo that Great Palm is a fine place to work as long as one stays away from the principal. Leon did her best to secure a cheap dye job that made her red hair look purple, and her favorite editorial gesture of putting a finger down her throat and pretending to gag endeared her to the Area 6 directorship, except during times when they had to field complaints from parents regarding her crude disposition. This was his mentor, and when she said, "Call me," Mark likened that happening to the chances of his winning the lottery.

At six thirty on this first morning of the new school year, he and Ray Devereaux, a security monitor, were seated on a golf cart in front of the school, checking in buses, diverting cars to the student drop-off area, and keeping an eye on the student parking lot. Between spits of tobacco juice, Devereaux gave him the lowdown on South Demming's finest, battling a speech defect that made him sound like Elmer Fudd.

"What ya got here," he started in a high-pitched voice that belied his big frame, "is one gang called TOYZ; they started out as a car club, but when one of them had a problem with a Mexican kid in MP, all of them had a problem. The kids in TOYZ are pretty well off; most of them are white Americans whose daddies made money in farming. A lot of the kids in MP are from migrant families, and some of their parents work for the parents of some of the kids in TOYZ."

"So what started the problem?" Mark asked as he deftly shook off the tobacco juice that Devereaux unknowingly spat on his thumb, rubbing it on the back cushion of the golf cart.

"This has been going on for so long that I'm not really sure anymore. I think it started out with one of the white kids making a green card joke about a Mexican kid."

At that point, a train horn sounded loudly, shaking them out of their conversation.

"That's fucking Nelson," Devereaux said, and he turned the cart speeding in the direction of the student parking lot toward a pickup truck with gigantic wheels. "I told him not to blow that horn, but he wipes his ass with anything anyone tells him.

"Nelson, get over here!" Devereaux yelled.

"Let me talk to him," Mark suggested.

"It won't do any good, boss, but go ahead," Devereaux gave in.

Nelson Taylor was a tall, clean-cut white kid who, if his ride was any indication, was somewhat spoiled. He walked toward them looking at Devereaux until the new principal stepped out of the golf cart to introduce himself.

"I'm Mr. M," Mark said, making use of the moniker that simplified things for people. "I'm the new principal."

"Nice to meet you, sir," Taylor said as he accepted a handshake. "I'm Nelson." He smiled and revealed a bottom row of gold teeth accenting his mouth.

"Let me ask you something," Mark started. "It's 7:00 a.m., and this school is right in the middle of a large community. Do you think it's possible that some people are still sleeping?"

"Yes, sir," Taylor said in a polite manner, looking down at his feet.

"And who do you think gets to field complaints from the community?"

"That would be you, sir," Taylor said, this time looking him in the eye.

"Do me a favor, Nelson. From now on, please don't honk that horn anymore. You could wake up the dead with that thing."

"I promise you, I won't do that anymore, Mr. M," Nelson said.

They shook hands, and Taylor joined his peer group, some of whom were giving him the good-natured ribbing that accompanies being called over to speak to any adult in authority.

"Hey, dumbass," Mark heard one of them say. "Who was that dude? What did he tell you?"

"That dude," Taylor answered, "is the new principal, and the fucking guy talked to me like a human being. I got no problem working with this guy. It's all about respect, yo!"

When Belinda Ruiz and Penny Wolf came to confess about a week prior to the opening day of school, Mark brought Melissa Franco into the picture. The four of them contemplated best case / worst case scenarios before arriving at a middle ground that would work from a cosmetic standpoint but would require follow-up in the weeks to come. For the first day, all students would have a homeroom to report to, thus creating the appearance of order. Perception is everything, and the last thing a principal wants is for a perception of disorder or chaos to reign. So the students made it to their homeroom classes that first day, and administrators along with support personnel manned their stations to point the incoming ninth graders to their new digs. This was going relatively smoothly right up until an announcement on the radio.

"Mr. M, Dr. Traynor is in the building."

Negotiating the sick feeling in his stomach, Mark traversed two hallways before he saw *the* silhouette. Alfred Hitchcock had nothing on Roger Traynor when it came to making an appearance. Seeing him go down a corridor, Mark beckoned.

"Dr. Traynor," he called to get him to turn around. He introduced himself.

"Oh, nice to meet you, Mark," Traynor said as he wiped his sweating forehead with the handkerchief from his lapel pocket. "Damn, it's hot out here!" He briefly looked around at the old decaying school and muttered, "It's a good thing they're tearing this place down." As a few wayward male students passed them, Dr. Traynor took notice of the low-riding pants and protruding underwear and asked, "So, you got anything planned for the way these kids are dressed?"

"I'm going to push for school uniforms."

"Good answer," he said, and then another interruption on the radio temporarily spared any additional interrogation.

"Mr. M, Mrs. Robreno is in the main office and wants to see you."

"Oh, Magda's here," Dr. Traynor said. "Come on, let's go talk to her."

At that moment, Mark regressed to his childhood thinking, back to those early discussions regarding which method of suffering or death is preferable. Would you rather freeze to death or die from the heat? What's better, to get the wind knocked out of you or to get kicked in the balls? Ya got to pick one; which is it?

Robreno was smitten by Dr. Traynor's presence. "Dr. Traynor, I am so honored to have you visiting one of my schools," she gushed.

"I'm just glad to have had the opportunity to greet this young man on his first day and wish him luck," Traynor replied, and as he departed shortly after some more small talk, Mark contemplated which exit was more abrupt. Was it Traynor's adieu, or was it the mother bear's smile?

For a moment afterward, the mother bear and he sat in the office and didn't say anything. During that time, he processed that she had known him for twenty years. She was his department chair when he started out as a middle school English teacher. She came to their first daughter's baptism. She came to celebrate New Year's Eve when Sylvia and he offered their house for a staff party, but that *was* yesterday, and this just happened to be today. The sunlight that was peeking into the office from a nearby window disappeared, and as shadows overcame them, the mother bear shared.

"Mark," she sighed, "I'm afraid that we have done you a tremendous disservice."

"I don't understand. What do you mean?" he asked, all the while wondering if she was taking or preparing blame.

"The job of a high school principal is the most difficult job of all," she started. "To place a first-year principal in a high school, especially one like this, is not something I support. Unfortunately, this decision was made without my knowledge or input."

"I'll be okay, Mrs. Robreno," Mark offered, wondering if she was done and he could pull his pants back up.

"I hope so," she said, and with this sentiment, she departed.

Upon her departure, the sunlight took its cue and returned to the office. Mark spent the rest of that early morning doing what principals need to do as often as possible, visiting classes until lunchtime rolled around.

South Demming students had the option of two dining arrangements. There was the traditional cafeteria setting for 330 kids, and pizza and snacks were available in the pavilion area, complete with picnic tables resting under a large covered area. The hallway leading from the cafeteria to the courtyard pavilion served as an additional mingling spot, so the students were relatively contained without feeling constrained. Anywhere from nine hundred to a thousand kids were fed during each of the three thirty-five-minute lunch slots.

"Hey, Magic, you got to hear this!" Joe Carrera yelled from down the courtyard hallway. In his tow was a young black man of average height but stocky build. As Carrera entered the courtyard where Mark perched himself, he picked up speed. "Magic, this is Landon Daniels; he gained fifteen hundred yards last season, so everybody knows he can run the football, but you got to hear this!"

"Hear what?" Mark asked.

"Go ahead, Landon!"

"Aw, c'mon, Coach. Don't make me do this!" the young man protested.

Carrera raised one eyebrow like a conductor raises his baton, and Landon Daniels, in the softest voice, sang, "It's not unusual to be loved by anyone. Do, do, do, do, do."

As Carrera and he both broke out in laughter at this seventeen-year-old black kid doing Tom Jones, Daniels stopped his singing and frowned. "Aw, man, y'all makin' fun of me, and all I'm doin' is tryin' to get me some girls!"

Still having fun at the young man's expense, Mark postulated in song, "Hey, Landon, if you really want to get some girls, you got to try, 'She's a lady. Whoa, whoa, whoa, she's a lady.'"

"Let me try that," the eager young man humored him. Having found his faith again, he approached a passing young blonde girl, probably a new student. He grabbed her hand, went down on one knee, and sang, "She's a lady. Whoa, whoa, whoa ..."

Before he could get out the next verse, the surprised girl rebuffed him. "Get away from me. What's wrong with you?" she said as she shook free her hand and walked briskly to the pizza line.

With his game crushed, Daniels bowed his head and shook it from side to side, pausing to tell his new principal, "Aw, man, that doesn't work. You the principal. You s'posed to give good advice."

Carrera began laughing uncontrollably to the point where he was gasping for air. "Magic, you kill me," he said as he went back into the shade of the hallway.

Chapter 5

OLD DIGS

When Roger Traynor said, "It's a good thing they're knocking this place down," he proved himself to be a quick study of the outdated, for South Demming more closely resembled a road-stop motel than a modern-day high school. With its open campus and classrooms built around neatly manicured courtyards, it likely was a hit in 1953, but its cement hallways had lost their polish; its sidewalks bore the etched names of people that were immortalized through a childish act but whose etched faces today would bear witness to their utter anonymity. Their caprice of yesteryear had given way to the unintelligible magic markings and spray paintings of graffiti aficionados and gangbangers.

In earlier days, there was logic to the layout, but as time progressed, a "method to the madness" became the kind apology for the labyrinth. One main hallway went north and south while two tributaries went east and west. North and south covered the area from the lunch pavilion to the auditorium and science wing, with stops that housed special-education classes, ROTC, math, English, and art classes. The first east and west hallway was an interior hallway that had a mixture of regular class offerings, was interrupted by a corridor that housed a stairwell to get to a smaller, second-story grouping of classrooms, and served as a waiting area to get into the library. This area also featured snack machines, and just west of it continued with a smaller hallway housing some foreign-language classes and ending with a double door leading out to the physical education field and twenty-two portable classrooms. The second east and west hallway was an outside hallway framed by the art courtyard patio at its western end and the more expansive social studies courtyard patio at its eastern point. The school sat on sixty-five acres that included a football practice field and track at its northern point, a baseball field further south, and a bean crop growing beyond this to serve as the crown jewel of the school's agriculture program. Woodshop, agriculture, and auto mechanics classes formed the southern frame of the lunch pavilion; the gymnasium formed the eastern boundary; and journalism and nursing classrooms enclosed the pavilion to the north, while a chain-link fence to the west afforded a view of the student parking lot.

During class transitions, students waddled out and continued waddling to their assigned destinations as the crowds grew so thick that shuffling took over, and they unwittingly bounced off one another trying to ferret a crease or opening in hallways built for 1,500 students as opposed to the 2,800 that engaged in this daily ritual of human pinball and its associated vernacular.

"Hey, bro, watch where you're going."

"Shut up, bitch!"

"Scuse you!"

"You grab my ass one more time, and I swear to God I'll kick you in the balls!"

From the beginning, Mark perched himself at this greatest point of congestion, the intersection leading from the auditorium and science wing, overlapped by the walkways serving the art and social studies courtyard patios.

"Keep moving. When you stand there, you're blocking other people. Excuse me works for me. Watch your language! Take off the hat. Lose the headphones, please. Let's go; you've got one minute left."

They looked at him with curiosity as if to ask why was he wasting his time, but he was adamant in his insistence upon at least a semblance of punctuality even while most of their teachers sat at their desks awaiting their arrival.

"Come on, gentlemen," he encouraged as he approached a gathering of young men who continued an animated conversation after the late bell had rung.

"Damn, dog, why you buggin'?" a Latino boy asked him as his friends followed the suggestion, leaving him in their wake.

"Listen," Mark responded. "Do you know me?"

"Yeah, you the principal."

"No, I mean, I've got a name. Everybody calls me Mr. M," and he held out his hand.

The young man sized him up and reluctantly extended his hand, providing a weak handshake complemented by diverted eyes. "I'm Felix," he answered.

"Felix, I want you in school every day, and it's good to see you today. I don't ask much—just get to class on time, and let's respect each other. I promise you that I will never disrespect you."

"Yes, sir," Felix said, and Mark thought he noticed a little pep in his step. That idea was put to rout immediately by Sarah Szemanski, who to her credit was at her assigned post. She had noticed his dealings with Felix.

"You're wasting your time with that one," she droned.

"Why's that?"

"Felix Mendez is a third-year ninth grader. He wanders all over this school like he owns the place, and he's dumb as a rock. The only thing he understands is how to get into trouble, and we owe it to ourselves to start processing him for opportunity school."

"It's the first week of school," Mark said in an attempt to engage her benevolent side. In this effort, one of those metal detectors that old men use at the beach would have come in handy, for The Manski's beady eyes were cold steel.

"And the beginning of the school year is when you need to start with kids like that." Having made her point and punctuated it with a loud sniff of the air, she headed back to her office.

The three-legged dog was the metaphor Mark shared during the staff faculty meeting prior to the first day of school. It was emblematic of his positive approach toward leadership. On the way home after the first week, he didn't see the dog, and there wasn't even a ripple in the canal. Construction on the new school had ground to a halt in recent days, and he found himself longing for the comfort of these archetypes. It was as if they had retreated to watch him, perhaps seeking in him what he had been seeking in them, a reason for being where they were and a purpose for doing what they did. His thoughts were interrupted as the red lights again flashed and the long wooden arm came down to allow for the passing train.

Chapter 6

CLASS IN SESSION

"So when we examine the wet-foot, dry-foot issue," a late fiftyish and professorial-looking gentleman offered, "what are your views in terms of how it is being applied in our neck of the woods?"

Coiffed in his Levi's, untucked white polo shirt, and with his sockless feet slipped into a well-worn pair of Topsiders, the red- and gray-haired and goateed Ron Shipman oozed social studies department and was a billboard advertisement for those more radical days of social conscience, campus unrest, free love, and more importantly, freedom of speech. While he guided his charges from the shelter of a lectern, he would sooner throw himself under a moving train than shelter them from their ideas and opinions. He was a college professor except for the fact that he made his living in a high school, and his high expectations earned him high marks and a cultlike following among the elite corps of students at South Demming. At this moment, he posed a question, and when he felt a representative sample of hands filled the air, he chose a respondent.

"Ah, Mr. Mathews, thank you for your input today. What do you think? What do you know?"

Matt Mathews, a senior, teen-idol handsome, the starting quarterback, the 5.0 grade point average, and the guy that every other guy wished he could be, rifled off his response with the same precision that he threw bullet passes between defensive backs. "It's being applied along color lines," he stated.

"Okay and I'm going to need you to expand upon that statement, Matt."

"I mean when the Cubans wash ashore, it's a news event, and this town paints them out to be heroes for making the trip. I've seen them helped to get to shore. I've seen their family members interviewed and seen how the media provides coverage of parties that their families throw for them. The other day, when a boatload of Haitians made it this far, the Coast Guard was spraying them with water from fire hoses and doing everything it could to stop their boat from reaching shore."

"I'm seeing some heads nodding in agreement. Who has something to add to this?"

David St. Jean, a student of Haitian descent, entered the discussion saying, "It boils down to how each group is defined. The Cubans are seen as seeking political asylum, and the Haitians are seen as economic refugees. It's a convenient way to package it."

"Interesting point, Mr. St. Jean, but what do you mean by packaging it?"

"It's like this, Mr. Shipman, black is black, and we're just the new niggers in town!"

"Woooooohhhhh!" the whole class emitted, almost drowning out the bell for the next period.

"Looks like we have some strong opinions, and let's not leave out the Mexican members of our school family; the immigration issue is not going away soon, but unfortunately you have to. See you in a couple of days. Read chapter 12 for next time. I know that's out of order considering it's the first week of school, but I stopped following orders after my third marriage."

Ron Shipman went out into the courtyard area to bid the students adieu and to welcome his next group of students. As the old went out and the new came in, many were kind enough to take notice of their principal and offer a "good morning," a "wuz' up," or a guilt-laden, "I'm not late, am I?"

The young lady who inquired about her timeliness was punctual, but Felix Mendez strolled into Ms. French's Algebra I class as the bell was sounding. Ms. French, a light-skinned, elderly black woman remained seated at her desk like the cuckoo clock bird stays upon its perch.

"Young man," she started, still not knowing Mendez's name even though she had him all the previous year, "you need to leave this class, now! Go to the office!"

"Why, Ms.? What did I do?"

"You are late," Ms. French replied with irritation.

"No, Ms., the bell was ringing, and I was in class. Three people walked in after me. How come you're not kicking them out?"

"Do I need to call security?"

"Fuck that shit!" Mendez blared, and he walked out of the room slamming the door and right into the arms of Ray Devereaux.

"Felix, what the fuck happened now?" Devereaux asked.

"Fuck that fat old bitch!" Mendez screamed.

"Man, you got to get the fuck out of ninth grade. I told you, you help us, and we'll help you. Let's go."

"Where we goin', bro?"

"Let's just go for a walk." Devereaux's approach brought calm to the young man, but South Demming had many corners.

"Now what?" bellowed Sarah Szemanski. "Felix, why are you out of class?"

"It's okay, Ms. Szemanski; he's with me," Devereaux pleaded.

"It's not okay. Bring him to my office. He's going home."

"You see, Ray, nobody gives a shit or even wants to listen. Fuck it! Let her send me home."

Szemanski, Devereaux, and Mendez made their way to the administrative office, and not until the third time someone summoned her via the radio did Szemanski respond. "I'm all tied up with a situation right now. Is there another administrator who can help?" Her lips pursed, her beady eyes grew smaller, and she shook her head from side to side.

Interrupting his morning rounds, Mark left the classroom to follow the drama. Ms. French, still on her perch, told her students to open up their books and do the pages assigned on the board. No buildup, no drama, no real teaching going on, there were more heads lying on the classroom desks than there were attending to the busywork at hand.

Szemanski didn't even bother to lift up her head from her suspension paperwork despite knowing full well that the principal had entered her domain. Still engrossed, she could multitask just enough to prove a point.

"I hate to say I told you so, but I told you so," she said in her Eeyore-like tone. "This one's going home, and we're halfway to opportunity school!"

With Felix Mendez seated resignedly on the other side of the judge's bench, Mark beckoned Sarah Szemanski to follow him out of her chambers.

"What are you going to do with this kid?" he asked.

"Simple. He's going home. Ten days."

"Listen, Sarah, I believe in backing up my APs, but I have to tell you that ten days is excessive for what this kid did."

"He cursed out a teacher. We have to support our teachers!"

"We have to support our teachers when they're right. Her job is to teach this kid, even if he comes in a few seconds late. I was there. I saw what happened."

"So what do you want me to do?"

"Give him work detail, a day in SCSI, whatever, but he needs to be in school. Let's save the ten-day suspensions for things that merit ten-day suspensions. I have to be able to justify these things when they go beyond you and me and end up at the area office."

"You're the boss, but I think you're making a mistake."

"I'll live with that if I turn out to be wrong. I would rather take a risk on behalf of a kid then condemn him for a situation in which the adult did not act like an adult. French handled this all wrong."

"Well, that doesn't surprise me, but that one's another story. You're going to need to get tough on her!"

"Sarah, you're the AP over math and science. If she needs to be monitored more closely, then I expect you to take care of that. I need you in classrooms to observe what's going on instructionally."

"Well, if you want that, then I'm going to need some help with the discipline in this place. I can't be the only one handling it."

"The school year is only in its second week. Let's see how things shape up."

"I know how they're going to shape up. Don't forget, I've been here for five years. I know this place and the people in it."

"And I will rely on your expertise and feedback. It's okay for us to disagree as long as we present the united front for our faculty and staff."

Szemanski didn't have a retort or even a snort. She went back to her cubicle and informed Felix Mendez that this was his lucky day, and she processed him for an indoor suspension. This she did quickly because her index finger was burning to make a phone call to a very special friend.

Rumors cavort with whispers around masculine women like Sarah Szemanski. Her significant other was alleged to be one Sergeant Holly Craft, the school resource officer assigned to Area 6. Craft's role was to supervise and support Louis Cruz, the school resource officer assigned to South Demming, but as a friend and minimally a confidant of Szemanski, she served as a sounding board for a lot of one-sided information.

"I'm telling you, he's too soft. The kids are going to walk all over him, and I'm going to have to bring out the stick!"

"That's not what South Demming needs," Craft opined.

"Well, that's what it's got. You know that piece of shit, Felix Mendez, right?"

"Yeah, what about him?"

"I had the chance to pin him halfway to the wall, and I got overturned."

"You're shitting me?"

"Listen, I need you to share this information with Captain Cook. The word's got to get out that this guy is going to get us killed."

Captain Pauline Cook was part of the sisterhood. She and Craft were bodily the opposite of the five-ten Szemanski. While all three had wide rear ends and sported Beatles-type haircuts, Craft and Cook, both in their forties, were generously five feet tall, a stature that was the butt of many jokes shared by male resource officers throughout the county.

For his part, Louis Cruz looked every bit the policeman and then some. At six foot two and 245 pounds, the twenty-eight-year-old had intimidation, youth, size, and supplements as his constant companions. His youthful side made allowances for patience and understanding in his dealings with South Demming's irregulars, and there were times when he was successful in counseling and serving as a role model to students, but Cruz's darker side would emerge anytime a student challenged his authority, and it didn't take much to get under his skin like a hypodermic needle.

In addition to Cruz, the security team at South Demming consisted of five monitors who had the task of maintaining safety on the multicorridor, sixty-five-acre campus. They were equipped with walkie-talkies, assigned rotational posts, and given two golf carts, which were mostly out of commission with one ailment or another. Nate Judson, a sixty-two-year-old, had the most tenure, and those twenty-one years along with his military background earned him the title of head of security. He raised five sons, all of whom went to South Demming, all who played football, all who were team captains in both high school and college, all who were solid citizens in life, and two of whom made it to the NFL. Coach Judson worked with the Buccaneers' (South Demming's current mascot) wide receivers and was head coach of the girls' track team. "I done all right raising my boys," he was fond of saying, "so I figure I can give back by working with some of these girls. If I can keep them active, maybe they won't get pregnant, and maybe they'll stay in school."

Judson stayed lean and fit with a six-three, 190-pound frame, but the same could not be said of those who worked under his supervision. While each in his or her own right was a decent person, each had a quirk that occasionally took away from the main mission of keeping peace among the 2,800 students.

Ray Devereaux was a fat six foot two, tipping the scale at 315 pounds, a stature that didn't help him negotiate walking well after a motorcycle accident that left him with pins and plates holding his foot and ankle together. He kind of dragged the foot along when he walked, giving him a Chester-from-Gunsmoke quality, and the speech impediment earned him the nickname Chester Fudd. He took the good-natured ribbing, which was part of South Demming's charm. The long-termers, and Ray who had been there for seventeen years counting his time as a student, were like family, and one couldn't consider oneself a Buc until this rite of passage signaled by the first time some infirmity would be stripped naked and exposed for the prodding of the fraternity.

Equally sized and about the same age as Devereaux was Coach Reinhold's son Bryan. He had a deep voice and a command of the English language that was impressive for anyone, let alone someone working as a security guard. He was fond of sarcasm, something he reserved almost exclusively for South Demming's students, most of whom recognized his good-natured ribbing. Like his dad, he had a big heart and a soft spot for troubled and underprivileged kids, especially the football players he helped coach. The other soft spot he had was for Jessica Roper, a divorcee and social studies teacher at the school. To most of the students, Bryan and Jessica may as well have been the class couple. In fact, there were times that Jessica's other job of being a mom to two elementary school-aged children caused her to arrive late to school. Bryan would fill in so admirably in her absence that when she arrived, the students teased her and told her she could leave because Bryan was doing a better job. Bryan Reinhold also was a lifer at South Demming. He graduated from there, played football for his dad, and was fond of saying, "Football down south is the only game in town. I wouldn't even think of playing any other sport. All the other balls are too damn round!"

From the fat and somewhat jolly, the graver side of the team was headlined by Ms. Essie Hunt, a devoutly Christian Baptist woman who believed the separation of church and state was an act against the vengeful God that balanced her soul on the tightrope dividing heaven and hell. In addition to her posts in front of the school and the student parking lot, the front of the school featured a pew-like bench from which she would pray for the buses to come in on time and for everyone to have a blessed day right up until it was time to chart the position of incoming buses along the dry-erase board directly above. Ms. Hunt's unwavering devotion to God instilled enough reverence in all the staff that she was the only security guard that was addressed as Ms. Everyone else went by their first name, and not a single one of them could control the parking lot as well as Ms. Hunt; no child dared park in any of the special spots reserved for seniors or even think to enter the parking lot without the requisite window sticker. She followed them in her golf cart and rounded them up to go in the right direction toward their classes like the sheep dogs on Westerns herd the flock.

Jerry Pierre was a fortyish Haitian man of limited English proficiency. Why Coach Judson decided to give him the megaphone to patrol the lunch pavilion area was beyond Mark, but he believed in giving latitude and trusting in the professional judgment of his employees. To the kids, he was known as "Hey You" because he would use the megaphone to remind them of proper decorum. "Hey, you, don't sit on the table. Hey, you, don't cut in line. Hey, you, stop running." He never learned a single student's name. He had a job to do, and it didn't include building relationships. When it was time to dismiss the pavilion area to go back to class, Hey You thought nothing of using the siren feature of his megaphone right next to the ear of some oblivious kid. This upset more than one student, who would curse him out in return, and Hey You would run to the nearest administrator requesting intervention.

In Abraham Maslow's Hierarchy of Needs, safety serves as the foundation, but Maslow wasn't around the modern-day high school where principals sit on safety like Looney Tunes characters sit on the keg of dynamite.

Chapter 7

MORE FLIES WITH HONEY

On the hump day of week three, 6:15 a.m., Mark was settling in with his first cup of coffee and shooting the shit with Joe Carrera.

"Magic, I got to tell you I'm pissed off."

"This early, Joe?"

"Doughnuts, Magic, doughnuts and the vending machines make the athletic department and this school a lot of money, and the county is on a fucking health kick. Nobody is going to buy granola bars and baked potato chips. We clear about $500 a week with doughnuts, and now they're on the hit list. The vending machines generate close to $100,000 every year, and that's thanks to all the fucking sugar they used to have in them."

"So what's the backup plan?"

"I don't know, Magic. I'm talking to an AD on the northwest side of town that has been dealing in pastelitos and has a guy willing to come down our way."

"Shit, Joe, pastelitos have guava, cream cheese, and a sugar glaze on top. Hell, they've got enough sugar in them to start a diabetes epidemic."

"Yeah, but they've got something that doughnuts don't have."

"What's that?"

"They're not on the radar."

At that moment, Melissa Franco did a light knock. "Mr. M, may I speak to you privately?"

"Magic, I'll get back to you on this," Carrera took the hint. "Our kids need the sugar, and I'm going to see to it that they get it, one way or the other."

"Melissa, come in and have a seat," Mark offered.

"Mark, I just received a phone call from Alberto Hernandez, the superintendent in Area 2."

"I've known Alberto for a while. My wife was his AP when he was a principal."

"Well, they're looking for a principal for Seaview Middle, and he has asked me to interview."

"Melissa, that's great. You're more than ready for this. I'll speak to him on your behalf."

"You won't have to, Mark. He's going to be calling you. I'm not supposed to say anything, but it appears to be a done deal regardless of the interview."

The words "done deal" traditionally have been followed by the admonishment "but don't say anything," during all the years Mark had worked in the county. There was an inevitable code of silence that was evoked during personnel shifts, and breaking this was worse than perjury.

"Mark, the schedule changes are happening, and I think that Penny has a strong handle on the inputting process. We should be okay in a couple of weeks."

"Melissa, I'm sorry we didn't get the chance to work together, but I don't believe in standing in the way of someone's professional advancement. Just keep me posted, so I'll have an idea of the time frame."

"Will do," and she left his office, leaving him with a bitter taste in his mouth and no fucking sugar anywhere to sweeten his disposition.

Divine intervention limped in with Ray Devereaux.

"Here you go, boss." And he deposited a huge cinnamon roll on the desk. It was dripping with sugar glaze and shining as though it was plugged into a wall outlet. "It's from Nottingham Farm Store just down the block."

"Holy shit, this looks good!"

"Boss, you got a minute?"

"Ray, we need to get outside, but what have you got?"

"I just want to thank you for yesterday. Felix Mendez, as fucked up as he is, likes South Demming and works with us to let us know when anything is going down. He's like an extra pair of eyes. He's a gang member, the MPs, and he keeps his peeps under control when they're in school. We give him a little extra rope with hall time and try to get him to go to his classes. He's not dumb. Come in here, Felix."

At that point, the stocky young man with the shaved head and gold teeth walked into the office.

"Tell him what you told me you wanted to tell him," Devereaux prodded.

"I just want to thank you for yesterday, sir, and I'm sorry I lost my cool. I'll apologize to Ms. French as soon as I get back from work detail."

"Felix, Ray tells me that you give us a hand once in a while, and I would like to keep that going, if that's something you're still comfortable with."

"Yes, sir, whatever you need, just let me know."

As the young man left, Devereaux looked like he still had something on his mind.

"Is that it?"

"No, can I make a suggestion?"

"About what?"

"I've got the perfect candidate to take Ms. Franco's place."

South Demming Park, immediately to the east of South Demming High, was one of those areas set aside when the community was planned so that homes could overlook its majesty, families could go on picnics, and children could play on the swings, go down the slides, and sift through the sandboxes it provided. Those children and several more generations worth all made the inevitable mistake of growing up, and the park with each succeeding group was witness to the metamorphosis of innocence, a condition that had mutated over time, making each rendering carry with it a unique flavor. For more than half a century, it also had served as the place where students skipped classes, smoked cigarettes, smoked pot, or parked their cars when no spots were available on campus or when a security monitor like Essie Hunt would notice and care that they were smoking something in their cars.

The first complaint from the community came in week four and revolved around the park and the fact that students were listening to their radios too loudly and just hanging around in the morning instead of going directly to their classes. When the front of the school cleared, Mark suggested to Ray Devereaux that they take the cart around the back to the park.

"Why we going to do that, boss? We never done that before. Mr. Heffernan told us not to go back there because it's not part of school grounds."

Thinking for a moment that Devereaux may have swallowed his plug of tobacco, Mark explained, "Well, I need you to get used to the idea that there will be things that I do differently from Mr. Heffernan. Whether it's part of school grounds or not has no bearing on the fact that those kids are either coming to school late or simply not coming at all."

"Got you," Devereaux said, and he turned the cart around and cranked the battery-powered vehicle to its maximum fifteen miles per hour.

This morning went down in history as one change in leadership philosophy. They knocked on windows of parked cars, drove the golf cart into circles of students who were mingling, and went into the public bathrooms to round them all up and usher them to class. Amidst a few "what the fucks" and some inaudible grumblings, their round up netted about fifty students that they followed back the two hundred yards or so to campus.

"Bryan Reinhold, Unit 12," Mark radioed, "get ready to usher some of our park residents to their respective classrooms." Reinhold's perch in the social studies courtyard area afforded him a view of the dejected throng.

"Yeehaw!" he bellowed into his radio. "We got ourselves a new sheriff in town!"

Glancing at Ray Devereaux, Mark asked, "You heard that, right?"

"Yes, sir!"

Also noticing the procession from Portable 8 was Rex Hoffman, social studies teacher, union steward, and self-appointed keeper of "what these students need."

"That's what these students need," he approved from his doorway, "some good old-fashioned expectations and some consequences. Where are you taking them, SCSI?"

"Uh, no, I'm taking them to class."

"How are they going to learn that way?" he questioned.

"How are they going to learn on indoor suspension?" Mark answered back.

"Hey, I don't really agree with that, but you're the boss," Hoffman said, and then retreated to his classroom.

Hoffman was a midfifties, bushy gray-haired man with a Captain Kangaroo visage and an *Addam's Family* classroom. His decorative tastes attested to his eccentric nature but endeared him to his students who were fond of "chillin'" by watching Vietnam war footage from the vantage point of an old sectional leather couch and a couple of well-worn La-Z-Boy loungers. While there were desks in the room, these were reserved for those who didn't arrive in enough time to sit in the first-class section. Surrounding the room, on the walls, suspended from the ceiling, or sitting atop a storage armoire were artifacts from "Rex's Realm" as he called this museum. There were the busts of Moe, Larry, and Curly, and Laurel and Hardy. There was a NASA space suit; there was a Vietnam-era soldier's uniform; there was a World War II flight jacket, varied gas masks, a scaled replica of the Spirit of St. Louis, and several *Life* magazine covers. Hoffman even had surround sound made up of some original Bose 901s and some cheap surround speakers bought at a yard sale. He constantly had the media center's LCD projector on reserve because he enjoyed showing movies.

Hoffman's claim to fame was his runner-up finish to Area 6 school board member Eileen Riordan. While he was her only opponent, and he lost in a landslide, he felt this brought him closer to her in terms of his sphere of influence, and he remained in constant contact with her regarding the happenings at the school.

The morning trip to South Demming Park became a ritual on this day, and while the numbers gathered dwindled next to nothing over time, the occasional wayward soul could be collected and saved on any given day.

Collecting and salvaging souls was Don Reinhold's mission in life, and this he did in an early 1980s Ford Aerostar. About thirty minutes before the South Demming Park reclamation project, Reinhold turned his van down 328th Street, right by the Mobil station, past the Modesto housing projects, and several blocks into the neighborhood that Pep Garces had described as "no-man's land." But Don Reinhold wasn't just any man, and he had earned his passage to such an extent that the whores, the drug dealers, and those who had simply retired from hope would offer an occasional wave or a "Wuz' up, Coach?" In their world of black and white, this burly, curly gray-haired man carried the trump card of caring for the kids.

"Hey, Coach, why we goin' here?" Felix Mendez asked from his perch atop a milk crate in the back of the van. Reinhold was there for all the students, including those who didn't play football but might need a ride on a given day.

"Marcus needs a ride this morning," Reinhold informed his passengers. Marcus Summers was among the four senior stars in a defensive secondary that was being heavily recruited by major colleges across the nation, but more importantly, he was the one kid who pulled the hardest on the coach's heartstrings.

As the van pulled into the driveway of a house on the corner, Mendez and the two other passengers let out a collective "Daaaaaaammmmnn!" This exclamation came at the sight of the home that had wood covering areas where windows had been, 50 percent of the shingles missing from the damage of the past two hurricane seasons, and crumbling paint and stucco exposing the concrete blocks underneath.

"Coach, somebody lives here?" asked Danny Baldwin as he tugged his exposed boxer shorts out of the teeth of the well-worn milk crate next to Mendez. Baldwin, a first-team all-state cornerback and wrestler didn't live in the lap of luxury, but his trappings at least resembled something fit for human habitation.

"Yeah, he's got it rough," Reinhold acknowledged, "but here he comes, so keep it to yourself." At that moment, a young man with a night-black complexion, shoulder-length dreadlocks, and a front row of grinning gold teeth sprinted toward the van with his book bag in tow.

"Hey, y'all," he greeted the contingent.

"Zup?"

"Zup, dog?"

"Hey, Landon, let me ride shotgun with Coach," Summers asked the Tom Jones impersonator who occupied the only passenger seat that wasn't a milk crate.

"Nah, dog; sit next to the white boy," Daniels said, pointing out Mendez.

"Fuck that shit!" Summers said. "Yo' mama," he referred to Daniels's foster mom from the group home in which he lived, "drives a damn school bus, but you can't get your ass up enough time to ride in with her."

"Yeah, but my ass is the first one that got picked up, so my ass been keeping the passenger seat warm for my ass."

"You guys need to shut up and watch your language!" Reinhold bellowed.

"Yes, sir, Coach."

"Sorry, Coach."

Reinhold's taxi service was entirely against school board rules, but the coach was fond of saying, "They also got rules that kids got to be in attendance every day; I'm just seeing to it that that happens."

Blocks away yet worlds apart, senior cheerleader Christy Del Pino pulled her silver Mercedes C-320 into the student parking lot. Riding shotgun with her was Matt Mathews. With their light brown hair, razor-precise smiles, and perfect-life resumes, they were as close to royalty as is allowed under school board rules. There was no discussion as to whose ass belonged where because each of their asses was kept warm through the heated seats of German automotive engineering.

"I love you," Christy yelled after Mathews as he bolted from her car.

Turning around and jogging in place, he held a hand up to his ear and said, "What?"

"I love you!" she repeated more loudly and with an exasperated tone.

"What?" Mathews again inquired.

"Never mind." She sighed to herself as she watched him disappear into the lunch pavilion area.

These were the varied forms of arrival to South Demming. Some were escorted. Some were transported. Some were imported.

Chapter 8

ON A WING AND A PRAYER

That morning, during the nine o'clock homeroom period, Cathy had scheduled some student council representatives who had a matter of urgent importance. At exactly 9:05 a.m., they appeared at the principal's office door, they being Christy Del Pino, head cheerleader, Jasmine Crawford, student council president, Veronica Sanchez, coeditor of the *Swashbuckler*, the school newspaper, and the thirty-two-going-on-fifteen activities director Kim Bennett.

"To what do I owe this entourage?" Mark asked.

"Mr. M, the students want to fill you in on how things have been and how they're looking to you to consider some changes," Bennett opened.

"You know, I haven't been around long enough to really see the need for changes. I feel that I have to get a grip on how things are before I start deciding how they will be."

"I, I mean they, understand that you're new here, so all they really want is for you to hear them out."

"I'm good with that, but let's sit down at the conference table where we'll be comfortable. Who wants to start?"

Christy Del Pino was smart enough to begin speaking without having to wave her pom-poms. "Mr. M, we want to know why we can't have pep rallies before football games."

Looking at Kim Bennett, Mark asked, "They haven't been having pep rallies?"

"No." Jasmine Crawford seized her opportunity. "There were a couple of fights in the past, and since two years ago, we haven't had a pep rally."

"All the kids want you to give us a chance," said Veronica Sanchez. "I can play it up in the paper that you're testing us to see if we can live up to our end of the bargain, you know, kind of a positive peer pressure."

"How bad was it for pep rallies to be cancelled?" He again turned to Bennett.

"I don't know if it was really that bad," she suggested, "but most of the adults in this building can't stand pep rallies because it takes them out of a routine."

Mark looked at Jasmine's pleading blue eyes peering out of her blonde and blue bangs and then focused on the pierced nose of Veronica. "Jasmine, get all of your homeroom reps to talk this up as an opportunity to have some fun around here as long as no one gets stupid. Veronica, do what you said you were going to do with the newspaper coverage, but you can't do a pep rally two days before the game on Friday."

"We know that, Mr. M," Kim Bennett said. "We're looking to do this before the Palm Coast game. The first three games are tune-ups. Palm Coast is a tough opponent and a traditional rival over the years."

"I want to thank you young ladies for your negotiations. Ms. Bennett, our next administrative team meeting on Monday will have this as an agenda item. This has to be planned to go off without a hitch. I'm looking for you to organize this and troubleshoot any eventuality, so that we can set a positive tone."

"Thank you, Mr. M."

"We love you, Mr. M. You'll be at the game, right?"

"Bye-bye!"

"Boss, I couldn't help but hear the last part of your meeting." Sarah Szemanski appeared as the group departed. "Did I hear correctly that you are allowing them to have a pep rally?"

"Why is that such a big allowance?" he asked. "At my previous school," and he referred to his days with Manny at Bronfmann Senior High, "we had two pep rallies to accommodate more than five thousand students, and the worst thing we had to deal with was an occasional rubber blown up as a balloon and filtering through the crowd."

"You're making a mistake," she concluded.

At that moment, someone summoned her via the radio, and probably sensing that she was about to be questioned as to her objection, she answered the call.

South Demming had a tremendous football team that went 11–0 during the regular season the previous year until having their season end with a difficult playoff loss to Hanover Lakes. Nevertheless, they were the reigning Area 6 champs, and Mark didn't fully grasp the magnitude of what a tune-up game meant at South Demming until Friday evening, the second week of September. Despite a poor-caliber opponent in Bronfmann, there were at least two thousand Buccaneer fans on the home side of Harnett Field in Hanford. The band was in full regalia to honor the start of a new season, and a few students painted their faces royal blue and white.

Prior to kickoff, Joe Carrera approached with his arm draped around a young black man of small stature. He held him so tightly that the kid's face pressed against the top of Carrera's chest. "Come here, Darryl. I want you to meet the principal. Mr. M, this is the number-one Buccaneer fan of all time." Darryl wore a South Demming football jersey and had two spirit chains around his neck, one royal blue and the other silver. He couldn't have been more than five feet tall, but his smile would have gone the length of the football field if he didn't have ears to stop it.

"Pleased to meet you, sir," Darryl said in a slow, calculated manner. "How do you like it at South Demming?"

As he accepted his surprisingly firm handshake and his greeting, Mark immediately realized that Darryl was mentally challenged. "How are you, Darryl? Very nice to meet you."

"I'm good, sir. I'm always good. It's a beautiful night, and we're going to win," Darryl said with words measured as carefully as the chains that determine whether it's a first down or time to punt. "Welcome to South Demming," he stated, and this time he gave the brothers' handshake that started with palms joined by interlocking thumbs and continued with the grip being released in favor of the four fingers being joined anew at the first knuckle. As they shook hands, Darryl pulled Mark toward him, gave him a hug, and walked down the sideline clapping his hands.

"Magic, Darryl was at South Demming for eight years. You know that special-education kids get to stay until they're twenty-one. He hasn't been able to let go, and all the kids here love him. I just wanted you to know that he's the honorary team manager, and as long as I'm here, and it's all right with you, he gets a field pass to all the games."

"That's why I love this place, Joe."

"I thought you might say that, Magic."

Under a semidark September sky, the game began with Bronfmann Senior High kicking off to the Buccaneers of South Demming. Kickoff was at 7:05 p.m.; the score at 7:06 p.m. was Buccaneers 7, Bronfmann Bulldogs 0. Danny Baldwin, briefly fumbled a kickoff, upset the timing of the charging Bronfmann kick-coverage team, led them to the left side of the field, and when he felt they all were pursuing him, stopped suddenly, changed direction, and ran up the right sideline for ninety-five yards and the score.

The Buccaneer kicking team lined up with Raja Horton, one of the defensive backfield studs on one side, and Marcus Summers on the other. The ball was booted high into the night, and by the time the Bulldog returner caught it, Summers hit him so hard that the crowd let out a collective groan.

"That's how they hit in the South!" Bryan Reinhold boasted. "You didn't see too much of that at Bronfmann, eh, boss?"

"Magic, this is probably going to get real ugly, but Don will call off the dogs early," Joe Carrera explained. "Hopefully, you'll still have some friends on the other side of the field," he laughed.

Bronfmann had to start from its own ten-yard line and faced a third and ten after two running attempts were snuffed at the line. The Bulldog quarterback dropped back to pass, faced fierce pressure from tackle Willie Ivory, and threw the ball up for grabs. Marcus Summers picked off this pass and sprinted down the left sideline for a second score.

The Bulldogs went three and out on the subsequent possession, punting and giving the Bucs the ball on their own forty-yard line. Nate Judson caught Mark's attention when he told him, "Watch this!"

"What do you got going, Coach? You going to go long?"

"Just watch. You'll see."

When Matt Mathews went back to pass on first down, he found a wide-open Tyrus Waters for a sixty-yard score. This was simply a matter of dropping back, throwing the ball in the general vicinity, and watching his receiver blow by everybody to catch up to it.

With a big smile competing to outshine the gleam in his eyes, Nate Judson explained, "They been playing up and in single coverage on Ty. You can't do that. He's too fast. I told you to watch." The glare off Judson's bald head complemented the luster off his teeth and eyes, and Mark suddenly got new meaning out of Friday Night Lights.

After another stop and subsequent possession, halfback and part-time crooner Landon Daniels hit a hole, made a nice cutback, and raced unscathed into the end zone, sixty-seven yards from where the play began.

After the first quarter, South Demming held a 35–0 lead, and Coach Reinhold retired his starters for the rest of the game. The problem was that the hungry second and third teamers were every bit as good so that when the final whistle sounded, South Demming won 62–0.

As the principal of a school with a kick-ass football team, Mark was proud but concerned how this victory would be perceived by his rival principal across the field, especially since it was Manny Hernandez.

"Marko," Manny said as they shook hands at midfield, "I asked my kids and my coaches what was going on, and you know what they told me?"

"What?"

"Not only did your kids pick up our kids after they kicked the crap out of them, but they were encouraging them to keep playing hard regardless of the score. They're just a much better team, Marko, but they're also some pretty good kids."

In the east end zone, the Buccaneers circled their coach for some words of inspiration. "That was one helluva show," Reinhold began, "and you did what you were supposed to do, so we're off to a good start, but each game from here on gets a little tougher, so enjoy this and get ready to get back to work on Monday. Let's take a knee."

The inner circle of players got on one knee, and a second circle of standing players each put a hand on a kneeling player to take the proper stance while awaiting the coach's benediction. "Dear Lord, thank you for giving us the strength to do our very best and for keeping both teams' players free from injury. Help us to remain humble in triumph and proud in our preparations. The great game of football is nothing in comparison to the game of life. Keep us grounded in this belief, for it is through your guidance and wisdom that we say amen!"

"Amen!" the players chimed in.

"There's no separation of church and state in Hanford, Magic," Carrera said as he handed over a game ball inscribed South Demming 62, Bronfmann 0. "Congratulations on your first win as principal."

The stands were still half-full, and the remaining fans, guided by the sounds of the band and the encouragement of the cheerleaders, sang the alma mater while Mark admired the football and thought of some witty retort.

"This isn't enough, Joe."

"Not enough? Well what the fuck else do you want, Magic?" Carrera asked.

"Signatures. I want signatures on the fucking ball, and I want a celebratory pastelito."

"From your mouth to God's ears, Magic," he answered. "It's going to happen; just keep your fingers crossed."

Crossing fingers was something he had done with regularity since becoming a principal.

Chapter 9

THE BACK OF THE BUS

There is no group of school board employees that is more underpaid and underappreciated than bus drivers, but Charlissa Streeter wasn't thinking of the deficits facing bus drivers when she took her seat at the back of the bus any more than she was thinking how Rosa Parks would turn over in her grave every time a black child passed up an available front seat. Her civil rights were violated when the driver took exception to Charlissa's feet being on the seat cushion.

"Girl, I'm the one responsible for keeping this bus clean," the driver started in a stern tone, her face visible to Charlissa in the rearview mirror, "and that ain't going to happen with your feet being on the seat." This reminder was unsuccessful in getting Charlissa to budge. The driver took it to the next level. "Now, get them damn feet on the floor!" she yelled.

While it didn't rain please and thank you in the Modesto Project very often, yelling accompanied by cursing had the same effect as the rope tugging at the bull's balls when the rodeo gate sets free the rage and brings new meaning to a bumpy ride.

"Who you to be talkin' to me like that?" Charlissa began her buildup. "You ain't my mama, and even my auntie don't talk to me like that!"

"I ain't your mama, but if I was, you'd have enough sense not to put your feet where people sit."

At this point, the twenty or so other students on the bus had their curiosity piqued enough to remove their earphones and offer their respective expertise.

"Girl, she be tryin' you!" was the sentiment from a neighborhood girl across the aisle.

"C'mon, Lissa. It's too damn early. Ain't nothin' good going to come out of this. Just put your feet down," Raja Horton pleaded. Horton was acting upon Coach Reinhold's calling out of his players to be leaders in the school as well as on the field. It appeared to work as she put down her feet, folded her arms, snorted, and turned her back to the onlookers, but the driver called the school requesting the presence of an administrator once the bus pulled in.

"None of y'all go nowhere," the driver directed the students as she pulled into the circular drive and came to a stop. At that moment, she opened the front side doors, and in walked Larry Jefferson.

"Good morning. What's the problem?" Jefferson asked as his eyes scanned the half-filled bus.

"I asked that young lady to put her feet down from the seat," the driver started as she pointed out Charlissa Streeter, "and she cussed me and refused to do what I asked her."

"I cussed you?" Streeter asked. "You cussed at me, and anyway, I put my feet down."

"You got yourself one of our finest this morning," Jefferson said loudly enough for all the occupants to hear. He dismissed all the students except for Charlissa, and when they left, he told her to accompany him.

"Man, I ain't goin' with you!" Streeter refused. "I did what that bitch asked me to do. Why we gettin' into all the drama?"

At that point, Jefferson lightly touched the young lady's arm to encourage her accompaniment, and she slapped away his hand.

"Don't fuckin' touch me!" she yelled. With it only being seven fifteen, ten minutes before reporting time, curious onlookers gathered outside the bus.

"You want me to have to call Officer Cruz, or you going to come with me?" Jefferson revealed the choices.

"I don't care. You call that fuckin' cracker," Streeter yelled as tears started streaming down her face.

"Officer Cruz, I need your assistance on Bus 3026 in front of the school."

Hearing this communication over the radio, Mark instructed Ray Devereaux to drop him off at that point.

Louis Cruz sprang from his squad car like a rodeo bull exiting the gate. Apprised of the situation, he went to the back where Charlissa Streeter remained, arms folded, looking nowhere in particular. "Let's go. I don't have time for bullshit this early in the morning." Cruz grabbed Streeter's arm; she resisted, sprang free, and opened up the doors at the back of the bus, jumping out and running into the crowd of about a hundred students. Looking to record the event, several students were conspicuous in their usage of the movie feature of their cell phones. At this time, the tardy bell had rung, and Mark and Sarah Szemanski were attempting to get the late students into first period. Nobody moved.

Cruz sprang out of the back of the bus, chased down Streeter, and tackled her like a Hanford rodeo cowboy tackles a calf, and then he roped her with a pair of handcuffs as his knee pinned down her head to the pavement.

Four or five black boys witnessed this event. They circled the officer as he cuffed his perpetrator; all had their fists clenched, their lips pursed, and their eyes squinted into angry slits that attested to their fury over the situation and their helplessness to do anything about it. Mark looked at them fearful of what they might decide to do, and then he looked at the crowd of students that ignored the directive to report to class, and he realized that control over his domain, his school, his home away from home, was something he simply borrowed.

When Charlissa Streeter was yanked to her feet by Officer Cruz and led away to his office for processing, the mob followed but eventually dissipated, with Coach Judson's cajoling over the bullhorn, into the varied hallways that held their classrooms. Cruz arrested Streeter for disruption of school function and resisting an officer, and Larry Jefferson tacked on the ten-day outdoor suspension, did the requisite paperwork, and called Streeter's family to inform them of the event.

A Mrs. Smith, Charlissa's aunt, requested an audience with Mark and was understanding of the decision to suspend but was unhappy that her niece was arrested. She was a sympathetic figure, likely in her seventies, overweight, and she relied heavily on a cane as she walked into his office. Her wispy white hair provided stunning contrast to her dark complexion, and she spoke softly. "Sir, I grew up in Hanford in the 1950s. Those were different times then. I been leaning on the crutch of Jesus long before I ever needed this here cane."

But Charlissa's brother Darryl Johnson, who provided transportation for his aunt, didn't care that her spirit died for the sins of others. He bore witness to the technology of a text-messaged video, and being a broker in the stock of dignity, Darryl was ready to trade insults the minute Louis Cruz walked into the office.

"Mr. M, I'm going to the JAC," Cruz revealed. The JAC stood for the Juvenile Assessment Center where Charlissa Streeter would go through the six to eight hours of processing before being released to her family.

"How'd I know it was you?" Darryl Johnson asked Cruz. Johnson, a South Demming dropout, had his share of run-ins with Cruz during his five years at the school, so they were on a first-name basis.

"Darryl, you should be telling your sister what not to do, so she doesn't end up like you," Cruz answered.

"Man, I ain't got to listen to your shit anymore," Johnson answered, and he stood up to leave, brushing against Cruz, a decision that immediately found him facedown on the principal's desk.

"Ahhhh! Get your hands off me, you fuckin' cracker!" Johnson screamed in pain and anger as Cruz twisted the young man's arm into an unnatural position, cuffed him, picked him up by the cuffs, and threw him onto a chair outlining the conference table.

The noise brought several clerical personnel to the door opening, led by Cathy who deftly closed it like a child who cleans a room by throwing things under the bed.

Mark looked at Mrs. Smith, and she had long tear streaks rolling symmetrically down her brown cheeks. They seemed to join somewhere under her chin in a noose-like arrangement. "Lord, I go to church every Sunday and pray for these children. They mama's in jail; they daddy ain't nowhere to be found. Please, God, help me!" She started rocking back and forth in her chair. It was Monday morning.

It was nine o'clock when he called the leadership team to the conference table, a long rectangular piece of furniture that rested perpendicular to his desk and took up a third of the room. Mark's agenda, which was to include making arrangements for the return of pep rallies, now had a new priority item, student discipline.

"Ha, ha, heh. It won't do no good, boss," Larry Jefferson offered when Mark insisted that they abandon whatever they were doing to man the hallways during class change and remain at their before- and after-school posts until students were tucked in or had bid adieu. "They fight. We suspend, and sometimes we arrest. They understand that, heh, heh, heh, wooh!"

"Jefferson's right, boss," Sarah Szemanski concurred. "You care about these students, and that's good, but you haven't been around here long enough to know that the troublemakers won't turn around. We've got to process them and get rid of them." Szemanski's lips pursed, and her eyes retreated to their familiar beady state. Mark imagined a forked tongue flickering or a rattling sound to accompany her words.

Mark had gotten wind that Belinda Ruiz had been campaigning for an open AP position at the much lower maintenance, wealthier, and newer North Kendall High. She remained silent on the matter, maintaining a distant proximity.

"Magic, you can't take this shit personally," Joe Carrera counseled. "Shit happens to these kids in their neighborhoods, their lives, and sometimes they bring it to the school. That's not your fault."

"You ain't lyin'," Jefferson agreed.

Mark assumed that Melissa Franco simply was awaiting her phone call, and while he suspected she was troubled by the morning's events, she likely was even more troubled that she was away from her phone.

Kim Bennett, a brunette ex-cheerleader, had pep rally on her mind. "I guess this means we'll have to cancel the pep rally?"

"I didn't say that. One thing has nothing to do with the other."

"When you get seven hundred kids in the auditorium, you're asking for a fight to break out," Sarah Szemanski warned.

"Uh, huh; dat's right!" Jefferson added.

There was an uncomfortable silence in the room until the voice of student services chirped in. "May I be excused?" Wendy Akins asked, breaking the awkward moment. "We still have tons of schedule changes to do, and I don't feel I have anything to contribute."

"You don't think that the counselors can play a role in the solution to this issue?" Mark asked.

"No, I don't."

Feeling himself fuming, Mark weighed her words and how they measured up against the students' needs. "I need you here," he told her, and then he watched her pout as she sat back in her chair with her arms folded.

Recently appointed dean of students, Craig the "Iceman" Isley fixed his steely blue eyes that complemented his white head of hair and said, "Boss, I'll do whatever you need. Just give me the word. I'm there." Ice was a team player who made a career out of occupying multiple roles, a special-education teacher, a work-experience supervisor, a golf coach, and now someone who showed his loyalty to a new boss after only knowing him for a few months. On the other side of fifty, the white in his hair didn't detract from his youthful appearance; he provided eloquent testimony to the notion that positive attitude keeps one young.

"I'll get the coaches to be out there, Magic. They won't have a problem with that."

"Thanks, Joe."

At that point, Mark turned his attention to Nate Judson. "You know we can use all the help we can get," Jud began. "I been saying for years that we need more than five security monitors. This place is too big, and when one of us is out sick, we're really strapped. Hanford High got ten monitors, and they got less students than we have. One of my boys works over there, and it's still crazy. This place and these kids ain't that bad, but it could be if we don't stay on top of it."

As Mark digested Judson's analysis, Cathy walked in with a worried look to inform him that Dr. Chandler-Lopez was on the hotline demanding to speak to him. He picked up the phone and felt like he was picking up dog shit from the yard.

"I understand that you had an incident this morning," she pounced upon his greeting.

"We had an ugly scene on the bus. That's correct."

"Uh, can you tell me why I don't have an incident report on my desk?"

"It's my understanding that I have twenty-four hours to get that to you, and this particular incident is under control."

"That is not how we do things in Area 6!" She raised her voice loudly enough for his cohorts to hear. Mark kept the phone about a foot away from his ear at that point. "If for some reason you can't immediately write up and fax me an incident report, then I expect a phone call apprising me of what happened. I need to know when you know. Are we clear?"

"I will get you that report within an hour," Mark said.

"Thank you," and she hung up the phone.

"That's the type of bullshit that chased Hef," Carrera offered.

"What? Does she think you have nothing better to do?" the Iceman sprang to his defense.

"Guys, it's been a long morning. Kim, we'll have to meet later to discuss pep rally preparations. I want everyone at their posts during class change, and, Joe, if you can get me some coaches out in the pavilion at lunch, I would appreciate it."

"Consider it done, Magic."

The rest of the day went smoothly as Mark managed to visit some classes and take his post in the pavilion during lunch, but it wasn't until he occupied the student parking lot and bus lanes at the day's end that he saw the most unusual thing. Hundreds of bubbles were floating around outside the front of the school.

"Hey, M," Landon Daniels said, "looks like someone been blowin' bubbles out here. How come I didn't get invited to the party?"

"Just don't start singing what I think you want to sing, Landon."

Scanning the campus up and down, Mark's eyes locked in on the chiller stations where bubbly foam was cascading from the rooftop, down to the ground like an overflowing washing machine. Stray bubbles freed by wind drifts entertained the kids on their way home.

"Don Scott," he called the zone mechanic. "Unit 17, come back."

"Come on back," Scott answered in his decidedly southern accent.

"Meet me out in front of the school. You need to look at something."

"If that ain't the damndest thing I ever saw," Scott said when he arrived as he looked at the chillers. "Them pipes got to be clogged. It's hot as shit out here, so they must be overworked, but I ain't never seen that."

Scott was appropriately named. Also more than fifty years old, he was Scotty on the Starship Enterprise. He may as well have said, "She can't take much more, Captain; she's going to blow!" But he managed to go into the chiller station and work some kind of miracle to end the bubble party.

"What was it?" Mark asked when Scott came back out.

"Boss, I didn't do shit. It just stopped."

"Look," Landon Daniels said as he presented his principal with a softball-sized bubble carefully held in both of his hands. Mark popped it.

"Aw, man, see if I ever give you anything again," and he ran away, darting between the buses until he found the one driven by his foster mother.

On the way home, Mark saw the old man and the three-legged dog. He wanted to stop to talk, to see if they were real or just some coping mechanism created by his overloaded brain. The train caught him again, and as it passed, he said to himself, "I must be crazy, but I really like that fucking place!"

Chapter 10

INDEPENDENCE DAY AND
THE CHESS MATCH

In the short time Mark had known her, Cathy had developed a keen awareness of the dread he faced each time his phone rang. Her sense of humor helped ease things a bit as she had developed some physical gestures to signal which area office tormentor might be on the other end of the line. For Magda Robreno, she would hold her hand over her forehead as if stifling a headache. For Alice Chandler-Lopez, she would go with the traditional circling finger pointing at the head to indicate craziness. For Wilma Hart, she developed a nauseous look that absolutely cracked him up. When the phone rang on this Tuesday morning, she had no cues, meaning he might be spared.

"Mr. M, Pep Garces is on the line for you."

"Thanks, Cathy." He exhaled. "Long time no hear from, Pep. Where have you been?"

"Keeping occupied, Mark, but I couldn't let this week start without touching base with you. September is a special month for Mexican people. This year, we celebrate the 195th anniversary of Mexican independence."

"Pep, I'll confess that I know little of your history, but I'm all for celebrating."

"Mark, that being said, I expect you will or already have seen some Mexican kids at South Demming coming to school with Mexican flags draped around their shoulders. I hope you will allow for this practice as I promise you it will only be for this week."

"I appreciate the advanced notice. Do you foresee any problems, or have you encountered any problems in the past?"

"Mark, most of the kids are willing to explain to anyone why they bring the flags during this time, but in some cases, other kids don't want an explanation. I don't want to pin labels, but in most cases, the kids with the least tolerance are the white Americans. There have been fights, so you need to be on the lookout."

"Pep, I will be sure to alert my administrative team and teachers. Has an effort ever been made in advance to educate staff and students regarding this practice? Can you come out to the school, maybe get on the PA, or let us record you for the morning announcements?"

"I think that's a very good idea. Let me see if I can get out there tomorrow morning, but you'll need to run interference until then."

At this point, it was a quarter after seven, and Mark was late for his morning ritual at the track, but when he got out there, he was surprised to see Dr. David Canales, the night school assistant principal, working a crowd. As Ray Devereaux's odds-on favorite to replace Belinda Ruiz, Mark had taken the initiative to invite him to some volunteer service on the school's behalf, particularly since David's Cuban heritage gave him the gift of gab in two languages. He didn't think he would see him out there but assumed he really wanted to show his interest in the impending AP vacancy. Canales already was talking to several Mexican students who had donned their country's flag. Speaking fluent Spanish and having an outgoing personality, he appeared to have quickly developed a rapport with this subgroup.

"Hey, man," he addressed Mark, "I think you need to know about this."

"David, first of all, thanks for taking me up on the offer. I just got off the phone with Pep Garces, the executive director of the Migrant Program. I know what this is about, so as soon as we clear our areas, this will be the main topic for the A-Team meeting. I hope you can stick around long enough to join us."

"I made plans to make a day of this," he said. "You can count on my fat ass being wherever you need it," and as he laughed, his belly shook.

"Tell you what, then," Mark said, "hop on board and join me for a quick spin."

David accepted the invitation for a golf cart ride, and Mark headed toward the portable classrooms and South Demming Park. As the cart began to move its considerable payload, Ray Devereaux announced his presence by hopping on the rear runner, causing both of them to turn around upon impact.

"Goddamn, Ray!" Mark said. "This job is hard enough without having to get whiplash riding a fucking golf cart!" Devereaux just had cleared his post in the student parking lot.

"Boss, Dr. C, we got a problem on our hands. The redneck kids are pissed off that the Mexican kids are doing their flag shit again. They was talking shit in the parking lot, and I had to get them to hurry up and get to class."

Ray was upset, so his speech impediment became even more pronounced, but Mark focused on his attitude. "What do you mean by flag shit, Ray? These kids are celebrating something of an ethnic nature. They're not doing this to piss off anyone."

Ray remained steadfast. "That might be true, but you tell that to Nelson and his boys."

"You talking about Train Horn Nelson with the monster truck? What does he have to do with this?"

"He just don't like Mexicans, boss." Ray hopped off before they turned into the agriculture field and the dirt road leading out to 165th Street and South Demming Park.

David and Mark just drove for a while in silence until David spoke. "You know, I don't like some people, but I don't let that dislike stand in the way of my better judgment. How do you handle a situation like this?"

"David, I drive around in the golf cart in the morning searching for ideas, and when I don't have them, I call a meeting." Mark pressed the talk button on the radio and reminded everyone, "All administrative team members, we will be meeting at 8:00 a.m. in my office. Please put aside what you're doing and be prompt."

As they drove back, Mark thought how nice it would be to have one Monday where white kids, black kids, Hispanic kids, and Mexican kids just went to class without carrying the burdens of their ancestry. They entered the portable area ten minutes after the late bell had rung, only to be greeted by Rex Hoffman who was perched in his doorway, poised to offer his perspective on things.

"Hey, boss man, we almost had a fight out here this morning. You going to let them Mexican kids carry their flags? You got a plan for this? Because it's likely to get worse."

Hoffman's lips couldn't be seen moving behind his unkempt mustache. Mark thought he would have made the consummate ventriloquist if he could put his words in someone else's mouth, but the shit that came out of his simply would leave a bad taste in anyone else's. "Hey, you're the social studies teacher," Mark answered. "Why don't you go back inside and teach your kids what all this is about?"

Hoffman retreated to his classroom, and David looked at Mark and said, "What a fucking asshole! Who is that guy?" David had a look of bewilderment on his face as his eyebrows formed a V-shape, and his nostrils flared.

"You're perceptive, David," Mark said. "He's a fucking asshole!"

"Contemporary history leaves Mexicans with few heroes, Mark," Pep began. "Criollos were Mexican-born Spaniards who were seeking political means to overthrow the Gachupines by convincing their military brethren to switch allegiance in reaction to Joseph Bonaparte's succeeding King Ferdinand as the leader of Spain and to drive out the pro-Bonaparte Gachupines. Hidalgo was a supporter of this movement, but when certain Criollo military leaders refused to back it, word was leaked, and Hidalgo made his decision to call the Indians to revolt rather than flee Dolores or simply await his inevitable arrest. This decision changed the character of the movement from a political ploy to a bloody movement fueled by years of resentment, powered by primitive weaponry, and led by Criollo Captain Ignacio Allende and Hidalgo himself. But Hidalgo may have been a reluctant hero."

"How's that?" Mark asked.

"He did not foresee the carnage that would occur and a year later retreated to Dolores where he eventually was executed by the Gachupines. The war lasted eleven years and was followed by decades of political strife, but at midnight on September 15, every year since, El Grito de Dolores, 'Mexicanos, viva Mexico' is remembered with pride."

"Thanks for the history lesson. This gives me a better understanding on how to address possible fallout."

"Mark, you seem to be a sincere person. I know you will handle this with the safety of students in mind."

Pep Garces left the office that morning, and his efforts had a calming effect on most of the student population for the duration of the celebration of Mexican independence, but his expertise would have been helpful throughout the week.

In the wild, animals recognize their status in the pecking order and organize their lives accordingly. They rest in carefully arranged habitats, some needing camouflage to hide from predators, and others using it so as to be invisible to their prey. Regardless of their status, thirst eventually forces them out in the open where water reflects the strengths and weaknesses that it sustains. It has remained the same in public schooling where the most open spaces house the vending machines that provide liquid refreshments. At South Demming, this area was by the media center, and before school, during class changes, and after school, the strong and the weak gathered there in a caste-like fashion. This area was Nate Judson's post, an assignment requiring him to be the most wary of animals.

From the improvised shelter of her office, Sarah Szemanski wrestled with the decision of which camouflage to don. Would she be the moray eel, striking unannounced but definitively, or would she be the snake, slithering in and out of the consciousness of others? "Guess who just called for a meeting?" Szemanski reached this rhetorical morsel from the top shelf of her pantry of sarcasm.

Holly Craft knew the answer but was more concerned with the questions presented by this delicate situation. "Look, Sarah. Things are tough all over Hanford. Shit happens on the weekend, and it continues in the schools. We're short, but I'll see if Pauline can get T. J. over there by lunchtime to back up Lou. Let me know how the meeting goes."

Szemanski hung up the phone, satisfied that she would have material to bring to the meeting.

Mark began the meeting by introducing David Canales and soliciting the level of understanding pertaining to Mexican Independence Day. While all had some background knowledge, their biggest concern was its potential to polarize the school.

"Boss, them redneck boys going to be waving their Confederate flags from the back of their trucks," Larry Jefferson opened up.

"And when you tell them to roll up and put away the flags, that just pisses them off even more," Nate Judson offered his voice of experience, "and you know the black kids don't like seeing that flag either."

"So what's the answer?" Mark posed. "It seems like you're damned if you do, and you're damned if you don't!"

"It'll blow over. It has in the past, but we've got to keep a lid on this for the next couple of weeks." Sarah Szemanski again sniffed the air as if trying to pick up the scent of approval.

Jefferson nodded and provided a quick, "Dat's right!" for the good of the cause.

"David, you were on the track this morning; what was your feel for things?" Mark asked, particularly because of David's fluent Spanish and the possibility he may have overheard some things being spoken that weren't meant for everyone's ears.

"I was talking to some of the Mexican kids with the flags when I got out there, and I remember one of the white boys saying, 'Hey, Mister! We're still in America, right? How come you're letting them wave the Mexican flag?' I ignored the comment, mostly because I didn't have an appropriate answer, but one of the Mexican kids, a girl named Migdalia, didn't keep her mouth shut. She yelled at the kid, called him a *come mierda*, a shit eater, and told him not to make her go over there to fuck him up."

"And she would have done just that, boss," Sarah Szemanski added. "Migdalia Santa Cruz has a mouth on her like I've never heard before."

"Thankfully," Dr. C interjected, "the first bell rang and gave me an excuse to shoo everybody in the right direction. I did spend a little time after that by speaking to Migdalia; that's how I got to know her name."

"This ought to be good," Szemanski interjected with something between a chuckle and a cackle.

"I told her that I could respect the fact that she was angry but added that I had never heard anyone speak with such a foul mouth. I told her I had a daughter of my own and suggested that her parents likely didn't raise her to speak like that. I added that she seemed like a smart young lady who had other choices of words."

"I'm sure that touched a soft spot," Szemanski added, getting Jefferson to add an "Oh Lord!" which he followed with something that sounded like "Woop."

"She said, 'So what are you going to do, suspend me?' I told her that wasn't my intention, and she looked at me and said, 'Then, can I go to my fucking class? The teacher's going to give me shit for being late, and I don't need you and him all up in my face!' I asked her to try using some appropriate language, and she said, 'Yeah, yeah, I'll do that. Could you please let me go?' I saw I wasn't getting anywhere, so I let her go."

"Don't feel bad, David," Szemanski consoled him. "At least you caught Migdalia on one of her good days." Szemanski and Jefferson giggled in unison like two schoolgirls taking turns pushing each other on playground swings. The rest of the administrative team members were strangely quiet, almost as if they were seeing this on rerun, but David revealed that he had an angry side.

"I'm glad that you guys find this funny," he said. "I'm fat and jolly, so I can laugh with the best of them, even if it's at myself, but how is any of this going to help the situation?"

"Well, Dr. C," Szemanski replied, "you'll be happy to know that right before I came to this meeting, I was talking to Sergeant Craft, and she informed me that Captain Cook would be sending T. J. Burns, an Area 6 detective, to back us up during lunch and until closing, so we should be good if the rest of us are out and about." Szemanski again sniffed at the air and let her contentment escape through the slits of her eyes and the straight line of her mouth.

"We going to need some help in the student parking lot, Mr. M," Nate Judson weighed in. "Did Ray tell you about the kids that got in each others' faces this morning?"

"Yeah, he told me about that, Jud," but Mark was seething over the fact that Sarah Szemanski would call to make these arrangements and not run the idea by him first. He dismissed the group, considering that the end of the first block was approaching and they needed to be at their posts, but he detained Szemanski.

"Look, Sarah, it's not a bad idea that you took the initiative to secure some assistance today, but don't you think you should let me know before you get the area office involved?"

"Boss, I'm just doing my job, trying to be proactive. I thought you would appreciate me bringing this to the table. Someone's got to make some decisions around here!" Along with pursing her lips, Szemanski had a way of making a biting comment, then tucking in her chin and moving her neck back like a cobra looking to strike again.

"Oh, so now you feel that I'm incapable of taking a stance?"

"No, I'm not saying that. I'm saying it's my job to advise you and act on your behalf."

"I'm not going to curb your having advice to give, and I don't want to deprive you of autonomy, but when it comes to communication with the area office, you're only acting on my behalf when I'm in the loop first."

"I will do that from now on," Szemanski conceded. "I've just been through this before, and you haven't really experienced this place when it heats up. I'm trying to look out for you."

"Then look out for me by letting me know what you would like to do to look out for me, okay?"

At that point, the bell for second block rang, and just as Szemanski and Mark were about to head to their respective posts, the hotline rang. He looked at Cathy and gave her the okay. Her finger working in circles and pointing at her head told him all he needed to know.

"Yes, I'll put him on right away." Cathy sighed, looked as if she just got word of a death, and said, "It's Dr. Chandler-Lopez."

"Hello."

"Mark, Mark, Mark." She said this quickly enough to seem as though she were imitating a dog. "What do you have going on over at South Demming this morning that you felt compelled to tell your AP to call for additional school police?"

He immediately explained to her about Mexican Independence Day, the need to be on their toes, but she interrupted him halfway into this explanation with a loud yawn that clearly was exaggerated in order to be audible over the phone.

"I'm sorry. God, I'm tired this morning. I'm glad nothing has happened. You'll get your additional resource officer for today, but from now on, make sure that it's you who puts in the request, not an assistant principal, you understand?"

"Yes."

"Good. Let me know if there are any problems. Good-bye!"

Mark wished that Sarah Szemanski could have been in the room to hear that phone call, but these thoughts of vindication were immediately put to rest by Nate Judson.

"We got a thirty-two in the media center hallway. I need help!"

For Mark, this involved simply exiting through the office, making a right turn into the hallway, and reaching the clearing, but by the time he got there, a large crowd was dispersing at the bell and at the urging of Jud, Ray, Bryan, and Sarah Szemanski. He saw Nelson Taylor and a Mexican kid whose name he didn't know picking up their book bags.

"You guys come here for a minute," Mark ordered, and as they walked his way, he asked Jud, Ray, and Bryan what they had seen.

"Crowd was too thick. Couldn't see, but something was fixing to happen," Jud offered.

"Jud's right, boss," Ray allowed. "They was fixing to get it on, but they must have seen us."

"It's a good thing that Ray and I are gravity challenged," Bryan added. "Our fat asses are hard to miss."

"Well, I'm going to the office," Szemanski informed the group. "I've got plenty of things to tie me up this morning."

Mark wanted to share with her his conversation with Chandler-Lopez, but he had both boys looking at him for some direction. With all the others who had gathered at this meeting place having fled to their respective lairs, the electric hum of the vending machines and the gentle buzzing of the fluorescent lights mockingly mimicked serenity. "Nelson, be straight with me," he started. "Something was about to happen here. There is no reason for your book bag to be on the ground when you're going from one class to another."

"Nah, Mr. M, we had a problem, but we squashed it."

"What's your name, son?" Mark asked the Mexican boy.

"Guillermo Santana, Chief."

"What was going on over here?"

"No, cuz, my father works for this white boy's old man. I don't want no problems with him, but he saw me with two of my homeboys in the parking lot. They was with the Mexican flags and all, so he was with his crew and gets all brave and shit and says somethin' to me about getting a green card."

Turning his attention to Nelson, Mark asked, "This true, Nelson?"

"Yeah, I fucked up saying that shit, and I apologized to him just now in the hallway, but his boys still want him to fight me."

"Look, Chief," Santana said to Mark, "this shit's squashed with him and me. I ain't going to say how it is with my homeboys, but he was a man and apologized, and it's all good. Can I go?"

"You can go, but maybe you can speak to your homeboys, so we don't have to deal with this all day."

"Maybe I'll do that, Chief."

"Go to class then."

"What about me?" Taylor asked.

Waiting until Santana was out of earshot, Mark asked, "Is this shit really squashed?"

"I think me and him are cool," he guessed, "but I don't know about his boys."

"What were you thinking when you said that?"

"I wasn't thinkin', Mr. M. That's always been my problem."

"This Santana kid said his dad works for your dad."

"Yeah, my dad's family owns a lot of farmland, and they've always used workers from the Hanford Center."

"So you know they're poor, and you know they're probably not citizens, at least not his parents, and you still come up with the green card remark?"

"What can I say? I'm an asshole."

"Yes, you are," said Bryan Reinhold who stayed for the conversation.

"Hey, fuck you, Bryan!" Nelson answered back.

"Too late. You're mother beat you to it," and they both laughed at their exchange.

"Nelson, go to class," Mark ordered. "Come see me if there's a problem." He then noticed Rex Hoffman exiting the media center. First block was his planning period on this day, and apparently he had spent it tending to some business. He anticipated some type of remark from him regarding this situation, which he had to have seen, but he walked by with a forced "Good morning," stayed close to the wall as if trying to blend in, and headed out to his portable to greet his students.

"Hey, boss man," Reinhold offered. "Hoffman was in the library typing away with two fingers for more than an hour. I don't think I've ever seen him doing that much work. You must be having a special effect on him."

Bryan Reinhold had provided something to think about. Why didn't Hoffman seize an opportunity to rub salt into the morning's wounds? What was he doing for so long in the media center? At least to an extent, the students were predictable, but Mark was growing increasingly more concerned about the adults in his midst.

Mark had known T. J. Burns since he was a rookie resource officer, and he was cutting his administrative molars at Bronfmann High. They had worked more than a few situations during their two years together and had developed a mutual respect for each other's style. Both believed in being communicators, a philosophy that served them well as they rose in their respective ranks. This day, Detective Burns arrived in his police blues and was escorted to the office by Joe Carrera.

"Holy shit, Mark," he began. "Congratulations. I always knew you would be a principal. Hell, it must be going on two years since I last saw you." T. J. had a massive white-toothed grin that only was outdone in brilliance by his thinning but naturally blond head of hair. He was almost six feet tall, and at the age of thirty-five, he was beginning to develop a pear shape. In his hand was a doughnut courtesy of Joe Carrera.

"Magic, I'll leave you two lovebirds alone. I just wanted to make sure I took care of the school system's finest."

"Joe, you know this fucking guy too?"

"Magic, if I told you all about what and who I know, then I'd have to kill you, and then I'd have nobody to bitch to and drink coffee with, ah, hah, hah, hah! Got to go count up the profits before the district pulls the plug."

"T. J., it's good to see you, man," and as Mark shook his hand, he pulled him forward to bump shoulders. "Look at you, dude! It didn't take you long to make detective!"

"Hey, thanks, Mark. So what's going on here this morning? Captain Cook said you could use some help."

Mark gave T. J. the background information and asked him if he could hang around during lunch and be a presence during dismissal.

"You got it! Let's get down to work!"

A solid blue sky was the canvas for the pavilion area. The grass outside the covered patio had grown golden from too many dry days, an atypical weather pattern for that time of the year. The Mexican boys and girls, as was their practice, congregated at two picnic tables in the uncovered portion and decorated a tree behind them with a Mexican flag that they draped among the branches. Some soft, almost indistinguishable Mexican folk music meekly accented the setting as it deftly crept through the speakers of a scratch-and-dent ghetto blaster, perhaps audible to the white kids who preferred the covered area but definitely inaudible to the black kids who tended to gather on the opposite side that flanked the gymnasium. The only air circulating in the pavilion was that provided by the ceiling fans of the covered patio, so the flag maintained its place of prominence, undisturbed.

Perching his frame against the first picnic table in the last row of the pavilion afforded Mark a view of the Mexican kids to his immediate right, the white kids in the middle, and the black kids to the far left. He angled under one of the fans to better withstand the ninety-degree heat. In the two rows that separated the picnic tables, kids of all backgrounds waited in line together for the one thing that seemed to transcend racial and ethnic boundaries, a slice of pizza. Behind him, all the way to the left, Carrera and T. J. guarded the hallway leading out of the pavilion. From this vantage point, they had immediate access to any trouble occurring along the gymnasium side and could see the entire lunchtime crowd. David stood in the opposing corner, closest to the Mexican kids, while the Iceman sat at a picnic table chatting with some black students. Hey You circulated throughout the area clutching his megaphone.

Mark's focus was interrupted by a gentle tap on his left shoulder. He turned around to face the sky-blue eyes and golden hair of somebody's perfect child. Her name was Chloe Owens, and if she wasn't one of those kids of summer who he saw swinging from the rope and jumping into the canal, then she was waiting her turn.

"Mr. M," she began, "if those Mexicans can bring their flag to school, can we bring the Confederate flag tomorrow?"

Mark digested the bile of her words, looked at her cherubic features, and with some incredulity, he angrily responded, "Girl, when you can show me that the Confederate flag is part of some ethnic or national celebration, then we can talk. Right now, you're just being a hater. You want to bring the Confederate flag as a reaction to their bringing the Mexican one, but you don't even know why they brought it, do you?"

"Well, thank you for at least hearing me out," Chloe Owens offered. Her fine hair was blowing wildly in the space she shared under the fan, and the blue of her eyes seemed to pour out of her lower lids like spilling paint.

Several minutes after the bell signaling the end of the first lunch period, Nelson Taylor sat in the sheltered area atop the last iron picnic table in the row nearest to the hallway entrance. He positioned his body so that sunlight divided it from the shadows. Intently, he worked his right thumb, index, and middle fingers to deftly roll up a piece of paper and attempt to force it into one of the holes afforded by the interlaced ironwork. It wasn't until his whole body became entrapped by shadows that he was enlightened to his new surroundings. Two Mexican boys stood at his right side, blocking out the sun. From behind him and to the left, four more circled him and then settled atop the picnic table facing his. They didn't speak a word; they simply stared at him, striking premeditated poses. One of the boys creating the new shade had his arms folded. Tall and skinny, he leaned against the metallic beam supporting the roof, while his counterpart, stocky and oval shaped, had his right hand in his pocket and the other functioning to hold up his oversize pants. His feet were spread wide apart to better support his considerable girth. When Taylor looked in their direction, both quickly flashed front top rows of gold teeth and resumed their glaring. The four occupying the picnic table positioned themselves directly facing Taylor. Mexican flags hung across the right and left shoulders of the boys on each end, a feature of their well-choreographed presentation as were their chins that rested on thumbs and forefingers with the remaining fingers folded and forming the barrels of imaginary guns.

"Wuz' up?" was all Taylor could muster as he took stock of his situation. This was a universal greeting that could signify interest, indifference, or something more primal. The Mexican boys said nothing, but to Taylor their eyes took on the glowing quality reserved for alligators during the night.

Students began arriving for the second lunch session, but T. J. and Mark remained transfixed by the development surrounding Taylor.

"You see that shit?" T. J. asked.

"Yeah, I see it," and with his power voice deep within his diaphragm, Mark bellowed, "Taylor, get over here, dude."

He escaped the horseshoe of people that surrounded him by exiting to the left and using the aisle formed between the first two rows of tables. Requesting his presence served the purpose of removing him from possible danger and allowing him to retreat with some semblance of dignity.

"What the fuck am I supposed to do now?" Taylor addressed his question to Mark and to Officer Cruz who had just arrived. "I apologized already," he continued. "I'm not going to suck anyone's dick."

Cruz and T. J. broke out in laughter, and Cruz said, "Look at you, Nelson. What makes you think anyone wants your ugly face hanging off the end of their dick?"

"Yeah, you're really funny, bro," Taylor said, "but y'all can arrest me, suspend me, do whatever. I'm not afraid to get my ass kicked, but I'll take out at least one of those motherfuckers if they continue that shit. If you wouldn't have called me, I'd of split one of 'em already."

"Son," T. J. came back, "the only splitting I saw was when you hauled ass to get over here when the principal called you."

"All right, so you tell me what I'm supposed to do," and he looked at Mark.

"For starters, go to class. How come I saw you at first lunch?"

"This is my lunch. I didn't go to math class," Taylor answered.

"Look, Nelson, that's another conversation we need to have. For now, I don't recommend sitting by yourself or going anywhere in this school by yourself until we can figure something out."

"I got my boys over there," Taylor pointed in the direction of ten or twelve white American kids who now sat where he had been unceremoniously greeted. The six Mexican boys had taken to their area to the right of the shelter.

"Go sit over there and don't say anything to make things worse."

Cruz, T. J., and Mark watched Taylor strut over to his group, waving his hands and pointing in the direction of the Mexican group on the other side of the courtyard area. Their eyes shifted over to the Mexican side where one of the boys, Guillermo Santana, held out his middle finger.

Looking at Mark, Cruz asked, "Is that kid retarded or what?"

"Mr. M, may I answer that question for Officer Cruz?" T. J. begged.

"Go for it, T. J., but I've got to believe Lou may have a better idea with him being here every day."

"Boss, things aren't always as they seem. I feel safe in saying he's retarded!"

"You feel better now, T. J.?" Mark asked.

"Yeah, I'm good!"

"Guys, what are the possibilities of detaining all these kids and talking to them, either separately or together?"

"I'm willing to do that, Mark," T. J. answered, "but I'm reading them the fucking riot act. You know as well as I do how easily this fucking place can blow up, and I've known you too long and care about you too much to let that happen. You know my nephew goes here as well?"

"No, I didn't know that, T. J. Who is he?"

"He's a work in progress, Mark."

"What do you mean?"

"He's Nelson Taylor."

"You're shitting me, right?"

"Nah, Mark, in my family we got folks on both sides of the law. Nelson's not really sure what side he's on yet, so I'm here to help him make good decisions, not like his piece-of-shit father that my sister married." T. J. took in Mark's startled expression and said, "I'll tell you about that some time, but right now we've got this show going on," and he moved his outstretched right arm, palm down, forming a semicircle that encompassed both groups.

For the next five minutes, the three of them studied the two groups. About a dozen white boys stood with arms folded staring at the Mexican contingent that appeared equal in number. From their parallel foothold forty feet away, the Mexican boys assumed the same stance. Both groups seemed not to blink or move as if doing one or the other might be viewed as a sign of weakness. The birds lining the trees on the grassy right side began an incessant chirping that grated on the nerves. The adults in charge remained transfixed, and the objects of their attention had crossed one another's imaginary lines, up to the challenge but not knowing the rules of engagement. Things had become more complicated than they initially had thought, and now they lined up, checkers on a chessboard.

"Nah, nah, fuck this shit!" T. J. exclaimed. "Mark, let's go with your plan."

"T. J., you're thinking what I'm thinking. Can you go over to the white kids and hold them until the bell rings?"

"Count on it," T. J. said.

Mark walked over to David, who had just planted himself on a picnic table amidst the Mexican group. "Doc," he said, "I need you to keep this group in this area even when the bell rings."

"You got it," David promised.

Running short on time, he radioed Craig Isley on the exposed side to the left of the covered area. "Ice, tell Joe to free up the gym. We've got a problem, and I need to walk a group of kids into it for safekeeping."

"I'm on it," the Iceman assured, and just like that they sprang into action, grand masters of their universe, thinking several moves ahead. Mark had just enough time to tell Carrera and Hey You that they needed to be extra emphatic in their clearing of the lunch pavilion area.

"Let's go." T. J. motioned to the white group of boys who had been joined by about five girls, including Chloe Owens.

"What about those Mexicans?" Chloe inquired.

"You let me worry about them," T. J. answered, and his response led to a group grumble with indistinguishable verbiage.

"Mark," T. J. requested as he led his assemblage, "once I'm in the gym with this group, have Dr. C bring in the other kids."

The ancient gym always had the invitation of one side of pulled-out bleacher seating because they no longer could be pushed back against the wall. Multiple pennants hung from the rafters advertising past district championships in football, basketball, volleyball, and softball. The walls to the immediate left of the entrance were reserved for pictures of nine state championship wrestling teams in the past decade. South Demming had its glorious embattled history waged on wooden, dirt, and grass surfaces, but for this afternoon, it played host to a conflict of interests with scars deeper than any caused by a sport.

T. J. brought his group to the left side of the bleachers furthest away from the entrance, and seconds later Dr. C emerged with his group that T. J. directed to sit on the right side, closest to the entrance. Roughly the same forty feet that separated the two sides in the pavilion area was afforded by the bleachers. Among the Mexican students, Migdalia Santa Cruz, the lone female, afforded her perspective immediately upon entry.

"Y'all better watch your fucking backs, especially y'all bitches," she started as she pointed in the direction of the females on the opposite side of the gym.

"I don't know who you think you are," T. J. started, "but you're not coming in here and disrespecting this man. Mr. M, get her out of here before I arrest her."

"Migdalia." Sarah Szemanski emerged by the entrance. "You'd better come with me!"

Recognizing that no one was impressed with her tirade, Migdalia Santa Cruz left with Sarah Szemanski, who would make an afternoon's work out of a moment, while making the most out of his moment, T. J. Burns was frugal with time and generous with clarity.

"Now, I want everyone to listen up and listen good," he began addressing both groups. "I have too much respect for this man and what he's trying to accomplish to let anyone or anything stand in the way. I also have too much respect for this place. I graduated from South Demming, and I'm not going to let anyone turn this place to shit. These kids," and he pointed to the Mexican side, "have the right to display their flag during a national holiday. It's not personal toward you. And one of you," he referred to his nephew, but pointed to the white kids in general, "fucked up real bad, and you'll have to excuse my language because I don't know a better way to phrase it, by making a dumb-ass racist remark. But he also apologized for being a dumb-ass, and I'm asking you," he pointed to the Mexican side again, "to please accept it as sincere. I want to let slide what I saw ten minutes ago, but I swear on my two-year-old son's life that I will arrest every one of your asses if this shit continues. Are we clear?" There was an overall grumbling that resembled acquiescence. "Are we straight?" Again there was an air of resignation and more likely an air of relief that there was some adult intervention into this situation that could have gotten out of control.

After the two groups were released to their classes, Mark had damage control on his mind. The needs of the migrant population didn't begin and end with Pep Garces; he merely oversaw the programs throughout the county. His immediate contacts were Omar Velazquez and Caridad

Garcia, who orchestrated the events and catered to the needs of the migrant students. They were housed in the 500 section of the building, the only second floor at South Demming. Mark nearly burst into their office with his proposal.

"Mr. Velazquez," he began, choosing him over Caridad Garcia because he was closer, "Mexican Independence Day celebrations, because of ignorance, have managed to divide sentiments on this campus and create the potential for violence. I hope you know that I'm supportive of your efforts, but I need both of you," and now he looked at Caridad Garcia, "to educate and involve everyone on this campus with regard to what's being celebrated. I know that Pep went on earlier, but this seems to have fallen on deaf ears. Maybe we can bring some food and music into the equation."

Velazquez and Garcia were the symbolic tandem for this moment. Olive skin and soft features gave away the thirty-ish Garcia as a Mexican-born Spaniard. The black hair and leathery tanned skin of the thirty-ish Velazquez left no doubt as to his Aztec heritage. Almost two hundred years ago, their sentiments would have aligned with the Criollos to end Spanish rule. Now, they combated a less transparent subjugator sheltered under the umbrella of ignorance. Mark broke into the school coffers to find $200 to assist in the planning of an after-school celebration of tacos, burritos, and Mexican music. Caridad went on the PA that afternoon to announce the plans, which would take place three days later.

The afternoon and dismissal went smoothly, and Mark drove home contemplating how much time was invested in things on the periphery of education. The train crossing rails caught him in the middle of thought. At about the fifty-car count, the train stopped dead on the tracks. After ten minutes of waiting what would become a twenty-five-minute debacle, he was infuriated. There was nowhere to turn around because dozens of cars were behind him, and this was a one-way road. He called Sylvia to see if she had heard anything on the news that would provide a logical explanation for this static situation. She hadn't heard anything, and he simply stared at a brown train car and resigned himself to finding solace in the fact that nothing was going on.

Chapter 11

TEACHER BURNOUT, BIGWIGS, AND ALLEGATIONS

Barbara French's flat feet ached with each calculated step she took. Her yellow, round face kept pace as lips puckered and parted, and eyes squinted and opened in a painful harmony. Swaying like a pendulum, her oversize purse traversed the distance between her shoulder blades, marking time as she had been doing for the past thirty-five years. Now as she stopped in front of her classroom, her pain subsided, she opened the door, flicked the light switch, and found the mercy of her desk.

Her five-foot frame held 240 pounds of inertia that challenged the structure of the swivel chair that she used to negotiate the whereabouts of sundry items on her desk, the most important of which was her coffee cup. Therein she viewed its stained bottom, grabbed a thermos from her purse, which now rested at her feet, and poured the first cup of the morning on top of the previous day's residue. Putting on her reading glasses and taking her first sip, Ms. French opened up her teachers' edition textbook and marked off enough problems from adjacent pages to keep her students busy for the one hour and forty minutes that she would hold them.

Dick Van Slyke arrived at seven in the morning, just as he had done for the past thirty years at South Demming. He set down his combination lock briefcase in the middle of his desk and stole a glance at his reflection as provided by the cathode tube monitor that took up space on the left side. The image provided resembled a film negative but managed to capture the considerable pouches under his eyes and the unkempt goatee and mustache array whose ghostly grayness took attention away from the yellowed teeth that were courtesy of a two-pack-a-day Newport habit.

The three-digit combination was easy to remember, 225, the time that the last bell rang to dismiss his students. The top of the briefcase contained travelers' stickers, resembling a suitcase of those who like to boast of places they've been. Van Slyke had seen many parts of the world on tours that he financed through a teacher's salary, but beyond the cover of his briefcase, there was nothing within to suggest he was anything but well-travelled. His eyes received the assistance of his 250 reading glasses, and his thumbs negotiated the 225 and light sideways pressure that popped open the metal snaps. Within there was a plastic baggie containing a ham sandwich on whole wheat bread, an apple, a tiny tub of cottage cheese, an unopened pack of Newports, and the early edition of the newspaper. He reached for the paper, grabbed the first section, propped his feet upon his desk, and began reading. There was a time when the briefcase held more of his responsibilities than his comforts.

They filed into Ms. French's first-period intensive math class at the last possible second, with more than half the class's twenty-five students coming in at intervals after the late bell. The work was on the board. The books were under the desks. Her students were among the neediest of South Demming's population.

The desks were set up in five rows of five, perpendicular to the doorway. There was no assigned seating, so students who arrived early had their choices of seat, which inevitably ended up being in any one of the back rows. Most came with their supplies, which included MP3 players or iPods as they used technology to tune out the world. Others simply put down their heads upon their desks and caught up on sleep. There were, of course, a few students who placed a premium on their educations and did what was required of them, including asking questions. These generally were the new arrivals from other countries whose language deficiencies landed them in less challenging classes and whose upbringing combined with insecurities to make them an attentive audience. Their raised hands carried the weight of Ms. French's intolerance until their shoulders burned, forcing them to use their other arms. When they sought her attention by calling out her name, she finally grew exhausted by their insistence, threw back her body, causing the wooden chair's legs to screech like tires against the linoleum. She pounded her hands upon her desk, and the impact startled even those who were wearing their headphones. Like shattering glass and cracking ice, the arthritis in her knees and hips accompanied her arrival to the board.

"I can't believe that I'm going over this again," she yelled. "Perhaps if you listened the first time, I wouldn't be repeating myself!"

Her desk rested parallel to the students and to the immediate right of Mark's entry point. With a dry-erase board behind her, demonstrations required students to turn their heads to the left. She easily could have arranged the desks across the width of the room and turned them facing her, but like gawkers passing a car wreck, they craned their necks to see. Ms. French took notice of the principal's arrival. "Yes, how may I help you?" she asked, seemingly annoyed by his presence.

"Don't let me interrupt. I'm just visiting classes this morning."

He perched himself in one of the student desks in the second row. Seated parallel to his right, rather lying upon his desk with his head of hair covering its surface, a young man was snoring lightly. Mark tapped him on the shoulder and asked, "Dude, rough night?" Not knowing it was the principal making the inquiry, he raised his head, his hair totally covering his face.

"What the fuck, bro!" he exhaled with a hoarse whisper. Parting the drapery that was his hair and tucking it into the brackets that were his ears, he drew a preliminary thesis. "Whoa! Did the bell ring?" He started to reach for the skateboard underneath his desk. Two female students in their proximity giggled softly.

"No," Mark answered, "I just thought you might want to catch some of your class before you have to leave for next block." He immediately sat upright, looked at Ms. French's desk, realized she wasn't there, and then located her standing at the dry-erase board.

"Oh, I get it!" He turned to Mark. "This is a dream, right?"

"What are you talking about?"

"No, cuz, I never seen that lady teaching before." The two girls again giggled.

"Just pay attention!"

"We have a visitor this morning, and I would like for everyone to pay attention," Ms. French began. At that point, the four heads arose in slow motion, all looking toward Ms. French's desk and then turning forty-five degrees to pinpoint her novel location. "Mr. M," she continued, "the students have been having some trouble with solving for x in algebraic equations, so when that happens, I believe in reteaching the concept. Now, who can explain what I mean by isolating the variable?" Not a single hand tested the air. For the next fifteen minutes, and for her visitor's benefit, Ms. French continued asking and answering her questions and providing demonstrations on the like-new dry-erase board. The students, mindful of the principal's presence, sat upright, most with hands folded on desktops. Having seen enough of this, Mark got up to leave. He looked into several of the students' eyes as they followed him out, and for a moment imagined prison bars in their pupils. He made his escape.

Save for switching which foot was on top and slouching a little deeper into his office chair, Dick Van Slyke maintained his paper-reading posture as students entered his first block class. The two bulletin boards at the front and back of the room were covered with yellow construction paper and nothing more. Upon entry, one could see the dry-erase board directly ahead and desks facing toward it beginning to the immediate right of the doorway. There were six rows of five desks in each, and those seated furthest from the door had the best view of Mr. Van Slyke's feet. A pair of Hush Puppies with thumbtacks in heels, gum and hair stuck to one, and a newspaper opened up were the only things to suggest that the entity behind them was human. As students glanced at the board upon entry, dropped their book bags near their desks, and began copying vocabulary words from the board, Van Slyke advertised his existence by turning the newspaper page and repositioning his feet.

Whether it was definitions, answering questions from a reading selection, or putting together a five-paragraph essay, the Van Slyke sweatshop could churn out production, all of which remained ungraded in a huge pile atop his desk like compacted cars readied for sale as scrap metal. This pile was recycled every four and a half weeks when Van Slyke would return the papers to students with checkmarks being the only suggestion that he had given them a glance. He determined interim grades and final grades by the percentage of assignments that had been completed.

Van Slyke pared down this basic staple to its current forty minutes, and free time usually lasted an hour because he hadn't made allowances for the block schedule that the faculty voted in three years earlier. On most days, students waged war against the code of conduct with outlawed weaponry like MP3s, iPods, cell phones, and the passive resistance of sleep.

On this mid-September day, five minutes before the end of first block, one student, David St. Jean, chose to wage a war of words. "Hey, how much money you make?" he asked Van Slyke.

"I don't think that's any of your business," he answered.

"Maybe not, but I wanted to know because I want to do what you do," the young man continued.

"Oh, you want to be a teacher?" Van Slyke inquired.

"Nope," David St. Jean replied. "I want a job where I don't do shit and get paid for it!"

At this point, the class let out a collective "Whoa!" and for the first time that morning, Dick Van Slyke put down his newspaper, rose from his throne, and recognized that his left foot was asleep. Not daring to take another step, he stayed to the right of his desk and continued the conversation with David St. Jean.

"So, on top of being a dumb-ass, you're a smart-ass!" he blared over the sound of the bell, which had rung.

St. Jean digested the retort and exercised his right to free speech. "Hey, fuck you, Old Man!" he yelled as he exited the classroom backward and bumped right into the principal.

Without an excuse me or even any surprise, he turned around and continued. "Hey, you need to fire that dude. I'm tellin' him he needs to teach us, and he starts cursin' at me."

"The only one that I hear cursing is you," Mark pointed out. "I think you'd better go to the office while I get the other side of the story, and we'll talk." David St. Jean abided by the suggestion, and Mark stepped into Van Slyke's classroom.

"Well, boss," Van Slyke said as he sat on his desk rubbing some life into his sleeping foot, "I really can't have that kid in my class. I assume you heard him in the hallway."

"Yeah, I heard him for sure."

Van Slyke sized Mark up and continued, "I need your support with this. He can't insult me and undermine my authority!"

"What exactly happened?" Mark inquired in an attempt to see if there was any validity to St. Jean's claim. "Because I got to tell you, the kid comes out telling me you were cursing at him!"

Van Slyke's face grew flush. "Let me tell you something," he started. "That little smart-ass told me he wants a job like mine, so he can get paid for not doing shit, to use his words. Am I supposed to put up with that? The whole class heard him."

At this point, students were filing into Van Slyke's second block class, so Mark cut to the chase. He said softly, "Before I call this kid's family, I need to know whether or not you cursed back at him."

"Damn right, I did!" he admitted. "They don't pay me enough to deal with that kind of shit! All right, people," he broke away from the conversation to begin his class, "the work's on the board; let's get started."

Outside the principal's office, David St. Jean was sitting by the Buccaneer statue and repeatedly placing his palm atop the sword portion to test its sharpness. Ken Ferguson, who was lining up substitute teachers for the week, viewed this over his reading glasses.

"Hey, kid," he warned St. Jean, "the last person that touched that sword got cut so badly that we had to call rescue for him."

"Wow!" St. Jean feigned incredulity. "So how long were you laid up for?"

Not used to being outwitted, Ferguson turned to Mark, who had just arrived. "Hey, boss, can I get a raise?"

"David, let's go talk," Mark said, and he motioned him toward his office. Once inside, St. Jean took notice of some of the baseball memorabilia that adorned the walls. Mark had some frames and cards housing Detroit Tiger memorabilia going as far back as their World Series title of 1968.

"All this from back in your day?" he asked.

"I'm not so sure I want to answer that."

"Why? You ashamed of being ancient?"

The young man was an expert at finding scabs to pick. About five eight and maybe 135 pounds, he wasn't physically imposing, but he put the "ban" in the urban look, going all out with baggy jeans that he constantly had to hold up with one hand. He topped those off with a Tupac Shakur T-shirt that he illuminated with the sheen of the golden grill that covered his upper teeth. In his left hand, but usually atop his head when an adult wasn't around to tell him to take it off, was a New York Yankees cap complete with the official Major League Baseball tag still tied to the cap with a string. Accessorizing with a gold choker chain and an electrocardiogram pattern shaven into his closely cropped hair, David St. Jean's penchant for going against the grain stood out even more boldly than the boxer briefs that resurfaced each time he could drop his guard and his pants when adults weren't around.

"Nobody likes being ancient, David," Mark answered, "but I age even more when I have to deal with situations like this. Tell me what happened."

"Why? You're just going to suspend me anyway."

"Because I need to know," and Mark found himself raising his voice considerably as he said this. He motioned for him to sit down, and the two of them occupied the chairs on the other side of his desk, facing each other.

Mark realized that raising his voice threw a rock into the lake, interrupting the gleam in the boy's eyes, and David St. Jean emerged from his cocoon of sarcasm and was different. "The guy doesn't teach, Mr. M. He just puts shit up on the board that'll keep us busy, and then he never grades it. Today, he gave me attitude as soon as I entered the room, and he rode my ass the whole period. Everyone gets done early. Everyone talks, but I always get singled out."

"How'd he single you out?"

"Hey says shit to me like, 'shut your mouth,' or 'shut the hell up,' or 'sit your ass down,' and today I wasn't in the mood."

"And that's when you made the remark about his job?"

"I told him that I wanted a job like his where I didn't have to do shit and could still get paid. He's stealing from you, from the students, from the system."

"Did you strengthen your argument when you told him 'fuck you'?"

"It's not an argument," he countered. "It's not a debate. He ain't worth anything more than the response I gave him. I say what's on my mind. I'm at peace with that. I ain't no hypocrite. It's how I roll!"

"And how has that worked for you?"

"Well, I'm in the principal's office, so I guess that's up to you."

"I'm going to have to get your mother in here."

"That's all you got? You ain't suspendin' me?" St. Jean stood up abruptly and pretended to head for the door before doing a quick 180.

"Yup! We're talking parent conference, counselor and administrator present, and a look at your schedule. What kind of grades are you getting?"

"I get by with Bs and Cs," he answered, and his brow furled. "Why?"

"For the benefit of both parties, I'm thinking of putting you in an Honors English section."

David St. Jean shook his head. "I don't know, bro; that's a whole lot of work."

"Yeah, it is, but from what you're telling me, you've had some time to rest up in Van Slyke's class, so this will be a change of pace, not to mention the fact you're already taking Honors American History with Mr. Shipman."

St. Jean was speechless. He just put his head down staring at the floor and shaking it from side to side.

"So what are you thinking?" Mark asked.

"I'm thinking my mama don't speak English. She speaks Creole, and she's embarrassed by that."

"She doesn't need to be. We've got people in the office who speak Creole and can translate for us. As a matter of fact, I'm going to get one of them to call your house and make an appointment for her to come in today or tomorrow. I may just let you translate for us if I can't get anyone who's free when she gets here."

St. Jean lifted his head, displaying anew the light in his eyes. It now was his turn to throw a stone. "How'd you know I wouldn't be sellin' you out?" he asked, baring his golden grin.

"Because in each of my dealings with you, there has been one constant," Mark reflected.

"And what might that be, Dr. Freud?"

"You don't lie. You say what's on your mind. You ain't a hypocrite. It's how you roll."

It rained hard that afternoon. Strong winds swept debris into fence lines, door entrances, and hallway corridors. Water washed away the sidewalk dust like a wet sponge on a chalkboard. Students rushed to their buses, awaiting vehicles, or their cars so that the campus emptied out with a choreographed precision. And in the aftermath of a fifteen-minute downpour, there was the illusion of cleanliness, orderliness, and freshness.

Fanning out his umbrella a few times, Mark entered the main office. Ken Ferguson took notice of his dampened state and offered a suggestion. "You know, boss man, those umbrellas work a lot better when you hold them over your head."

"You know, Ken," Mark countered, "I didn't see you out there taking one for the team."

"Yeah, but I think I paid my dues when you had me babysitting that kid earlier today."

With the reference to David St. Jean, Mark entered his office, opened the closet, and placed the umbrella in a corner, out of plain view. He took his seat at the desk, put up his feet, and thinking of the closet and the rain, he wondered how many other principals had problems they wished they could tuck away or set adrift.

Immediately after the rain storm, the ninth-floor vista from the school board building was spectacular. The foggy film lifted from the windows and parted in deference to a rainbow that seemed to stretch beyond the limits of the ocean that it framed with its opulence. One day urban sprawl would bully its way into this picture, but for this day, Tonya Barton, the new deputy superintendent of Demming County schools, spoke of having vision, and through the clarity afforded by her thick prescription lenses, she could see for miles. Turning away from the view and walking back toward her conference table, she cast herself in the role of a most hospitable host to Sylvia Mahovlic, handing her a Styrofoam cup of coffee and pointing out her neatly arranged paper plate of Pepperidge Farm Milano cookies. Four o'clock in the afternoon was a time for self-indulgence, and Ms. Barton, who insisted on being called by her first name, was an elegant, tall, but seriously overweight middle-aged lady for whom a little pampering had become a rite of her station in life. She added cream to her cup of coffee and stirred until its hue matched that of her skin, and resting the plastic spoon on a napkin and taking a seat opposite her guest, she began the conversation with a decidedly masculine voice. "So, Sylvia, tell me, and be honest, how's your man making out at South Demming?" Her tone inspired confidence, and in their previous conversations, Sylvia had grown to admire this articulate and majestic woman, often sharing with Mark their exchanges and placing her on the pedestal that they both reserved for only the most special of people.

"Tonya, I've got to tell you. He's doing fine, but it hasn't been easy. South Demming always has been a tough school, and Mark is the kind of person who wants things to turn around right away. He's big on school safety, and that place has a history of violence, so he knows that he needs more security personnel."

The big woman digested these words with her cookie, took a sip of coffee to cleanse her palate, and spoke. "We need to get Chief Starling over there to do an assessment and see if we can get him some help. You let Mark know that I'm thinking of him, and I look forward to meeting him. If he's anything like you, he must be a special person. Sylvia, I'm sorry, but I have a conference call in five minutes," and with that she rose from her chair, a new cookie in hand, and hugged Sylvia as she nudged her toward the door.

After handling the afternoon e-mail, Mark had one foot outside the office door when the hotline rang. Contemplating the tree that falls in the forest when no one is around to hear it, he let out the loudest "Fuck!" he could muster prior to beginning his conversation with the mother bear.

"Mark, I just faxed you a copy of a very disturbing letter that Eileen Riordan received," she began.

"Really," he answered. "Who's it from?"

"The person didn't sign it."

"Mrs. Robreno, why are we giving such concern to an anonymous letter? Why isn't that letter in the trash?"

"Well, you see, when your school board representative gets a letter, and she forwards it to Dr. Traynor, and Dr. Traynor sends it to me with a written note, 'Magda, please look into this,' I'm less prone to dispose of it, and I have to be honest; it is an indictment of your leadership. Please look it over and call me with your thoughts tomorrow. Good afternoon."

Mark hurriedly retrieved the fax and imagined its edges curling up with fire as he began to read.

Dear Dr. Riordan,

As a school board member serving Area 6 and a Hanford resident, I know that you have a personal *intrest* in the welfare of South Demming High School. I share this concern with you and feel obliged to make you aware of a growing cancer that is taking over this school. Administration has been ineffective in *it's* dealings with the student population, and the *moral* of the faculty and staff *have* never been lower.

Yesterday, during lunch, there were at least 400 students in the hallway area outside the media center, instead of being contained in classrooms or the designated lunch areas. I'm sure a fight was going on, but no security or administrators were there to control this mess. Furthermore, students leave the campus and roam the surrounding neighborhood, causing complaints from nearby residents. We are only a moment away from a campus riot. Mexican kids have been allowed to carry their flags, and the white American kids have responded by bringing the Confederate flag. A firm hand is needed to weed out the delinquents and thugs that roam our school. The good kids in the school deserve better and feel cheated by *whats* going on. The message that is being sent is that you can get away with murder and come out with a slap on the wrist. I hope that you can use your influence to *interveen*. Please help South Demming before it's *to* late!

Mark's hand shook as he read this semiliterate rendering of the school's climate, and he probed his memory to weed out the spineless bastard, and words and moments came to light because he desperately needed them. And he remembered.

"That's what students need, some good old-fashioned expectations and some consequences!" And he remembered, "You going to let those Mexican kids carry their flag?" And he remembered, "You got to plan for this because it's likely to get worse." And he remembered the two-finger typist skulking out of the library, clinging to the wall like a chameleon but unable to change his color because backs weren't turned.

And he remembered David Canales's words, "What a fucking asshole!"

And he remembered the fucking asshole that once ran against Eileen Riordan for the school board. And he remembered Rex Hoffman.

"Mark, I know you too well. You sound upset. What's wrong?" Sylvia inquired when he called to tell her he would be running a little late.

"Something is wrong. I'll tell you when I get home in about an hour or so." He wasn't in the mood to go into detail. He figured he'd just let her see the letter when he got home, but in the meantime he was going to formalize his response to Mrs. Robreno by putting it in memo form.

"Are you going to be all right?" Sylvia insisted.

"I'll survive," Mark gave in. "Right now I'm just really pissed off, and I got to get something done. I'll see you in a little bit."

"Promise me you'll be careful driving home!"

"Don't worry about me. I'm fine."

At six thirty in the evening, exactly twelve and a half hours after he had arrived, Mark began his trek home. The train, too, was delayed, and he made it home in twenty minutes.

"I was worried about you," Sylvia began as she hugged him close to her. "What happened?" Mark led her to the bedroom, so the kids, who were doing homework, wouldn't see or know. He handed her the letter, and as they sat on the edge of the bed, and as he watched her read it and shake her head, tears of frustration filled his eyes. He wanted to hit something but instead simply bowed his head. Sylvia rubbed his shoulders, and in so doing, she both felt and absorbed his pain.

"Fucking Robreno wanted my response to this," he began. "All the years we've been told to ignore anonymous shit like this, and the bitch wants my response. She said it was an 'indictment of my leadership.' Can you fucking believe that?"

"Babe, I was talking to Tonya today, and she said something that I've been telling you all along. She said Chief should visit South Demming. He might be able to get you the help you need."

"Sylvia, I'm not closed to that idea. Everyone chooses to ignore South Demming, and when something bad happens, they look to point fingers. None of these assholes could walk in my shoes and do what I do for one single day. They would shit their pants, but because they are who they are, they've been anointed experts. What's wrong with this fucking picture? Everybody in the Area 6 office has an elementary school background. They don't have a clue about high school, and I have to follow their lead and listen to their fucking shit! I should've just stayed back and waited for a piece-of-cake job in Area 5."

"Mark, the kids at South Demming and the teachers at South Demming need you," Sylvia attempted to change his track. "You're there for a reason."

"Look. I know and believe what you're saying, but you can only be a martyr for so long. Sooner or later, I'm going to lose it, and it's not going to be good."

"You're too smart to ever let it get to that point. This too shall pass," Sylvia offered. "What you need right now is a shot and a beer."

The Americanization of Mexican Independence Day went off without a hitch Thursday afternoon. Students and adults of all ages and backgrounds filtered into the cafeteria after school to sample tacos and burritos ordered from El Matador, the Mexican contribution to Hanford's historical downtown area. Folk music played from a portable stereo system, and Mexican students donned the garb of their country and performed dances. They invited a few of their non-Mexican classmates to get on the floor and learn some of the steps. Danny Baldwin, Marcus Summers, and Landon Daniels gorged themselves courtesy of Coach Reinhold, who footed their entrance fees, and with a burrito in his hand, Daniels allowed himself to be tutored in some of the dance steps. That sight got everyone laughing as the clown prince of the Buccaneer backfield unveiled a few new moves. Coach Reinhold had stopped in with the boys at the tail end of the festivities, right after a good practice in the late summer heat. He also would be their ride home and endure the belches and farts that made him rue the fact that he didn't have a radio or air-conditioning in the old Aerostar van.

Having yet to receive any feedback regarding his response to Rex Hoffman's anonymous letter, Mark had reserved Friday as the day to confront him. As he contemplated this confrontation with the folk music serving as his theme, the BlackBerry buzzed, and he answered the five o'clock caller.

"Mark," Dr. Alice Chandler-Lopez began, "Dr. Warner and I are going to need to see you Monday at 10:00 a.m. at the area office. Please adjust your schedule." There was no inquiry as to whether or not he had a commitment; he simply was to be there at their beck and call, at their convenience.

"What's this about?" Mark asked.

"Dr. Warner and I are working on your professional development plan, and we need to go over it with you and have you sign off on it."

"Why am I going to be issued a professional development plan?"

"Oh, it's nothing bad," Chandler-Lopez said. "It's simply a map to assist you in your professional transition."

Mark immediately drew the correlation between Hoffman's anonymous letter and a knee-jerk reaction on the part of Robreno to show her proactive nature. On the chance that Roger Traynor might inquire as to her handling of the situation, she would offer him the fact that he had been placed on a PDP and was being held accountable to the objectives within.

In his days at South Demming, Mark learned never to relax for a moment. He learned never to call an end to a successful day. The minute he would let his guard down, bad news would hit him from an obtuse angle like the flashing red lights and long white guard rail of the train crossing. And sure enough, it got him again, and as he watched and counted the segments of its passage, he had the deepest admiration for its routine.

Chapter 12

LOOK WHAT THE WIND BLEW IN

With Melissa Franco's appointment to principal imminent, Belinda Cruz's escape plan in the works, and Ray Devereaux campaigning for his choice to replace one or the other, a number of things were blowing in the wind, not the least of which was the just-anointed Hurricane Katie. On the way home, Mark stopped at Publix to buy bottled water and some foodstuffs with long shelf lives. The lines of people in the checkout aisles resembled South Demming's hallway processions during class changes. Preparing for the worst had become a way of life for people in the Hanford area and beyond ever since Hurricane Alex had flattened the town thirteen years earlier.

Prior to this, almost thirty years of no close calls had bred a generation's worth of complacency characterized by people who seemed to wish a hurricane would come so that they could have a party. In September 1992, they got their wish, but Alex was a party pooper, flattening homes, killing hundreds of undocumented and uncounted in-the-death-toll aliens, knocking down trees that in their death throes grasped at the lawns they once adorned, tearing them out of the earth and leaving shards of roots resembling worn-out mops. Chainsaws became a tool of freedom in a suddenly primitive world as tribes from surrounding neighborhoods pooled this resource to cut paths to allow for travel by foot or by car or to simply allow for egress from a home. The trees that dared to stay in place had their limbs amputated by two-hundred-mile-per-hour wind bursts, rendering them as little more than giant toothpicks for the teeth of Alex's wind. In the storm's aftermath, most of the people of Hanford and several cities north could not recognize their neighborhoods, but they would forever recognize nature's fury.

The mother bear lived in one of the impacted cities north, and when Alex huffed and puffed and blew her house down, it also prepared her to lead her children in disaster preparation. Not needing to be cajoled by district-wide efforts to coordinate plans, Magda Robreno called her principals into an emergency meeting at the Area 6 office at four o'clock the next afternoon. "Thank you for being here on such short notice," she began as though choice was an option. "As you know, Katie is spinning in the Atlantic, and while it is several days away from making landfall, we need to prepare for the worst while hoping for the best."

"You give her another face and some nice tits, and she'd be the fucking weather lady," Don Torrento whispered in Mark's ear.

In Demming County, some schools served as hurricane shelters that principals were expected to operate in conjunction with the American Red Cross. The mother bear passed out the shelter schedule, which included all of her cubs as backups to the shelter school principals. She reminded them of the normal precautions to take with school equipment and to secure any objects that may become projectiles in hurricane force winds. In short, she spent thirty minutes going over the memorandum that was e-mailed by the district earlier in the day. "Keep your BlackBerrys charged. Use your car chargers if you have to," she said. "We must stay in touch in the event of a storm, especially so that we may do preliminary damage assessments and determine when schools may open again. I understand that most of you have families and would like to be making your own preparations as we speak, but remember that this is what you signed up for, and if you don't care for this or have the stomach for it, you may need to reconsider being a principal."

When Mark got home, Sylvia was watching the weather channel while preparing dinner, and Jesse and Janet, their ten- and eight-year-old daughters, were doing homework. He looked at their impossible perfection and boiled inside over Robreno's casual reference to taking care of one's family. What did she know? Just like nature had blown down her house, it chose to leave her barren and in an unhappy marriage.

Ninth grade had planned its Holocaust unit to start out the year, and in English I classes, they had been reading the *Diary of Anne Frank*. Having taught this unit during his classroom days, Mark still remained transfixed by Anne's notion that "People are basically good." How she could have been so charitable in her assessment of those who altered and eventually would end her life was a stopping point for class discussions.

He stopped by the school on the way back from the Area 6 office to clear off his desk of some paperwork and answer some e-mail. When he got there, Ray Devereaux, who also worked South Demming adult night school a couple nights per week, stopped by with David Canales.

"David, it's good to see you and thanks again for your help last week."

They shook hands, and Dr. C said, "Hey, man, it was my pleasure to be in the thick of things. Thanks for asking me. I know you probably got a difficult decision, but I owe it to my family to pursue your AP opening. I'm grateful for the night school job, but it's a dead end. I want to advance in this profession. My wife just had our first, a baby girl."

"Congratulations," Mark said. "Your wife and daughter are lucky to have someone as supportive as you."

Dr. C grabbed hold of his considerable belly girth with both hands, presented it to Mark and Ray, and said, "I grew this to support my wife during her pregnancy," and he amused himself enough to chuckle softly. "I saw you come in one night when you first got hired. You were with your wife and two girls," he alluded to their having helped him decorate his office. "I saw you guys interact, and I said to myself that you're the kind of person I could see myself working for."

"Well, if you can see yourself working for someone who doesn't know what the hell he's doing, then you've knocked on the right door," Mark said. At that moment, Dr. C emitted a loud belly laugh complemented by an infectious smile that brought enough levity that Mark found himself laughing along with him.

"You know we have mutual friends in Luke De La Hoz, who you worked with at Bronfmann and who taught with me at Coral Ridge, and Elisa Bravo, who tells me she's your children's godmother," Canales continued. "They tell me that you're as good a professional as they come and an even better person."

"It's a small world," Mark mused.

"Yes, it is. Just today, I could barely fit at my desk, and the cafeteria lunch portion they gave me was minute," Dr. C added with another brief but hardy laugh. Again, Mark found himself laughing with this person who perpetuated the "jolly" stereotype, but more importantly, got him thinking about being able to bring aboard some new blood, someone who seemed to have a positive outlook and didn't take himself too seriously.

"Listen, thanks for your time," Dr. C said, "but I've got to get back to work."

He left Mark in his office with Ray, who was staring at him. "Well, say what you want to say."

"Boss, Dr. C's smart as hell, and he speaks Spanish, which can come in handy around here, and he's got good people skills."

Mark began his drive home deep in thought. While he beat the train to the crossing this evening, he couldn't escape from an irony inherent in how children are weaned in education. In the earliest literary renderings, there is the celebration of innocence with the inspiring story of a little train that could, and how "I think I can" gives way to "I know I can." And they are given enough confidence to negotiate a pathway out of the frail state of childhood and into the tenuous state of puberty. It is here where they learn that trains also stop at places like Auschwitz, Bergen-Belsen, and Dachau.

"Damn; it's colder than my ex-wife in here," Ken Ferguson said, invoking a timeworn but suitable metaphor to describe the temperature in the main office. There had been a bite in the air ever since the chillers went amok two days earlier, and the main office, which normally gave substance to the argument of global warming, seemed to have entered the Ice Age. "Look at my fucking nipples, boss!"

Ken Ferguson's current business found him as, hands down, the ugliest secretary on the planet. At sixty-three years of age and packing about 290 pounds on a six-three frame, he sported a full head of salt-and-pepper hair to season the pot roast that was his belly. His pants and belt struggled against his girth, angling like a wrist and forearm on the losing end of an arm wrestling match. Ferguson was the big partier in a house rented out by him and two South Demming physical education teachers, twenty-eight-year-old Mike Landry and thirty-year-old Robbie Wolf, Penny Wolf's son and another lifer at South Demming. Instead of being a father figure or at least a mentor to these young men, he reveled in his ability to drink each one "under the table," utilizing another timeworn hyperbole borrowed from the same old act that got his ass kicked out of the house by his ex. Mark struggled not to look at his nipples, but Ken Ferguson was a sideshow in every sense of the word.

"Caught you looking," he said, and he held up a thirty-gallon plastic garbage bag to cover his chest area. Ferguson's South Demming connection was his ex-wife, Linda, who was part of the Fighting Gray in the early sixties and continued to make a good living as a general practitioner of medicine in Hanford. A Viet Nam War vet, he had a modestly successful house-painting business in Hanford and had most recently semiretired into his current role as the procurer of substitute teachers and a softball coach for the school. The garbage bag was on hand because he was orchestrating the conventional covering up of computer hardware and other office equipment in preparation for the potential flooding brought by an incoming hurricane. Late the previous evening, Superintendent Roger Traynor ordered that schools take the necessary precautions to safeguard equipment in preparation for a closing of schools. With the storm an estimated thirty-six to forty-eight hours away, Traynor made his decree that beginning Wednesday afternoon, schools would be closed until further notice to allow families time to prepare and to allow for an aftermath.

The winds of Katie would reach shore Friday night at about eleven o'clock, but her full fury spared Demming County to the tune of occasional gusts in excess of one hundred miles per hour and intermittent torrential downpours, breathtaking but not deadly if one remained inside.

The storm was hospitable enough to allow for sleep, albeit a restless one as wind-tossed projectiles periodically came to crashing halts, engraving their signatures atop aluminum shutters like the shadowy figures of South Demming's past anointed the first pouring of concrete into sidewalk frames. Nature left its mark with no ill intent and in a random fashion, unlike human beings who leave theirs with calculated precision.

Magda Robreno awakened Saturday at precisely 7:00 a.m. Her battery-operated radio was tuned into the weather station, and while most of the hurricane had crossed the state and begun to reconstitute in the gulf, strong winds and the promise of thunderstorms still prevailed in the Hanford area and further north. The Hurricane Center cautioned against going outside, given that there were downed trees, downed power lines, and significant flooding in lower lying areas. Power was out in more than a hundred thousand homes.

Hearing this, the mother bear did the prudent thing. She initiated the Area 6 phone tree by calling her directors and setting in motion an executive order that would guarantee her area would be the first to report conditions among its sixty-three schools. Mark received his call at seven thirty.

"Mark, what can you tell me about the condition of your school?" asked Alice Chandler-Lopez.

"Right now, Doc, I can't tell you anything because I'm checking out my home, and the window in my kids' room blew out, and Sylvia and I are cleaning it up. Besides, we aren't even supposed to be out on the roads yet."

"Mark, I understand the need to look out for your home, but please remember that Dr. Traynor is going to be expecting a report as early as possible so that he can make a decision as to whether or not school can open on Monday."

"I'm going to head out there now."

"Good!" She hung up the phone with an abruptness reserved for telemarketers.

Mark recognized that he and Sylvia had been playing Russian roulette for years with their home, never having bothered to secure shutters or storm windows. He felt they got lucky again with only a small hole and a crack in the kids' side bedroom window. Their lack of preparation was why they spent the evening at Sylvia's mom's house.

The roads were in pretty bad shape on their side of town, with palm fronds spread across them, pockets of flooding, and some downed but dead power lines that road crews already were working. Against Sylvia's wishes, Mark dropped her off at her mother's house and ventured south to check on the school.

"You're crazy," she stated, "but I understand."

Road conditions along the way were pretty much the same, with an occasional need to veer to one side or the other to avoid a smorgasbord of debris. He arrived at South Demming to discover that Don Scott already was there, and much to his surprise, so were Ray Devereaux and Bryan Reinhold. But there was one person whose presence pleasantly surprised him.

"Hey, man, I live in the area, so I thought I'd check things out," said David Canales.

"That's really nice of you," Mark said.

"Well, you know I work night school, so it's my responsibility to check things out."

"You're the man!"

"You don't believe me, do you?" Dr. C asked. Then he added, "Okay, I just want to show you my dedication because I want the fucking AP position when it opens up."

"I appreciate your honesty," Mark encouraged. "It's yours if my input has anything to do with it."

For the next two hours, the task force divided up the building, which still had no power, and used their flashlights to negotiate the hallways that were internal, taking time to make notes of any leakages or damage that they saw. The school looked no worse than it did after any big thunderstorm. It was so old that its lack of pristine condition served it well during times of scrutiny. Twice during their inspection, the power went on and turned off again, trading hope and despair.

The school was not ready to open on Monday, which was still two days away. The rest of the county, mostly due to power outages, reported the same, and the entire next week required essential personnel only to report to work. This, of course, included the principals, their custodial crews, and any other twelve-month employees. Mark thought this to be a time for him to exhale after a breathtaking beginning to his executive career, but he caught his breath when Ray Devereaux limped into view.

"Boss, three of the portables are really fucked up," he revealed, "and the bleachers along the practice football field got tossed all the way to the other side. That had to be a twister!"

"I'll add that to my report. Thanks, Ray."

"Katie gave us a pretty good blow job," Bryan Reinhold extrapolated. "We're going to need to house those portable classes somewhere else once we open up again."

Two of the portables' roofs were peeled off, each looking like a potato skin dangling at the precipice of the garbage bag, awaiting just one more slice of the knife.

"I'm going to let them know in maintenance," Don Scott added. "Them bleachers cost a pretty penny, and they're FUBAR."

Joe Carrera pulled up in his old Cadillac and stepped out to survey the scene. "I was here earlier, Magic," he began. "Seems like we take one step forward and two steps backward. The money for those bleachers was donated by Community Bank, so whatever insurance kicks in isn't likely to help in that area. Goddamn! Hey, your family make out okay?"

"Yeah, we're fine; nothing that a few bucks won't cure."

"Same here."

"Hey, what about you guys?" Mark looked at the contingent.

Everyone had pretty much the same experience at their respective homes. All Hanford natives since before Hurricane Alex, to them this was not much more than Winnie the Pooh's "very blustery day."

Mark slept all that Saturday afternoon and woke up in enough time to enjoy a couple of cold ones. The power had returned to their home, and they had a quiet evening. He didn't remember any dreams he had that night, but he remembered hearing a distant train horn attempting to interrupt his fall into a deep sleep.

For the next week, Mark presided over the skeleton crew of the day and night custodial team and his secretary. These were the "essential" personnel as mandated in that they were responsible for building and grounds upkeep, and in Cathy's case, answering the phone to disseminate the latest district perspectives on when school might open again.

Joe Carrera was hanging out periodically during this time and was in the office when Cathy came in to tell Mark that Magda Robreno was on the hotline.

"Mr. M, how are you?" she began.

"I'm fine, Mrs. Robreno. How are you?"

She didn't bother to extend the pleasantries to a report on the welfare of her family; rather she opted to conduct the business end of this phone call. Segues were not part of her conversational repertoire. "What can you tell me about Dr. David Canales?"

"Well, he works South Demming adult, and I've had the opportunity to talk to him, and I think he would be a good fit for the open AP position. Hell, he came here right after the hurricane to check up on the place."

"I agree with you; he is one of three people that have applied that we need to interview to go through with the formalities. This is a good opportunity for you to bring on board someone that is your hire, but I do have one problem with Dr. Canales."

The word "but" served as the filtration system to rid Magda Robreno of any particles of benevolence. "But" was the syringe that she used to inject venom into innocuous statements. "When he applied for your opening, we called him to find out if he had an interest in the vacant AP position at Hanford," she began. "He made it clear that he only had an interest in South Demming. Now, Mark, you have known me for a long time, and you know how I operate."

He envisioned a surgeon with a rusty chainsaw. He envisioned amputating the wrong leg, or extracting the wrong kidney, or taking out the good eye. Mark knew exactly what she was going to say because, as she had indicated, he had known her for a long time.

"We are all soldiers. We don't have the luxury of choosing our assignments. I agree with you that Dr. Canales is the best choice, but rest assured that as long as I'm the superintendent in Area 6, he will never become a principal."

Giveth and taketh away were the weekly specials at the Area 6 commissary. For want of something better for himself and his family, Dr. C sold his soul.

"Now, you are aware that Belinda Ruiz has put in for a transfer as well?" Robreno added.

"Yes, I am, and that's probably for the best. I don't want anyone who doesn't want to be here."

"Agreed!" Robreno said. "Of course, once she transfers, we will have to interview for that position as well. We will have to be extremely careful, considering that this is for an assistant principal over curriculum. Have a good day."

Having waited out the conversation at the doorway, Joe Carrera surmised its gist and inquired, "So, Magic, we got a replacement for Franco yet?"

"Looks like it's going to be David Canales, Joe."

"Oh, you mean the fat guy from night school?"

"Hey, I resemble that remark." Dr. C appeared at the office doorway. "The fat guy from night school at your service," he said and added his patented chuckle that Mark knew had a place somewhere amidst the twisted metal and shorn rooftops that refused to let go, spitting into the wind.

"Magic, I'll see you tomorrow." Joe Carrera left abruptly.

"Hey, man," Dr. C began. "I need your advice. Earlier today, Mrs. Robreno called me to offer me the AP position at Hanford. I refused it, telling her that I had an investment in South Demming, with my working night school and all, but I think she was pissed off. Man, that school is out of control, and I don't want to be part of any wrecking crew that's sent down there. This is where I want to be. I want to work for you. Do you think I fucked up?"

"David, I think you are going to be working for me, and I can't speak for Mrs. Robreno. She probably wasn't happy that you turned her down," I spared him the grisly details, "but in the school system in which we work, she could be gone tomorrow."

"I fucked up, didn't I?"

"Yeah, you fucked up, but welcome aboard."

David Canales was there at seven in the morning, Monday, October 2, and he was there for the rest of the way. He joined his new boss and Ray Devereaux out on the track that morning, and rather than send him back in when the hallways cleared, Mark invited him to accompany them to South Demming Park on the reconnaissance mission. There was a spot for one more rider on the golf cart, a step in the back. Dr. C took that position and held on as the cart groaned against the more than nine hundred pounds of human beings it contained. Mark looked back at him, the morning sun in his face, the wind blowing his wavy hair, the ever-present smile, and he was left with only one thought. "You look like the fucking pope riding back there."

"No," David Canales said. "I'm not the pope. I am San Gordo, the patron saint of fat asses everywhere!" And he chuckled, and suddenly everything seemed right, and the weight of the world left Mark's shoulders and landed on Dr. C's like two birds on a clothesline in winter.

Chapter 13

THE SWEET AND THE SOUR

"Thirty-two, thirty-two, we've got a thirty-two by the main office!" Sarah Szemanski yelled into her radio.

"What is that? Who is that? Where are we going?" Dr. C yelled, losing his breath as he chased Mark down the social studies hallway and made the sharp left turn to the main office area.

Dr. C got the visual quickly. Lying on top of a black female student, Bryan Reinhold had her on her stomach with her hands pinned to the ground, using his 340 pounds to his advantage.

"I can't breathe! I can't breathe! Get off me, you fat fuck!"

"Hey, if you've got enough air to get that out," Reinhold noted, "then you can breathe. Enjoy the oxygen, and I like to think of myself as gravity challenged if you don't mind."

"Boss, I got a call into 911," Sarah Szemanski revealed. Immediately to the left of Reinhold's pin, Ms. Essie Hunt lay in a fetal position, her right cheek visibly swollen. A long tear streak accented her pain, and she only responded with a moan when Mark inquired as to whether or not she was okay.

The ambulance siren sounded in the distance, and he looked ahead to see Officer Cruz on the ground atop another black female who was more subdued. He got up and, holding her arm, walked her to his office.

As the paramedics worked on Essie Hunt, Sarah Szemanski proffered a greeting to Dr. C. "Welcome to South Demming. I guess you didn't see too much of this in night school."

"What happened? Is she going to be okay?" Dr. C couldn't hide an astonished tone.

"I wouldn't be surprised if her jaw is broken," Szemanski diagnosed. "Latonda kicked her in the face trying to get to Chantel. Ms. Hunt lost her balance and found herself on the receiving end of several kicks."

"What was this about?" Mark inquired.

"Who knows?" Szemanski answered the question with a question. "Things happen in the neighborhood over a weekend, and they spill into the school. I'm going to go to the hospital with Essie. It's starting to heat up!" She stared at Mark. "This is your first go-round; you may want to take notes," and she sniffed the air with the exuberance of a dog sniffing another dog's ass.

The orbit bone around Essie Hunt's eye was slightly fractured, and she sustained a concussion. She would not return to work for six weeks. Latonda Rowe and Chantel St. Pierre were arrested and charged with battery on a school board employee, suspended for ten days, and recommended for expulsion, a formality that generally yielded the desired result of removing malcontents from the South Demming campus. The argument was over a boy and which of the girls was more of a "ho." Essie Hunt prayed for her attackers; there was no venom in her makeup, and healing was a given variable in her ecclesiastical existence.

Mark looked directly at David Canales. "I'm sorry that your first official moments here had to be so unpleasant," he offered, "but you kind of already had your indoctrination," he added in, referencing Mexican Independence Day.

"I'm still trying to figure out Szemanski," Dr. C answered. "She spoke to you so disrespectfully, and she almost seemed glad that this whole thing happened."

David was perceptive. He handed over a palette and canvas to paint the picture, but it only would lend color to the conclusion that he already had drawn. Mark wanted to agree with him, but it wouldn't have been fair, so he went around the cavernous opening rather than echo his sentiment.

"David, I'm only going to be able to give you today to get yourself situated in your office. I'm letting Belinda Ruiz go to her new school tomorrow. I don't want someone here when her heart is somewhere else. South Demming requires being guarded at all times, and I need all hands on deck."

"No offense," Dr. C came back, "but if you think I'm going to be decorating on my first day here, that won't happen. I've got the weekend to move in. Tell me where you need me."

"I appreciate it, David. You can hang out with me during lunch duty. I need you in the media center hallway during class transitions, and out by the flagpole during dismissal. Try to take care of getting situated as much as you can, but I may need you to deal with some of the fallout."

Dr. C looked puzzled and said, "I'd be happy to do that if I knew what you meant."

"David, when we arrest kids, the worst part often is in dealing with their parents afterward. Jefferson is working on the paperwork with Isley. Why don't you pass by there and see if they need a hand."

"Will do."

Mark had retreated to his office to check e-mail and provide requisite signatures on myriad documents when the hotline rang. He spared Cathy the inevitable unpleasantness from whichever Area 6 executive would be on the other end.

"I'm surprised you answered your line considering what I heard just happened there," said Wilma Hart with her New York drone. Dr. Hart, not his immediate supervisor, was filling in for Dr. Alice Chandler-Lopez, who had indicated in a recent e-mail that she would be taking some "spa" days. Recalling that e-mail, Mark tuned out Dr. Hart and envisioned Chandler-Lopez cloaked in a kimono with cucumber slices on her eyes and a pickle-length slice over her forehead exclamation point. He laughed to himself.

"Are you listening to me?" Hart's angry voice interrupted his daydream. She must have said something requiring a response.

"No, I'm sorry. I got distracted. We have a lot going on this morning."

"I am well aware of that. I have my sources, Mark. It's getting to be as bad as Hanford over there. You have to take control. You can't bury your head in the sand. You can't be in denial. Make sure I have an incident report. Call me if you need me."

Dr. Hart likely didn't appreciate having to do double duty, particularly since her feeder pattern contained all the lower-maintenance schools in Area 6. Nevertheless, Mark was certain that she felt she fulfilled her obligation by reminding him of his. To her, he was an ostrich with its useless wings, unable to grasp the gravity of the complexities weighing down his school. While she didn't boast of "spa" days, she was fond of revealing details of shoe-shopping expeditions, and for someone of her less-than-five-feet-tall stature, she did have some remarkably big feet. He surmised that this was part of nature's way of compensating by balancing out her even bigger head, a head that would suffice as the top of a PEZ candy dispenser, tilting back and delivering one sour morsel after another.

Back to reading his e-mail, Mark started thinking about what Hart meant when she said she had her sources, but before he could break into an analogy, Ken Ferguson's voice took him back to the present.

"Excuse me, ma'am, but you can't just go in there. Who do you need to see?"

"Who the fuck you think I need to see?" a heavyset black female screamed. "Where the damn principal?"

Mark stepped out and introduced himself. "Ma'am, you've got two choices. You can stop screaming and cursing, and I will give you all the time you need, or you can continue this, and I'll call for the police."

"This yo office?" she asked.

He pointed out the way with an underhand gesture, and she walked in like a bull in preparation for charging the matador. In her tow was another female who appeared to be about the same age.

"Excuse me," Mark said, "and you are?"

"I'm her neighbor. I'm her ride."

"Then I'll need you to please sit in the office." She obliged, taking her perch on the couch in front of Ken Ferguson's desk and immediately adjacent to the replica of the Buccaneer, and Mark went into his office to greet his guest.

He sat down next to her in one of the two chairs in front of the desk. Before he opened, he took in the appearance of his angry visitor. He was certain that she was the mother of one of the girls from the morning's escapade. She was in her late thirties, sporting cornrowed hair with purple braided extensions. While she wasn't wearing any jewelry, she had long, elaborately detailed fingernails and an RIP gravestone tattoo resting peacefully between her ample breasts that struggled for freedom against the encasement of a tank top, like two children on their tippy toes, peering over a fence.

She began speaking without looking him in the eye, opting instead to pout at a twenty-degree angle from his face. "Where my baby at?" she asked, still looking away.

"I'm going to assume you are the mother of one of the girls who fought this morning."

"I'm Ms. Rowe, Latonda's mama," she revealed.

"Latonda got into a fight this morning and—"

"You ain't tellin' me nuthin' I don't already know." Ms. Rowe pointed her right index finger and waved her hand as if she were swatting away gnats. Her fingernail knifed through the air as though it were tangible, cutting it into ribbons. "Latonda and Chany been havin' problems for some time. I been askin' Mr. Jefferson to help, but he ain't done shit. This past weekend, I brought Latonda to Chany's house, and her mima and I agreed to let 'em have it out on the front lawn. They kicked they asses, and I thought we was done with dis shit. Now I just got a phone call tellin' me she been arrested. How come I get called after the fact?"

"Are you aware that your daughter kicked one of my security guards in the face?" At this point, Ms. Rowe looked him in the eye. "We had to call an ambulance to have her checked out because she was barely conscious, and it looked like her jaw might have been broken." These words succeeded in having Ms. Rowe once again look away from him.

"My baby wouldn't do that!" she stated while continuing to look away.

Mark wanted to question her sanity at that point. This woman just admitted that she hand-delivered her daughter to a neighbor's home so that her kid could fight with another kid, and in the same breath she had the temerity to imply that this was not part of her child's nature. "It's not going to do us any good to argue over who did what," he said. "Your daughter is at the JAC, the Juvenile Assessment Center. You need to go home and wait for a phone call—"

"I ain't got no phone," Ms. Rowe interrupted. "My baby know to reach me through my neighbor."

"Then I'm sure she will let officers know to call that number, but I guarantee you that the processing part will take you well into the evening. You won't be able to see her even if you go there now. In the meantime, you need to know that board rules require that Lantonda be suspended for ten days and be recommended for expulsion."

"Oh, so now she won't even be allowed to go to school? Look, she might of fucked up, but she's a smart kid with good grades. So now what?"

"Take it one step at a time. Let the courts decide; let the system make a determination."

"Mr. Principal, dat system ain't never worked for me." Ms. Rowe looked him in the eye. "Thank you for your time. I do what I got to do. Someone should of call me before my baby go to jail. That ain't right. I do what I got to do." She departed with an angry gait that had her purple braids bobbing up and down with each stomp of her feet.

There never came a query from Ms. Rowe as to the welfare of Essie Hunt. In her world, Ms. Hunt likely was collateral damage to more pressing concerns. Mark had no idea of the meaning behind "I do what I got to do," but he suspected it was more of a pacing mechanism, cloaked as an idle threat, but the school system provided many exploratory avenues so that those who were justifiably cornered and helpless still could lash out.

Chantel St. Pierre's mima proved to be unreachable, and it required a visit to the home by the school social worker to deliver the associated paperwork. There never was a confrontation or the request for a confirmation. Chantel simply was adjudicated and went to opportunity school, as did her foe, Latonda. To say that assuming a posture of resignation appeared to be the more time-efficient choice would be accurate on the surface, but the question remained as to whether this was an example of choosing one's battles or simply giving up the fight.

Two hours later but worlds away, Wilma Hart had a shoe salesman slip her foot into a pair of Etienne Ainger stilettos. This diversion concluded her business lunch with Magda Robreno and further lightened her wallet by $120. She had to put her best foot forward.

At the end of the third and last lunch, Mark ventured into the hallways to encourage kids to get to class on time. On the football practice field's track, about fifteen kids were walking toward the back exit instead of heading to class. As he called out to them, they broke into a unanimous run, a flight that found them scattered about the surrounding neighborhood. Bryan Reinhold was perched in his golf cart in this area.

"Boss, you want to hop in, and we'll see how many we can round up?" he offered.

"No," Mark said as he watched them grow smaller and well out of reach. "Bryan, this is just great. I'm the principal of a school that students would rather run away from than attend."

From the vantage point of his portable doorway, which was perpendicular to the track, Rex Hoffman surveyed the scene. When he saw Mark look back at him, he closed his door.

"You can't take it personally, boss." Reinhold attempted to comfort him. "They've been doing this since I've been here. Hell, I used to be one of them."

"That doesn't make me feel any better, Ryan."

"Yeah, but it makes me feel better. I've been carrying that guilt and have wanted to get it off my chest for years."

"What do I look like to you Ryan, a fucking priest?"

Reinhold looked at him for a moment, grinned, and said, "Maybe not, but what the hell. Forgive me, Father, for I have sinned."

That afternoon, Mark stayed late to get caught up on some e-mail. At about four thirty, two hours after dismissal, the hotline rang. Knowing that everyone pretty much had gone home, he contemplated not picking it up, but within the context of this day, and knowing his surgical link to the BlackBerry, what would one more source of aggravation mean?

The voice on the other end was that of Ron Hofer, a retired principal, who picked up some part-time dollars working out of the Area 6 advocacy office. His job was to field complaints, usually from parents, regarding unresolved issues at given schools. During this day, he had met the acquaintance of Ms. Rowe, and she had painted a picture of the principal's performance in relation to her daughter that was more colorful than the bouncing purple extension braids that dominated her head.

"Mark," Hofer started, "as a former principal, I know how these things can get out of hand. Ms. Rowe's biggest concern rested on why she wasn't called when her daughter was arrested."

"Ron, I don't know how many times you've been involved in having to arrest a student, but the only thing that apprising a parent in advance guarantees is that the parent will be on the school's doorstep demanding to see his or her kid. Some of the time, parents lose their cool, and they end up getting arrested. What would you have me do?"

"Hey, don't shoot the messenger. I just need your stance for my report, and as far as I'm concerned, I would have done the same thing."

"Ron, look—there's an incident report to which you have access. It outlines everything that happened. Her kid broke my security monitor's jaw by kicking her, and you and I are debating the merits of my actions. If I would have brought this lady in while her daughter was still on campus, my resource officer could have had me arrested for obstruction of justice."

"Mark, that's why I never wanted to go beyond elementary school in my administrative career," Hofer answered. It was that answer which was emblematic of a big problem in Area 6. Not only were those in charge incredibly impersonal; not a single one of them had ever been a high school principal, so their perspectives were meaningless on many issues.

"Look, Ron, I'm sorry to go off on you, but it's been a shitty day and a long day, and I just want to go home."

"I don't blame you," Hofer said. "Hang in there."

As he grabbed his keys to head out, Mark thought that Hofer, at least, seemed decent and understanding. He poked his head into the APs' offices to see if any were still around. Dr. C was still in his office while Jefferson had long since gone, and he figured Szemanski likely left the hospital to take a long lunch and call it a day.

"Hey, man, you okay?" Dr. C asked.

"No, man, I'm not. Sometimes I wonder what the fuck I'm doing here," he found himself confessing to David.

"Hey, man, I've been around here at night, and now I've seen you at work by day, and I've spoken to enough kids and adults to know what you're about. You're a rock star here!" he exclaimed.

"Dave, if I ever need a publicity agent, I'll know who to call, but thanks!"

Sylvia was a great cook who couldn't find the time to do so during the week, so as they waited for the pizza to arrive, they did what two educators who live together do; they vented, they commiserated, they tried to make sense out of the nonsensical. They were fortunate in that these debriefings proved cathartic. They had each other as sounding boards, and as such, the relationship was strengthened.

"I don't have an answer to fix the violence in this place," Mark started. "They expect me to keep the peace with five security monitors in a school that has a thousand more kids than it's built to handle. I don't have the budget to bring any more full-timers on board, and the part-timers are either unreliable or they leave once they get a full-time position. How can they give Hanford eleven full-timers when they have the same amount of kids, and their campus is nowhere near as open as ours is?"

"Babe, why don't you let me talk to Chief? He works down the hall from me, and he's always asking how you're doing." Sylvia mentioned her meeting with Tonya Barton and offered her connection to the school system's chief of police, Harold Starling. "As a matter of fact, he's a big football fan and was asking if you can get him field passes to one of the games."

"Joe can hook him up. That won't be a problem. Go ahead and ask him if he can pay us a visit."

"I will."

The Palm Coast game ended up being South Demming's second game of the season with the two weeks lost to the hurricane. It was scheduled for that Friday, October 6. This also brought to Mark's memory the promise he had made regarding allowing for a pep rally on that afternoon. To complicate matters, he would be out of the building the next three days to attend a district-sponsored principals' workshop on building positive school cultures to assist in ushering in the Continuous Improvement Model as a means to tackle the dilemma posed by the state test, the MARI (Math and Reading Inventory).

Along with its students, Demming County's schools were receiving grades for their performances. It was no secret to anyone that Dr. Roger Traynor's arrival had coincided with the county's dismal overall performance on the MARI. His message was clear. He intended to bring in people from the outside to fix the mess on the inside, and despite surrounding himself with a handful of imports he knew from earlier times, no one among his guest experts and recently arrived intimates could grasp the magnitude of the Demming County dilemma. Their PhDs and newly anointed status kept them flying below the radar but right into being bugs on the windshield. So it was in the opulent trappings of a Hilton Hotel, complete with complimentary breakfast and lunch, that principals received the professional development and strategized to create a more perfect world on their respective campuses. There were no expenses spared on the part of a school district that had no spare change, so the eggs Benedict were digested in enough time to enjoy the chicken cordon bleu, and everyone at least whet their appetites even if they didn't develop a taste for change.

"So how's it been going?" Angela Leon inquired as they waited their turn in the buffet line during lunch. "I hear they let Belinda leave, so who's your new curriculum AP gonna be?"

"I don't know yet," Mark answered. "They haven't scheduled any interviews."

"What?"

He watched Leon's nostrils flare, each one almost as wide as her perpetually open mouth. She always carried with her a someone-just-farted face. As she scooped up some scrambled eggs and placed them on her plate, she left him with some food for thought.

"Call me if you need me. You'd better hope you don't end up being an F school."

Choosing to focus on something within his control, Mark used the BlackBerry to e-mail Kim Bennett and mobilize her and David Canales to see to it that the arrangements for the pep rally would be meticulous and that the students would understand they were being trusted to handle themselves in a dignified fashion, not only during the pep rally but during the days leading up to it. He looked around to see his fellow principals doing the same thing. It pained all of them to be away from their buildings, and during every break in the proceedings, they contacted secretaries or APs to check on the status of things.

Worry was something that principals carried with them long before the advent of the BlackBerry; the technology simply allowed them to worry with greater efficiency. And whether they were typing with thumbs into the BlackBerry or appearing to talk to themselves via the Bluetooth headset, the circles under their eyes and the frown lines on their foreheads provided more telling stories. With the exception of a power failure on Tuesday that caused the classrooms to be unbearably stuffy, the three days of Mark's absence from campus were free of any catastrophe. When Thursday came to a close, and Dr. C gave him a positive report, he breathed in deeply the air of satisfaction, and he held it in his lungs, not because he was reveling in the moment but because he had forgotten how to exhale.

As a follow-up to the three-day workshop, Magda Robreno was the only region superintendent who reconvened her principals the next morning. On a whim, she decided, via her telephone tree, that it would be beneficial to reflect upon "where we were and where we were going."

From 8:00 a.m. to 10:00 a.m., they reflected, and because Robreno was multitasking this morning, she met with her directors after modeling what she wanted from the principals. They had about an hour's worth of material and spent the next hour waiting to be dismissed. Robreno returned and, appearing preoccupied, dismissed them minus the characteristic negativity that was her gift. Mark returned to his campus feeling that he had been spared an indignity.

Arriving during the bell for third period, he grabbed his radio and headed out to the major intersection that was his post. Before he made it, Joe Carrera caught up with him in stride. He seemed unusually giddy in keeping with his nature, and by this time, Mark had learned to be his audience.

"I've got two words for you, Magic," Carrera began. "Cha ching, Magic; Cha fucking ching! Ah hah, hah, hah, hah, hah!"

"It's great to see you in a good mood, Joe. To what do we owe this moment?"

It was still transition time between classes, and Carrera pointed out the obvious. Every other kid had a pastelito in his or her mouth as they made their way to class. "It's the return of sugar, Magic!" Carrera explained. "Look around you for God's sake!"

"Hey, Coach," Matt Mathews said, "what do you call these things?"

"Why? You like them?"

"Hell yeah. Can you lend me a buck, so I can get a couple more?"

"Here you go," and Carrera handed the quarterback a dollar.

"Hey, Coach. Them pasta whatevers are good!" Danny Baldwin exclaimed. "Can I pay you back tomorrow?"

"I'll start a tab for you, Danny," Carrera acquiesced.

"Joe, what are you, a fucking pusher?" Mark asked as he took in the scene.

"Magic, I ordered five hundred pastelitos figuring I would take a bath on this. We just sold the last one, and the supply is not meeting the demand. It's Economics 101. It's butter and guns. It's he said, she said," and he rambled as saliva began to bead up at the corners of his mouth.

"Hey, Coach, can you lend me a buck?" Marcus Summers inquired.

"Here you go."

"Joe," Mark said, "have you actually sold any of these?"

"Magic, we've sold plenty, but it's all about marketing. Once the football players put these in their mouths, everyone will follow."

"You're a fucking pusher," Mark insisted.

"Nah, Magic, I'm a businessman. Five hundred pastelitos times fifty cents, and you've got $250 gross revenue. Multiply that by the five days in a week, and you've got $1,250. We get to keep sixty cents on the dollar, so that's $750 profit each week. Multiply that by thirty-six weeks, and you've got $27,000 cleared from the sale of pastelitos!"

Carrera initiated a high five and slapped Mark's hand so hard that it stung for the next ten minutes. "I love you, Magic! I love life! Look at me! I can speak Chinese! Cha ching! Cha motherfucking ching! I love you, Magic!" Carrera gave him one of his bear hugs, almost lifting him off the ground, and he went into his office to count his profits.

With the one-minute warning bell sounding, Chartavia Thompson, the coeditor of the school newspaper, the *Swashbuckler*, looked at her principal and was pointing at her watch.

"Mr. M, that's three days. Where have you been? Everybody misses you. You're always in our classes. You're always out at lunch with us."

"Well, I missed you guys too," Mark said. "They had me at a principals' training for the past few days."

"Well, don't do that anymore. You hear me?"

The architectural scheme for the original South Demming featured the gigantic auditorium as its focal point. The first built of the nine buildings comprising the campus, the auditorium still boasted the original cherrywood seats and a solid maple stage. In its time, reel-to-reel movies beamed from the projection booth to entertain members of the farming community on a Saturday night. As the community grew and new churches were planned, the auditorium substituted as a place of worship on Sundays. Local thespians and aspiring play writers once unveiled their productions in this venue of so many memories. The auditorium was not only the proudest among the South Demming edifices; it was the centerpiece of a proud and prospering community.

But pride made of concrete and stucco has a lifespan, and memories not passed on to succeeding generations lived only within the aging walls and gave birth to folklore. Custodians had told of indistinct voices when they opened up the auditorium in the dimness of the morning. Neighboring homeowners had called the school to report lights flickering and silhouettes moving about during nonoperational hours.

Now the soulless cast-iron wrecking ball loomed in the near future, and in anticipation of this day, neglect became an unchecked fungus, leaving leaks unplugged, burnt bulbs unattended, and peeling paint undermining the memories, cornering them in the unlit recesses so that they crouched in fear of what daylight might bring until the night came to signal one more day's reprieve. Perhaps it was in jubilation that the memories found life in the present. A common thread that bound all the tales of strange lights, strange figures, and strange voices was that they all began shortly after 1992 when Hurricane Alex struck and the first talk of building a new South Demming commenced.

Kim Bennett was a senior and captain of South Demming's cheerleading squad in 1992. For her, restless spirits would always give way to school spirit, and she had it down to the exact detail required for the pep rally. This event would be for the classes outlining the social studies patio, portables one through eleven, and the science wing. Any future pep rallies, should this one be successful, would include other sections of the building. In the meantime, BUC TV, the school's closed-circuit broadcast, piped the sights and sounds into classrooms. In all, about seven hundred students were invited to the 930-seat auditorium. This left room for the band members, the cheerleaders, the Blue Tide Steppers, and, of course, the football team. At the beginning of seventh period, Bennett went on the PA and governed the pace and the order of rooms reporting to the auditorium. The security team and the leadership team dotted the path with their presence, and teachers of invited classrooms led their students to assigned sections where they could monitor the proceedings.

The cheerleaders, led by Christy Del Pino, positioned themselves at the foot of the stage and waved their pom-poms and danced as the brass-laden band at the back of the stage blared out the song "Are You Ready?"

Seizing the moment and the stage microphones, senior defensive backs Danny Baldwin and Raja Horton began the proceedings.

"Wuz up, South Demming?" Baldwin yelled. The crowd yelled in a deafening unison that still didn't meet the players' standards. It was Horton's turn.

"That's all y'all got? Y'all got to give it up. We playin' Palm Coast!" At this point the fifty-two-year-old auditorium had its ghosts exorcised along with the cobwebs and the dust that had yet to find their way to the creased eyes and gray hair of Coach Reinhold and Joe Carrera. Mark tried to read Carrera as he stood next to him along the right side wall of the auditorium. He had a sour look on his face, an expression that even one of his pastelitos couldn't sweeten. Once the noise subsided enough to be heard via yelling, he looked at Mark and began shaking his head.

"I hate fucking pep rallies, Magic," he screamed.

Returning the favor, Mark hollered back, "Why?"

"They're a pain in the ass and a distraction. Don hates them too."

Mark looked to the stage as Danny Baldwin introduced his coach. "Y'all going to have to do better than that when I introduce Coach Reinhold. He's not just a coach; he's a father figure and a role model to all of us. None of us wanna win for ourselves; we wanna win for Coach. Come up here, Coach. Give it up for Coach Reinhold!"

At this point, the cheering attained its previous crescendo and was complemented by the band again playing "Are You Ready?" Reinhold climbed the five steps to the stage, pushing on his knees with his hands. He took the mike and was bear-hugged from front and behind by the football-playing emcees.

"You guys need to make sure you wrap up like that tonight against Palm Coast," Reinhold began. "I got to tell you; it's been years since we had a pep rally, and I really miss them. I'm excited, and if you kids can't get excited about the game tonight, then you need to have your oil changed!"

"I thought you said he hated pep rallies, Joe?"

"Magic, there's something you need to know about Don."

"What's that?"

"He's fucking senile! He just forgot that he hates pep rallies."

At this point, Mark didn't know who was more nuts. Was it the coach who chose to work when he didn't need to, or was it Carrera who came close to humping him to celebrate pastelito profits?

"I got to tell you," Reinhold continued. "This is an experienced, mostly senior team. I've been with these guys from the time they went four and seven two years ago, and now they've won twelve straight regular-season games. They're a great bunch of guys, and their time has arrived. They've learned how to lose together, and they've learned how to win together. But the common word is together. This is a team, and I believe that this a state-champion-caliber team, and tonight we start by sending Palm Coast home with a loss!"

The crowd cheered loudly once again, and the band played its theme. The players all got on stage to surround their coach, and sixty-five-year-old Don Reinhold balled his fist and did an uppercut in the air, taking his best and last shot at the one thing that had eluded him despite his great work over the years. The same way there could be only one Don Reinhold, there could be only one state champion. But his legacy went beyond being a coach. He settled down the band and the crowd with a few waves of his hand, and he spoke one more time.

"I want to bring someone up here who has been a Buccaneer all his life and is the number-one fan of the football program. He's our honorary team captain. Darryl, get up here!"

The crowd grew frenzied as Darryl, in his number 1 South Demming jersey, took the stage. The band again played, and Darryl busted a few good moves to the music. The crowd laughed. The crowd cheered. The players, the band members, the cheerleaders were all giving one another high fives, and for one glorious afternoon, South Demming was the happiest place on the planet.

The music and cheering brought the pep rally to a close, and everything was timed perfectly as the dismissal bell rang, and students shuffled out of the auditorium and to their classrooms. There were no fights, no bus delays, and no complaints from teachers about the disruption to their programs. In all, Mark felt that the afternoon experiment yielded desirable data.

"So what did you think?" Mark asked Nate Judson as he appeared in the office doorway. Expecting his approval, he was surprised to see him shaking his head and looking down at the floor.

"What's the matter?"

"You got a group of girls going to want to be talking to you Monday."

"Who?"

"Those girls in the Blue Tide never got to perform. The band got to play. The cheerleaders cheered, but the steppers never got their chance, and they been practicing all week long. Now, that ain't your fault, but this place got a bit of history attached."

"What are you talking about?"

"My first year here in '85, the black kids rioted after a talent show. There were some good performances like dancing, singing, and even a country music band. The talent show was scheduled for fifth and sixth periods back in the day when we had a traditional bell schedule and a seven-period day. The last act was three black boys doing a rap. This act brought the house down right up until the bell rung for seventh period."

"What did that have to do with anything?"

"You know Tim Suits, the activities director over at Andersen High?"

"I know of him. What about him?"

"Well, he used to be South Demming's AD before Coach Carrera, and he decided the kids had to go to class, went on stage, and pulled the plug on the act. The black kids thought he was disapproving of the act, and that's when it got bad."

Judson's eyeballs became movie projector bulbs, and Mark was the canvas screen upon which his memory flashed. He agonizingly detailed, as if film frame-by-film frame, the ensuing events. "There was about twenty black boys and even a few girls who when they got out of the auditorium were making racial slurs at Suits. Now, they was walking in the right direction, but they wasn't going quietly."

"So what was done about that?"

"Well, you know Fred Rogers over at the area office?"

"Yeah, what about him?"

"He was an assistant principal over here in those days, and he grabbed one of the loudest girls by the arm, and she pulled away from him, calling him a motherfucker. At that point, the resource officer arrived; I don't remember his name, and he wasn't here for long, but I remember he slammed this girl into the ground and cuffed her. As he led her away, things got worse." Judson paused long enough to look at Mark, look at the floor, and shake his head anew.

"Go on," Mark pleaded.

"The black boys found some rocks to start throwing at classroom windows. They ran down the inside hallways, and whenever they got the chance, they was punching white boys and girls in the back of their heads. You know the cafeteria hallway?"

"Yeah."

"Well, the concrete walls that support the windows looking into the cafeteria used to be all windows. That changed that day because all the glass was shattered by the boys throwing rocks, and when they ran out of rocks, they threw garbage cans through the windows."

"So how did this end?"

"Mr. Rogers called 911, and they sent out a SWAT team with tear gas and rubber bullets. It took a couple of canisters, and there was no need for the rubber bullets, but they shot one of the boys in the butt anyway, probably to make a point."

"So who was the principal, and where was he?"

"Well, he was a she, and she was Marianne Renick, and she just stayed in her office with her door closed the whole time."

"You're kidding me, right?"

"Ain't everyone like you, willing to stick their neck out."

"So, how did the community react? Did it make the news?"

"Oh yeah, the five o'clock, the six o'clock, and the eleven o'clock. They arrested ten kids and expelled all of them. Ms. Renick couldn't hide from the parents of those kids the next day. Now, nobody got hurt too bad, but we had a police presence at the school for a month after that. The white farm kids flew their Confederate flags from their pickup trucks, and when Ms. Renick ordered them to be removed, she had to deal with a whole other set of parents."

"So how did this finally calm down?"

"The Allied Church Ministry, black and white reverends and ministers, preached peace during Sunday sermons and brought some healing over time."

"Wow!"

"Yeah, might of done something different if I was old Tim Suits."

"I hear you."

"Yeah, might of maybe let them black kids do their rap and not worry so much about the late bell."

"You think Suits had a problem with the act?"

"Nah, he had another problem," and Judson smiled as he said this. "He was just plain dumb!"

"Is that your professional opinion?"

"Nah, I got me an editorial opinion," Judson offered.

"And what might that be?"

"Well, some folks say that rap causes violence. I say that stupidity causes it. Got to go get me some spaghetti before the linemen go for seconds." Judson started to leave the office to participate in the pregame meal held in the cafeteria.

"Wait!" Mark said. "Do you think the Blue Tide girls might have the same kind of feelings?"

"Nah, they like you. They just want to talk."

"So, why the history lesson? Why the drama?"

"You seem like the guy who might be able to help with the healing. Figured you would want to know."

"Yeah, but I'm not a minister; I'm an educator, and I have no idea what that makes you."

"I'm hungry—got to go!" Judson jogged in place backward, turned around, and headed out of the office, making a sharp right into the cafeteria.

In 1953, the world was black and white. The older films that played in the spectacular new South Demming auditorium were black and white. The color and controversy of the issues of that time were cloaked in black and white. Flash forward a half century on a kaleidoscopic journey through time, and land in a place of multiple hues and multiple views that miraculously still manage to polarize in terms of black and white. The Blue Tide steppers were black girls with an urban edge who would sooner set fire to a pom-pom than wear it. To the uninitiated observer, this situation would seem to smack of segregation, but it really was a matter of personal preference that might be attributed to the differences that exist between black and white.

Chartavia Thompson bridged the gap by operating in the gray area. As it turned out, she was the Blue Tide stepper who wanted to talk to Mark. An honors student, a newspaper editor, a track athlete, and a trainer for the football team, she still found enough time in her busy schedule to put her foot down. "All we're asking is that you recognize the need for better planning of pep rallies in the future. We worked for two weeks to perfect our act, and we didn't even get the chance to showcase it," Thompson revealed.

"Look, I can do that. I'm sorry that you guys didn't get the opportunity, but I'll see to it that you go front and center the next pep rally. I promise."

"People here respect you, Mr. M. Thank you for always being there for us."

Chapter 14

MORE THAN A GAME

When Matt Mathews's foot catapulted the football to stadium-lights level, end over end, hope and despair traded places, luck and misfortune played leapfrog, and the haves and the have-nots prepared to collide. There were no numerators or denominators in Coach Reinhold's equation; his formula for success was a multiplication problem where X equaled preparation and Y equaled determination, and their product was another notch in the win column.

As the ball began its downward descent, Tyrus Waters was at full speed, his head tucked into his shoulder pads, his arms and legs a blur, and his vision focused upon the kick returner so as to enable him to instinctively take the perfect angle. The blockers along the way became inconsequential, neither reactive enough to set up a wedge nor possessing enough lateral movement to impede Waters's path. Aerodynamics mixed with geometry and exploded upon impact as Waters collided with the ball carrier, lifting him off the ground, setting into motion a whiplash that tore off his helmet and relieved him of the football, which, as misfortune would have it, bounced ten yards ahead and out of bounds, end over end.

"Goddamn it!" Don Reinhold exploded. "We do everything right, and they get a break like that. Jesus Christ! Jesus H. Christ!"

"We're going to stop them, Coach." Kenny Judson, Nate's son, and coach of the defensive backs took notice of Reinhold's red face, which complemented by his gray hair gave him the appearance of a burning cigarette. In this case, the breath was being sucked out of him, and his aggravation was being dragged out into the tenuous position of an unflicked ash.

Palm Coast started with the ball on its own thirty-yard line and blended in a few short passes with some up-the-middle runs to stun South Demming by scoring the first touchdown. Along the way, it became apparent to Don Reinhold that the officiating was slanted toward providing an advantage for the Panthers of Palm Coast. There was an offside call that should have gone the other way. There was holding occurring that wasn't flagged, and on another occasion, the Panthers should have been called for delay of game. After the score, Reinhold slammed down his headphones and began a tirade directed toward any official within earshot.

"Hey, let's call it both ways," he implored, and when Danny Baldwin's forty-yard return of the ensuing kickoff was negated by an illegal block, Reinhold grew even more animated. "You know we pay taxes too, Goddamn it!" Seeing that the official who threw the flag couldn't immediately identify the guilty Buc, Reinhold seized editorial opportunity in the form of the thirty-yard-line marker. "Who's it on?" he beseeched. "Who's it on!" he yelled louder. "You need a number?" And with that, he lifted the yard-line marker, his arms fully extended high over his head and said, "Here's a number; call it on thirty!"

Joe Carrera, along with a couple of assistant coaches, turned his back on the head coach so as not to be seen laughing. "Shit, Magic," Carrera said as he wiped the tears from his eyes, "Don's going to have another fucking stroke."

"What do you mean another stroke?"

"You mean I never told you about that? Magic, about two years ago … Oh yeah!" Carrera's story was interrupted by a long touchdown strike from Matt Mathews to Corey Watson. Just like that, South Demming tied the game and began a dominance that would see them win 34–13. The excitement shelved Carrera's tale, and after the game, Coach Reinhold looked nothing like the guy who was bordering on a stroke as he addressed his players.

"You did it! You did it!" he exclaimed as he jumped in the air five times, his leaps covering a semicircle in the end zone. "This game was pivotal. We can't let up, but this game was pivotal. Let's take a knee!"

As the coach led his players in the postgame prayer, Carrera provided some more insight. "Magic, don't mind Don. He's making a bigger deal out of this game than it was, but he just hates Palm Coast."

"What's the story there?"

"Nothing other than he thinks the school and its community is filled with people who have their noses up in the air. I don't blame him."

"Why?"

"Because they have their noses up in the air, Magic. Ah hah, hah, hah, hah! Shit, he hates them almost as much as I hate Hanford."

"And what's your problem with Hanford?"

"It's the other end of the spectrum, Magic. You see, Palm Coast people have their noses up in the air, but Hanford people have their heads up their asses."

Mark looked into his eyes to see a hint of sparkle, the crinkled corners that foretell an impending smile or the indirect side-to-side or up-and-down movements to suggest hyperbole. Carrera kept his eyes upon his, refused to blink as if it were a sign of weakness, and Mark watched as his pupils became nail heads. He blinked and chose another route. "Yeah, but *hate*?" He emphasized the word to illustrate his extreme view.

"You're absolutely right, Magic. Hate's a strong word. We really don't hate them; we just fucking can't stand them!"

"You people have issues!"

"Nah, Magic, we have wins! Losers have issues. Let's talk over coffee on Monday."

As he parted to shake hands with the coaches and a few of the players, Mark continued watching Carrera until he reached Don Reinhold, shook his hand, and put his arm around his shoulder. The old coach then put his arm around Carrera's shoulder. With the stadium lights and the scoreboard as their backdrop, they walked this way, as if posing for a timeless photo, two icons, two relics from a bygone era, two guys going out for a beer.

"Magic, your fucking coffee has got to be cold, so I got Cathy to grab you another cup. It's on its way."

"Thanks, Joe. The train got me this morning. That's what I get for leaving ten minutes later than usual."

"Magic, one thing I've learned in the twenty-seven years I've been here is that this place will still be here even if I don't get in on time."

"Yeah, you say that, but your heap is always the first one in the parking lot."

"What can I say? I'm competitive in everything I do. And what do you mean my heap?" Carrera drove a vintage sky-blue 1963 Cadillac Coupe de Ville. It had a collector's license plate certifying its antique status, a license that made allowances for the black cloud that accompanied its start-up and the periodic stalling that characterized its stay at traffic lights.

"I'm sorry. Have I offended you in any way?"

"Magic, that Caddy was the original cruiser mobile. I got it in 1967 when I was a junior in high school. I can't begin to tell you how many crazy nights were made possible thanks to that piece of Americana. You know, I've got a brand-new Monte Carlo. It sits in the driveway, and I park the Caddy in the garage. I only live two miles away, so I drive it to work, and that's it. They don't make them with tail fins anymore. They don't make them with engines that size anymore. They don't make cars that turn peoples' heads anymore!"

The same guy who had no regard for personal space also was a master at summoning a melancholy distance, even in matters of suspect significance. Carrera clearly had a sense of history and an appreciation for its artifacts, so Mark chose to change the subject.

"Hey, during the game you started to tell me about Don, but we both ended up getting caught up in the action."

"Oh yeah, you mean about the stroke he had."

"Yeah, that kind of caught me by surprise."

"It caught us all by surprise, Magic. You know, Don's bigger than life, so to see him get laid up was a shocker."

"So how did it happen?"

"It was about four years ago, Magic. To know Don is to know first and foremost he's a teacher. He believes in giving kids visuals. So when they didn't understand how to hit the sled to get it to move maximum distance, Don demonstrated how to get a quick start and hit low and keep driving the legs. He did this for a few times, then just went to a chair along the track and sat down. It was about ninety outside that afternoon, so Nate saw Don, went over to him, and didn't like the way he looked. He called me on my cell to come out, and when I went up to Don, he looked like shit, all pale with this crusty shit on his lips. I asked him, 'Hey, Don, you all right?'

"'Goddamn it, Joe. I've been doing this for thirty years. It's just hotter than shit out here,' he told me, but I already made the decision to call 911. When I did this, he got up, walked a few steps like he was drunk, and fell down. I asked him to just sit there and take it easy, but he ignored me, and I continued to follow him. He got up again, walking like a drunk, shading left to right, but making it to the locker room."

"So how long did it take the paramedics to get there?"

"That's the best part, Magic. They check Don out, don't feel comfortable with what they see and have heard, and tell him he needs to get transported. They want him to get on the gurney. Don gets up and says, 'You want me to get in that ambulance, then I'm not going to get wheeled in.' Everybody followed him as he wobbled to the ambulance, which was parked along the track, about a hundred yards from his office. He stumbled but didn't fall and made it to the hospital."

"So what did they find out?"

"He had a mild stroke, Magic. He was there for about three days before they released him, and they never found a physical cause, but they told him he needed to stay away from coaching and teaching for a couple of months. Don was at work the day after his release from the hospital. He taught his driver's ed. course, but the coaches were under my orders to make sure he didn't go out to the practice field."

Sipping from the fresh cup of coffee that Cathy deftly weaved into their conversation, Mark looked at Carrera and guessed, "Something tells me that your decree fell upon deaf ears."

"If you mean nobody fucking listened to me, then you're right, Magic! Goddamn, you're a silver-tongued devil!"

"So what happened after that?"

"I'm getting there, Magic. For about a week, Don watched the practices, sitting on a lounge chair perched behind a tree on 165th, right across from the park. Everybody could see him, but nobody wanted to call him out. He started getting braver, like a raccoon approaching food left behind at a picnic. By the end of the second week, he was watching practices from the back of his van parked by his portable, only about fifty yards away from the practice field. He even yelled to Nate and Robbie a couple of times, and they pretended not to notice. They had too much respect for him to abide by my, what did you call it, a decree? I like that, Magic. Decree kind of sounds like decrepit, and nobody was going to keep that old bastard away from coaching. By the third week, Don saw his offensive linemen holding and missing assignments, and he couldn't take it anymore. He jogged toward Jud and Robbie and said, 'I don't care which one of you gives me the whistle, but one of you'd better give me a Goddamn whistle.' Jud parted with his whistle, and Don took over the practice. I'm surprised he lasted that long."

"Why's that?"

"Asking Don Reinhold to stay away from a football field is like asking a gambler to fold when he's got a full house with five face cards winking back at him."

"Damn, Joe, that's a real good way to put it. I didn't think you had that in you."

"Magic, I drive a 1963 Cadillac Coupe de Ville. That's got to make me good for something!"

Chapter 15

CHRISTMAS IN OCTOBER

As was its routine, the morning sun rose over the track and the football practice field that it framed. Partially obscured by the largest oak tree in South Demming Park, the seven o'clock sun parceled out its orange rays through the eclipse of leaves, seeking a place to shed its warmth. It first found the faces of the Mexican kids who had made it their practice to gather around the track and speak to one another in Spanish. It wriggled a few of its digits of light into the social studies patio where many of the black kids sat on benches, exchanging pleasantries that included a good-natured trading of insults, but it had yet to reach the front of the school that faced westward, a blessing in that drivers of those cars dropping off students in the inner circular drive, the buses utilizing the outer loop, and the vehicles pulling into the student parking lot would otherwise be blinded. By seven fifteen, nature abruptly released its hair-trigger rolling window shade, and the entire campus was exposed.

From the comfort of the golf cart that he parked along the track, Mark saw Rex Hoffman squinting and attempting to use his right hand as a visor as the sun attempted to block his path to the portable. With the sun at his back, Mark joined in this effort and pulled the golf cart in front of Hoffman. This time a near riot and a beckoning hurricane weren't in his way.

"Morning, boss," Hoffman greeted. "Boy, it sure is bright out here!"

Basking in Hoffman's discomfort, Mark reached into his pocket and pulled out the anonymous letter, handed it to him, and watched as the slits of his eyes opened wide, letting in the light. "This you?" he asked Hoffman as he got out of the cart to add a suggestion of intimidation.

"Yeah, boss. I wrote this," he admitted.

"You couldn't come to me to discuss this? You felt you had to write an anonymous letter? What possessed you to do that? I haven't listened to your concerns? I'm not approachable?"

"Look, I care about this school," he started, "and I don't like what I'm seeing happening around here. You're not going to get anywhere with the convicts in this place unless you go by the letter of the law."

"The convicts?" Mark asked.

"You know what I mean. At the beginning of the school year, I gave you an entire school-wide discipline plan that I created, and you never gave me any feedback. That wasn't fair," and he sounded like a five-year-old who hadn't gotten his way as he alluded to a twenty-five-page, poorly written and ill-conceived manifesto that was as eccentric as the decor of his classroom. Mark hadn't given it a second thought until he made that moment possible.

"So that's what this is about? I don't go with your plan, and you go underground."

Hoffman's face grew red as he handed back his letter and said shrilly, "Somebody has to do something about this place!"

"You know what, Rex," Mark offered as he placed the letter back in his pocket, grateful to have something to occupy his fist, "if you want to make the decisions somewhere, go back to school and take your administrative coursework, pass the leadership exam, interview for a position, and grace some other campus with your expertise in writing anonymous garbage. In the meantime, you're paid to teach social studies, and your kids are waiting for you."

Hoffman turned around without another word, and with the sun now in his face as he watched him walk away, Mark squinted in anger.

David Canales appeared from his spot amidst the portable classrooms, and Mark got back in the golf cart and drove it toward him, so David could join in the ride to South Demming Park. "What's up with Hoffman?" David asked.

"Here you go, Dave," Mark reached into his pocket and handed him the letter. "Here's a little reading material for your morning transit." Watching him from the corner of his eye, he heard David grunt and saw him shake his head as he digested the material.

"Whoever wrote this shit didn't have the balls to sign it," he said.

"Well, Dave, that's the answer to your question regarding what's up with Hoffman."

"Then that's nothing to worry about. Who would believe anything that comes out of that asshole?" David attempted to reassure him.

"Well, Dave," Mark continued his sarcastic tone, "look at the handwriting in the upper right corner."

David read the note from Dr. Traynor to Magda Robreno expecting her to look into the letter. "Oh, Marko," he said exasperatedly, "they should have thrown this shit in the garbage!"

"That's not how it works in Area 6, my friend. Robreno faxed this to me and told me that it was an indictment of my leadership."

David's face grew flushed, and he shook his head from side to side. "You can't possibly be serious!" He probed for signs of some elaborate prank.

"I can't make up shit like this, Dave. I don't have that good of an imagination, and to top off all this, Chandler-Lopez and Warner want to see me at the Area 6 office today to have me sign off on a professional development plan."

"Is that something that they do with all beginning principals?" David looked to find something of a coincidental nature.

"David, the people who supervise us are extremely transparent. I'm on the radar, brother, and this job is tough enough without being micromanaged."

"I don't know what to say, Mark," he offered. "I can't believe an anonymous letter can be allowed to have that type of clout."

"It isn't anonymous, Dave. Hoffman knows Eileen Riordan. He writes the letter, e-mails it to her, and she backspaces over his name and shows it to Traynor, probably before a board meeting. Riordan calls Robreno to let her know that a teacher at South Demming is the author. Instead of protecting a principal and telling him to watch his back, Robreno puts a knife in it and brings Chandler-Lopez and Warner on board to twist it."

As they resumed their patrol, Mark's thoughts rested on the dread he felt over the impending morning meeting with Chandler-Lopez and Warner. As they pulled into the dirt-road service drive of the agricultural field, he noticed a handful of older migrant laborers tending to the recently planted bean crop. Among them was a woman whose weathered face couldn't be softened by the fifty yards that separated them. Mark selfishly wondered about her worries and how his would make hers seem insignificant. He envied the simplicity of her existence, working from dawn to dusk, day to day, and job to job.

"Hey, man," David interrupted his self-pity, "I look at shit like that, and suddenly my day gets better!"

Mark had grown to rely upon David's perspective on things, another somewhat selfish indulgence. "You know, Dave," he said, "I really appreciate you being a sounding board for my problems, but I don't know how fair that is to you."

"Hey, man, I feel close to you," his portly passenger revealed. "I mean our thighs rub together every morning when we ride this golf cart. I don't get that close to my wife half the time," he chuckled. "Besides, I want to be a principal. If it wasn't for your sharing, I wouldn't know what a miserable fucking job this is!"

David got him laughing again. They returned the golf cart to its waiting place for Bryan Reinhold, right next to his dad's portable, and as they entered the main office, Cathy had some good news to share.

"Mr. M, Dr. Chandler-Lopez wanted me to give this message to you," and smiling, she handed him a note which he read out loud.

"No meeting today; will reschedule at a later date."

Cathy had developed a keen awareness of the shit flowing down the Area 6 stream. She had learned to read his body language, and being that she was best friends with Chandler-Lopez's secretary, Savannah England, she had the inside scoop regarding any trouble brewing in the caldron of the Area 6 coven.

"Hey, boss," Ken Ferguson had heard Mark reading the message, "I guess I'll have to postpone playing solitaire on my computer now that you'll be in the building."

"Absolutely, Ken," Mark answered, "solitaire right after the sports page might be too much strain on your body."

"Magic," Joe Carrera bounced out of the office, "guess who I just got off your hotline with?"

"Damn, who's the principal around here? Cathy deals with the directors. You're answering my private line, and Fergie over here is doing a crossword puzzle."

"Magic, Ken was lining up subs right after he got stuck on one across. Cathy was on the line with the bitch from the area, and your hotline rings. Am I supposed to let it ring? Now, you want to hear what the fuck I got to say or what?"

"Go ahead."

"Sit down, Magic," and he led them back to the office, taking the seat across from Mark's desk. "This is some good shit! As a matter of fact, let's get Jud in here. He needs to hear this. Unit 12, Jud, come back."

"Go ahead," Judson said.

"Jud, meet me in the principal's office."

As they awaited the arrival of Nate Judson, Mark looked at Carrera and couldn't help laughing. "You're a fucking drama queen, all giddy and shit after picking up the phone. If you were a woman, you'd be a dick tease. This better be good!" he forewarned him.

"Magic, you're going to love this! And by the way, if I were a woman, you'd better damn believe I'd be good!"

"Okay, I'm here," Nate Judson announced in his raspy voice as he appeared in the doorway.

"Nate, sit down. You need to hear this. I just got off the phone with Harold Starling, Demming County schools chief of police."

"Damn, you know him too?" Mark interrupted.

"Magic, I told you a couple of times already that if I told you about everything and everyone I know—"

"I know. You'd have to kill me."

"Exactly! Now, can I tell my story? After I promised him a sideline pass for the game against Williams High, he told me he's planning on paying us a visit on Monday. We play this right, and maybe we can get some additional bodies to watch this place."

"I got a couple of people in mind if that happens," Jud offered as he contemplated the possibilities.

"Now, wait a second, Joe," Mark said. "Wasn't he calling me? Didn't he want to talk to me to see if Monday works on my schedule?"

"Magic, Cathy checked your schedule. He's coming in at ten thirty, right before the lunch periods begin. If it's about credit for this, you can take the credit," the wily AD offered.

"That's not it. I'm glad he's coming. I just thought he might want to talk to me."

"I get it, Magic," Carrera revealed. "I just shook your Christmas present and told you what it is."

Ken Ferguson appeared in the doorway and was laughing. "Hey, you're a regular grinch, Joe!"

"Come on, Magic, cheer up. It's Christmas!" Carrera proclaimed.

"It's fucking October, Joe."

"And there are less than a hundred shopping days left. You're just getting an early start. Magic, if there were mistletoe, I'd have to kiss you! But seeing how there isn't, I'll just give you a hug."

Mark withstood another bear hug and felt used as Carrera left the office abruptly, leaving him and Judson in his wake. Nate never did take a seat. His vigilance and his military background conspired to take it out from under him.

"If you don't need me," he said, "I'll head back to my post."

"Nate, I'll need you here at ten thirty Monday morning."

"Oh, you bet I'll be there, and I'm bringing my list."

"Your list?" Mark asked with some confusion.

"Oh, yeah," Jud said with his pearly grin, "my Christmas list, and if he lets me, I'll even sit in the brother's lap!"

At four thirty that afternoon, Mark left South Demming, and as he drove down Minneola Street, he saw the old man and the three-legged dog for the first time in many weeks. He again resisted the temptation to pull over, to introduce himself, and in so doing, ascertain that they were real.

That evening, the Bucs convincing win over crosstown rival Flagler High, a 31–7 route, took a backseat to Mark's restlessness, as that night his overtaxed brain relieved itself through the sieve of a dream. In the first light of dawn, he was arriving to the school and saw the old man and the three-legged dog exiting the auditorium. He veered to the part of the parking lot closest to them, exited his vehicle, and approached them.

"Excuse me," Mark said in a voice that wasn't his. Neither the old man nor the dog reacted to the sound of the voice. "Excuse me. How did you get in there?" he asked again in a voice that was foreign. Giving up this means of communication, he resolved to shorten the thirty or so feet of distance between them by picking up his gait. No matter how fast he walked, the distance between them remained the same. He felt his heart race as he went to a jog and then a run, and even with these efforts, the distance between them remained the same. They hadn't moved from where he spotted them, maintaining the same proximity to the auditorium doors, yet he couldn't reach them.

"Mark!" someone behind him called out his name. He turned around, and no one was there.

"Mark!" someone in front of him called out his name. He turned around, and no one was there.

"Mark, what is it? What do you want?"

Now emerging from his sleep, Mark realized he had been dreaming, and he groggily asked Sylvia, "What's the matter?"

"I was about to ask you the same thing," she revealed. "You kept saying 'excuse me' with a weird voice. Are you all right?"

"Yeah, I just had a stupid dream, that's all. I'm fine." And he looked at the clock, and it was two thirty, and he didn't fall back asleep until the first light of dawn.

"Never seen them, Magic," Joe Carrera said between sips of their Monday morning coffee chat.

"You mean to tell me that as long as you've been working here and living in the general area, you've never seen an old man walking a three-legged dog?" Mark asked him with a hint of disappointment. "All the fucking people you know, and this guy probably lives across from the faculty parking lot, and you've never seen him?"

"Magic, why is this so important?"

"Because I think I'm going nuts," and he looked for some reaction from Carrera.

Carrera took another sip of coffee and said, "Well, Magic, if they ever take you away, can I have your sports memorabilia?"

"When were you planning on telling me that Chief Starling was coming in today?" Sarah Szemanski invaded the doorway, interrupting their rumination. No good morning; no how was your weekend; no excuse me; just a quick strike and recoil.

"Uh, Magic, I'll catch up with you later," Carrera said, and he walked toward the doorway, forcing Szemanski to give up her scarecrow position that had been blocking the opening.

"Look, Sarah," Mark started, "considering the complexity of my role in this school, you'll have to forgive me if I occasionally don't exercise certain courtesies. You're more than welcome to meet the man and stay for any meeting that might happen."

"I just thought that considering I'm over security, you might've wanted me present at some point. Coach Judson told me he's been invited."

Jud obviously had mentioned this to her, thinking that she had been made part of the equation. In assessing his obligation to her as her leader, Mark believed that he subconsciously had omitted her.

"He supposedly will be here at ten thirty," he offered her this morsel to soothe her self-pity, all the while likening her to the unwanted guest who has stayed too long.

"I'll have to check my schedule," she said with an indignation that rivaled that of Rex Hoffman, and she left his office, weaving her way between the desks of Cathy and Ken and winding until she reached the partitioned area that defined her lair.

Chief Harold Starling was a local product, having graduated from Williams High in 1974. After a four-year military stint in the US Army, he earned a bachelor's degree in criminal justice from Florida

State University in 1983. Coming back to Demming County, he got in on the ground floor of the county's school resource officer experiment and blossomed with it. He worked his way up the ranks, and at this time, he was part of the superintendent's cabinet and the final say in safety issues for the more than 350 schools that he and his charges oversaw. A model African American gentleman, he recently had graced the cover of *New Era*, a "with-it" local magazine that ran feature stories and exposés on the movers and shakers in the county. And when Harold Starling moved or shook, he brought with him the requisite entourage that characterizes the mobility of the nobility who turn heads and travel by the light of flashbulbs. His arrival to South Demming came minus this glamour, most likely understated as a result of the sixty miles separating his downtown office trappings from the rural rawness of the school's setting. In his tow, however, was the Area 6 SRO tandem of Captain Pauline Cook and Sergeant Holly Craft who wobbled in like the Keystone Cops from silent film shorts.

After exchanging pleasantries, they adjourned to the office. Mark manned the head of the conference table with Chief Starling to his right, followed by Joe Carrera, Sarah Szemanski, Nate Judson, Cook, and Craft. Nobody partook of the bagels, cream cheese, coffee, and orange juice that were centerpieces to honor the significance of this meeting. Aside from Carrera's firming up of the arrangements for Friday night's South Demming vs. Williams game, an awkward silence of about ten seconds was broken when Chief Starling took command.

"So it's Mrs. M and Mr. M, the M and Ms. You know your wife is one special lady. I've been meaning to come out here at some point, but she convinced me that earlier would be better." In his charcoal-gray suit and perfectly placed necktie held erect by a gold tiepin, Chief Starling firmly embraced his status, legitimizing the term "tight."

"Well, you know that I appreciate your being here," Mark said. "I've got great people here who are doing their level best to keep a lid on this place so that we can go about the business of education. The only problem is that I don't have enough of them."

Chief Starling took in his words, bit his lower lip, and spoke. "Well, one of the problems with how they dole out the security personnel rests with numbers. They don't take into consideration that you've got an open campus, that you've got a construction site, that you've got some rough kids."

"You know," Jud jumped in, "one of my boys coaches and works security at Hanford. They got a closed campus, the same amount of kids, but they got eleven full-time and five part-time. I ain't no math genius, but something's wrong with the calculations."

"I don't have an answer for that," Starling gave in, "but I'm hoping I can get you some relief by using the construction angle. You need at least one more body to monitor that fenced-in area. That's a safety issue, and that's how I'll portray it."

"Well, I don't know if one more body will do it," Sarah Szemanski cut in, "but we'll take what we can get. It's a nuthouse out here! The inmates are running the asylum!"

If he could have reached over and grabbed her by the neck and squeezed until her eyes popped out, Mark would have. The last thing a principal wants is for one of his deputies to suggest that things are out of control, especially when the audience is a cabinet member. His rage became tangible, palpable. He looked at Carrera, who was in tune with him and shaking his head at the comment, but the serpentine Szemanski who had put her twist on the situation avoided eye contact.

"Well, I'm interested in hearing from Captain Cook," Starling redirected. "Pauline, you and Holly have been working Area 6 for a few years. What's your take on things?"

As Cook prepared to speak, Mark noticed Craft looking at Szemanski, and they appeared to nod at each other.

"Mark," she began, "I've known you for close to ten years, going all the way back to Bronfmann. You are a true gentleman and one of the finest people I've come across in the system."

"I'm sensing a 'but' somewhere in here, Captain," Mark guessed.

"Well, I don't want you to take this the wrong way, but the kids here view you as being a little soft. You might be too nice a guy."

As he weighed her words, Mark saw Craft nod again toward Szemanski, looked toward Starling, and counted to ten in his mind. And with slow, calculated precision, he prepared to answer, but Carrera beat him to the punch.

"Now let's wait a Goddamn minute here!" he began. "You're going to have to excuse my language, but this man busts his ass every day, gives a shit about kids that other people, me included, have given up on. This place needs a lot of attention, but things have never been better since he got here, and I am not going to sit here and let anyone question his effectiveness. That's all I've got to say!"

"Damn right, I'm a nice guy," Mark seized the opening. "I've gotten this far in my career, one of thirty-eight jobs in the entire county, by being a nice guy, but nobody should be confusing niceness for weakness. Besides, who, when you speak of the 'kids here,' sees me as soft?"

"Why is that important?" Cook inquired.

"It's important because you obviously are making it important. It's important because I view it as an indictment, like I'm some kind of pushover, not tough enough to handle this place. Are you here to help, or are you here to blame me for the years of neglect that have built up to this moment? I've got to tell you, Pauline, years of knowing each other aside, that I take that comment as an insult and view it as counterproductive to what needs to be happening in this meeting."

"Captain Cook," the chief intervened, "we're here to find solutions. This man is about the kids, and so am I. You can be a nice guy and get results!"

Thankful for Starling's support, Mark cast aside his ire but could not do the same with his curiosity. "Chief, Joe, I appreciate your comments, but now I'm the one who needs closure. Who thinks I'm soft, Pauline?"

"You know Nelson Taylor?" she offered.

"Don't tell me that kid is throwing me under the bus?"

"Well, we had some OT on the weekend, Holly and me, and we were patrolling US 1, and who should we pull over but good old Nelson and his monster truck. He's stopped in the middle lane talking to some friends in the left lane, and meanwhile horns are honking in both lanes behind them. I pull his dumb-ass over to the shopping mall on 296, and when he sees it's me, he goes into his charm mode. So I tell him that he's not getting a ticket, but I was going to let his principal know that he's a dumb-ass. So you know what he tells me? He says, 'That guy won't do shit to me. He's soft.'"

"So, on the basis of a comment from someone that you acknowledge is a dumb-ass, I get the soft label pinned on me. First of all, Pauline, if I were you, I'd have given his 'dumb-ass,' as you say, a ticket. I guess that makes you soft this one time. And damn right I'm not going to do shit to him! What jurisdiction do I have regarding some kid that gets a traffic ticket on the weekend? How does my name come up? I'm trying to get these kids in school and in class. I can take constructive criticism, but you're so far off base that it's a huge disappointment to me."

Chief Harold Starling left hope that Mark could use to replenish the hope he had been mortgaging since his arrival to South Demming. After the meeting, they walked the campus together, took a look at the kids in the pavilion eating lunch, and shook hands.

"Mark," he said, offering parting words, "let me apologize for the behavior of my two officers in there. They were off the chain and totally out of hand. You need to know that I know you're doing your best here and that I'll work to get you some bodies in here."

Chapter 16

LOVE ADVICE

At the beginning of the last period of the day, Nelson Taylor stood in the office doorway, all six feet, 230 soft pounds of him, blocking Mark's view to the outside world so that they wouldn't be interrupted.

"Mr. M, bro," he started, "I need some advice."

Unable to avoid some sarcasm given his recent revelation, Mark came back with "Nelson, bro, you sure you've come to the right person?"

He looked at his principal with a puzzled expression and said, "What do you mean? You and me always been able to talk."

"Well, I'm hearing that I might be soft, so I'm wondering if any advice I have might be too soft," Mark offered.

Taylor laughed, displaying the golden grill on his bottom teeth. "Oh, I get it. I saw those dyke school cops in here today, so they told you what I said?"

"Exactly! Man, I made you an office aide this period to get you out of weight training and hopefully get you to walk graduation. So I cut you slack, try to work with you, and you come up with that!"

"C'mon, Mr. M, they just pissed me off, so I came up with that shit. C'mon, man, you know I respect you, and I've seen you in the middle of enough shit to know you got heart. If you want me to say sorry, I'm sayin' it. C'mon, dude." He looked pathetic standing there and pleading.

"What's going on?" Mark gave in.

"I got me some female problems," Taylor revealed. "You know my girlfriend, Leisy?"

"I've seen you with a girl—so that's her name? What's happening with the two of you?"

"Man," Taylor said, "I think I fucked up. I had sex with this girl, and now she's all attached and shit, and she's talkin' about bein' in love."

"So why did you have sex with her?" Mark asked.

"C'mon, M, you seen her. She's hot as hell! That just-say-no and abstinence shit is for losers."

"So when are you guys getting married? Am I invited? Are you having an open bar?"

"Hey, man, I came here for advice, not to have you help me plan a wedding. I'm only eighteen. I ain't ready for that shit. There's too many other women out there." He ran his hand over his close-cropped hair.

"You want to sit down?" Mark invited his distressed visitor to the conference table. Taylor exhaled, moved toward the table, and sat in the seat at the head.

"Nah, man. That's the advice-giving chair. You sit there." Mark pointed out the chair to its right. He watched as Taylor, with pitiful eyes, looked to him for something that he couldn't find anywhere else. Mark sat down next to him and rubbed his chin, thinking of a good place to start.

"Nelson, women look at things differently. Men get caught up in the chase and the conquest. Women don't mind being chased; some even slow down so they can get caught, but there's a toll to pay at the end of that road. You the first she's ever been with all the way?"

"She says I am," Taylor answered.

"You don't believe her?"

"How the fuck should I know? Bitches lie about that shit all the time."

"Is that all she is to you, a bitch?" Mark probed.

"Nah, man. I got feelings for her," he confessed.

"Let me ask you, then," Mark said. "Did you wear a rubber?"

"Nah, bro, it's not like it was planned. It just happened."

At that point in the conversation, Mark couldn't resist a subtle jab. "You know what, Nelson? It might have been better if you were the one who was soft."

Taylor laughed lightly and said, "That's cold, dude."

"That's reality, brother!" Mark emphasized. "Now what happens if she gets pregnant?"

"I guess I would do the right thing and marry her. I don't believe in abortion," Taylor revealed.

"You love this girl?"

"Yeah, man, I love her. I got to tell you this, but you got to promise it doesn't leave the room."

"What happens in Vegas stays in Vegas," Mark said, borrowing from a timeworn cliché. "Say what you got to say."

"Up until this weekend"—Taylor looked him squarely in the eyes—"I was a virgin."

"You're still too damn young for the adult drama," Mark said. "Hopefully, she doesn't get pregnant, but you guys need to slow down."

"Mr. M, can I come back and talk to you some more, you know, kind of keep you posted about my crazy life?"

"The door's always open, Nelson."

In looking back at this conversation, Mark didn't believe they really arrived at any solutions or that he offered him any solace beyond being an active listener. But Taylor got up from his chair, came over to him, and hugged him as if he would never let go.

Leisy Pinto's eyes were black and beautifully odd. They didn't look at you. They didn't look through you. They looked past you, not willing to commit to the moment, choosing instead to survey the environment that encased it. US born, she learned at a young age that privileges and freedoms that were her birthright did not extend to her Honduran migrant parents. When Mark first met the Iceman, Ice was supervising the work experience program at South Demming, and he relayed a scenario that brought this concept to light for him.

"Hey, boss," Mark remembered him starting a conversation in the office one morning, "I just got back from Frank's Nursery in South Hanford to check up on one of my kids in the program, and I had no idea how fast Mexicans can run."

"Ice, you lost me," Mark said. "What's one thing got to do with the other?"

"That's right. I forgot," Ice said. "You don't know this area to know that Frank's is right next to a big farm that uses migrant workers. So they see me coming, white hair, blue eyes, and all, and all they see is immigration. One points me out to about four others, and they haul ass."

"Maybe you could get a part-time job with them," Mark suggested. "That's a pretty fucked-up way to have to live."

"Yeah, it is," the Iceman agreed, "but those Mexicans sure can run!"

Before she could read, before she could generate sophisticated ideas, Leisy Pinto was introduced to the notion of a bogeyman, white and angry, who could take away her parents and leave her alone. But when she was three years old, it was Hurricane Alex who took away her mother, collapsing a portion of their labor camp home on top of her and killing her. Leisy remembered very little beyond a pine crate being laid next to other pine crates in a deep hole and being covered with dirt. She remembered her father whisking her away to a colder place where she stayed with strangers as he worked until night, coming back in enough time to eat and go to sleep. This was the father she always had known, and while their lot in life improved so they could afford to live in an apartment, he worked too hard building homes, block by block, to build a home, moment by moment, for his daughter. So dumb-ass Nelson and his overbearing mother represented love and family to Leisy Pinto.

Chapter 17

HELP ON THE WAY?

"So did your wife kick you out of the house, or do you just come to a South Demming football game to relax?" Mark asked T. J. when he saw him at the entry gate prior to Friday night's game.

"Mark, I'm getting time and a half to watch football. Only in America is life this good!" T. J. smiled and extended his hand. "Listen, man, I've been meaning to thank you."

"For what?"

"For looking out for my dumb-ass nephew. He thinks you walk on water."

"Well, T. J.," Mark said, "there's hope for him, but last time we spoke, you told me you were going to share some insight."

T. J. motioned to Louis Cruz that he was temporarily abandoning his post, and he led Mark to his squad car about fifty feet from the gate and lit up a cigarette. "We can talk for a few minutes here," he said, and they both leaned on the car's hood.

"Man," Mark said, "either you've got a flair for drama, or you really need to smoke."

"Both," T. J. said, and he took a long drag off his Marlboro and let the smoke come out of his nostrils as the plumes signaled the entry of his words. "Mark," he began, "Nelson's mom, Dina, is my sister. She and Nelson's dad were married for about nine years before I found out that he was abusing her for most of their lives together. Whatever smarts he had in business didn't translate into his life choices."

"What do you mean?" Mark asked as he watched T. J. take another drag off his cigarette.

"The guy was a drug addict and an alcoholic, and he used to beat her up, not around the face where you could see marks, but he'd punch her in the head, or kick her, or pull her hair until she cried. Well, one day when he was about seven, Nelson decides he's not going to see his mom get hit, and just as the asshole is throwing a punch toward Dina, Nelson gets in the way and takes a shot to his right ear. Mark, in some ways, that was a good thing."

"Why do you say that?" Mark asked T. J., who had discarded his cigarette butt and was crushing it under his heel. As he looked at Mark, the glare of the orange ball that was the setting sun broke free from the grasp of an old oak tree and hit both of them in their faces. While Mark squinted, he noticed that T. J. wasn't even blinking.

"I say that, Mark, because I probably wouldn't be standing here right now. I'd be in a fucking jail cell for having killed that son of a bitch. You know Nelson lost most of his hearing in that ear, and he only hears what he wants to hear out of the good ear."

"Wow, so what happened?"

"He did two years, and they got divorced. I guess my sister never told me before because she knew how I would have reacted."

"You have any contact with the guy right now?"

"Minimal, at any kind of family function, and I told him when he got out to just stay the fuck away from me. Nelson's better off without a father in this case. We got to get back."

As they made their way to the entrance, Mark changed the subject. "Hey, what do you know of this girl Nelson's been seeing?"

"I know that she's got to be as blind as he is deaf," T. J. chuckled lightly.

"A bit harsh, don't you think?"

"Mark, that girl is drop-dead gorgeous, and look at Nelson. I mean he's my nephew, and I'm happy for him, but for him to get called up to the big leagues like that, he must be swinging a big bat or something.

She's there all the fucking time, and my sister loves her so much that she even got her a room in the house, so she stays a lot of nights. I guess her old man works all the time and doesn't really pay much attention to her, but Nelson's got a sweet deal with his mom seeing to it that he gets laid, but there's an even better benefit." T. J. studied Mark, awaiting his response.

"At this age, what could be better than that?" Mark asked.

"This girl takes school seriously. She even helps the big dummy study. Dina has tried everything to get this kid to pass. Forget about tutoring and all the money she spent on those learning centers. I have stumbled upon the perfect learning technique." And again, T. J. looked at him, barely able to contain a grin.

"Go ahead," Mark gave in, knowing full well what the revelation would be.

"You got to put your nose in a book before it goes anywhere else. She's got Nelson trained like some floppy-eared dog."

"Hey, you two going at it again?" Joe Carrera interrupted and then pointed out Chief Starling, who was accompanied by Sylvia's boss, Deputy Superintendent Archibald Kreinfeldt, both of whom stood on the track portion of the football field, looking like secret agent bookends in their multilayered wardrobes of gray suits topped off by black, knee-length overcoats.

Kreinfeldt and his wife, Carolyn, had made a dinner visit to the Mahovlic home earlier in the year, but Mark's knowledge of him was limited to that visit and some of Sylvia's anecdotes. He was a nonconfrontational problem solver who banked on the human resources around him, notably Sylvia, to go about business in a fashion dignified enough to do justice to his taste in clothing. A college anthropology professor by trade and a superintendent by fate, his kinship with Roger Traynor dated back to both of their days working up the ladder in the New York school district. Kreinfeldt's small stature did little to support his claim to fame as an Ivy League baller with Princeton University, but he liked to bring it up, particularly when he attended sporting events and wanted to fit in with those whose tastes in life were best exemplified by chicken wings and beer. Hugo Boss attire, Ruth's Chris steaks, and Hennessey cognac disguised the brother beyond recognition, and between him and Starling, the only black would be the night sky. As Mark excused himself from T. J. and walked over with Carrera to greet the guests, his puzzled athletic director probed.

"Magic, I don't give a shit, but who's the other guy with the chief?"

"That's Dr. Kreinfeldt, my wife's boss. I guess he's tight with the chief."

"Magic, it's still eighty degrees out here. Why the hell are they wearing overcoats? Listen—I've got to go; I just wanted you to know they're here."

Mark pondered that question as he approached the distinguished guests in his basketball shorts and South Demming football T-shirt. "I'm glad to see you could make it," he offered Chief Starling, "and it's good to see you, Dr. Kreinfeldt." The trio exchanged handshakes.

"Well, I'm here to support my alma mater, but from what I hear, it might be a long night in Hanford," Starling gave in.

"Well, according to the paper this morning, you're picked in an upset," Mark exercised his diplomatic side, "but you can't believe everything you read."

The game in some ways didn't take center stage. While Williams High took a first possession fumble by South Demming into the end zone, that was it for their scoring. The Buccaneers defense and special teams scored three touchdowns, highlighted by Willie Ivory's quarterback sack and thirty-five-yard fumble return for a touchdown. Marcus Summers picked off a sideline pass and returned it twenty yards for a score, and Danny Baldwin returned a punt sixty-five yards for yet one more highlight. In the end, the efficient offense tacked on a touchdown and two field goals, making the final score, Bucs 34, Cougars 7. This would have been more special to Mark if it had occurred minus his powerful guests; their presence had him dwelling more on what they could do for his school than on what was happening on the field. The chief was gracious in defeat, and Dr. Kreinfeldt heaped on the superlatives as he fiddled with his cufflinks, but it was Starling's departing words that further diverted him from enjoying the evening.

"I haven't forgotten our conversation. We're going to get you the help you need, I promise," and Mark watched as the two dandies departed, blending in with the night.

"Magic, tonight was another big win, but let me ask you," Joe Carrera offered as he poured out the last bit of the pitcher of beer into Mark's glass, "you think this fucking guy is going to be able to help us, or did I waste two field passes?"

Mark looked at several of the younger coaches who accompanied them to the postgame haunt at Grady's Bar and Grill, and he thought about how nice it would be to go back to being naïve as he watched them chug beer, rip meat off chicken wings, and laugh at the simplest things.

"I don't know, Joe. I think he will if he can, but if he can't, I don't know where I'll go next." He took a courtesy sip of beer and repeated, "I don't know."

"Go home, Magic. Get some rest."

Mark shook hands with Carrera, got chastised by the young coaches for calling it a night, and picked up his plate of chicken wing bones, tossing them into the trash.

Sylvia got home at the same time he did, having been unable to attend the game due to a late-night meeting. Their arrival tasted the first few drops of a thunderstorm that would go on for several hours. They lay awake watching the news, and Sylvia shared some news of her own.

"Oh, I forgot to tell you. I was speaking with Tonya this afternoon, and I've got some good news."

He played along with Sylvia's flair for spinning a tale, gave into her pause, and stated, "And how'd that go?"

"Well, she'd like to see you on Monday afternoon if you can make it. Mark, that's one more person who is in a position to really help South Demming. You need to go see her. So what are you thinking?"

The rain pounded out a steady beat for the thunder and lightning that danced outside in close proximity, and Mark thought of the unpredictability of nature and equated it with the unreliability of human nature. "I'm thinking that I've got to reach for every straw that's out there. I've got nothing to lose but gas money, and maybe something good will come out of it."

"So I'll tell her to expect you at around four?"

"Yeah, four would be about right," he said, and as he turned to attempt sleeping out the storm, he thought to himself, *When it rains, it pours.*

"Snoop Doggy Dog, my brother! Y'all got some change you can spare to help me out?" Conducting his business flanked by the very institution that had failed him, a thirty-something black man with an omnidirectional Afro, a worn-out hunter's jacket, badly ripped blue jeans, and laceless Converse All-Star sneakers held out his palm. Mark took notice of the man's talon-like fingernails as he placed his pocket change in his hand, and the panhandler looked at him with smiling brown eyes and said, "God bless you."

The School Board Administration Building afforded accommodations for all its denizens on nine floors. A model of efficiency on the first eight floors, the school board workers were housed within partitioned portable walls. They were equipped with telephones and computer stations and had the luxury of a general waiting area to help them govern the pace of their days.

"Thank you," Mark told the security officer as he affixed his pass and kept his appointment to see Deputy Superintendent Tonya Barton. To his right, Renaissance-like framed photos of past superintendents decorated the path to the first-floor elevator. Like paintings of dead family members hung in staircases, the countenances screamed their common ideal of "change." And with each succession, the only things that really changed were the number and the order of the photographs in this makeshift gallery. Beyond this payment of homage and again to the right was the corridor leading to the board room. Again, each of the nine board members had his or her nameplate in front of a segmented long table, and because they were not unlike their less-endowed fellow inhabitants, their general lack of true human contact often found them making stinging remarks to one another in unnecessarily long-drawn-out board meetings, some of which had been known to conclude as early or late as three in the morning.

The echo chamber of the elevator shaft recorded ghostly conversations whose indiscernible words likely were owed to the building's architecture. What Mark found to be odd was not how he couldn't make out what people were saying but how they immediately stopped talking once the elevator doors opened. On this Monday morning, two suits and a dress sauntered by him all abuzz with their secret, and he entered alone. As he looked at the floor numbers lighting up, he tried to remember what function each one served. He remembered that the second floor held the offices associated with risk management. He remembered that the third floor housed human resources personnel and that the fourth floor dealt with personnel investigations, but the hum of the elevator matched his inquisitive nature as he couldn't remember the functions of the fifth, sixth, and seventh floors. Now, his wife worked on the eighth floor, and they were all about school improvement planning and testing and accountability; hers was perhaps the only floor where the drones were far too busy to partake in extraneous subcultures. His early morning ascent went uninterrupted, save for another suit and another dress who averted their eyes, and like department store mannequins caught in the act, they ceased their conversation when the elevator doors parted.

Tonya Barton parceled herself out to her suitors in fifteen-minute slices. Having arrived about twenty minutes early, Mark witnessed one meeting conclude and two others begin and conclude as he sat in a modest waiting area that also afforded him the view of Dr. Roger Traynor's closed door and a formal-looking young man in his early thirties who popped in and out of the superintendent's quarters like some bellhop. While he couldn't hear the details of Tonya Barton's snippets, there was light laughter and a few bellowed words of praise from the deputy superintendent. Her generosity this afternoon included two "good for yous," one "that's my man," and two "you go, girls."

At precisely four o'clock, the big woman commenced to honor her commitment to him. She emerged and reserved another bellow in his honor. "Mark, I am so glad you could make it up to see me today!" she opened, and as he extended his hand, she stated emphatically,

"Oh no you don't. Come here!" She unfurled her ample wingspan, both embracing and encasing him, and directed him to have a seat at her conference table, which was garnished with her Pepperidge Farm Milanos, a freshly brewed pot of coffee, and an incessantly buzzing BlackBerry phone.

"Have a cookie, please. Make yourself comfortable. Now tell me, what's it like to be a high school principal? Nope, let me tell you," and in one amazing breath, she sucked in and filtered all the air in the room. "We have put up all these planes in the air, and we don't have enough pilots. We have placed all these initiatives and demands in the principals' laps, not provided the resources they need to execute them properly, and literally cut them off at the knees. Am I right?"

Borrowing from the oxygen she graciously placed back into the room, Mark refused to give credence to her self-flagellation and came up with a general enough response. "Ms. Barton," he began but couldn't get in the thought.

"No, no, no," she scolded, "we are not on a formal basis here. Call me Tonya," and she washed down a Milano with a sip of coffee.

Seizing one more opportunity to get a word in edgewise as she sipped from her cup, he began anew, "Thanks for taking the time out of your busy day to see me."

"Now, Mark, we will have a longer sit-down in the near future. I just wanted to meet you and wish you the best of luck and congratulate you on becoming a principal. Thank you for allowing me to serve you. That's what I'm here for. I am a firm believer that you catch more flies with honey than with vinegar."

The fifteen minutes were uplifting, and Mark stopped on the eighth floor, as he promised Sylvia he would, to give her the gist of the encounter. Archibald Kreinfeldt invited himself, shook his hand, and punctuated Mark's sentiments of what he thought was at least a positive encounter, the whole time ignoring the incessant buzzing sound made by his BlackBerry.

"Yeah," Kreinfeldt stated, "that's a good lady, but she pulls metaphors outta her behind sometimes, and I get lost," he said laughing. "But she sho' do eat some fine cookies, don't she? Hey, Sylvia, you got any idea how to shut off the vibrating thingy on my BlackBerry? Every time I get an e-mail, it buzzes and scares the hell out of me."

As Sylvia reprogrammed her boss's phone, the young man Mark had seen going in and out of Dr. Traynor's office suddenly appeared at her office doorway.

"Mark," Sylvia said, "I'd like you to meet Nick Agnello. He's a graduate student from Harvard, and he's doing an internship under Dr. Traynor, but get this—he's from the Detroit area originally like you. I asked him to stop by so you guys could meet."

Nick Agnello was a short, nondescript man who wore a suit to complement what Mark came to view as a somewhat tight-assed disposition. They exchanged some pleasantries but didn't bond in a Detroit sense. Agnello grew up on the expensive side of the tracks, and Mark's imagery wasn't Agnello's by any stretch. He was as much Motor City as Dr. Kreinfeldt was an Ebonics-spewing brother. As Mark left, he noticed both men fiddling with their cufflinks, and he noticed that Agnello's BlackBerry also was emitting a buzzing sound.

Working his way back to the side street and the parking meter, Mark noticed the panhandler working the other side of a now busy, rush-hour street. This time, he was providing a windshield-washing service to those unfortunate enough to have gotten the red light. Mark got in his car and headed toward the street parallel to his and made his way toward the I-95 entrance ramp but caught the red light immediately before it. From his home underneath the freeway ramp, another homeless black man, older and barefoot, approached his car with a squirt bottle and a dirty rag. As he got closer, Mark studied his round frame and even rounder face. He reminded him of Chubby Checker, the rock 'n' roll icon from the fifties and sixties. Whatever had hardened his life left his skin alone, as it appeared baby smooth.

Rolling down his window, Mark told him, "I'm good. I'm good, and besides, I don't have any change on me."

The man looked at him, began squirting and wiping anyway, smiled a toothless grin, and said, "That's all right, my brother, but look to me like you need to change them wipers. This one's on the house, and besides, I'll holler at you again," and he pointed to the now green traffic light, saying, "Hey, bro, don't get stuck at the station."

Mark hit the gas and pulled back the control governing the windshield washer fluid, so he could clean up the mess left behind from the man's efforts to provide him with a better view.

Chapter 18

SERVING THE STAKEHOLDERS

Freshly returned from her brief suspension as the only casualty of the averted Mexican American War, Migdalia Santa Cruz carried a trump card with her as she made her way to David Canales's office. Her pretty face was hardened by impatience, obstinacy, and martyrdom, and it was framed by long, straight Aztec-black hair that she pulled around her ears so it, like everything and everyone, wouldn't dare to get in her face. She studied Dr. C as he read the narrative on the referral.

"So, you don't even know why you called me down, so why don't we call it even and let me go back to class?" she offered.

Glancing at his family picture, Dr. C began, "Migdalia, this referral says that you were playing with your cell phone in Mr. Ogden's class. You know the school board rules about that, so why would you have the phone out to begin with?"

"Oh yeah, Mr. Assistant Principal," the fifteen-year-old punched back, "but what do them rules say about teachers who play with themselves?"

Stealing another glance at his picture, Dr. C studied the smug face of the angry girl and sought the clarification that he dreaded. "What are you talking about?" he asked.

"If I can't play with my phone, then you need to tell that fucking pervert teacher he can't play with himself. He wears those sweatpants half the time, and his hands are always in his pockets when he walks around the room while we're working."

"Migdalia," Dr. C began, "that's a very serious accusation. What proof do you have of this?"

"I got at least two other girls that seen him. He likes to stand behind the whiteboard on wheels, and the other day, all three of us heard him undo his zipper. You're givin' me shit about a fucking phone; meanwhile you're hiring sick fucks to teach us."

"Migdalia, please watch your language! What are the names of these other girls? Are you prepared to write a statement?"

"I can't help my language; I'm fucking, sorry, friggin' upset. Yeah, I'll write a statement. Hey, you gonna give me back my phone?"

"No, you're going to need a parent or another adult on your contact card to get the phone back," Dr. C revealed.

"Then, that won't be good for either one of us 'cause that person will be my sister!"

Canales chose not to probe that remark as he took another look at his family picture.

The allegations stemmed from new teacher Bill Ogden's fifth-period science block, and Dr. C managed to get Migdalia's statement and those from two other girls before he confronted Mark shortly after dismissal. The statements he gathered were similar in their innuendo but also in the fact that none mentioned actually seeing their teacher masturbate. Together they picked up the phone and called Dr. Alice Chandler-Lopez.

"Boy, what is wrong with people in your place? Mark, has this teacher left the building yet?"

"I don't believe so," he answered.

"Then get David or Sarah or Larry or somebody to bring him to your office now. Let him know what has been said. He is to report to the area office tomorrow. You'll need a sub in there until further notice; you understand?" she asked between heavy breaths.

"Yes."

"I will call Joyce downtown to let her know. Make sure you call the girls' parents to apprise them of the situation. Stick around campus for at least a couple more hours. I don't want anyone showing up on your doorstep with you not being there."

Moments after Mark got off the phone, Dr. C walked in with Bill Ogden. Clad in loose-fitting blue jeans and a bulky sweatshirt, he didn't look much older than the kids he taught. "What's going on? Did something happen?" he asked.

"Bill, have a seat." Mark motioned to the chair in front of his desk. He instructed Dr. C to remain and to close the office door.

"Bill," he started, "talk to me about Migdalia Santa Cruz."

"Mr. M, there's not much to say. I sent her to Dr. C's office with a referral because she was using her cell phone to text. She's got a bad temper and uses inappropriate language all the time. I've tried calling her home, but no one returns my messages."

"Bill, I don't know how to go about this delicately, but three girls in your fifth period are accusing you of masturbating in class." Mark studied his face and saw the color red appear both in his cheeks and his shaved head.

"Wow," he said, dumbfounded. "I don't know how to respond to that. I mean I didn't do that obviously, but wow!"

Mark thought his response to be somewhat odd and not very emphatic. When he explained the protocol of his having to report to the area office, he didn't put up much of a protest. Mark was expecting something along the lines of "so I'm guilty until proven innocent," but that never came out in any form.

As they had grown accustomed to doing and immediately after the young science teacher left the office, David and Mark simply stared at each other for about thirty seconds before Mark said, "Let me look at those statements again."

Migdalia Santa Cruz's statement was much like she revealed in her conversation with Dr. C, but the other two girls, also Mexicans, didn't have really good command of the English language as evidenced by their writing. Dr. C also had them write statements in Spanish but indicated that those were even less literate. One read much like the other:

Me and Rosa was in Mr. Ogden's class, and we notis that he like to go in back of the white board. Today, I here him undo his zipper back there and see him looking at me. It make me afraid, and I no want to be in that class no more.

"Damn, Dave," Mark said after reading this, "I mean I don't think I'd want my kid in that class, but does this statement prove anything?"

"Marko, I thought the same thing, but I've got to tell you that guy gives me the creeps! There's something in his eyes. He doesn't look all there."

At that moment, the hotline rang. "Mark, this is Joyce Adams from School Operations. I guess you're not having a good day today."

"That would be a good guess, Ms. Adams," Mark agreed. "None of this has anything to do with education."

"Now, this might be a little tricky," she dispensed with the small talk. "What kind of statements were you able to get?"

"I've got three statements from girls in his fifth period, and my assistant principal called down another five girls and asked them the generic, 'Have you seen anything unusual happening in your classroom?' They didn't bite on that, so what we do have suggests something unusual but doesn't seem to be enough to incriminate."

"I'm going to need you to fax me those statements," Adams directed. "Whatever you give me, make sure to give to Alice at the area office. Oh, and before you go, I have one more bit of evidence for you."

"What's that?"

"Your Mr. Ogden was accused of similar behavior at Lincoln Middle School where he worked last year. They couldn't prove it, but he was investigated, and they had a situation where they were able to surplus him. So lucky you, I guess."

"Yeah, thanks. Lucky me. Thanks for your help."

"Let me know if you need anything, Mark. Hopefully, tomorrow will be better for you."

Sitting back at his desk, Fred Roberts glanced at the clock on the wall perpendicular to his supine frame. It indicated four forty-five, fifteen minutes beyond the acceptable minimal departure time for an administrative director. He grabbed a dart that he housed in a coffee cup adjacent to his gamer and hurled it with all his might at a dartboard that hung on a barren beige wall ten feet in front of him. It missed the board entirely and emitted a spark when it hit the wall; both events precipitated the drawn out "Goddamn it" that Roberts reserved for times when he had to reach for the telephone.

"I'll be damned!" he said when Mark picked up the hotline. "You really take this principal shit seriously, don't you?"

"Well, I'm not sitting here just pulling it," Mark answered, not thinking that was providing him with material.

"Too bad I can't say the same about your science teacher."

"Word travels fast."

"Nah," Roberts interrupted, "all the women around here move fast. Seeing as how I'm biding my time until retirement rolls round in June, they got to find something for me to do. I'm the jack-of-all-trades, so I get the jack-offs. Ah, hah, ah, ho, oh sheeeeit!" he laughed at his own musing.

"What can I do for you, boss?" Mark massaged his ego.

"Well, you got a Ms. Santa something or other on her way to see you first thing in the a.m. She's pissed off about one of them form letters y'all sent. Claims she's the sister of a student that y'all suspended for 'fucking bullshit' to use her words, but you got perverts teaching kids, so I made an appointment for you. Now, I'm your fucking secretary."

"Thanks, I guess."

"She'll be in around eight thirty. Bring your umbrella. She spits a lot when she yells. Ah, hah, ah, ho, oh sheeeeit! Go home and rest up. You'll need it."

Mark looked at his wall clock. It was five o'clock. He decided to take Roberts up on his suggestion to get some rest and called it a day. On the drive home, he tried to figure out who his morning visitor might be. "Ms. Santa something or other," Roberts had said. "Claims she's the sister of a student y'all suspended." The wind was blowing briskly down Minneola Street, so much so that a dozen or so apples were strewn across both lanes, freshly fallen from a tree whose limbs had stretched too close to the road as if in defiance.

At six o'clock, Magda Robreno was sending out e-mails reminding her principals of upcoming deadlines. She typed diligently at her desk which framed her with three hanging plants neatly placed along its L configuration. Two chairs were arranged in front of this barrier so that her visitors would see her profile when she was typing and occasionally get acknowledgment from her full face when the loss of a thought permitted her to break away. Her plants, her computer, and a handful of souvenirs from faraway places she had visited were generic and impersonal decorative touches. There were no pictures of her deceased parents. There were no pictures of her with her husband. There were no mementos from her career in education, and most importantly, there were no cobwebs to be found. She logged off her computer, rose from her desk, flipped the light switch, and said good night to the evening custodian. She emerged from the elevator, walked out the metal and glass door, entered the parking lot, and found the comfort of her Mercedes Benz. Wilma Hart loved her shoes. Alice Chandler-Lopez loved her days at the spa, and no ride was too good for the mother bear of Area 6.

Landing atop a thin white tank top, her shoulder-length blonde hair was supported by black roots that belied the weathered look of her gaunt brown face. She had what appeared to be a knife-drawn jagged path on her left shoulder that had healed without the benefit of medical attention, and her other shoulder was authored by a tattoo artist who drew red and yellow flames under a casket. Her calloused hands were dressed up by French-manicured inch-long nails, and two cell phones were clipped to the waist band of her black cotton sweatpants. Her similarly manicured toenails protruded unabashedly from her Dollar Store rubber flip-flops. She was rich, and she was poor. She was young, and she was old, but she had arrived on time. Ms. "Santasomething or other" had a young lady in her tow who had Aztec-black hair tucked behind her ears and a jagged path of dried tears interrupting her face. Migdalia Santa Cruz had a sister, and at that moment, Mark understood.

He introduced himself, looked into her bloodshot, deep-set eyes, and awaited her response.

"I'm her sister," she said as she firmly pressed her index finger into her sibling's temple, leaving an imprint and the silent protest of a humiliated frown. Anticipating an invitation, they occupied the seats in front of his desk.

"The old black dude at the area office," the sister began, "said you'd be the one to talk to about a couple of things."

"You could've come to me first, and that would've saved you an extra trip," Mark revealed.

"Yeah, but when I get shit like this," she said, holding up what appeared to be a form letter, "and it's got your signature, I ain't figuring on having a conversation with you. You know what I mean?"

"Let me see that," Mark said, and he reached for the letter. She handed it to him like it was a piece of used tissue and looked over her tattooed shoulder.

"This is just a letter explaining why Migdalia was suspended for a day," he said. "We were trying to control a tense situation between two groups of students, and she walked into the gymnasium where the groups were and started cursing and questioning what we were doing. She made a bad situation worse."

"So how come I find out about this shit now? How come I got to read a fucking letter to know my dumb bitch sister got her ass suspended?"

"I'm sure my assistant principal attempted to make a phone call but couldn't reach anyone." As the conversation evolved, Mark studied Migdalia Santa Cruz's sister and felt like a child turning the handle of a jack-in-the-box.

"I ain't questioning you, Mr. Principal; I'm questioning why this little bitch couldn't tell me this happened."

At this point, Migdalia Santa Cruz's sister began a tirade that had the word "fuck" take a distant second to the vulgarity of the facial contortions and actions that accompanied it. Her lower cheeks filled with air, giving her the look of a trumpet player. Her upper teeth bit into her lower lip to ensure the accuracy of the F consonant, and the sharpness of the K sound emitted like the stroke of a flint lighter, but the spittle that splashed with it prevented ignition. As if her incendiary remarks could not inflict the requisite pain, she took to standing up and flailing away at the top of her little sister's head.

"You stupid fucking little bitch!" She started with two slaps to her sister's exposed ears. "You think you're some kind of badass, Dalia? I did two fucking years hard time because I thought I was a badass gang-banger. Look at me when I talk to you," and she nearly scalped her little sister as she pulled on her hair and twisted her neck backward. "You probably thought Papi was going to handle this shit, but he's too tired, soft, and old to deal with a dumb fucking cunt like you, so he sent me, and I will beat your ass dead before you end up like me. You understand? I'm talking to you, bitch. You understand?"

"Yes, let go of me," Migdalia Santa Cruz pleaded, and the tears followed the same path etched out by the dried ones.

"I'll let go of your ass when you apologize to this man," and she pulled her hair so far backward that her eyes resembled golf balls.

"Ahhhhh! I'm sorry, Mr. M. I'm sorry."

Taking in all this, Mark couldn't react to prevent it because it was foreign to him. He just looked at Migdalia's big sister as the humanity returned to her eyes, and he looked at Migdalia, who seemed so insignificant and humble.

"Mr. Principal, my little sister, I love her to death, but I will kill the bitch if she ever so much as does anything that reminds me of me. I'm twenty-three years old, and look at me. Two years of prison were dog years. I had to learn the hard way. I paint rich bitches' nails to earn a living, but I'm going to school to be a paralegal. Dalia's got it easy; she just makes it harder than it needs to be."

"Let me ask you something," Mark said, redirecting the conversation. "Mr. Roberts at the area office said you had some concerns about the allegations regarding her science teacher?"

"Oh yeah. Dalia told me about that, but I ain't worried about that shit no more. If that turns out to be true, I'll just rip off the motherfucker's balls," and she smiled for the first time, revealing two gold eye teeth. She extended her hand, which Mark gladly shook as it signaled the end of her visit, and she offered, "I got a bad temper sometimes."

No fucking shit, he thought and resolved to visit a couple of classes, taking care to avoid Ms. French's and Mr. Van Slyke's offerings.

Rejuvenated after a handful of enjoyable visitations and a noneventful lunch period, Mark enjoyed the beginnings of cooler afternoon air in the student parking lot at dismissal. The breeze chipped away at his emotional residue, and a bright sun reheated his passion. He shook hands with his students, engaged in good-natured chiding, and permitted himself to lapse into a state of well-being until Sarah Szemanski appeared on the radio.

"Officer Cruz," she whined, "we're going to need your help on bus 6241. We're about the middle of the bus lane."

"On my way, Ms. Szemanski," Cruz responded.

Remembering the last time they solicited Officer Cruz's assistance aboard a bus, Mark immediately interjected, "Lou, let me check it out first."

"All right, Mr. M, let me know if you need me."

"David St. Jean has been asked to get off the bus, and he won't," Szemanski apprised him upon his arrival. "You should've just let Lou handle this. This is delaying the other buses from leaving."

"Do me a favor, Sarah," Mark said, "let the driver's behind us know that it'll be a minute or two."

"You're the boss," she reminded herself, all the while looking downward and shaking her head from side to side with each step she took toward the other buses. Her cadence made it appear that there was interdependence between the movement of her legs and the turning of her head, making her the embodiment of a windup, pain-in-the-ass doll.

A fat black female bus driver sat sideways at her wheel with her arms folded across her heavy chest and her right foot tapping quickly to provide a beat to her impatience.

"I axed him to get his sorry butt outta my bus, and he said he ain't goin' nowhere," she explained. "He got them headphones on, and he be singin' so loud, ain't no way I can concentrate."

Sizing up the driver and suspecting that her limitations likely couldn't extend beyond the scope of her route, Mark looked toward David St. Jean, but he was beaten to the punch.

"What y'all got here," he addressed Mark, the driver, and about thirty-five other students, "is passive resistance. Learned about that in social studies this morning, and I'm applying it this afternoon."

163

"David, I've got to call in one of my trump cards now. Can we talk about this off the bus, in my office?"

"Can't let you use that card now, boss." At that point, there was a general grumbling among the other passengers.

"Hey, Mr. M," a husky black boy requested, "what say you make me yo' aide, and I drag this boy's behind off the bus?"

"David," Mark pointed out, "people are starting to get upset with you, including me."

"It's like this, Mr. M. That driver, notice I didn't say *bitch,* watches my every move. I may as well be one of them traffic dummies, so I can meet her requirements. If both my cheeks of my butt, notice I didn't say *ass,* ain't parallel to the seat, I'm in violation. Now, I can't sing? Screw that crap. Notice I didn't say, *Fuck that shit.*"

At this point, Mark felt his authority was being challenged, and he was one press of the button away from calling Louis Cruz and giving David St. Jean a reason to curse. He moved toward St. Jean and noticed that his head was scraping the top of the bus's ceiling. Pulling out a last stop, he pretended to be stuck and began flailing away with his arms as if to free himself. "Now look what you made me do," he pointed out as the bus broke out in hysterical laughter. "Why you doin' me this way, bro? Now, how'm I gettin' home?"

Laughing harder than anyone, David St. Jean did something very uncharacteristic of him. He picked up his book bag, walked off the bus, turned, and asked Mark as he followed him, "So when can I ride again?"

"Next week, David. Monday," Mark told him.

"That's okay," he said. "Learned about the benefits of power walking in PE today. Got my complementary pedometer. Might just win that class contest for miles logged."

"You know you were probably this far away," Mark separated his thumb and index finger about two inches apart, "from getting your ass kicked by Officer Cruz."

"And you were about that far away from having to watch me get my ass kicked," St. Jean answered, holding his thumb and index finger about the same distance apart.

"What do you mean?"

"Well, if you were that much shorter," he explained, "I wouldn't have laughed my ass off that bus."

As the bus pulled away, Mark decided to stop by the football practice field and look in on the Bucs as they prepared for their next opponent, Eastridge High. Coach Reinhold had the offensive linemen off to the side and was demonstrating blocking technique, utilizing the practice sled.

"You got to explode on the snap," he barked. "You got to go low and get the leg drive. Don't ever stop moving your legs," and he slammed into the practice sled with surprising force for anyone, let alone a sixty-five-year-old. He repeated this a few more times and provided psychological advice with each thrust. "Get angry. Get pissed off. Think that the guy on the other side of you has said something about your mother. Use that to motivate yourself."

As Mark watched the man at work, it occurred to him that they both were in the business of controlling violence.

Chapter 19

UNTOLD STORIES AND THE PREGAME

Corey Watson and Matt Mathews had lived the moment countless times, dating back to their backyard acrobatics and childish flair for drama to their early heroics playing Pop Warner football, but the stage was grander, and the stakes were higher this time around. With the ball on the Eastridge thirty-yard line and six seconds left in the fourth quarter, chased by a faster and larger Eastridge defender, Mathews ran vertically to his right and heaved the football across his body, high into the air in the general area he knew that Watson would occupy. The crowd of five thousand-plus people attained a unanimous silence to better study the ball's flight and not disturb its path. Desire and desperation accompanied Watson more closely than the two defenders who rose into the air with him. His six-foot, three-inch frame stretched to its fullest, and his two hands were a little bit higher and far more practiced than the four other hands that grabbed at the same moment. As the ball landed in his hands, he clutched it with all his might and braced for the inevitable collision. The two Eastridge players hit Watson simultaneously in the right and left rib cage areas, tearing the helmet from his head, but the impact was spread throughout the sandwich that they made of his body, and he landed in the end zone on his feet with the ball still held high in his hands. The official put his hands in the air signaling a touchdown; Matt Mathews put his hands in the air signaling his elation. The fans erupted with joyous noise, most putting their hands in the air. The Buccaneer players put their hands in the air and shared hard high-tens among one another. The coaches pumped their fists. The final score was Bucs 16, the Eastridge Spartans 14.

"Goddamn it, Magic!" Joe Carrera yelled, so he could be heard, "a win's a win, but this should never have been this close. You see, Magic," and he pointed at his mouth, "I'm not smiling. We play like this against Hanford, and they'll kick our asses."

"Come on, Joe," Mark begged to differ, "we pulled off a miracle! Corey pulled that out of the sky!"

"Nah, Magic," he shook his head, "Don pulled that win out of his ass!"

From their sideline berths, Carrera and Mark watched Mathews and Watson being interviewed by the *South Demming News Leader* reporter. Coach Reinhold waited for the interview but began to gather his troops to take the postgame knee.

Mark studied Carrera for about twenty seconds as he watched his jawbone clench and unclench.

"Goddamn it!" he said, and he kicked the thirty-yard-line marker causing it to travel about ten feet into the playing field. "Don's going to need to pray if we can't get any better performance than that," and he waved his hand disgustedly at the circle of players and coaches.

"Joe, I got to tell you," Mark started, "we won the game. I'm going to hate to see what you'll do if we lose one."

"You're absolutely right, Magic, but you also don't understand. Call your wife. Tell her I'm taking you out for a beer. There's something you, as the principal of this great school, have got to know."

Homes on either side of Lucinda Road do not face the traffic; they turn their backs to it. Behind chain-linked fences, the dogs yelp at passing cars until their tongues jut from their mouths like surrender flags, and they find shade on dusty, cracked earth landscapes where they lap at garden hose-fed water bowls, recoup their energy, and continue their pointless pursuits. The south-side dogs run east, and the north-side dogs run west. This is the unwavering makeup of their daily existence until the sun sets, and darkness resets the stage.

"Luci Street," as the locals called it, was one of those places that even the train had chosen not to interrupt, opting to take the long way around. But its geographic purpose remained its status as the dividing line between those who would attend Hanford High to the south and those destined for South Demming to the north. And for local historian Joe Carrera, it may as well have been the Mason-Dixon Line.

"Magic," Carrera apologetically handed Mark a beer, "I know it's not Grady's, but Sherry's working late, and the kids are doing sleepovers at friends' houses, so it's just you and me and the High School Sports Wrap-Up edition."

"Yeah," Mark answered, "but you didn't bring me here to watch TV. You said there's something I have to know."

Carrera sat down at a La-Z-Boy across from Mark's perch on his couch. He kicked out the footrests, took a sip of his beer, let out a loud belch, and installed his can on a coaster. "Magic, I'm going to tell you why I hate Hanford High and everyone, kids excluded, associated with the school, but to do that, I have to give you a social studies lesson."

With his can of beer in his hand and his propped up feet, Carrera looked anything but professorial. Mark gave in, once again, to his flair for drama and prepared himself for yet one more revelation, a ritual that the people long associated with South Demming felt the need to give him in small doses.

"Magic," he began, "just south of us is Luci Street. It's got a fancier name than that, but that's what everyone calls it. Well, Luci Street is the boundary line that determines which school kids attend. Hanford High's football program is run by a bunch of cheaters. They recruit our kids and furnish them with bogus addresses. Everyone in this part of town is related in some way, shape, or form, to everyone else. There are plenty of aunts, uncles, and cousins who in the name of Bronco football will do their part to help the team."

"Joe, we don't have kids playing for the Bucs who live too far south?"

"Yes, we do, Magic, but we don't go out recruiting them. If they want to play for Don, we'll help them get to us legitimately. They will live with family members at the address in the computer, but they need to come to us to make this happen. We don't cherry-pick south of Luci."

"How big is this difference?"

"It's huge, Magic, because what we do is legal under the high school sports guidelines for this state. Recruiting isn't legal anywhere, and that's what they do at Hanford. They are lying, cheating, and backstabbing motherfuckers!"

At this point, Carrera's pupils once again became nail heads, and like a traffic cop at a busy intersection, Mark couldn't adequately direct the flow of this conversation. "But how do you really feel about them, Joe?" he asked in an attempt to usher in some humor.

"Two years ago, Magic, we beat them for the first time in nine years, and we beat them again last year. When we lined up, the kids shook hands; they've known each other and have grown up playing against each other, but their coaches, their AD, and their former principal, Jim Clarkson, waved us off."

"So what did you do when this happened?"

"Something I shouldn't have done, Magic, but when I approached Clarkson, and he accused me of being a cheater, let's just say we were forehead to forehead before Jud and Bryan got between us. You can say what you want about me as long as you don't call my integrity into question. I've got the letter outlining the whole situation for you. I was just saving it for this time."

"But this game isn't for another two weeks. Why do you feel the need to tell me now?"

"Because this game is the biggest sporting event in this city, and the preparations must begin now."

"Okay, so it's a big game, but how are the preparations that different that we need to be sweating this now?"

"Magic, you'll need a six-pack to swallow this, and I won't send you out on the road that way. Let's make the beverage coffee, and let me fill you in on Monday. Let's watch the sports wrap-up for now."

When Mark pulled into South Demming Monday morning at 6:05 a.m., Joe Carrera's '63 Caddy already was parked in its spot to the left of his. He touched the hood as he passed it, and it was cold.

"Fucking guy must've woken up with a hard-on," Mark laughed to himself.

"Magic, where have you been?" he asked as he handed over a Starbuck's coffee cup. "Thought we could get an early start and let Ice, Kate, and Fatman have first crack at Cathy's brew."

"What's your problem with David, Joe? Why can't you call him by his name?"

"No problem here, Magic," he offered. "Everyone here kind of has a nickname, and that's usually based on some physical quality, but hey, we're here this morning to talk South Demming slash Hanford football. Magic, sometime early next week we need to schedule a meeting—you, me, their new principal, and their new AD. I'll be the first one to tell you that I'm glad Clarkson isn't there anymore, but the new guy, Lowell, came straight from an elementary, and his AD was his PE coach there, and neither one of them is ready for this, and they're the home team for Christsakes!"

"You're moving too fast for me," Mark interrupted. "We both use the same field for our home games. What difference does it make whose home or visitor?"

"Magic, we alternate each year. It's their turn, so they get to put in the orders for police presence, security overtime, and they get to run the concession stands."

At this point, Carrera looked away from him, but Mark detected the tensing of the jaw as it drummed against his temples. "What's the bottom line, Joe?" he asked. "You obviously have a strong handle on this, so what's the bottom line?"

Turning to face Mark again from his chair on the other side of the desk, Carrera raised his hand, index finger pointing toward the ceiling, and said, "Money, Magic, is the bottom line with everything, but for this game, we've got to take safety into account."

"Go ahead. What does South Demming stand to make from this game?"

"Magic, we will have easily nine thousand people at this game. It's a standing-room-only situation. Times six bucks per ticket, you're looking at $54,000 just in gate. Now, these folks get hungry. The concession stand does about five grand of business at this game, and souvenirs go strong as well. We'll be close to $60,000 gross. Divide that between the two schools, and you're looking at a $30,000 payday minus the time and a half that we have to pay school resource officers, Hanford Police, and our own security. That amounts to about five grand, so each school still takes away more than twenty-five grand from this game."

"Five grand in security?" Mark asked incredulously.

"Magic, among school police from the district, Hanford cops, and security monitors from both schools, we're looking at twenty-three bodies out there, patrolling the field and making sure that it's safe for America."

"Look," Mark said, "you've done this before, and I don't want to call your expertise into question, but twenty-three fucking security people?"

"Plus a paddy wagon," Carrera added.

"A paddy wagon? What the fuck are you talking about?"

"Doughnut, Magic?" Carrera asked as he opened the box on top of the desk, revealing a dozen glazed temptations.

"What the fuck are you talking about?" Mark repeated.

"All right! Don't have a fucking doughnut." He closed the box and put it at his feet. "Magic, have you ever lived up north?"

"What does that have to do with anything, Joe?"

"Think of dog shit in the spring, Magic," he started. "All winter long it's hard and cold. Now, the weather warms up, and it starts to thaw, and it stinks beyond belief. That's what happens in this game. Every piece of shit on both sides of Luci Street comes out of hibernation. We've got hangers on, gamblers, dope dealers, hookers. It's Hanford's sorry-ass version of the Super Bowl. They have got to know that their bullshit won't be tolerated, so the paddy wagon is a visual to keep them in check. And going back to the bottom line, Magic, a sorry-ass elementary school principal and a first-year AD do not have a clue in terms of preparation, but the control is in their court because they're the fucking home team."

"So, what's your plan to enlighten them?"

"You sure you don't want a doughnut, Magic?" he asked anew.

"I'm sure," Mark answered. "Let's bring this to closure."

"Closure, Magic, is your letting me handle this through their AD. He's green, and he's been asking me a lot of questions. I can convince him to follow my lead, and the end result will groom him for the future."

"Go ahead and set up the meeting."

"That's why I love you, Magic. I'd kiss you, but apparently you wouldn't like doughnut breath, so I'm just going to give the rest of these to Fatman."

As he walked, the pant leg cuffs broke over his wingtips as though their tailor were also a choreographer. His perfectly knotted tie allowed its tip to lightly touch upon the top portion of his brass buckle, and his neatly manicured hands protruded from dress shirt sleeves that he rolled up one rung in anticipation of business. He accessorized on his right hand with a leather planner, and his left hand snaked out of hiding just enough so that the draped jacket that concealed his forearm served as a backdrop for the Rolex watch that punctuated his punctuality. The sharp lines of his jaw were only outdone in their precision by his immaculately groomed mustache and closely cropped, slightly graying Afro. The earth tones of his attire were a perfect match for his dark copper skin because Dr. Henry Lowell, the tall, slender, and suave new principal of Hanford High, wore brown like he owned it.

"Magic, that is one *GQ* motherfucker." Joe Carrera nudged him as they happened upon this arrival that coincided with their tucking students into first period. "For the next meeting, we'll get you down to Macy's or Lord & Taylor or something, but you'll still have to get a stick up your ass to walk as straight as that fuck!"

Mark digested Carrera's words, sized up their mutual preppy look with polo shirts provided by Bucs' Athletics, and could only come up with, "Shut up, Joe! You want the guy to hear you?" At this point, Lowell and his two companions had closed the car door and were about thirty feet from where they stood at the school's entrance.

"Magic, I don't give a shit who hears me," Carrera toned it down to a gruff whisper. "The little white guy has to be his AD that I've been talking to over the phone. The big dude is Robby McGrady, their head coach and a piece of shit."

The trio to whom Carrera alluded couldn't have been more mismatched. McGrady was a monstrous, middle-aged black man, likely six and a half feet tall and nearly that big around. He wore an untucked Hanford Broncos athletic polo shirt over blue jeans and sported a scraggly salt-and-pepper beard. The little guy was their new athletic director that Lowell moved up with him from the elementary school. His name was John Forrester, and he too wore a monogrammed polo shirt that he tucked into his khaki pants, but there was nothing to make him stand out between his two companions. He appeared to be an afterthought in the arrangement, a throw pillow in the decor, or a hastily hung picture.

The acknowledgments seemed bellicose in nature as though this were a summit between warring countries. Dr. Lowell accepted Mark's extended hand and provided a decidedly firm and castrating handshake that squeezed in his four fingers but shut the door on the knuckles. John Forrester oozed out between his two companions and gave Carrera and him two quick little handshakes and then darted back inside his comfort zone. Coach McGrady nodded to them and grunted. Mark gave them a "Thanks for being here," and he received from Lowell an ambivalent, "No need to thank us," in return. They entered the main office, and Mark pointed the entourage toward his door, following them in tow. As he passed by Ken Ferguson's desk, Ken reached out and slapped him on the ass.

"Sorry, boss," he said when Mark turned around startled. "My Tourette's is acting up again. Go give 'em shit—I mean hell, I mean heck—I mean, well, you know what I mean." He made him laugh, but Mark shut down his smile when he reached the conference table.

"Mr. M," Carrera addressed the gathering, "if you and Dr. Lowell don't mind, I'd like to take point on this." He turned his eyes to the trio directly across from them at the side closest to the doorway.

After studying them for a few seconds, Lowell said, "Mr. Carrera, John here tells me that you have been a big help to him in his new role. For that, I am grateful, so by all means, get us started."

"Boss man?" Carrera inquired as though they hadn't orchestrated this opening move.

"Joe," Mark said, "you've been doing this back to when the players wore leather helmets. You're on!" His comment drew some light laughter and set the stage for Carrera.

"Gentlemen," he began. "Hanford vs. South Demming is this area's biggest sporting event." He went on to highlight the camaraderie that continued to exist between the players and the money that stood to be made as a result of this storied rivalry. He discussed the ticket-selling process, the concession-stand operations, and the gate security. Heads were nodding in agreement until he outlined the entire security plan, and Lowell began to drum the fingertips of his left hand into the conference table.

"Mr. Carrera, if I may interject?" Lowell moved his right index finger in quick bursts against his lips and became even more erect in his seated posture. "Out of deference to your years of experience with this event and my newness to it, I've been happy and wise to let you speak, but your security measures worry me."

"Look, Dr. Lowell," Carrera replied, "it's a lot of people and a lot of money, I know, but we're not doing anything we haven't done before. The crowds were out of control in the past, and we've had some fights. Hell, one year, we even had the concession stand robbed at gunpoint. There's strength in numbers. If you're not confident about what I'm saying, ask your head coach over here." He pointed to Robby McGrady.

McGrady, who had been twirling a ring on his finger, suddenly came to life. "Look, Dr. Lowell. It ain't no secret that me and Joe's had some differences, but this is one thing that we're on the same page with."

Dr. Lowell rather forcefully let some air escape from his flared nostrils. "Let me ask the other new principal here what he thinks," Crawford turned his attention to Mark and continued. "We're looking at a total of twenty-three security folks, beginning with Hanford Police, to Demming County Police, to school-site security, and then, to top it all off with, we're bringing out a paddy wagon. How's that going to look to the communities we serve?"

"I'm hoping, Dr. Lowell, that it looks like we're taking every necessary precaution to ensure public safety. There has been a precedent for all the preparation as Joe mentioned."

"Gentlemen, although it goes against my nature and everything I know about proper public relations, I'm going to acquiesce this time and not rock the boat." Lowell stood up, gestured for his companions to do the same, handed his hosts some glossy, foil-embossed business cards, shook both of their hands, thanked them for their time, and as they walked the group toward the main exit, he turned to his head coach and said for all to hear, "Outta all dis, we damn sho' going to be able to keep our niggers in check!"

Mark's eyes immediately darted toward Carrera, who wore a wry smile to cover his naked sentiments and shook his head from side to side. He spit on the sidewalk, tucked his hands in his pants pockets, and stared at him for a moment before speaking.

"And that, Magic," Carrera started as he watched the visitors enter their vehicle, "is one more reason why I fucking hate—read my lips— *hate* Hanford High."

"He's new there, Joe. You've got to understand where he's coming from."

Carrera examined Lowell's business card and stated, "He's coming from Hanford High, Magic, where their motto is and always has been We Hire Assholes. But there is a good thing here," Carrera said as he continued to look at Lowell's business card.

"And what's that may I ask?"

"We're still doing it my way. Ah hah, ah ha ha ha!" and he gave his principal a hard slap on the back and began looking at the business card again as they walked toward the main office. "Hey, Magic!"

"Yeah?"

"Let me look at your business card."

"Hey, boss." Ray Devereaux popped out between the many rows of parked cars. "I saved you a parking spot. Ice is holding it for you just up ahead." Mark rolled up his window and headed in the direction he pointed, only to see the Iceman talking on the radio and waving him toward a reserved spot marked off with a traffic cone. This was no more than fifty feet away from the entrance gate.

"Boy, that's some service!" Sylvia exclaimed. She knew of the hype and history of this game and wasn't going to miss it.

"Yeah, they heard you were coming, so all of a sudden I get the VIP treatment," Mark played along. The truth was he usually got to games early enough to get a good spot without the preferential treatment. For this one, one hour early appeared to be one hour too late. The lines outside the two ticket booths stretched in serpentine fashion, befitting Sarah Szemanski, who monitored the visitor's gate and taxing the ticket-taking Larry Jefferson whose bulging eyeballs fought for the space in his skull like the standing-room-only crowd members who jockeyed for position along the fence line framing the football field. The silver bleachers held so many bodies that they no longer could reflect the sun.

"I don't know, boss," Jefferson greeted him while extending an "Evenin', ma'am," upon spotting Sylvia. It was a hot humid night, and the sun was beginning to set, and Jefferson already had the exasperated, sweaty brow look of a beaten man. "This place can't hold much more than we already done got." He shook his head and repeated, "I don't know. I don't know."

Out of earshot, Sylvia turned to Mark and asked, "What's his problem?"

"He already told you when he said, 'I don't know.' That's his problem."

"Well, at least he said hello," Sylvia offered. "What the hell is Szemanski's problem?"

"She's too busy. She's too tied up to engage in any pleasantries," Mark answered. "Sarah's the only one of us who works, so you'll have to forgive her."

Sylvia weighed the sarcasm and appeared ready for a retort when they were interrupted prior to entering the field. Walking with a limp and approaching them from a bent-over perspective, an unshaven, gray-haired, and tattered man stopped Mark's progress by placing his head directly against his chest.

"Pretend you don't know me," he whispered harshly as he looked up at Mark. "It's me, T. J."

"T. J., what the fuck!"

"Shhh! You don't know me. I'm undercover. We're expecting some drug deals to be happening here tonight, so Carrera let me borrow some of his clothes," and his laugh revealed a blacked-out tooth to complement his vagabond vogue.

"Oh shit!" Mark said. "Don't let him hear you say that."

"Hey, Sylvia." T. J.'s forceful whisper caught her attention.

"T. J., oh my God!" Sylvia exclaimed.

"Sylvia, keep it down," Mark reminded her. "T. J.'s working under cover," and he started to laugh.

"Listen," T. J. said, "I just wanted to say hey to you guys. I'll try to clean up next time. I promise. Got to go!"

For its part, South Demming had maintained its undefeated status by summarily disposing of some lesser opponents over the previous two weeks. Hanford had sustained its first blemish the previous week with a loss to parochial school power Ponce de Leon High. This left Ponce de Leon and South Demming undefeated in the division and placed Hanford in a must-win situation. Their mission was to defeat the Bucs and root them on when they would take on Ponce, thus forcing a three-way tie.

The immaculately kept grass of Harnett Field stretched north and south. South Demming won the toss, deferred, and elected to defend the north end zone to start the game. As the visitors, their sideline occupied the west side of the field. The moments before kickoff represented the time for school officials and ancillary personnel to examine all directions. Despite twenty-three security folks, administrative personnel from both schools, and the bold statement of a paddy wagon that settled like a gallows on the north side of the stadium, Mark felt the extreme uneasiness that comes with a crowd approaching ten thousand people, half of whom have something to settle with the other half. He couldn't pick out Henry Lowell on the other side of the field but wondered what he was thinking and whether or not those thoughts might have included a sigh of relief that such security measures were undertaken. Mark saw many people, mostly black men that he hadn't seen at previous games, and they had prominent perches along the fence line and in the north-end bleachers. Their shadows would soon stretch into the end zones and hash marks as the stadium-lit evening silhouetted street credibility.

"How ya doin', sir?" Mark was interrupted from his speculation to find Darryl, dressed in his South Demming regalia that included a rosary of royal blue and white football-shaped prayer beads dangling from his neck. "We going to *win* tonight!" and he offered a high five and a hug to seal the deal.

"I spoke to Darryl's boss at Publix to make sure he had this night off," Joe Carrera explained. "The kid may have some shortcomings, but he enjoys a good ass-kicking as much as the next guy."

"And you're that sure that's what's in store for Hanford tonight?" Mark asked.

"Magic, I will kiss Henry Lowell's brown ass if that doesn't happen. That's how sure I am." Carrera clenched his jaw as he looked to the scoreboard, which was clicking off the last minute before kickoff.

Matt Mathews kicked the ball high and deep southward. The Hanford recipient caught the ball on the five-yard line, dodged an attempted tackle by Raja Horton, moved east to west for about ten yards before having the extreme misfortune of meeting Tyrus Waters, who in missile-like fashion separated player from ball, with both ending up out of bounds. The hit, which at this point of the season was to be expected, drew the oohs and ahhs from the crowd and set the tone for the rest of the evening.

Hanford went three and out, gaining only one yard from scrimmage. On their subsequent punt, Danny Baldwin took the ball at the Bucs' forty-yard line, found a crease in the coverage, and returned it for a touchdown. Bucs 7, Broncos 0.

After his early heroics, Baldwin sought out his principal. "This is fun, Mr. M! They ain't that good!"

Because Hanford could match South Demming athletically, they never were out of the game, despite eventually losing 28–14. Mark's elation was mixed with dread when the teams lined up to shake hands after the game. He remembered the fiasco Carrera recounted from the year before, but he wasn't worried about the players who shook hands with one another and were very civil. His eyes were on the Hanford entourage and frankly his highly passionate athletic director. He watched as they all shook hands and noticed Carrera handing something to Forrester, McGrady, and finally, Lowell. The proceedings were more than amicable, and Lowell provided him with what he felt was a genuine congratulations.

As the crowd filtered out of Harnett Field, Mark eavesdropped on the interviews that were being conducted with Danny Baldwin. Whether he had a microphone and a camera in his face or simply had a reporter with a notepad confronting him, he seemed to bask in his moments of glory. He had a kerchief covering his head and looked every part the professional, guarding his image with humor and humility.

"Oh Lawd, I'm getting too old for this!" he exclaimed to a throng of reporters who chuckled at his remark.

Suddenly, Mark felt the bear hug, and this time Carrera succeeded in lifting his 250-pound frame off the ground. "How about them Bucs, Magic? How about them motherfucking Bucs? Ah, hah, hah, hah, hah, hah! Lowell would probably like it if I kissed his ass, but it never happened."

"We did great, Joe, and I'm just as happy that we didn't have to deal with any bullshit tonight."

"Magic, if you put your trust in me, you can't go wrong. Oh, and, Magic, I've got one more thing to say. Go ahead! Ask me what it is," Carrera ranted as the foam formed in the corners of his lips like waves breaking at the beach.

Mark gave in. "Go ahead, Joe. Get it off your chest."

"Cha ching, Magic! Cha motherfucking ching!"

"Yeah, there was a shitload of people here tonight, but let me ask you something. What were you handing to Lowell and his people when we were shaking hands?"

"You're going to love this, Magic," and he handed him a card with a glossy, foil-embossed crest of South Demming, and before he could read on, Carrera confirmed what Mark suspected. "Before you go crazy, Community Bank foots the bill for these. I got some for me too. It's your new business card, Magic. I'll be damned if the Hanford High principal has a better-looking business card than you do. I wanted those arrogant sons of bitches to walk away with another reminder of their inferiority."

"So winning tonight hasn't tempered your distaste for Hanford?"

"Magic, you silver-tongued SOB. If that means do I hate them less, then the answer is *no*!"

That being clarified, they both turned their attention to the north end zone where Coach Reinhold was giving his postgame sermon.

"Looking at that, Magic, I'm left with one conclusion."

"I've got one more conclusion left in me for this evening, Joe. Go for it!" Mark encouraged him.

"God's a Buccaneer, Magic. God's a Buccaneer!"

Chapter 20

ENTER THE DRAGON

And the Buccaneer God did battle with the devil when the students arrived Monday morning; several devils, a number of vampires, nurses clad in triple X-rated uniforms, and a homeless schizophrenic were among a few of the cast of characters who took liberties with Spirit Week and ignored the restrictions against masks, face painting, and tasteless depictions of any kind. Monday was Mardi Gras Day, and the spirit of *anything goes* did not work out too well for a handful of students. They sat in the main office awaiting their turns to call their parents to bring clothing and, in the extreme cases, take them home for the day.

Ken Ferguson took notice of an eye shadow and mascara-wearing, gigantic-breasted young man who complemented his rubber boobs with a long red wig and sported a spring-loaded plastic penis that sprang to attention each time he opened the raincoat that hid his endowments.

"Hey, haven't we met before?" Ferguson asked.

"My mother is going to kill me," was all the young man could say as he looked at his feet.

"And I can't say you deserve anything less," Sarah Szemanski said as she entered the front office to claim her next client. "What in God's name were you thinking?"

"That one, boss"—Larry Jefferson appeared and pointed one of his long fingernails at the gender-bender boy—"that one gets my prize for the most foolishness!" Mark looked at Jefferson with his cat claws and catlike contact lenses, and he almost expected him to hiss and arch his back in defining his space.

Angela Leon never sponsored a Spirit Week. Her school had a uniform policy and a strict academic focus, so she didn't know it was Mardi Gras Day when she pulled up into South Demming's parking lot, right behind Mark's pickup, even though two spaces ahead there was a spot clearly within her view. It was two in the afternoon; the students were tucked into their last block of the day. She shut off the engine of her Sedan de Ville, sucked the last bit of life out of her cigarette, and left a bloody lipstick stain on its filter, crushing its remains in her already butt-filled ashtray. The legs of her gray pantsuit made little whooshing sounds as her short, stubby legs pounded a heel-echoing staccato into the pavement leading up to the school entrance.

"How can I help you, ma'am?" asked Essie Hunt as Leon passed by her, ignoring school-entry protocol. "Ms., please!" Essie Hunt implored. "Please check in with me. It'll only be a moment," she said assuredly.

Without either stopping or turning around, Leon blared, "You can help me by not wasting my time."

Noticing that her path was headed directly toward the main office, Essie Hunt used her radio like a matador uses a red cape. "Main office, please come back. Come back, please!"

The front office door swung open as if propelled by a quick force of wind at the same time that Cathy reached for her radio to respond. Essie Hunt called again, but a warning at this juncture was akin to saying, "Stop or I'll shoot," when the gun's already smoking.

To the amazement of Cathy, Ken Ferguson, and the conscientious Essie Hunt, the principal of Great Palm High, disposed of the "May I help yous" with the precision reserved for hazardous waste.

"Where is your principal? Never mind," she said as she unlatched the partition door and stomped into the office where Mark was discussing school-wide attendance with David Canales.

"I told you that you should have called me," she began when she noticed that they recognized her arrival. "Now, I'm taking time out of my day because Magda seems to think that high school principals can just rearrange their fucking schedules."

"Who is she?" David whispered. "What's going on?"

Mark took notice that Angela Leon's face had the same maroon shade as the blouse that complemented her business attire, and hoping to temper her unpleasant demeanor, he opened by inviting her to sit at the conference table even though he would have preferred opening his mouth for a root canal or his ass for an enema. All the while, David looked at Mark with his mouth partially opened as if to plead for his next words.

"David, this is Angela Leon, the principal of Great Palm High, and she's here to go over some things with me. We can finish up later on today or early tomorrow." David no sooner lifted his big frame inches from his chair than Leon was cordial enough to include him.

"Sit down, David; you're not going anywhere. You're his AP. You're supposed to have his backside, so if I start chewing on it, you'll know what to do to keep him out of harm's way in the future." She turned to Mark and with a horse-toothed, lipstick-stained staged grin, and said, "I'll need to look at your most recent attendance printout, your school-based budget, and your master schedule, pronto!"

"I'll get Cathy to get those for us," Mark said, and after he summoned her to retrieve those documents, Leon began to shake her head.

"Mark, those three things need to be at your fingertips at all times. Nobody should have to dig those up for you. You're lucky it's me who's requesting them this time. If it were Chandler-Lopez, she'd have your balls on a silver platter!"

The twenty to thirty seconds that it took Cathy to gather the documents seemed like twenty to thirty minutes. Mark noticed that David's face was getting red as though he might have forgotten to exhale and gather his next breath or that he was feeling the effects of Leon's large, flared nostrils sucking up most of the oxygen in the room.

Now armed with her reports, Leon began picking them apart like a buzzard going at carrion. "Mark, which AP did you assign to attendance?"

"He's sitting across from you," and as Mark indicated David, he felt like he was Judas making Sophie's Choice. David rubbed his temples and later confided that he tightened his asshole.

"Okay, David," Leon turned her attention to Mark's right-hand man, "let me ask you something."

"Yes, ma'am, please." David reserved a professional distance and leaned back in his chair with his arms folded.

"You have a number of students who already have five or more absences. How is this being handled intervention-wise?"

David leaned forward, a pilgrim placing his head in the stocks. He beamed; he sat upright; he readied his index finger for action. "Well," he began, "we have our automated dial-out system that lets families know when their children are absent on a given day. We send out letters to the families of those students with five or more absences, and these letters reiterate the attendance policy and how nine or more unexcused absences will result in the student being failed due to excessive absences."

"Okay, so you have a robot calling homes," Leon extrapolated, "and you send out letters. How do you know that the right people have heard the messages or received the mail? What are you personally doing? How many phone calls have you made? How many doors have you knocked upon? To how many of these situations have you applied the riot act?"

David didn't have an immediate answer, and after Leon concluded her savage interrogation, she made the gesture. Her index finger rose from her lap and floated into her open mouth where she made gagging sounds to indicate her disapproval. "I have got tell you, David," she continued, "if you were my AP, you'd be one step removed from being back in the classroom. South Demming is next to last in the entire county in attendance, and it's sending out form letters."

David's eyes became enlarged, and he cleared his throat, and Angela Leon turned her attention to Mark. "I'm looking at your budget, and I already see two big problems. Look at all the substitute hours you've purchased. Why aren't you coming down on the people who don't show up to work every day? Mark, you've got to write their asses up. Look at what you've got in your discretionary funds. How do you expect to run a school on $70,000? That'll buy you gas for your lawn mowers and some toilet paper, so your teachers can wipe their asses, which is what it appears they have done with your leadership style." She shook her head from side to side, and he saw her index finger twitch, but she spared him that gesticulation.

Leon took longer in her perusal of the master schedule, and Mark imagined that she was reloading, but she changed gears. "Well, your class sizes are too big. You probably need to assign your deans some students to relieve these class loads, and I still can't believe that the area office is dragging its ass in getting you a curriculum AP. Who have you pissed off?" she asked him as she reached for her purse and rose to leave. "You've got your work cut out for you. We can't solve your problems in an afternoon. I'll be back, and I'll see what I can do to call the dogs off in the meantime."

Mark and David walked her out of the building. Her advisory session lasted all of one half hour, but it likely took at least twice that much off their respective life expectancies. As she opened up her car door, she turned to Mark and said, "Call me."

Mark and David looked at each other as she sped off. Mark spoke first, saying, "Welcome to my world, Dave."

David let out a huge breath of air from his nostrils and said, "Mark, I felt like a baby curled into a fetal position with my thumb in my mouth. That's leadership? I thought she was supposed to help you. Didn't you tell me that she was your mentor principal? Don't get me wrong; she made some suggestions that I will use, but there's a way to not rob people of their dignity. She could have said, 'You might want to try this; it's worked for me,' or she could have offered some encouragement with the criticism. She couldn't do your job here. She wouldn't last a day." Even in his pain, David attempted to make his boss feel better. "Let me know, and I'll give you my letter of resignation right now. I don't want to be the reason for anything bad happening to you."

"David," Mark sighed, "if that's what it's coming down to, then I'll join you in the unemployment line."

During the drive home, Mark's thoughts were occupied with respect to the unexpected visit and the trail of ghosts, witches, devils, goblins, and other apparitions that should have foretold her arrival. Despite the plethora of festive creatures, it wasn't until the appearance of Angela Leon that the monster had arrived.

The train caught him at five o'clock, and rather than count cars to stay awake, he chose to dwell on the word *monster*. He laughed to himself as he conjured all the negative words it contained. There was stern. There was stone in the verbal form. There was rent. There was rose, the kind that appears at funerals, and there was stem, what's left after a rose has dried and died. There was sermon, the kind that no one wants to hear, and most importantly, monster held in its claws the word *mentor*.

At four o'clock the next day, Fred Roberts held the first dart of the afternoon. He twirled it in his big right hand, tested its sharpness against the index finger of his left hand, and smiled to himself as he put it down to pick up the phone.

"Bro, do yourself a favor," he skipped the formalities after Mark's hello, and as he gazed across the room, his eyes glazed over, turning the twelve-foot expanse ahead of his desk into an inconsequential blur.

"Who is this?" Mark asked, not recognizing the giddy tone Roberts reserved for special occasions.

"Not who, my brother, but what it is, and it's your lucky day!" he spoke in riddles long enough for Mark to recognize the person behind the guise in his voice.

"Dr. Roberts, what can I do for you?" he asked.

"Mark, my man," he said, "it ain't what you can do for me but what you can do for yourself. And you can do yourself a favor, bro." Again, his eyes appeared to look into the immediate distance but not acknowledge the presence of any of the objects in the room.

"Talk to me," Mark urged him to continue all the while feeling that Roberts had something to gain in this transaction.

"Well, I know that you need a curriculum AP, and I just found out who the candidates are, and one of them used to work for me before I became a director. She's working at Green Grove Middle up north, but she just bought a house down south after her divorce, so she's looking to relocate."

"So, we've got candidates?" Mark asked incredulously. "Do we have any interview dates? You know who they are? Am I going to be a part of this process at some point?"

"They're setting up the interviews for next week. Magda's going to call you to sit in, but before you do that, you might want to bring in my little darling." This time he smiled, which cued his eyes to focus with pinpoint accuracy across the room.

"What's her name?" Mark asked.

"Her name's Alana Tavares. She's one of them little Latina hotties." As Roberts revealed her fringe attributes, including a vivid description of, as he called them, "her breasteses," a huge grin raised the gray of his temples, and his dart became a baton among his thumb, index, and middle finger.

"That's all good," Mark acknowledged his appreciation of the female form, "but can she run the academic program at South Demming?"

"Let me put it to you this way," Roberts went on. "She was just starting out in administration when I got her on board. She did my master schedule. She prepared my budget. She found extra money I didn't even know we had. Do yourself a favor, bro!" His gaze became transfixed with a now blazing accuracy, bringing his immediate world into focus.

"I'll call her at her school and see if she can come in before the end of the week."

"You're going to thank me," Roberts closed. "You'll sleep better at night. Your worries are over, my brother." And he paused before uttering his last, "Do yourself a favor! And besides, she's mighty nice to look at!"

So Fred Roberts played Cupid during Spirit Week. Only, in this case, he was armed with a dart rather than an arrow. Feeling it important enough to lower his feet from his desktop, he seized his dart, eyed his target, and struck his first bull's-eye in many weeks. His joyous laughter complemented a perfect conclusion to his day, an ending in which his aim was never more precise.

For her part, Alana Tavares's aim was obvious and every bit as precise as she walked the short distance across the room and handed the dart to Dr. Fred Roberts.

An hour and a half after dismissal, the dormant parking lot came back to life resoundingly upon the arrival of its newest visitor, Alana Tavares. The tires of her gold C-230 Mercedes squealed as she pulled into a spot in front of the school. The parking lot did its part by announcing her arrival, but Tavares had some work to do before announcing her presence. With the console of the dashboard and the rearview mirror serving as her vanity, she relined, restroked, dabbed, puckered, and adjusted. Tavares stepped out of the vehicle, and as each heel struck the pavement, the sound echoed so that her gait was accompanied by castanets. The swaying of her yellow sundress kept in sync with the beat as it negotiated the curves of her backside.

Ken Ferguson's fingers drummed against his desk as he contemplated his next move in solitaire. He raised his eyebrows so that the lines in his forehead became more pronounced. He stroked his chin contemplatively and pursed his lips to assist in the thought process, and with a final gesture geared toward liberating his genius, he reached between his legs and adjusted his crotch area. Shortly after doing this, he surveyed the office, and his eyes met with those of Alana Tavares, who had taken in the whole scene. Looking over his reading glasses, Ferguson did something he generally avoiding doing; he got up out of his seat.

"What can I do ya for?" Ferguson asked as he deftly unhooked the latched gate that separated them as though it were a bra strap.

"Thank you," a poker-faced Tavares muttered as she entered. "I have an appointment to see the principal."

"Let me see if he's in his office," Ferguson said as he took two exaggerated steps backward, peered within the partially closed door, and entered just beyond Tavares's vision. "Your appointment is here," he told Mark and David Canales, and Ferguson puckered his lips and placed both hands on his hips in a charade to indicate the presence of a female.

"Let her in, Ken, and stop doing that; you're starting to worry me," Mark said right as Ken began to reach out over his chest with cupped hands. As she entered, he positioned himself to smell her hair and ogle her behind.

For both of their parts, Tavares and Mark were business people. In her he saw the knowledge she possessed with respect to creating a master schedule, assisting in budget preparation, and driving the school's curriculum. These priorities allowed him to recognize the extra layer of makeup and perfume, the heels that made her brief legs seem long, and the overly sprayed hair that matched her rigidity. She morphed accordingly into a demure, educational-buzz-word-spewing prodigy, someone who he was willing to hire on the spot after a twenty-minute exchange of ideas.

About five minutes after her departure, David Canales agreed that Tavares possessed the knowledge and skills necessary to move South Demming in a positive direction.

"Yes, yes, she's very knowledgeable," Canales acquiesced, "but it doesn't hurt that she's so nice to look at."

Ken Ferguson had elected to stay past his four o'clock quitting time and came in to grab a spot at the conference table. "So if you ask me," Ferguson started.

"We're not asking you," Mark and David said simultaneously.

"Jinx! Somebody owes me a beer," Ferguson continued. "If you ask me, your office ain't never looked or smelled this good. Go ahead and hire her, and you can reassign me to be her slave."

"You're sick, Ken," Mark told him.

"I think you're right," he agreed, and then a smile started to turn up at the corners of his mouth, right about the same time that the silent fart he ripped began to let its presence be known. "My stomach has been bothering me today."

"Oh God!" David screamed as the odor grew strong. "Why do you even let him in your office?"

"Damn, Ken!" Mark said. "What the hell did you eat?"

"I got to go," he answered. "It stinks in here."

Right around five o'clock and about the same time the scent of Ferguson's deposit finally grew faint, the office hotline rang, and Mark thought, *No sooner do I get rid of shit, then someone tries to stir up some more.* Cathy had gone home for the evening, so he couldn't even screen the call.

"Mr. M," the mother bear growled. "I'm glad I found you. I understand you're doing some preliminary research into finding someone for your curriculum position."

"Yeah, she was pretty impressive, and I think she's a good fit for this place."

"I hear some very good things about her," the mother bear said, "but there are two caveats."

Mark knew that with Magda Robreno, nothing ever was easy, and progress necessitated negotiating a minefield in most cases. Two caveats might mean two bullets in the chamber.

"Go ahead," he said.

"Well," she started, "we still have to follow protocol and conduct interviews, and we can't put anyone at South Demming until after the state test. The departure of a curriculum AP is too damaging at this time of the year, so you'll have to wait until March."

By this time, he had grown accustomed to the second-class treatment of South Demming, so he didn't bother to say what was on his mind, starting with how it was acceptable to allow Belinda Ruiz to leave to serve the needs of another school, but same consideration wasn't afforded to them. It was mid-November, and their salvation would have to wait another four months.

Armed with this new knowledge, Mark stopped by David Canales's office prior to heading home. He looked at David and asked, "How'd you like to be the curriculum person here?"

David furrowed his brow so that its rows matched those of the bean fields. "Why? What happened? I thought we were going to go with Tavares," he said.

"Just got off the phone with Ms. Robreno, and she's all for that as long as we wait until after the MARI," and he watched as the contemplative Dr. Canales emerged. He logged off his computer, rose from his desk, bit his lower lip, and scratched his goatee in preparation for his response.

"What in the flying fuck is she thinking?" he began. "How in the hell is that going to get us off the fucking radar as you say?"

"Let me repeat the question, Dave. How'd you like to be the fucking curriculum person here?"

"Mark, I would love to do that at some point," he answered. "I mean it would be tremendous for my career, but I'm not ready for that. We can't do that to the school."

"We don't have a choice, David. Do you think I could ask Jefferson or Szemanski this question? Between the two of us, we'll have to make something happen."

The November sun was orange and looked much as it had when it rose that morning, its destination never challenged. From point A to point B in this case went from east to west, but Mark's life seemed to be traveling between north and south, a route impeded by trains and apparitions that surfaced for reasons he did not know.

The old man and the three-legged dog appeared less than a mile into his journey home. He watched as it managed to squat slightly to pee, but he made up his mind never to stop because he truly feared that they didn't exist.

Chapter 21

THE GAME PLAN

"We stop him, we stop them; it's a simple as that," Robbie Wolf said as he remained transfixed on the game film footage of Ron Dozier, Ponce de Leon High's star fullback.

"Yeah, but why do you want to mess with the game plan one day before the game?" Don Reinhold asked his linebackers' coach. "I mean look at the kid," he continued while shaking his head. The film showed a stocky white kid being stopped at the line, bouncing to the outside, and with a tremendous burst of speed, running untouched seventy yards down the sideline. "Nobody even got close to him. He's better than anyone we've seen."

Ron Dozier led all high school running backs in yards from scrimmage, breaking the thousand-yard mark by halftime of the fifth game of the season. Notre Dame bound, he was a rich white kid and a good enough Catholic. At five nine, he didn't like being on the short side, so he pumped enough iron to sport 220 pounds of muscle, a work ethic that was good enough to earn him third-team status as a Parade All-American.

"Willie," Robbie Wolf yelled out the door of Coach Reinhold's portable classroom. "Get your ass in here." At that point, South Demming linebacker Willie Ivory came into the room.

"Son, why are you still here? Practice was over an hour ago," Reinhold noted.

"Got nowhere to go tonight, and me and Coach Rob been doing some thinking."

"It's like this, Don," Wolf went on, "when they run their offense, everything goes through Dozier. They run sweeps. They run up the middle. They dump off passes to him. They even have an option play they use a couple of times per game, and he throws better than their QB."

"We've been watching the same game film," Reinhold noted. "I'm old. I'm not blind. We've been over this. What's your point?"

"Coach," Willie Ivory chimed in, "they ain't going to get penetration past our front four. Their O-line ain't nothing but a bunch of tuba players in the band. They got some beef, but they ain't the athletes we are."

"This better be good," Reinhold said as he glanced at his watch.

"It'll be where we stand them up at the line, and the kid's got no choice but to bounce to the outside. We don't need Willie backing up the line. We need him on Dozier's ass and Dozier's ass alone. The other kids will pick up Willie's slack."

"He ain't as strong as me. He might be a bit faster than me, but I'll cut out his legs before they get to moving too fast," Ivory petitioned his coach.

"Now wait a damn minute!" Reinhold exclaimed. "We've been practicing all week with our corners playing up, and our safeties ready to go one on one in long yardage situations. We've been talking about taking away the middle and forcing them to the outside where our corners can stop them from turning up field," he reviewed.

"And I'm talking about doing the same thing, with the addition of our boy here," Wolf agreed. "Willie's going to be a heat-seeking missile, and Dozier's gonna feel the heat for the first time this year. What are you thinking?"

"I'm thinking that we go with the original game plan and play them straight up, but I'm not opposed to mixing in your idea if things start to go south for us," Reinhold gave in slightly.

"That's all I'm asking for, Coach," Wolf said as he offered his hand to Reinhold, who was positioning himself on the chair in order to get up and leave. "When are you going to get those knees looked at? They probably need replacing."

Reinhold received this gesture; his puffy, large-knuckled hand pressed into the younger man's palm and interlocked thumbs as he pulled himself out of the chair and grimaced, saying, "If you're going to replace me, do me a favor; don't do it body part by body part. My knees are killing me. It ain't fair. You young guys got all the ideas, and you got good legs. What the hell do you need me for?"

Ponce de Leon High had been one of a handful of schools in Demming County that could match South Demming in terms of having a rich history. Established as an all boys' school in the middle of Florida Everglades land in 1955, it housed 150 male students in a modest eight-classroom building. Catholic leaders sought an educational refuge for young men with the vision of producing citizens of sound body, mind, and values. That incarnation had been resurrected over the years to currently include 1,500 able-bodied young men on a nineteen-acre campus with twenty-first-century classrooms and an athletic program with enough boosters to offer scholarship opportunities to students who might otherwise be unable to afford such a quality education. This luxury set Ponce apart from the rest of the competition because its populace wasn't dictated by public school boundaries, and its athletic programs could recruit athletes to fill any perceived or existing void in any sport. The end result had been that the college and professional sports world was filled with Ponce graduates in baseball, basketball, and football, and the academic all-stars had gone on to grace the business world and contribute handsomely to their alma mater, thus furnishing the means for present and future athletic prowess.

Joe Carrera had his particular spin on it as he talked moments before kickoff. "The jock sniffers keep the money flowing, Magic. They're running a fucking university program over there. Kids get to go to the highest bidder. It makes me sick because they can get away with it legally."

"What about this Dozier kid?" Mark asked.

"He played for Palm Coast last year. He's like half the kids on our team; he can't pass the reading portion of the MARI. Only in his case, rich Daddy makes a contribution. The kid passes their watered-down entrance exam and does his senior year at Ponce where you don't need the MARI to graduate."

"How do you know all this stuff about this kid?"

"It's not about the kid, Magic; it's about the program. I know about the kid because I play golf with his old man, and he's doing whatever he can to help his kid out. I understand, but what you got over there is the best of both worlds. They get to play our game, but they get to do it by their rules. It's like they got the only ball, and if we complain, they go home."

"Well, considering that we're playing the game at Harnett," Mark threw in his opinion, but he felt like a quarterback being chased to the sideline, "they're going to have a long ride home."

"Magic, they really believe that they're going to beat us on our home field, but there's the anthem."

As they awaited the conclusion of the national anthem by the South Demming band, Mark glanced at Coach Reinhold, whose hand was over his heart, and noticed that his shock of gray hair waved in the wind like the flag. He also noticed Joe Carrera looking toward his old friend, biting his lower lip, and nodding his head up and down as the "home of the brave" portion was drowned out by the cheering crowd.

The opening series quieted the home crowd, which accounted for about six thousand of the eight thousand people present at the game. True to what the coaching staff had scouted, Ponce played its power game, and the tuba players that Willie Ivory alluded to proved to have enough bulk to hold their own at the line. After Ron Dozier bounced outside, dodged a corner, and literally ran over Rajah Horton en route to a thirty-three-yard touchdown and a 7–0 Ponce lead four minutes into the game, it became apparent that plan B might be needed early on.

Moments after the score, Robbie Wolf sidled closer to Coach Reinhold's left side and stood in his peripheral vision.

Viewing his assistant coach, Reinhold exploded, "Goddamn it, Robbie! I already told you I'm not blind. Did you come here to say I told you so, or did you come here to prove to me that you can wear these headphones because I'm not going to be around forever?"

At that point, Joe Carrera, who had been occupying the right side by Reinhold's bad ear, stopped the venerable coach from taking the headphones off his head and begged, "Come on, Don. Don't be stubborn. Everything Robbie knows about the game, he got from you. Give his idea a chance."

Reinhold stared at the field during the water timeout and saw his defensive players drinking like neglected dogs, and he heard the Ponce band greedily playing its fight song, but with instinct as his sixth sense, he obeyed his gut. "You guys are right. Robbie, when we get the ball back, huddle up with the D and get Willie fired up. He can stop this kid, and we can win this game."

The offensive strategy for South Demming was to grind out the running game to keep the ball away from Dozier, who couldn't hurt them if he wasn't on the field. To this end, Landon Daniels, inspired by his competitor on the visitor sideline, wasn't to be outdone. In surgeon-like fashion, he cut through the holes opened by his linemen and carried the ball eleven times for seventy-seven yards, the final carry being a ten-yard burst up the middle and into the end zone. Matt Mathews didn't throw a pass. He didn't need to. South Demming rode that drive until the end of the first quarter, and the teams were tied, with neither one being able to stop the other's star player.

The Bucs' first break of the game came upon the ensuing kickoff, which Dozier bobbled behind him; he had to dive on it and eat it to prevent a turnover. This gave the Explorers the ball on their two-yard line and started Willie Ivory salivating.

Lining up in an I-formation with Dozier's heels almost out of the end zone, the Ponce quarterback faked a hand off to his up back and pitched right to Dozier, who began looking to pass up field. With his new marching orders, Willie Ivory's feet traced the footsteps of Dozier, and his eyes saw a singular fixation in Dozier that didn't include him. When he finally realized that Ivory had him in his sights, Dozier did the only thing he could do; he surrendered the two points for a safety by tucking away the ball and absorbing a massive hit from Ivory. The Bucs took a 9–7 lead into the locker room at halftime.

The plan B was working as intended and helped South Demming hold onto its two-point lead. With less than six minutes remaining in the third quarter, Ponce pitched the ball to Dozier, who was forced to run laterally by Ivory. Backing up the play was Danny Baldwin, who jumped on Dozier just as he turned the corner and rode him into the sideline. Maybe five or ten years ago, Coach Reinhold would have been able to adjust and avoid the collision, but in this case, he bore the residual brunt of the impact between two of the fastest and strongest players on the field. Danny Baldwin had tackled Ron Dozier, and in so doing, met with his coach's expectations, a lofty set of standards that had the eggshell-like protection of a sixty-five-year-old arthritic body. Coach Reinhold's feet were lifted off the ground, and his body was thrown backward with such force that his head whiplashed against the grass.

Recognizing the impact of his deed, Danny Baldwin cried out, "Oh my God, Coach, are you all right?" And all eight thousand of the people in the stadium could hear him.

Several of the cheerleaders, most notably Christy Del Pino, began sobbing, and all eight thousand of the people in the stadium could hear them.

The entire South Demming defense left the field oblivious to calling a timeout to join in the circle around their fallen coach, and their frantic footsteps stampeded into the consciousness of everyone in the stadium so that this moment trumped all the previous drama that led up to it. To Coach Reinhold, few things in life were more important than the game. In this twisted tribute, it became clear that his fans felt the same way about him.

For several moments, he lay motionless and appeared to be unconscious. His inner circle of coaches, Robbie Wolf and, of course, Bryan Reinhold, saw that the iconic coach was alert but suspected that he had the wind knocked out of him, a condition in this case that rendered the victim as speechless as those who witnessed the event. As his lungs refilled with air, he looked at the entourage that hovered above him and said, "This is embarrassing. Somebody get my ass off the ground."

As he had done less than twenty-four hours earlier, Robbie Wolf extended his hand, and Don Reinhold accepted it again, rising to his feet. It was then that he felt the sharp pain in his left knee, lifted it off the ground, put his left arm around his son's broad shoulders, and agreed to await the golf cart to transport him to the locker room area under the bleachers where the team physician could better evaluate his situation.

From their vantage point, the fans in the bleachers exhaled, sucked some fresh air back into their lungs, and cheered and applauded so loudly that it begged the question of what spoke in greater volume. Was it the respect of the silence or the din of the cheering?

The third quarter ended with the score still at 9–7, but the subplot took center stage when Coach Reinhold came back to the field via golf cart and reassumed his position on the sideline with the aid of crutches, five minutes left in the game, and the score still 9–7.

After the second round of cheering had subsided, Mark ventured out to meet Coach Reinhold during a water break. "Don, you okay?"

The coach looked at him with a hint of impatience and said, "I might have a torn meniscus. Didn't think anything was left in there to tear." He provided a slight grin and said, "You know, I zigged when I should've zagged. Anyway, I don't need a leg to coach."

With Ponce moving the ball to the Bucs' forty-yard line with about 2:30 left in the game, they broke away from the game plan of Dozier left and Dozier right because everywhere Dozier was, so was Willie Ivory. This time they relied on their quarterback to complete a series of short passes, which moved the chains and made them a legitimate threat to take a lead with little or no time left for the Bucs to retaliate.

On a third-and-ten situation from the Bucs' thirty, the Explorers hoped to let their star dictate the course of their season with an option play. Followed by Ivory to the left side of the field, Dozier was forced to throw a pass across his body, a pass that Raja Horton anticipated, picked off, and raced untouched seventy-five yards down the sideline. The final score was Bucs 16, Explorers 7.

The next morning, Mark went to South Demming to catch up on some office work, which took a couple of hours, allowing him to leave around ten thirty. Departing via the gravel road by the bean fields, he saw a Mercury Sable approaching him, kicking up a lot of dust in the process. He stopped his pickup, and the Mercury stopped as well. The driver was Glenda Reinhold, the coach's wife.

"Glenda," Mark asked, "how the hell is Don? What are you doing here?"

"Why don't you ask the stubborn old coot yourself?" she answered while pointing to the backseat where her husband laid stretched out.

Mark saw the big gray head become visible and asked, "Don, what the hell are you doing?"

"He's here to watch game film and get some lesson plans ready in case he can't make it to work on Monday," Glenda answered for her husband. "Maybe you can talk some sense into him."

"Look, boss," he started. "I got a doc's appointment this afternoon. I'm just taking care of some business until then."

"Do you know why he's laying down in the backseat?" Glenda asked and then provided the answer. "It's because he can't bend his leg at all."

"I'll be fine," Reinhold assured him. "The wife's just being a wife; that's all."

When it all played out, Don Reinhold had a partially torn meniscus that would require a brace for immobilization and crutches to avoid placing any pressure on the joint. The recommendation was four to six weeks on crutches with the first two weeks away from work.

The coach was back to work two days later on Monday. At this point in his career, he taught driver's education, but he'd be damned if any kid got hurt because he wasn't there to do his job. The only request he made of his principal was to allow him to park his van by his portable classroom.

During the ensuing weeks, Mark watched each morning as the man pulled up to his portable and struggled with his crutches to negotiate the walkway leading up to his door when he could have taken the easy way out and leaned on the crutch of workman's compensation.

Chapter 22

THE DISENFRANCHISED

She was in her dark place, a wooded area just in front of the trailer in which she lived and just behind a freeway. She struggled against a stiff breeze to light a match, and on the sixth try she succeeded, providing enough flame for the cigarette and enough light to frame her mascara-stained face. She took a long drag and leaned back on a tattered nylon beach chair, blew out several smoke rings, and watched as the wind ended their brief existence. She liked how the sound of the passing cars competed with the rustle of the leaves.

He was there to receive the cigarette from her in a rite of passage. There wasn't another chair, so he simply sat cross-legged on the ground and to her left side. He took a slight puff, reached out for her left arm, and holding her wrist firmly in his left hand, he touched the lit end into the crook of her elbow and held it there for a second. She let out a groan and then shuddered but didn't pull back from the pain.

Taking the cigarette from him and holding it in her mouth, she joined him cross-legged on the ground, sitting directly across from him so that their knees touched. She placed his left arm, up to the elbow, across her right knee, and she secured it in place with her hand holding his tightly. She then placed her left hand over his mouth and leaned forward toward his trapped arm with the cigarette dangling from her mouth. She took a long drag to liberate the ember from the ashes and touched it to his forearm. Her left hand muffled his anguished cry, and her pinkie finger felt a teardrop. She removed her hand from his mouth and turned it toward her, so she could lick it off and enjoy the salty taste.

Reflecting at the end of a noneventful Monday, Mark conversed with Lou Cruz by the flagpole during dismissal. Emboldened by a recent relative calm that made him hopeful, he chose his words frivolously.

"Ain't shit happening around here lately, big boy," he laughed. "You might need to find some action over at Pineapple," he suggested as he brought the nearest elementary school into the conversation.

Cruz laughed, but as he did this, Mark still noticed some tension being outlined in the temple region. The clenching and unclenching of his jaw came with the rapidity of a Morse code signal even as the last bus pulled out of view. "Don't say that too loud, Mr. M. It's still South Demming," he said, and this time his jaw clenched so tightly that his temples pounded outside his skull as if trying to break free.

For a few minutes they enjoyed the fall breeze that punctuated their comfort. The flag percolated above them, and thoughts of what could be brought Mark back to the kids swinging from a rope and jumping into the canal, shattering its glass-like veneer and sending little shock waves into motion. And the ripple in his mind coincided with the call from central dispatch that sent Cruz running to his squad car and speeding down Minneola Street with siren and flashing lights rudely interrupting everything that could be.

"Fuck. You talked too soon, Mr. M," Cruz yelled as he ran toward his car.

"Why? What happened?" Mark asked as he ran next to him trying to keep pace.

"There's a car upside down in a retention pond by Luci and US 1, and there's somebody still in the car. I got to go. I'll call you later," he said breathlessly as he picked up speed and left Mark to watch him nearly fly into his squad car.

"Hey. Please tell me it's not one of our kids," Mark said, but he was already out of reach of this question.

At three fifteen, only about a half hour later, the hotline rang, and Lou Cruz confirmed Mark's worst fears. Alexis Sanchez was a seventeen-year-old tenth grader and part of the school's self-contained unit for the severely emotionally disturbed. She left campus shortly after lunch that day with two males later identified as Hanford High dropouts. Joyriding in a stolen vehicle, the trio's afternoon concluded when the driver hit the right curb at about fifty miles per hour, causing the tire to blow and the car to flip twice, end over end, and come to its resting place upside down in a six-feet-deep retention pond. Sanchez's forehead had hit the dashboard, and she was rendered unconscious. The two males escaped the vehicle as it filled with water and left Sanchez to drown as they fled the scene.

Lou Cruz got there in enough time to see the car submerged and to recognize the outline of a body within. Trouble had arrived too early, and help had arrived too late. Now, bubbles reached the surface, and he gazed as windblown waves arrived to burst them one by one.

"Was she in school at all today?" was all Magda Robreno could ask when Mark apprised her of this event.

"Yes, she was up until about fifth period," he said, having already answered the inevitable question for himself once Lou Cruz had given him the girl's name. Showing restraint for once, Robreno didn't dwell on how the kid could've left campus but offered her prognosis for the next day.

"Mark, brace yourself for the media tomorrow. Mobilize your counselors, and I'll send the district's crisis team out to assist with the grief-stricken kids. It will be a long day for you," she concluded.

Mark was grateful for the employment of the district's help and even more grateful that it appeared from their conversation that the mother bear would not be deploying anyone from her immediate shop of horrors.

It was five o'clock when he picked up the phone to call Wendy Akins to apprise her of the potential for disruption to her and her staff's day.

"Just another day in the hood," Akins commented. "If we had fewer interruptions, maybe we could counsel some of these kids to avoid something like this happening again in the future." She perched a political platform atop a child's grave as though she were hanging a picture.

He never got to know Alexis Sanchez, and schools are filled with countless other students who play bit parts and never appear in the credits. Mark wondered if she had been part of the group scene weeks earlier when Bryan Reinhold and he watched their blurry figures run off campus. Then, he wondered if she was, and he had stopped her, would she still be here today. Was it simply her destiny to have her life narrowed down to a food basket and a sympathy card arranged for by the South Demming Social Committee, or were there alternative endings that could have occurred if the main actors had acted?

When Mark arrived at a quarter after six, two news crews from Channels 7 and 10 already had their vans perched across the street with their satellite dishes erect. One of the Channel 10 reporters, Vicki Brown, he had known for a good number of years through her work on the educational beat. They had formed a positive relationship to the point where there was a mutual trust. He approached her first. "Hey, Vicki," he said, "we meet again."

"Mark, I'm so sorry that this has happened," she offered her sympathies.

"Yeah, me too," he concurred, "but I'd like to offer both of the news crews"—and he looked toward the Channel 7 contingent—"complete access to my office and anything I know will be happening to address this situation. I'm afraid some of the kids still might not know what's happened, and you guys might catch them by surprise. Why don't you come in?"

Both groups' street reporters followed him to the office, and he apprised them of the district and staff measures that would be taken to provide counseling services to grief-stricken students. They recorded his response rather than solicit the hysteria that he knew was possible if they were allowed to randomly approach students. They assured him that they would be across the street to simply record backdrops to the event, including crowd scenes of arriving students and shots of the school. This approach, one of honesty, was what had helped him avoid the misinformation that gets out when one tries to shut out the media. In previous years, the county had a minimal-contact-with-the-media approach that was akin to leaving principals in the roles of little children who shut their eyes so their parents won't see them misbehaving. Magda Robreno's perspective was born during this era, and Mark suspected that her laissez-faire approach toward this situation likely was killing her.

Mark had prepared a public address announcement to relay the tragedy to the school population, and he had asked via e-mail for his teachers to keep an eye on their students and send to the office anyone who appeared to be out of sorts, rather than open the door to everyone and risk the possibility of students taking advantage of the situation and trying to get out of class.

There was no massive exodus toward the counselors' offices, and the grief team managed to beat the news teams out the door, leaving prior to the start of the lunch periods, realizing that the anonymity of Alexis Sanchez left room for neither a news event nor a teachable moment. It was too late to resuscitate her when the rescue crew had arrived, and it was even later to attempt to resurrect a memory sufficient enough to illustrate that a tragedy had occurred.

At around one thirty, Sarah Szemanski stopped by the office carrying what appeared to be a large rolled-up scroll. The thirty students who comprised the SED unit had determined to memorialize Alexis Sanchez via writing their sentiments on this scroll, which in actuality was simply bulletin board paper.

"Boss, the kids from the SED unit were hoping you or someone might be able to drop this off at Alexis's house this afternoon," Szemanski revealed.

Vicki Brown was saying her good-byes at this time and asked that the scroll be unraveled so that she could film some of the messages written upon it. As she did this, Szemanski pulled Mark off to the side and said, "You might want to stop by the SED unit. One kid, Paul Simpson, is really distraught. I mean, he won't stop crying. Maybe if you talk to him, it'll work."

Mark didn't know Alexis Sanchez, and he didn't know Paul Simpson, but if his attempting to know him might save another tragedy, he was primed for action.

He arrived to Paul Simpson's classroom, and there was no doubt as to where he sat. His head was down, and he was heaving so heavily that his chair was moving as though it were on an Ouija board. Mark placed his hand upon the boy's left shoulder, which prompted him to lift his head. He wore gold wire-framed glasses, which were stained with his grief, and trickles of tears rolled down both cheeks with a symmetry that attested to true suffering. His long, curly light brown hair made him look as though he belonged in the seventies. His Pink Floyd T-shirt sealed the deal.

Paul Simpson held onto his principal as though they knew each other. His grip was that reserved for a mother or a father, not the talking-head stranger that Mark believed he must have been to him.

"Thank you so much for coming here," he sobbed. "I loved her so much. She was someone I could talk to about anything. I'm going to miss her. She was always there for me."

Mark only listened as he rattled off his sentiments, not knowing what words might work to console him. At that moment, the student's index finger pointed to some markings on his left arm that looked like they might be burns.

"She really loved me," he said. "She gave me these."

Upon leaving that day, Mark had only two thoughts. He didn't know her, and he didn't know him. He chose to keep it that way by not unrolling and reading the scroll that her classmates had created. It lay there on his conference table, its inscriptions destined for no grander memorializing, and Mark wondered if she ever had written her name in fresh cement or carved it into a tree. He wondered what were the unspoken wounds of her childhood or if she even had a childhood. He replaced the rubber band holding the scroll in place, and placed her paper tombstone under his arm.

At six in the evening, the setting sun hid below the old treetops, and the trailer park experienced nightfall a little earlier than the treeless cookie-cutter communities sprouting up to its immediate north and south. As he looked for Alexis Sanchez's address among the peeling white facades, Mark wondered why these homes are referred to as mobile or trailers. Few if any of the families populating Hanford Estates had any mobility or transportation means by which to drag themselves from this place. Dirt paths worn by countless treks to and from the dwellings were the sidewalks of necessity. A tattered nylon chair guarded by crushed cigarette butts served as the welcome mat twenty feet in front of the plastic-paned aluminum door that couldn't quite close or open without assistance.

"Who are you, and what do you want?" came a voice from within. The silhouette and the timbre of the voice suggested a young woman, but the lack of light within and without gave him no more information.

"I'm Mark Mahovlic, the principal at South Demming, and I was hoping to speak to the mother or father of Alexis Sanchez."

"They're not speaking to anyone," the voice proclaimed, "and why the fuck are you here anyway?" Now the body moved forward, and a tear-stained face came into view. She was probably twenty or twenty-five years old, likely a sister or an aunt. She wore a kimono, and her black hair ended in ringlet curls at her shoulders. She might have been pretty.

"I'm just here to find out if there's anything I or the school might do for the family at this time." Offering the scroll, he added, "The kids in her class wanted the family to have this; it's stuff that they wrote about Alexis."

"You can keep that shit; nobody here wants to see it," she snarled, "but there is something you can do. You can answer me what the fuck kind of security you have in that place that kids can get up and leave?"

He had no answer to placate her and remained speechless, struggling not to look away from her. This gave her fuel for her next move.

"Get the fuck out of here," she screamed, and then she spit into the plastic window before shutting a wooden door behind it.

Mark bent down slightly to place the scroll propped up against the trailer's wall. He looked back at the aluminum door and watched as the spit bubbles moved their way down the plastic window and disappeared, leaving only a stain in their wake.

Chapter 23

THE DARK SIDE OF SPORTS

Propped up by his crutches, Coach Reinhold spit tobacco juice into the sideline as he awaited the kickoff. This district playoff game against the Kendale High Vipers came after the bye week earned through the Bucs completing a second straight undefeated regular season. Again it presented an opportunity for the Bucs to put away a lesser opponent and earn an opportunity to make it to the State Final Eight. They conducted business as expected and ran away with a 35–0 victory, earning home-field advantage as the only undefeated team in their bracket.

On the opposite end of the county, Northeastern, an inner-city high school, disposed of its opponent, Madison High, by a similarly lopsided score of 42–7. Northeastern played a schedule that afforded them no easy opposition, and their one loss came to Ponce de Leon in a 17–14 thriller. Now, despite more than fifty years of fielding football teams, Northeastern and South Demming had never played each other. State classifications rested with school populations, and until the past five years, the two schools played in different brackets, but with both now boasting nearly three thousand students, the stage became set for what was being billed as the battle of the "City Boys versus the Country Boys." Nevertheless, this convenient media labeling could not do justice to the true battle between two schools with parallel pasts that, like newspaper print, boiled down to black and white.

Opening in 1955, Northeastern High was the pride of Freedom City, a historically black community in Demming County. While it had become a no-man's land for those on the outside looking in, Freedom City staked its claim to Northeastern's athletic accomplishments, feats that served as galvanizing elements for the community so that the law-abiding citizens, the ministers, and the proprietors rubbed elbows with the gamblers, the armed robbers, and the drug dealers every Friday night during football season.

By 1984, Freedom City had long since cemented its reputation as a US urban community with its moments of disfavor and its place on the radar of law enforcement. While it hadn't had its pivotal event like Watts, Chicago, and Detroit almost two decades earlier, it rested on the precipice, awaiting its place in history. In February of that year, a young black motorcyclist named Artis Caldwell obliged.

Kawasaki had put out a bike that year that commanded attention because it could more than double the posted speed limits, and at one in the morning, February 10, twenty-four-year-old Artis Caldwell demonstrated his bike's potential to Demming County's finest, leading them on a three-city, twenty-mile chase starting on US 1 in North Hanford and culminating one mile before exit 67 off I-95, the exit for Freedom City, Caldwell's hometown. Depending upon whose ending one would choose to believe, Caldwell either died in a crash during the chase, or he pulled over and was beaten to death by four white policemen who were involved in his pursuit. The police relayed the former; the community subscribed to the latter. The NAACP found its footing, and a media circus began.

As evidence emerged during the ensuing trial, the common belief grew among reasonably minded affiliations that the police may have been overzealous in their handling of the situation, and blunt trauma came at the end of batons rather than concrete. Eight months later, an all-white jury ruled to the contrary, and an all-black community demonstrated its outrage. Despite NAACP leaders' pleas to demonstrate peacefully, dissenting parties lit matches and threw them into the fuel. One white man had the misfortune of his car breaking down while passing through Freedom City on the afternoon of the ruling. He was pulled from his vehicle by several black men and beaten to death. Riots continued for four days and nights, and the National Guard was called to the scene. While this eventually ran its tragic course, its root causes were treated topically, and no true healing ever occurred. Now, the Northeastern Bulls were poised to begin their trek. They had a December 8 meeting with South Demming at Hammett Field, literally tracing the path backward from where Artis Caldwell began his fateful ride.

Bobby Coles loved his 1977 Cadillac El Dorado. With its two-tone navy and gold custom paint job and a set of bullhorns adorning its grille, the Caddy transported the Northeastern football coach in style. After twenty-five years, Freedom City loved the coach even more, as evidenced by the street on which the school was built being renamed Coles Court after him. At seven in the morning, he pulled into the parking spot reserved with his name right next to the one that read principal. Shutting off the engine and awaiting the unfurling of the automated ragtop, Coach Coles opened his door, rotated his six-five frame ninety degrees, placed both of his size 15 navy-snakeskin boots on the concrete, and with assistance from his arms managed to straighten his 320-pound frame into walking position. Reaching back into the car's rear seat, he retrieved a gold Stetson that he placed on his horseshoe bald head and made his way to the principal's office.

With his index finger pointing in gun-like fashion toward Northeastern's newly appointed Principal DeWayne Browning, Roger Traynor growled his sentiments. "I'm telling you that it was the height of irresponsibility to let out information like this without a proper investigation. The boy has to be allowed to play!"

"Dr. Traynor, with all due respect," Browning came back, "the girl's mother went to the media; we, I, didn't offer them anything." His fingers fumbled with a folded piece of paper he retrieved from his desk drawer.

"This situation, if it did happen, happened two weeks ago," Coach Coles audibled before even being seated. "Why did this girl wait so long? What evidence does she have?"

"She's fourteen years old!" Browning came back. "Maybe she was too scared."

"Maybe won't work here!" Traynor exploded. "Maybe you need to get your ass out of this office and find out where the fuck your security is that two kids can get it on in one of your bathrooms in the middle of the school day! He plays. Last time I checked in this country, people are innocent until proven otherwise!"

Coach Coles contained a smirk as he glanced at his principal and then watched as the superintendent of schools left without any good-byes. "Boss man," he pitched, "dat's da way it is here. You keep sittin' in that seat and makin' the good money, but football is bigger than both of us. Matter of fact, it's bigger than that big fella who just left your office. He's smart enough to know that."

Browning continued to manipulate the folded paper in his right hand to the point where he was rolling it between his fingers, from his index to his pinky. "Coach, I'm going to ask you to leave. I need to be alone for a minute."

DeWayne Browning was the district's golden child among young black administrators. At thirty-five, he was a family man with a ten-year marriage and two preschool daughters. He was handpicked to assume the principal's role at Northeastern, following his meteoric predecessor who parlayed his four years at the school into a superintendent's job in Philadelphia. Browning's problem was that his nature wouldn't allow him to look the other way. At this time, his focus was geared on the folded paper in his hand, which he began to unfold because he needed to verify that it said what it said when he first opened it up. As he read it to himself, he moved his lips.

"Mr. *Principle*," it started. "Either Dre plays or you die, motherfucker!"

D'Andre Bannister was the star eighteen-year-old running back who had been vilified in the newspaper for allegedly raping a fourteen-year-old girl in the boys' locker room. The details were late in their arrival, and the timing for the Freedom City community couldn't have been worse. It didn't take long for the identity of the girl to become public knowledge, so much so that she stopped attending school and eventually moved to Georgia to live with relatives.

Bobby Coles, like his coaching counterpart, Don Reinhold, was a pillar in his community, but his community constructed pillars atop capricious platforms. Coles had the charisma, but more importantly the know-how, to tell influential people exactly what they wanted to hear. The high-end drug dealers loved Coles because as football boosters they attained some legitimacy through their generous monetary donations to the athletic department over which Coles also presided as athletic director. The gamblers loved him because, as rumor had it, Northeastern's dominance often allowed him to control point spreads. The business community loved him because if he frequented an establishment, it lent credibility. Indeed, Bobby Coles's picture was a decorative staple in one barber shop, two soul food restaurants, a Cadillac dealership, and the mayor's office. The local ministers loved him because he regularly attended Sunday mass and was most vocal among those who punctuated the sermons with words of approval like dat's right, uh huh, and amen.

At five thirty, DeWayne Browning left his office hoping to get a head start and make his way toward Harnett Field. December twilight had set in already, and as he opened his car door, he had to do a double take to make sure his eyes weren't playing tricks on him. Looking more closely, he realized that the driver's side front tire was completely flat, and to leave no doubt as to how this might have happened, a knife handle stuck out of the tire at a perpendicular angle.

City Boys versus Country Boys began to take shape during warm-ups. Several of Northeastern's crew of coaches taunted the Bucs' players. While Bobby Coles did not participate, he did nothing to stop it.

"Hey, boy!" a coach, probably in his late twenties, caught Danny Baldwin's attention. "Y'all ain't played no one yet; you ain't shit."

Baldwin thought to remind this person of the fact that Northeastern had lost to Ponce de Leon but remembered Coach Reinhold's two-weeks' worth of preparation, some of which allowed for the possibility of poor sportsmanship and intimidation tactics.

"Now, understand that most of these kids and their coaches are good people," Reinhold had stated prior to the game, "but a few might try to push your buttons and talk some trash. You ignore that. Don't let them get into your head," he warned.

"Hey, white boy!" a huge lineman got Corey Watson's attention. "Yeah, I'm talking to you, pretty white boy. I'm going to fuck you up bad, and I'm going to start with your pretty-ass hair."

Matt Mathews's kickoff was long and deep; the brown pigskin turned end over end with a tight rotation that rendered its white laces invisible. It joined the moon and the stars in the sky, spinning like a sideways roulette wheel so that right gave way to wrong, the past chased the present, and good invited great. The kick was returned all the way to the Bucs' forty-five-yard-line, and on the first play from scrimmage, Northeastern's quarterback dropped back to pass and found a receiver wide open in the end zone for the game's first score. Raja Horton was in single coverage and bit on the play action to the point where he couldn't recover.

The Bucs went three and out on their first two possessions, and Northeastern awarded their defense by scoring on its next two possessions, making the score 21–0 with two minutes left in the first quarter. This deflated the Bucs because their secondary, their greatest strength, was being picked apart by Northeastern's tall, skinny, sophomore quarterback.

The Bucs offense finally got something going, and a couple of solid runs by Landon Daniels led to Matt Mathews finding Corey Watson on a slant pattern to the right end zone.

The Bucs got their first stop of the Bulls and began another impressive drive. With the ball on the Bulls eighteen yard line, Mathews found Ty Waters open in the end zone, but the ball bounced off of Waters's shoulder pads right into the arms of the safety he had shaken. The safety ran this back all the way, and the half ended with the Northeastern up by 28–7.

For three-quarters of the game, South Demming dominated the action, completely shutting down the Bulls' offense in the second half and scoring two touchdowns, but it turned out to be too little, too late.

Time expired, and the Bucs' glamorous season of hope and their dream of sending their coach out as a champion died.

Coach Reinhold proceeded as he always had. His players, most in tears, took knees to give their thanks. At the postgame press conference, he acknowledged that this was the last game of his lengthy career, a statement that caused reporters to approach this story from that angle, but the old coach wouldn't oblige.

"I'm only going to say this once," he started. "This isn't about me; it's about the kids. Those Northeastern players played their butts off and deserved the win. Go talk to them! Our kids had a great season and have nothing to be ashamed of."

After all sixty of his players gave him their teary-eyed postgame, post-career hugs, Mark seized a moment to give Reinhold his condolences and to thank him. The coach thanked him for all the support he had given him and his team, and in what still could have been a grand departure, he remained true and humble.

"I just feel bad for the kids," he said. "I just feel bad for the kids."

Chapter 24

IMMIGRATION ISSUE HITS HOME

The holiday break had come and gone, and upon their return on January 8, the South Demming citizenry brought in a new year with an inconspicuous start. Whether it was part of the beginnings of a culture change or a vacation hangover, the grace period that normally accompanies the start of the second semester extended to a full month.

On a mid-February Friday morning, ignoring the spot marked "guest" and choosing to park a hundred feet further away in an unmarked spot, the driver of an old van chose to make a statement. Proud alumnus Pep Garces and a balding white male of about fifty years of age emerged from the Astro. Despite having been turned off, the engine still sputtered and continued in its obstinacy. Looking back and laughing, Garces said to the companion, "That old girl there, amigo, she's a lot like me. You can shut me off, but you can't shut me up. You're going to like this guy," he continued as they made their way to the front office.

Pointing out the Buccaneer statue upon their entry, Garces proclaimed, "That there is a tough hombre. Could've used his help with the Conquistadors," and his laugh caught Mark's attention from his office desk. Fiddling with the partition latch, he looked at Cathy and asked, "Is he in?" right at the same time that Mark came out to greet him.

"Pep, what brings you here?" he asked as he extended his hand.

"Mark, old habits are hard to break," he began. "I have a habit of arriving unannounced, and you have a habit of still making me feel welcome, and today I," he stopped to point at his companion, "we really need to give you a heads up."

Ushering the two men to his conference table, Mark began to feel the familiar heart pounding that always seemed to come with the words "heads up."

Prior to taking their seats, Garces began with a formal introduction. John Walters came with a title as the director of the Alliance for Change in Immigration Law, a group with a nationwide protocol to address and reform the practices that had migrant families looking over their shoulders and living in fear of being caught. In jackets and ties, the two men took the stage in contrast to Mark's Dockers and Bucs athletic shirt, one of the many he received from the Joe Carrera haberdashery.

"Mark," Garces began, "I come to you outside the context of my job and as a strong supporter of all you do for this community. You know firsthand the underground war that migrants experience on a daily basis. Hanford is a battleground at a national level given its population."

"Pep, you've enlightened me to a large degree and don't need to qualify your business with me, so what's brought about this sense of urgency?"

"You need to know that a student protest is being organized by a female tenth grader at Henry Ford Technical School." He allowed Mark to absorb this for a brief moment and continued. "This will be a precursor to many more that are being organized nationwide. This will involve Hanford-area schools and will be happening two weeks from today on Friday, the twenty-sixth."

Having been handed the deed to this information, Mark stared at the bookcase of three-ring binders behind Garces and grew self-centered. "Okay," he said, "what will this mean for South Demming? What can I expect will happen here?" At this point, Walters took the initiative.

"At 10:00 a.m. that day, you can anticipate hundreds of students walking out of your classrooms and marching to city hall. Most will be those impacted by immigration laws, but all are being encouraged to participate."

Mark looked at Walters with incredulity. "You mean to tell me that all this is being put together by a fifteen-year-old girl?"

"No. She's getting some guidance from our organization, particularly with respect to what is acceptable and unacceptable. This will be a peaceful and respectful demonstration, first and foremost," he emphasized.

"Mark," Pep jumped in, "as the principal of South Demming High, we need to know how you will handle this situation. I'm sorry to do this to you again, but there still are a few snakes in the pit."

"Obviously, I'm going to need to get some guidance from the area office. Do they know about this?" Mark asked.

"They do, and I suspect that their approach will be to stop it from happening, and that won't be possible," Walters added.

Looking at both men, Mark weighed their words and remained noncommittal for the most part. "I mean I always worry about student safety with these things, but I'm not going to have my teachers stand in front of their doors like barricades. I'm not going to lock down the school. That would guarantee safety issues from my perspective. I need to speak to our people for guidance."

"Your people are going to instruct you to stop this thing from happening, and this will create a bigger problem," Pep prophesized. "You're the principal, Mark. Ultimately, you have to do what is right for the safety of the students in this school. I trust that your heart will guide you, and you will make the right decision."

After another ten-minute discussion, mostly generated by Mark's questions, he escorted the two men to the parking lot in silence. They had spoken their parts, and at this time Mark took his thoughts for a walk around the campus. Pep Garces placed a lot of confidence in his heart's ability to navigate his actions, but Mark simply hoped it would remain beating under the strain. As he passed the agricultural area, he stopped to watch what appeared from the distance to be a very old woman in a sunhat picking beans. Methodical, purposeful, and with a rhythm, this was her mundane existence. He watched her with a trace of envy.

"Hey, Magic, nice shirt!" Joe Carrera greeted him as he entered his office. He was seated at the principal's desk with his feet propped up. "So, how's your day been?"

"Well," Mark offered, "it's only nine o'clock, and I'm ready to call it a day."

"Yeah, I saw the merry Mexican was here. What did he do, put some more crap on your plate?" Carrera inquired.

"What's your problem with him?" Mark asked, wondering from where the animosity was coming.

"I just don't like him, Magic," Carrera explained. "When his kid was here a few years ago, he was pissed because he didn't make the varsity baseball team, so he made my life and the coaches' lives miserable by accusing us of making a decision based on his being a Mexican. I just don't like him!" he restated emphatically.

"Is there anyone you like?"

"I like you, Magic. I like you enough to help you get these kids in uniforms even though I think the idea sucks. That's what I came here to talk to you about."

At that moment, T. J. Burns and Lou Cruz appeared in the doorway. Mark surmised that their sudden appearance had something to do with the meeting he just had.

"Joe, we're going to have to table that discussion, but I'm going to need you to stay for this." Looking at the time, they had about twenty-five minutes before the class change bell, and he decided to assemble the leadership team to discuss the walkout.

Once everyone had gathered, T. J. outlined a coordinated effort between school police and Hanford Police that involved letting the students leave the campus and walk to city hall. "We're going to guide them there via the back roads and follow them along the path to make sure that some redneck doesn't pull up in a truck and take some pot shots at them," he explained. "Hanford and Demming Schools units will stay with them once they're at city hall to ensure that there is no violence."

Sarah Szemanski wove her way into the conversation. "Are you telling me that we're just going to let these kids leave campus? There has to be a consequence for this."

"Sarah, we don't have a precedent for this," Mark answered. "You could be talking about hundreds of kids standing up for what they believe and then being punished for it. That has whole other ramifications. You can't oversimplify it."

"Well, that's where I stand on the issue. Now may I be excused? I have someone waiting in my office."

She initiated her pirouette of disdain before he could excuse her. Like an umpire upset with a ballplayer who heads toward first base, not awaiting the call of ball four, Mark changed her perspective. "Nah, you need to sit through this until it's over. The person in your office can wait."

As it turned out, the meeting only lasted a few more minutes, but he had grown immensely tired of Szemanski trying to escape his authority like a wet dog jumping out of the tub. Sensing his dissatisfaction with her, Lou Cruz spoke up.

"Don't worry, Mr. M. We've got this covered. It'll be smooth."

Waiting for everyone to leave, Joe Carrera took the initiative. "Magic, don't think for one minute that Garces doesn't have something to do with this. He's one of the fucking snakes that he's always telling you about. You know I don't keep my mouth shut."

Mark looked at him, with his glasses perched crookedly on a nose with flared nostrils, and really couldn't deal with his intensity at that moment. "Yeah, I know," he answered halfheartedly, once again feeling alone in a place with more than three thousand people.

Clutching the microphone end in her palm as she punched out the numbers, the phone resembled a gun in her hand. The mother bear had six more calls to make in her chamber. She liked to stand by the window and look down when she called on her underlings like a sniper in high heels.

Cathy fielded the call at three in the afternoon. She entered Mark's office with deference suitable for entering a funeral parlor. Exercising what appeared to be a tiptoe gait, she solemnly whispered, "Mrs. Robreno's on the phone for you." Cathy had added some new twists to make some light of the misery she knew he felt anytime he had to receive a call from the area office.

He picked up the phone and held it to his head. "Good afternoon, Mrs. Robreno," he began. "How are you?"

"Fine, thank you," and not sparing any time for a cursory check on his well-being, the mother bear spoke in a calculated fashion. "Mark, I suspect that you are aware of an immigration policy protest that would appear to be impacting our schools two Fridays from today."

Beaming with pride left over from his proactive stance, he shared, "Yes, I am. I've already met with my administrative team and school police to go over safety precautions." He waited on what he had hoped would be a forthcoming "attaboy."

"Mark, there only is one safety precaution," Robreno countered. "You are to see to it that these students do not leave their classes, and you are to lock the outside gates of your campus. Place your faculty on alert beginning with an e-mail communication before you leave for the day. The students are to know that there will be consequences for anyone leaving campus. Emphasize this each day leading up to next Friday. Go with PA announcements, classroom visitations from your administrative team, and anything else you can come up with to drive home this point."

With her words, Mark became the monkey in the middle and could only think to ask, "Mrs. Robreno, have you spoken with school police because they, along with Hanford Police, have a plan that's allowing for students to leave the campus and demonstrate safely?"

"They are there in the event of any unrest," Robreno responded. "You are to follow my directives. Please tell me that I've made myself clear."

"Mrs. Robreno," he came back, "based only on information from my meeting with school police, it would appear that what you want and what they're anticipating are two different things."

"Good, then," she responded. "Do what I want, and they can anticipate all they want. Are we clear?"

With South Demming the last item on her afternoon agenda, the mother bear crumpled the to-do list and tossed it in the garbage pail under her desk, a fitting burial for a recipe for disaster. Looking out her window one more time, she surveyed the street below pausing to view the orderliness brought on by a red light that stopped progress.

When Mark touched base with T. J. the following Monday morning, T. J. had some choice words regarding the mother bear. "First of all, Mark, she's not in charge when it comes to these situations. She and all the other dumb-asses in that area office take orders from us. She's out of her fucking mind, and everyone knows that!" he added.

"Is that your final answer?" Mark kidded, but T. J. was hot and businesslike.

"Mark, my advice is that you pretend to go along with what she wants. This will cover your ass and keep things a lot safer for everyone. Discourage kids from leaving the campus, but don't put your teachers in harm's way. If they want to leave, the operative word is 'olé.' You guys bring out the matador capes, and we'll roll out the red carpet. Trying to stop this is guaranteed to cause a riot. What the hell is she thinking?"

"So that's what it comes down to, covering my ass?" Mark asked.

"That and keeping your balls off a silver platter," T. J. came back, "but really, Mark, it comes down to doing what's right."

When he said this, the words of Pep Garces came back. "Ultimately, you have to do what is right for the safety of the students in this school. I trust that your heart will guide you, and you will make the right decision."

In all this, Mark still had one more person to guide him. Ron Shipman had to have an opinion and some likely words of wisdom, and as he assessed Mark from the professorial comfort of his gray goatee and strategically perched reading glasses, all he needed was a pipe to accessorize the advantage he had.

"Ah, Mr. M, my friend," he began, "so you come to me now seeking advice."

"Ron, I love you, but please kill the *Godfather* routine," Mark said, and they both laughed.

"You singly are in a no-win situation, but we as an educational haven are in a win-win situation," he postulated. "You know all too well the passion I have for the immigration issue, and it has served as a platform for highbrow conversations in my classroom. No matter what, you've already stuck out your neck in this dilemma."

"So now it's my neck as well?" Mark interrupted. "I've already had my ass and balls threatened," he added, trying to lend some levity.

"Then don't be afraid to bare your ass and show some balls in the process," Shipman advised.

"How?" Mark pleaded.

Like a beauty pageant host with the winning envelope, Shipman studied him at length, adding drama to their conversation. "No matter how this thing turns out," he started, "recognize that it will become a teachable moment, and that is when you will come back to me."

Mark digested his words and studied his face for a moment before shaking his hand.

"Da, da, da, da, da, da, da, da, da, da, da dum," Shipman began singing the notes from the *Godfather* theme song, providing a musical accompaniment for his departure.

"So, basically, you're nothing more than a Cuban redneck!" Mark joked with David as they sat on the golf cart, out on the track, at six fifteen the morning of the planned walkout.

"Marko, call it what you will. I prefer to think of myself as a young conservative Republican. There are ways to make a point without disrupting the function of a school. I don't approve of this," he stated with emphasis.

When he looked at David's pained expression, Mark saw a touch of dread in it. David went on, "These kids are going to give Robreno what she wants. They'll make their point and make you look like shit in the process."

"It'll work itself out," Mark answered, and while David brought to light concerns that he refused to entertain out of self-preservation, Mark couldn't help but notice the role reversal afforded by this topic of conversation.

Studying him, David continued, "My father, your father, their fathers and mothers in some cases, all came here and had to go through the legal system to become citizens. Why should it be any different for these folks?"

They went back and forth for a few more minutes as a growing gathering formed on the track. Mark asked David to position himself within earshot, particularly among the Spanish-speaking students, to ascertain if anything was being planned beyond what was expected.

"They're mostly talking about keeping the walkout peaceful, Marko," David revealed when he hopped back in the cart a few minutes later. "They don't want to end up looking stupid so that people lose sight of the cause."

Like the first raindrops of a spring shower, students gradually spilled out of their classrooms at precisely 9:00 a.m., five minutes before the end of the first block class. Eventually, they began pouring out, inundating the grassy area at the front of the school. Some were onlookers. Some were supporters. Some were in it for the long haul, but within five minutes, more than half the school's population was out of its assigned area. Mark took a quick glance at Sarah Szemanski and wondered what her disciplinary plan would be for this situation, and while she was on the opposite end from his position, he could see her face contort to allow for the snort of dissent.

"Mark, *mi hermano*," Pep Garces tapped him from behind as he helped corral the crowd, "for the first time in history, we are witnessing a Chinese fire drill conducted by Mexican people." He laughed, and Mark just shook his head out of admiration for his intense pride.

Like a well-choreographed dance, the throng formed a circle around the flagpole. A couple of signs spoke their cause with messages like, "Immigrants United Will Never Be Divided" and "United We Stand." Conspicuous in its absence was the Mexican flag, but there were hundreds of hand-held American flags being waved.

Bryan Reinhold was by Mark's side and waxed poetic. "Boss," he began, "look at this," and he pointed to a news helicopter that just arrived and was hovering overhead. "I bet that from that vantage point it all looks like some kind of patriotic cake."

"You didn't eat this morning, did you?" Mark asked.

"Nah, just some coffee," he admitted, but their collective instinct took them away from the small talk. Blonde-haired, blue-eyed Chloe Owens walked briskly toward Migdalia Santa Cruz. She stopped within arm's distance. Her left fist held a small American flag, and as time seemed to freeze, Reinhold and he raced to this scene, both knowing they would be too late.

"Can I help you?" Santa Cruz asked Owens.

Owens said, "Look, I just want to say that I'm proud to be an American, and I want you to feel the same way. Good luck!" She handed the flag to Santa Cruz.

"What the fuck! No shit!" was all she could say to this advance.

As Mark and Bryan arrived, Chloe looked at her principal and said, "Even a hater has the God-given, inalienable right to change her mind," and she headed back toward the social studies wing where her second block teacher Ron Shipman awaited any late arrivals.

Mark looked at Bryan for any reaction, but a growing chant from the throng caught their attention.

"Hey, boss, can you hear that?" he asked. "They're saying, 'Paul's not dead,' or 'Block that kick,' or something like that."

Fist-held flags punched the air as the crowd moved in unison down Minneola Street, beginning its trek to Hanford City Hall, crying out, "Si, se puede. Si, se puede." Yes, we can. Yes, we can.

In all, probably five hundred students left campus to exercise their right to protest. They did so with the promised cadre of law enforcement to guide them there. Mark watched as the crowd turned the corner of 288th Street and listened as the chant grew more distant, but his thoughts were interrupted by T. J. Burns.

"I don't have much time, Mark," he began, "but it might interest you to know that there's an ambulance at Hanford Middle right now."

"What do you mean?"

"I mean that the lady running that show took Robreno's advice and locked up the place. Kids hopped the fence anyway, but two of them got hurt. One's probably got a concussion, and another one got cut pretty bad. You did the right thing. Got to go."

As he watched T. J. jog toward his squad car, Mark caught a last glimpse of Pep Garces punching the air as he turned the corner. Even in the back of a crowd, he was the Pied Piper, providing a very personal tune to guide the march toward city hall, a place of promise and a place where promises are broken.

A little prior to the lunch period, at about eleven o'clock, Mark found himself answering e-mails and wondering how things were shaping up at city hall. He felt helpless not being able to be there, but he knew his presence would be an overt show of support, which would be perceived as insubordination. He contemplated the lose-lose nature of this predicament for a few moments and had the self-pity interrupted by his hotline ringing.

"Mark, it's Mark Thayer," said the voice on the other end. "You'd be proud of your kids, bro! They're making their points and staying calm. Very classy."

Mark could hear the crowd in the background as they spoke. It sounded like a gusting wind, occasionally being pierced by amplified voices that cracked like thunder. Mark Thayer was the school district's media liaison and someone he had known casually over the years. He obviously had been sent to monitor the protest, guard the release of information to the public, and help the area office weather this storm.

"Well, Mark," he answered. "That's good to hear, but what other schools are represented?"

"Bro, you got Hanford High, Hanford Middle, Henry Ford Technical, and Eastridge High, but all of them together don't add up to the South Demming numbers, and your kids are doing most of the talking."

"Yeah, that sounds about right," Mark said. "Most of them won't shut up in class either. Hey, give me an idea about when this thing ends. Could you call me back?"

"I'll do that, but, man, I wish you were here to see Robreno," Thayer offered. "She's been down here a couple of times already, but she hasn't said shit because her jaw is too tight."

Mark wasn't sure where Thayer stood in regard to the mother bear, but his words convinced him that he wasn't a fan. He was glad that she was suffering in silence. "So about how many people are there?" he asked.

"Over/under is about nine hundred, maybe," Thayer answered. "I'll get back to you in a while. It looks like Fred Roberts finally dragged his old ass out of the chair."

Speakers from the crowd volunteered to step up to a dais that city hall had provided. One by one they spoke to the message of unity, lent personal anecdotes, and with the conclusion of each piece, the crowd cheered and chanted, "Si, se puede. Si, se puede."

At twelve o'clock, the mother bear called Fred Roberts to her office and told him to close the door.

"Fred, I have arranged for school buses to arrive and pick up these students to take them back to their schools. They will be there within the next half hour, which still will give them time to run their afternoon routes."

Roberts digested her words for a moment and then said, "Now, that's a fine idea, Magda, but you're missing a key part to this plan."

"And what's that?" Robreno snapped, and her jaw clenched so tightly that it wrestled with her ears.

Smug but pointed, Roberts asked, "Who's going to say that they're getting on those buses? Hell, Magda, they walked there to begin with."

Unhinging her jaw, the mother bear remained steadfast. "That's where you come in, Fred. Get on the phone to those principals, and if they can't make an appearance, be sure to have them send someone with a personality to talk to these kids."

Shortly after Roberts left with his directive, the mother bear rose from her chair and again witnessed the traffic scene six floors below. It was too early for congestion, and at this moment the light was green.

"Mark, who you got over there that speaks Spanish that these kids respect?"

225

"Mr. Roberts," Mark answered. "My Spanish isn't that great, but the kids respect me." He didn't hesitate for a moment, knowing what the job would be, and contrary to Roberts's ignorant statement, Spanish wasn't a prerequisite.

"Then get your ass over there right now!" Roberts directed.

Mark's ass, his neck, and his balls made it intact to the dais where he was announced to the crowd with "Mr. M's here. Mr. M, come up and say something. Talk to us."

The crowd cheered and applauded his appearance, and he had to wait about ten to fifteen seconds in order to be heard. Emboldened by his superiors' obvious need to rely on him to bail them out, Mark accepted the microphone and spoke from the heart that had guided him to this moment. "I'm proud of each and every one of you," he started, and as he spoke, he heard cameras clicking and saw television cameras pointing his way. "You all want to pursue the American dream, and you've started this journey by engaging in an American right, doing so in a peaceful and organized way. You have modeled how this moment should look!"

Again, the cheering rose, accompanied by the battle cry, "Si, se puede. Si, se puede." This time, Mark had to wait about a minute for the opportunity to speak again, and this time, Pep Garces joined him on the dais.

"Okay," he started anew, "there's an old game show called *Let's Make a Deal*. Today, it's going to go like this. You've walked two miles to get here. You've been out here for a couple of hours at least. You're tired, your hot, you're probably hungry, and you're definitely thirsty. He pointed to the fleet of buses with the school names on them. For safety reasons, I want to take you guys back to school. We've got snacks and water on the buses. Oh, by the way," he added, "nobody's in any trouble for this!"

With this revelation, the crowd thundered in approval and began their chant again. Pep Garces waited with him, holding his hands in a pushing position, attempting to get their attention. It took at least another minute, but they finally regained their focus, allowing him to speak. "In a moment, I hope that all of you will accept Mr. M's invitation, but before you board your buses, I want to say something to Mr. M that all of you need to hear." Garces embraced Mark's hand in his and grasped his forearm with his other. "Gracias *por venir, mi hermano.* From this day forward, you are a hero in this community. *Vaya con Dios.*" He looked at the crowd, which began its chant again, and yelled over them, "Now, hop on the bus, Gus!"

Mark watched as the group filtered to the buses, and he looked at Pep. "Man, you've put me through some shit since I've been here," he said.

"Yeah, Mark, but you can handle it," he came back. "There's a saying, 'He who can walk in shit avoids stepping in it.'"

"Is that some kind of Mexican proverb?"

Garces studied him for a moment and said, "Nah, I just made that shit up."

Mark was smiling as he drove back to school but was very concerned how they were going to handle the arrival of nearly five hundred students at midday. He called David to make sure he and some security would be in the bus loop to greet the kids and usher them to class.

"Marko, it's already taken care of," David assured. "We've been watching this on television and have the auditorium prepared for their arrival. We'll hold them there until last bell. That'll probably be about twenty-five to thirty minutes worth."

"Good. Thanks, Dave. In all the excitement of the exit plan, I didn't think about the arrival."

"No problem," David answered. "Oh, and so you know, television really does put some weight on you. Better you than me; they'd need the wide-angle lens to fit my ass in," and he gave the hardy laugh that said things would be okay.

Mark arrived in time to see the buses emptying out and watch Bryan, Ray Devereaux, David, and Larry Jefferson ushering students to the auditorium. He parked and made his way to the old building.

The students were seated and listening intently as Ron Shipman, with PowerPoint assistance, congratulated them on their peaceful assembly and provided them with the names of government officials to contact who might make a difference. After his handling of a few questions, the bell rang, and this group joined the others in last block as though nothing ever had happened.

Mark looked at the impromptu greeting party with admiration. "You guys are amazing to have pulled this off." He then looked specifically at Ron Shipman.

"I may come back asking you for a favor," Shipman said in his best Don Corleone voice.

Mark laughed, put his arm around Shipman's shoulder as they walked out, and said, "Gracias, amigo!"

He left for home pretty much right after the kids got out that day. The anticipation of the event and its successful implementation had taken its toll, and Mark's body was telling him to get out of overdrive. Never caring about his schedule before, the train interrupted the drive home, assuring that it would cut three or four minutes out of his life. Then his BlackBerry rang. It was Mark Thayer.

"Mark, I'm calling you as a courtesy and to give you a heads up, so what I'm about to tell you didn't come from me," he began.

Mark thought, *Great, another heads up, and this one's a double secret. Now what?*

"Bro, I was standing next to Robreno the time you were up there speaking. I got to let you know that she's pissed as hell."

"Mark, I've never seen her not pissed. What the fuck did I do wrong?"

"In my eyes," he explained, "you were textbook, bro, but I got to tell you that Robreno took exception to your telling the kids that you were proud of them and was bitching about it to me for a couple of minutes."

They talked about the event and his handling of it for a couple of minutes with Thayer assuring him the whole time that he was masterful and suggesting that Robreno was a bitch. "You did something she could never do, bro, and she obviously doesn't like being showed up. Not your fault. Just be aware. Keep doing what you do." He hung up.

A horn honking from behind snapped him back to attention as the train had since passed. Mark looked in the rearview mirror to see a woman likely mouthing obscenities at him and holding up both of her hands, karate chopping the air.

Chapter 25

A UNIFORM PUSH

"So the fashion show is the way to get the message out?" Mark asked Joe Carrera as they drank their six-thirty cups of coffee and sat on one side of the conference table facing each other.

Carrera took a big slurp and shouted, "Fuck, that's hot coffee! Now I've got a burned tongue and throat." He placed the cup roughly on the desk, sloshing its contents and further burning the knuckle of his index finger. "Goddamn it!" he shouted and looked at Mark for some sympathy.

"Well, maybe if you took time to smell the coffee and weren't always in such a big-ass hurry, you wouldn't be in such pain."

"Point taken, Magic," Carrera came back. "You've got a couple of hurdles to clear, and you're home free for the year. Set the stage for your uniform policy and set the stage for graduation," he offered, "but you might be in a bigger hurry than I am right now," and he freed up his scalded finger and pointed it at Mark.

"What do you mean?" Mark asked, soothing his ego and indirectly taking some pain away. Carrera always managed to make him rely on his wisdom and experience and liked to dole it out in small parcels like some Fed-Ex courier looking for an address.

"Magic, the fashion show is the culminating event. It only happens if you do all the other things the right way. My job is to make you look good and support you, even when I don't agree with you." He again pointed and said, "Magic, you got any toothpaste or something? This thing hurts like a son of a bitch. Damn!"

"What do you think this is, *Let's Make a Deal*? Why would I have toothpaste on me?" Again somewhat irritated, Mark continued the main conversation. "Why are you so opposed to this?"

Still blowing on his finger, Carrera studied his boss. "Why are you so in favor of it?" he countered. "I got to tell you that how you answer that question is a predictor of whether or not you can get these kids in uniforms. How are you going to sell this to them?"

Mark already had thought this part out, so he began, "Joe, first and foremost is student safety. With almost three thousand kids on our campus, it's tough to spot a trespasser."

"All right, Magic. If I'm a parent, which I am, I'm probably going to buy into that, but how are you going to sell this to the kids because they'll drive their parents crazy enough to stop the momentum?" Carrera raised his left eyebrow, tilted his head, and cupped his palm over his left ear as Mark formulated his response.

"I'm going to take out the competition and guesswork regarding what to wear. The uniform will be comfortable and probably be like some of the stuff they already have in their closets—you know, khakis, polo shirts, and so on."

"That might work, Magic, if it comes with sincerity and no hidden agenda. So what's the hidden agenda?" He leaned forward in his chair, holding Mark to task like a sealed envelope held up to the light. Pointing his burnt finger, he asked, "What's the real reason?"

Even as he watched Carrera wasting time by blowing on his finger, his temporary condition could in no way compare to the scars Mark was hoping to heal. He measured his words carefully. "People visit here, and they're afraid to step foot on campus because of our reputation and the population we serve," he began. "You can go to the schools just north of us in the nice neighborhoods, and nobody thinks twice if a kid is wearing baggy pants or a hooded sweatshirt. You got just as many of those kids or more at Bronfmann."

"I agree with you," Carrera replied. "Go on."

"Bottom line, I don't want our bosses, community members, or anyone coming here and prejudging our kids on the basis of how they dress. I want them coming here and seeing a neatly dressed group of kids that deserve to be regarded in the same sense as the higher socioeconomic kids in other schools. I can look past a kid whose boxers stick out of his pants that are so baggy that he waddles like a duck. I can look past a girl wearing gym shorts, huge hoop earrings, purple hair, and too much eye makeup. I can see these kids for who they are. Most of society can't, so they, meaning our kids, probably have to conform sooner than the kids up the road."

"Brilliant answer. Magical, Magic. That's what you got to tell them." He again punctuated his words with his burnt pointer brandished in Mark's direction. "They want you to be straight, agree or disagree with you. They're like anybody else; they don't want to be bullshitted," Carrera explained.

"So where do we go from here?" Mark asked.

"They already know that you're thinking of this, so it would be wise to involve them in the process. Have an assembly, answer their questions, be straight with them, but most importantly, give them some general ideas as to what will make up the uniform, but let them have some input and allow them to negotiate some flexibility."

"For example?"

"Well, Magic. I hope you aren't so tight-assed as to expect that these kids tuck in their shirts. The fat kids will have esteem issues in some cases if you go that route. You may want to listen to the girls because uniforms can be a sensitive issue with the choices available, like skirts, skorts, shorts, culottes, capris. You got to listen to them."

"I'm with you 100 percent on that," Mark said. "Let's get the ball rolling then." He looked as Carrera struck up his cynical grin, once again placing him in a needy role.

"What else is there?"

He looked at Mark, squinted his eyes, and said, "Grasshopper ..."

"Don't call me Grasshopper!"

"Sorry, Magic. This all involves getting the word out in numerous ways over numerous days. We'll start in-house with the assembly and letters to take home to the parents. We'll back that up with prerecorded message you'll do that our List-Serv will dial up for all the families. You'll get the word out in the school paper, the *Hanford News Leader*, and through some town hall meetings."

"Town hall meetings?" Mark interrupted.

"Magic, if you host an informational meeting at the school, you'll give people a chance to say they couldn't make it or the time wasn't good for them. If you go into the community, and you do it during evening hours, they won't have an excuse. We'll couple that with some public service announcements on the radio, and that should flood the market in terms of getting out the word."

"Is there more?" Mark asked, truly thinking that there couldn't possibly be more.

Using his left hand, Carrera did the universal gesture of rubbing thumb, index, and middle finger together and stated, "Money, Magic; there's the money issue. In some cases, our families rely on hand-me-downs to keep their kids dressed for school. For them, annual clothes shopping is not their reality. Now, we're asking them to dress all their kids a certain way, and the funds might not be available for that."

"Don't uniform stores have a way of helping with that?"

"Glad you asked that," Carrera started. "It's called the preferred vendor, Magic. We steer them in the direction of a particular uniform store without telling them that they have to go there, but they are our preferred vendor. We make them a business partner, and for every x-amount of dollars they make, they provide uniform vouchers to be used by our needier families."

"It makes sense," Mark acknowledged.

"Oh, it makes perfect sense, but there is one more thing you'll have to deal with," Carrera offered. "You'll have to deal with the families that won't support this move and will request a waiver to dress their kids however the hell they want. Bottom line is that you can't mandate uniforms; you only can suggest them."

"So despite busting our humps," Mark stressed, "we have no answer for that."

Carrera studied him momentarily and broke into song. "The answer my friend is pissing in the wind; the answer is pissing in the wind," a rendition that he followed with his bellowing laugh, pointing his bad finger in Mark's direction.

"You enjoying yourself?" Mark asked. "Are we done?"

"Not yet," Carrera answered. "We're still going to need to go to the local churches and have them spread the word."

"What will they do for us?"

"Magic, they'll support what we're doing. They always have, and besides ..." He hesitated.

"Besides what?" Mark asked impatiently. "What else is there?"

"Magic," Carrera studied him, "frankly, without them, you haven't got a prayer. Ah, ha, ha, ha, ha, hah. That's the good word, Magic, and there's one final thing to tie it all together." He paused for Mark's indulgence.

"You're exhausting me," Mark gave in.

"A theme, Magic; this is a campaign, and every campaign needs a theme. Now what can that be?" he asked as he regarded his finger and blew on it once more.

While the old auditorium didn't exactly swell with people, it swelled with anticipation. Perhaps two hundred people, including students, younger siblings, parents, and a few grandparents filled in some of the gaps among the seats. They generally strew themselves about the place, staking their claims in respective comfort zones. Upon seating themselves, they were afforded the view of diversely clad high school students, standing in varied frozen poses to the extreme right of the stage. They were mannequins awaiting their call to life. Beyond them, flashed on a movie screen, was the message for the evening in simple bold black italics. "Dress for Success. Get the Point!" To the far left of the stage, Activities Director Kim Bennett signaled for a musical cue behind the curtain, and with the first pulse, the mannequins came to life and were introduced to the audience.

"When she's not carrying her pom-poms, Christy Del Pino carries herself with class and grace in her khaki capris and black polo shirt." The cheerleader-turned-runway-model gracefully walked across the stage with Kim Bennett's cue, stopping with a midway pirouette to provide a 360-degree view of her attire and a curtsy to accept the applause. She then scanned the audience with her index finger, pointing at the group, going from left to right, and shouted, "Get the point!"

"Showing off his sporty legs, Matt Mathews opts for black Bermuda shorts and a royal polo top," Bennett continued her narration as the quarterback nodded his head approvingly, spread out his arms with palms facing upward, then struck a Heisman pose. He repeated Del Pino's gesture and remark before exiting stage right.

Not wanting to lose momentum, Kim Bennett went on, "And how about Danny Baldwin keeping it real in his khaki Dockers and white and tight polo shirt?" The immensely popular athlete did his pimp walk, stopping to face the audience with arms folded high over his chest in a defiant posture. "Get on it! Get the point!" he yelled.

"And let's give it up for Raja Horton," Kim Bennett urged. "Tonight, it's all black and white with the black Dockers accessorized by the white polo top. Raja's opting for the untucked look because he tends to wear his pants a little low."

Horton added a most muscular pose to his promenade and pointed across the audience blaring, "Get the point!" His was the final strut across stage. The audience was then invited to the stage area to more closely inspect the uniform choices that were hanging on portable racks.

As parents and students filed out of the auditorium at around nine o'clock, Mark sought out Don Reinhold, who had brought in the football players to serve as the models. Coach Reinhold occupied an end seat all the way up in the last row. Despite the ruckus and chatter accompanying the departure of about two hundred people, he was fast asleep.

"Oh, hey, sorry about that," Reinhold offered as Mark gently nudged him awake. Scanning the auditorium, he saw the expanse of empty rows of wooden seats, a desolation punctuated by the echoing creakiness of his seat as he got up. Attempting to salvage the situation, he added, "But you got to understand that this is pretty much my bedtime."

Mark's regard for this man didn't permit him to engage in the good-natured ribbing that Joe Carrera no doubt would have conjured, and besides, he hadn't put in the time to engage in that type of familiarity. Instead, he simply said, "No worries, Coach. Thanks for bringing in the kids."

Reinhold looked in their direction and said, "Aw shit! I still got to bring them back, don't I? I may as well put up a taxi sign on the roof of the van. See you tomorrow." Looking in the direction of Danny Baldwin and Raja Horton, he said, "Let's go. I ain't got all night."

"Hey, Coach," Baldwin started up, "can we stop and get something to eat?"

Reinhold frowned and studied the boys for a moment and said, "Sure. Let me guess who's buying. Hold on. Wait a minute." He tapped his temple with the knuckles of his right hand and gave a vacant look before revealing, "Yup, I guess it's me."

"Damn, Coach," Horton chimed in, "you always guess right. You a good guesser!"

"And you're a pain in the rear. Let's get out of here."

The coach and players were the last to leave, and Mark followed them out thinking that this Monday evening assembly was the culminating evening event before the impending spring break set to begin the following Monday. From the snail's pace of the summer preparations, to the continuously issue-driven first semester indoctrination, to a new year where national issues found expression on the Buccaneer campus, everything now seemed to be moving at warp speed. Accompanying these thoughts was his hope that, at least in terms of safety, South Demming had turned the corner to access a path running perpendicular to Luci Street.

Chapter 26

SPRING BREAK HEARTBREAK

The events that led up to the moment have remained a mystery to this day. The young teenage couple was on a date that involved dinner, a late movie, and a ride home sometime after midnight. Among those who knew them intimately, there was no talk of tensions; there was no sign of unhappiness; there was nothing to remotely suggest that one or the other had gone astray. To those who arrived on the scene, there was no immediate sign that drugs or alcohol were involved; there was nothing to indicate the presence of another vehicle; there were no skid marks.

On a dark country back road illuminated by flashing blue lights, a 150-year-old oak tree remained firm and tall despite the crushing impact of a large, big-wheeled pickup truck that moments earlier had slammed into it at more than a hundred miles per hour, sending its unrestrained passengers through the windshield. Their carved and broken bodies lay covered in a yellow tarp some fifty feet beyond the tree, and obeying the laws of physics, the truck rested nose down with its hood, roof, and payload area bent enough to be wrapped tightly around the tree trunk as if giving it a hug. An ambulance waited its calling to become a hearse.

An old farming couple in pajamas and kimonos answered questions from a police officer. "Only heard the crash. Didn't hear no brakes. Only heard what sounded like a train horn right before the crash," the man said.

The female, concerned about the vehicle's occupants, asked, "Who was in the truck? What happened?"

As if spurred on by the luminescence of the utility vehicles, the sky began to flash. A breeze dared upon the scene, and a hard rain arrived to cleanse the blood and mix with it so that it could be interred in the soiled scene. It hadn't rained hard in Hanford for a couple of months.

T. J. Burns called Mark at his home on Saturday morning at seven o'clock. For the next ten minutes, he fielded inquiries and filled him in on as many details as he knew. The whole situation just didn't add up as unanswered questions and sudden sorrow made a date to dance over the freshly dug graves of a couple who five months earlier danced at their homecoming.

"Mark, my sister has all the respect in the world for you, and there's another reason I'm calling. Nelson shared things with her about you that almost made you a father figure. She's asked me to make certain that you're there for at least the memorial. Nelson would want you there if he could tell you himself."

"You might want to consider not seeing them in their coffins," Sarah Szemanski suggested. "They probably should have done this with closed caskets." Szemanski found an angle that cast her in the role of the resident expert, but given what Mark knew of the tragedy, he took her advice and kept his distance.

Nelson Taylor's family paid for both funerals and saw to it that they would occur concurrently. For Nelson's mother, this was her final tribute, and she did her part to orchestrate a memorable and storybook farewell. Nelson and Leisy were displayed together, despite their torn faces, and they were remembered together in her eulogy, a gut-wrenching chronology of her son's warmth and the undying love of Leisy Pinto, whom she regarded as her daughter. There were no dry eyes.

The burial on Tuesday drew a huge crowd, due in part to the Pinto side of the equation. Honduran migrant workers stood at attention with their hats or ball caps in their hands and paid their respects. In Leisy Pinto they had lost one of their own who carried hope and freedom from the bondage of immigration policies. At eight o'clock, minutes before nightfall, her coffin was placed adjacent to that of Nelson Taylor's, and their last moments were destined to be debated for years after the last shovel of dirt blanketed their graves.

T. J. Burns had some final details to iron out and left the burial site even as people were paying their condolences. He wasn't much for hearing the same thing over and over again. He had borrowed some flowers from the funeral, and with them he drove the five miles to the site of the tragedy. There, at the base of the oak tree, he placed the flowers. He then reached inside his pocket and extracted a folding knife. He slowly carved a heart, not much bigger than a fist, and within it he dug the inscription, "N.T. loves L.P." He stood back to admire his primitive tribute and said, "Rest in peace, you dumb fuck." T. J. then took a seat on the ground, his back supported by the tree, and pulling up his knees with both arms, he made a resting place for his heavy head.

Chapter 27

GRADUATION DAY

Black and white were the colorless schemes among the choices afforded with the uniform policy, yet they served as dichotomous symbols for the right and the wrong in an oversimplification that helped Mark Mahovlic survive his first year as a principal. Khaki and royal, which he never came across even in the sixty-four-pack of Crayolas, bled in a little color, while Bermudas, capris, and cargo pants helped fashion a plan that had a real chance to be successful.

These were among his many thoughts as he reflected upon the teeter-totter totality of the school year and gazed out at the auditorium floor full of 636 graduating students and more than two thousand of their family members and friends surrounding them in a ceremonious group hug. The Hanford Auditorium was an arena that was good for events ranging from demolition derbies to basketball games. For this midafternoon rite of passage it represented just how well conformity could take hold when presented in the right context. Every student walked in unison. Every student fit into rows. Every student donned the royal caps and gowns and traded tears for smiles or smiles for tears. This was their day, and nobody was going to compromise any of its moments.

"Mark, just make your speech short and sweet," Magda Robreno insisted while they were in the courtesy room. "We have two more of these to attend today," and she pointed to the dignitaries with whom he would share the stage. Alice Chandler-Lopez was there, as was Fred Roberts, both of whom were investing in the chicken wing platter and sampling some of the cheese cubes. Wilma Hart dipped a celery stick into the ranch dressing that accented the veggie platter and left a white blotch on the right corner of her lips.

"Please tell me you're not going to be long-winded up there," Chandler-Lopez stated as they made their way to the curtain call.

"Remind your students to not throw their caps in the air at the end. Someone could get hurt," were the words of caution from Wilma Hart.

The ROTC Color Guard began the festivities with their flag display and presentation of arms. The band played the national anthem. The chorus sang the alma mater. The salutatorian and the valedictorian delivered their speeches, flawlessly and filled with time-tested clichés. It struck Mark that though he knew them and their names, he did not really have a handle on their impact on the school, other than making great grades and improving their test scores. He could have thought of dozens of other kids at South Demming who really made the school what it was during its finer moments, but that was the rebel in him.

"Parents, family members, friends, and most of all grads," he began. "My bosses have told me to not be long-winded and to keep this speech short and sweet. They told me that they've got other places to go, and I don't know about you, but this right here is the only place to be!"

Raucous laughter and applause accompanied that remark and set the tone for his speech, outlining a grocery shopping excursion, metaphorical aisle by metaphorical aisle, going from the childish whimsy of poking a hole in the toilet paper wrapping to stopping and smelling the coffee when life seems to be going too fast. In its conclusion, he thanked the students for shopping at South Demming and for allowing the school and its staff to be the proprietors of their hopes and dreams.

They filed out of the auditorium accompanied by music from the orchestra with a pace and order as orchestrated by Kim Bennett. Mark watched them with a feeling of pride and accomplishment and did so minus the company of his management team who, as promised, had other places to be and made their respective exits as if someone had yelled, "Fire!"

Outside, Mark accepted the well wishes of the handfuls of remaining students and parents who extended the moment with photo ops, some including him. He negotiated a friendly cease-fire by acting like he had some place to go besides the local beer and wings joint that a few of them conspired to attend following the event. Among the coconspirators, David Canales caught him in the parking lot and felt the need to give him the perspective from behind the podium where he sat with the administrative team.

"Marko," he started, "Robreno, Chandler-Lopez, and Hart were in rare form tonight. Next time, please just let me sit in the audience!"

"What now, David?" Mark studied his pissed-off face. "What the hell did I do wrong now?"

"From my view, nothing," he answered, "but all these bitches could do was complain about how long everything was taking and argue as to whether your speech was appropriate or not."

"That was to be expected, I guess. Anything else worth mentioning? Anything to spoil my appetite for the after-party?"

"Well, Chandler-Lopez asked me to remind you to bring your binder to the area office luncheon on Monday."

He had almost forgotten about the binder that he had to do for professional development purposes. This was given to him by Mitch Warner after a principals' meeting rather than a scheduled meeting that originally had been planned and put off several times. Along with the binder came Warner's admonition regarding taking care of the contents within or risking having Chandler-Lopez serve his balls on a platter. It had been completed a few months ago and was collecting dust on a shelf in his office. Ripe with little tasks, sign-off sheets, and checklists, this inane annoyance was a compliance document to show that the area office, notably Robreno and Chandler-Lopez were being proactive in bringing Mark along in his career.

"So," Mark looked at David, "I guess that binder will be my ticket into an event that I'd rather not attend. Can we just fucking get a drink right now?"

"I'm one step behind you, my friend." Dr. C chuckled and let out a fart, which Mark chose to not acknowledge, instead being glad David was not in front of him.

Word had gotten out beyond the inner circle, and when Mark arrived, it appeared that the whole faculty and staff were there. Joe Carrera had saved a seat of honor for him and already had ordered him a shot and a draft beer, clearly after having begun taking care of his immediate needs.

"Magic, that was a fucking great speech." His words came out with the tone and cadence reserved for the shit-faced. "Great fucking, fucking great speech, best outta all the ones I've heard, and I've heard a lot of 'em. Ya wanna know how many I've heard, Magic?"

"How many have you heard, Joe?" Mark indulged him, but Carrera was distracted by a game of darts being played by Robbie Wolf and Bryan Reinhold.

"I'm sorry, Magic. What did you say?"

I said, "How many have you heard?"

"Yeah, that's right," Carrera agreed to something somewhere in his mind and got up gingerly to negotiate the twenty feet or so toward the dartboard stations.

Mark followed him and asked Bryan Reinhold, "Please tell me he's got a ride home tonight?"

"Yeah, boss," Reinhold explained, "I'm the loser that gets to take him home tonight, provided he doesn't kill me with a fucking dart. Jesus Christ, he doesn't even drink like a man. Vodka and cranberry juice—are you fucking kidding me?"

The burly designated driver kicked back a big swig of Budweiser and let out a gargantuan burp that permitted the words "fuck me" somewhere in the middle of its emission. He studied Mark for a moment and said, "Nice speech tonight. I damn near got misty when you stopped by the frozen pizza aisle."

"Glad it moved you," Mark answered.

"Oh, it didn't move me, but a couple more beers, and I see something moving pretty soon."

"I thought you were the designated driver tonight?"

"Nah, we got the little woman picking us up. She has a dinner date with her cousin and can swing by to get us."

Limiting himself to a beer and a plate of ten wings, Mark made his way home. There was nothing to stop him. He beat all the lights except two, the blue ones that took turns flashing on top of the police car that pulled him over for speeding. He was a Metro cop, wearing his khaki-colored uniform, accented with a black utility belt and black patent leather shoes. This early evening he took pity on him, and Mark got off with a warning, so he was less offended by the warning lights and long white arm of the railroad crossing that signaled that the train was coming.

Final exams were the order of the next three days for the underclassmen. Mark contemplated the school year as he made the ten-minute drive from South Demming to the area office. He likened his situation to that of the graduates, having already passed his tests, and on this morning, he would be handing in his binder for one final scrutiny of his neck, his ass, and his balls. Cracking his neck, pulling the underwear out of his ass, and straightening his package, Mark completed the trinity before entering the area office big conference room and handing over the binder as though it were the Bible.

"What's this?" Alice Chandler-Lopez inquired as he handed the binder to her. She already was in her bipolar nice mode, enjoying some of the party fare, and couldn't be bothered. "Oh. Okay, just put it on the table in the storage room for now," she said and made no mention of it ever again.

Chapter 28

COLORFUL BEGINNINGS

A principal's job over the summer is to oversee plans and preparations for the forthcoming school year. For South Demming, this involved interviewing for open positions, monitoring Alana Tavares's building of the master schedule and aligning it with the school-based budget, and watching the custodial staff work its miracles to get the building ready. Gum was scraped off the bottom of desks and walkways. The plastic covers of light ballasts were removed and washed. The concrete floors were polished, and in general, the old girl received her fifty-fourth facelift.

"I got to hand it to you, boss," Bryan Reinhold said as he surveyed the campus minutes before the first bell of the school year. "I never thought I would see this!"

As far as the eye could see, there were students dressed in school colors, sporting their Dockers, khakis, Bermudas, capris, and polo shirts, all within the outlined arrangements of royal, khaki, black, and white. There were no students for the football players to remind to get with the new uniform policy. To find someone out of compliance was to spot the needle in the haystack. "See what a little advance work will get you, Magic!" Joe Carrera exclaimed. "This is unbelievable, beyond what I expected," and he slapped Mark on the back.

Sarah Szemanski nodded her head, pursed her lips, and even complimented some of her regulars on their appearance.

A change of culture had taken root like a freshly planted tree. A start in a new direction had the wind behind its back. As the sun's fingers caressed the trees, and the trees swayed gently at the wind's prodding, a voice on the radio cracked like a falling tree, disturbing Mark's euphoria and self-absorption. It was David Canales. "Mr. M, I'm going to need you in my office," he said as the bell rang in the new school year and summoned Mark to the world of apprehension with only one cup of coffee inside him.

"David, I can't begin to tell you how disappointed I am with this decision," he heard Dr. C addressing someone in his office. "Of all the people in this school I thought would support us, you would have been on the top of my list."

As he approached his office, Mark's eyes caught the scarf-wrapped head of a fat middle-aged black woman. She wore the clothing of a domestic laborer and a badge identifying her as an employee of the Holiday Inn. Immediately to her right and visible upon his entry was David St. Jean.

"Mr. M," Dr. C began. "David's mother is here to request a uniform waiver for her son. She doesn't speak English, so David is his own agent, filling his mother in as we go along." The Haitian woman smiled sheepishly and stared at her watch.

Unable to contain his disappointment, Mark let David St. Jean have it. "I can't believe after all I've done to support you that you would make this choice!" he said in a raised voice, undoubtedly heard throughout the office area as Ken Ferguson came by and closed the door.

"This isn't about you and me," St. Jean answered. "It's about exercising my option, and I'm opting out of being told what to wear, no disrespect toward you."

For a moment, Mark studied him. He wore baggy jeans that undoubtedly were two or more sizes too big because his boxers showed even in his seated position. He wore a shirt with Bob Marley's likeness on it, and as he nervously smiled, he flashed his golden grille.

"I'm exercising my individuality," he elaborated.

"Yeah, nobody quite like you anywhere," Mark said sarcastically. "I've never seen a Bob Marley shirt before, and I guess you're the only person whose pants don't fit."

Then Mark looked at his hair, which was close shaven with a design going from his forehead area to the back part of his head. There were two lines, one going straight and one eventually breaking off to the left of his head. "Nice hair too!" he added.

"Yeah," David St. Jean explained, "did some summer reading. This is my representation of 'The Road Not Taken,' a Robert Frost poem. Good reading has made all the difference for me, Mr. M," and he flashed his grille again as his mother began signing a couple of documents to pave his path.

Mark just walked out disgusted.

The honeymoon period of the first month had few highlights. There were minimal schedule glitches. The budget meeting went without a hitch, and beyond David St. Jean, there only were a few more students exercising their options with respect to the uniform policy. There seemed to be an implied expectation of better behavior that came with the uniform look, but given the tumult of his first year, perhaps the suffering they all shared had bled through and given way to better times.

Chapter 29

A MASTER PLAN

The bloodred nail of her middle finger touched the first knuckle of her thumb as her hand wrapped around the receiver and swept it away to the window part of the office overlooking US 1. The sixth floor was of sufficient enough height to acknowledge her climb. From there, she moved about in little circles as she spun her words.

"So we agree then on the tour you'll give your visitors?" Then, continuing after a brief pause to digest the response on the other end, she offered, "No, he'll be occupied elsewhere, but timing is everything. You fully understand your part then?" After another pause, she concluded, "Good. Monday should be interesting to say the least." Widening her last little circle, she broke free of this path, swooped down from the altitude of her sixth-floor view, and deftly cradled the receiver, guiding it into its nest.

On the other side of town in the school board building, Roger Traynor's fingers pounded the eighteen-seat conference table stage like Cossack dancers. At four thirty, a time when most people's work days were coming to an end, Traynor reveled in the knowledge that his cabinet members, composed of an array of nine people with chief or deputy as titles, and his six area superintendents, were on their way to the bimonthly STARS meeting, an acronym for the intended purpose of this illustrious crew assembled to provide Support and Training for At-Risk Schools.

"So let's review the plan for Monday," Traynor began. "Magda, you will bring Alice with you to Hanford High, and I'm going to send Tonya and Nick to South Demming. Spend quality time there. Visit some classes and let me know what you see."

As the superintendent of schools droned on and assigned his other problem-solving teams, the mother bear smiled contentedly.

As the Harvard intern, Nick Agnello got to be the fly on the wall in all these meetings. His five years of experience as teacher and dean at an all-boys school in Massachusetts were, frankly, a blemish on his resume, but Agnello was given a sense of entitlement through people who knew people who knew Roger Traynor. STARS was a program that Roger Traynor initiated during his days in New York, but the size of the centralized Demming County system precluded his knowing whole truths about anything, so he was reliant on those around him to speak the truth. Nick Agnello quickly joined the ranks of people who told Traynor what they believed he wanted to hear.

One floor below, Joyce Adams fiddled with her phone. "Mark," she began, "I'm sorry to drop this on you on a Friday, probably when you're just heading out the door, but I'm going to need you to give a deposition first thing Monday morning." She then sipped from a cup of coffee that was the last in a pot that had been servicing her caffeine needs since early that morning.

"Joyce, I don't have my roster of players in front of me, so you'll have to tell me on whose behalf."

"It's Ogden, Bill Ogden," she revealed.

Since his possible indiscretion at South Demming, Ogden had been moved to yet another school, a middle school in the western part of the county, and according to Joyce Adams had since hired an attorney to challenge this move. "What time do you need me there?" Mark asked.

"Nine o'clock sharp," Adams revealed. "With your drive, going to work first won't make any sense. You'd never get here on time. I've already contacted Alice at the region office, so they know you won't be at South Demming, at least for the first part of the day."

"That's fine, Joyce," he acknowledged, "but all I've got to say about that situation is what I was told secondhand. I don't get it."

Adams took a glance at a picture of her two sons, six and eight years old, and she gathered her strength. "I guess they'll want you to attest to his work ethic or reliability or something," she said. "You know how it is; we just do what we're expected to do."

The old man and the three-legged dog were on Minneola and 280th Street immediately on his way home. This time Mark honked and waved. The dog didn't react, and the old man didn't bother to look in his direction.

"Hey, Mark, how'd we get so lucky to have to fight Monday morning traffic on 836?" Dr. Alice Chandler-Lopez asked, concluding this query with a giggle.

"I'm sorry?" he answered. "You're going to this meeting too?"

"Yeah, but I'm getting a late start with some unfinished business here. Where are you at right now, big guy?"

"I'm probably still at least a half hour away, because the traffic is starting to back up, and I left plenty early," Mark answered, wondering whether someone had slipped her a happy pill.

"Okay, I'll see you later," and she hung up the phone just long enough to pick it up again and begin pressing out another number.

It was seven thirty, and Mark planned on being downtown one hour before the scheduled nine o'clock deposition. One hour early was the new punctual forced into existence by an urban sprawl that left two choices, either very early or likely late.

Another fifteen minutes into his drive, the BlackBerry buzzed again, and again it was Chandler-Lopez on the other end inquiring, "Hey, where you at right now?"

"I'm getting off at the exit on Northwest Second Avenue," Mark answered, still trying to figure out why she was at the point of plotting out his trip, and even more importantly, why was she being so nice and conversational.

"Well, I'm still stuck at the office, but I should be able to sneak out of here in a few minutes. I guess the traffic's bad?" she asked.

"Yeah, it's been busy for sure."

"Call me when you get there," she stated and hung up, picked up, and pecked out anew.

Joyce Adams greeted him and sat him at a long conference table. At 8:05, Mark was the only person present except for her secretary, who apparently was organizing a filing cabinet. Remembering Chandler-Lopez's request to call her when he arrived, Mark picked up his BlackBerry and got a busy tone. He tried two more times, once at 8:15 and again at 8:25, and each time there was no answer, so he left a message lest she think he ignored her request to touch base.

At 8:30, Adams came in from her office across the hall. This time he took notice of her black business pantsuit and red high-heel shoes, which were the perfect complement to the dark circles framing her bloodshot eyes. "Mark, Alice just called me to tell me she won't be able to make it," Adams started. "She wanted to know if you had arrived, and I told her that you've been waiting patiently." Then looking at the empty conference table, she stated, "I'm surprised that no one has arrived yet."

Adams excused herself again, entered her office, straightened out the picture of her boys, and picked up the phone.

At 9:00 a.m., from the comfort of her office chair, Alana Tavares listened attentively to the conversation Cathy Acker was having in the main office, and ascertaining the unmistakable timbre of Dr. Tonya Barton, Tavares intercepted the proceedings and inserted herself.

"Dr. Barton, I'm Alana Tavares, the APC," she began, extending her hand, and looking at Nick Agnello, she gave him a nod.

"Very nice to meet you," Barton said, "but tell me, is your principal here?"

Tavares was aware of Mark's detainment downtown but answered with, "No. He's not in the building yet."

"I see," Barton said with a disappointed tone. "Then perhaps you would be so kind to show us around your lovely school?"

"I'm happy to do that," Tavares stated. "Is there anything specific that you would like to see?"

"I'll tell you what," Barton's voiced boomed enthusiastically. "Why don't you take us to see your three best teachers?"

At 9:05, Joyce Adams reentered the conference room where Mark remained alone. "Mark, I'm sorry to say that the attorney's office just called, and they won't be in to take your deposition this morning."

"So, that's it!" he said disgustedly. "They interrupt my day, spend my gas money, and don't have the courtesy to offer an explanation. That's bullshit!"

"I'm sorry, Mark, but this wasn't my show. I couldn't agree with you more," Adams provided her condolences.

As he got up to leave, Adams gave him a quick hug and told him, "Please be careful driving home. Just be careful period."

Mark got stuck at the light before the expressway entrance, and this time he gave a couple of bucks to the Chubby Checker look-alike.

"God bless you, my brother," he said as he began cleaning the windshield. This time there appeared to be a clean soapy liquid in his bottle, and the rag looked unused. He was giving Mark his money's worth as the windshield looked appreciably cleaner. "You gettin' the executive wash this mornin', boss ... because a man like you gots to get a clearer picture of what's goin' on around him."

At 9:05, Alana Tavares headed out of the main office with Dr. Barton and Nick Agnello in tow and led the duo into the room of one of South Demming's finest, Mr. Dick Van Slyke. Upon entering, Barton took off her glasses and checked for smudges. Half the students in the class had their heads down on their desks while some of the others appeared to be copying words from the image cast by the overhead projector. Van Slyke had his feet propped upon his desk and was engaged in a phone conversation. Noticing his visitors, he dismissed the party on the other line and stood up to greet them.

"Yes. Who are you?" he started.

"I'm Dr. Barton, the deputy superintendent of curriculum," his visitor revealed, "and this is Mr. Agnello from Dr. Traynor's office."

"And how can I help you?" Van Slyke offered.

"We're just making some rounds of the schools and visiting classes," Barton stated.

The deputy superintendent moved about the aisles as though she were walking the plank. A few of the sleepy heads rose to the sound of her heels heavily hitting the tiled floor, sounding like distant gunshots going off. Then signaling a bemused Agnello toward the door, they both left with the South Demming APC in their wake.

"I'm so sorry, Dr. Barton," Alana Tavares offered her explanation once the trio found sanctuary in the hallway. "Grades are due today, and some of the teachers probably are giving their students some busy work. Let me take you to another classroom."

"Yes, please," Barton responded quickly.

Tavares led them past the social studies wing where Ron Shipman was building independent thinkers and responsible voters, and instead she made a sharp ninety-degree turn into Ms. French's math class. Therein, a combination of heavy heads and starving minds greeted their arrival. Like she had done many times in the past, Ms. French took her cue, rose mightily from the chair at her desk, and freeing a fart with this sudden movement, she began teaching the problems left on the board over the weekend.

Once outside the classroom, Agnello turned to Barton and said, "If these are the best teachers, I'd hate to see the worst," he concluded with a sarcastic chuckle.

Tonya Barton turned to Alana Tavares and said, "Thank you for your time. I think I've seen all I can stand for now."

Tavares followed the visitors to the entry gate and watched as they left. Hurrying back to her office, she had a phone call to make, and now forming like cracks in plaster, a smile turned up in the corners of her mouth.

"Marko, I'm afraid I've got some bad news to tell you," David Canales opened his conversation as they talked during Mark's drive back to the school.

"Bad news can take a number and stand in line with the rest of the bad news as of late," Mark answered. "What happened, David?"

"We had some visitors from downtown, and they asked for you, but because you weren't here, they asked Alana to take them on a tour."

"Who were they?"

"I recognized Tonya Barton, but she had some young yuppie-looking guy with her that I don't know. Anyway, Alana takes them into classrooms, and from her reaction after they left, I guess it didn't go too well."

"Whose classes did they go into?" Mark asked. "What was going on in those classes?"

"I don't know, Mark. All I know is I asked Alana the same questions, and she burst into tears and closed the door to her office. That was about thirty minutes ago, and she's still in there."

As Mark arrived to the main office, Cathy was shaking her head, and Ken looked at him, circling his index finger near his right ear and pointing to Alana's office. David joined Mark as he knocked on Tavares's door. She opened it like she was opening a casket to mourners. Long tear lines were traced by her mascara like some connect-the-dots coloring book of woe.

"I feel like the biggest fool on the planet," she started. "I've never felt so stupid. I'm so sorry!"

"Alana, what the hell happened?" Mark asked. "What the hell went wrong?" He felt himself growing flush and recognized the sick feeling in his stomach.

"They, they, asked me to, to, t-take them on a tour of some, some classes," she heaved as she attempted to speak. "I, I wanted to take them to some good teachers, but Barton asked me to let her pick."

"So what classes did they visit? Please take a deep breath and tell me where the hell they went," Mark said, trying to check his anger in deference to her considerable guilt.

"Out of all the people they could choose, they went to Van Slyke and French," and then she began sobbing uncontrollably.

Part of him wanted to kick her for letting this happen, and the other part of him did the gentlemanly thing by shortening their distance and giving her a conciliatory hug. She accepted this for a brief moment and then pulled away.

"You should fire my ass for allowing this to happen! What they said on the way out was humiliating. They left laughing like we're some kind of joke over here."

Remembering hugs and Pepperidge Farm cookies and too many fucking planes flying up in the air, Mark attempted to console Tavares, saying, "I'll make this right. I've got a solid relationship with Dr. Barton. I'll call her and invite them back. Fuck! Out of all the classes to visit!"

Back at the school board building, Dr. Barton made her way to her office to attack a bevy of tasks and prepare to greet the impending arrival of about five appointments scheduled for her late morning and early afternoon. Her days held too few hours to reflect on much of anything. In essence, she was a black woman enslaved by a black man. Her $200,000 salary could buy her most things in life, save for the most precious, which was time.

Nick Agnello checked the time on his Rolex, and he knocked on Traynor's open office door and accepted the invitation to enter.

One half hour later, Tonya Barton picked up her phone to receive a call from Dr. Traynor. "Tonya," he began, "we have much to discuss. I'm going to need you to clear your calendar for the rest of this afternoon. Time is ticking."

Lunch duty beckoned, but Mark first needed to confess his sins to the mother bear.

"Let's see now, Mark, you are calling to tell me about your visit this morning," Magda Robreno prophesized.

"Mrs. Robreno, I wasn't even there this morning. I was downtown to give a deposition," he surrendered. "From what Alana tells me, it was bad."

"Yes, and from what Dr. Traynor tells me, it was very bad," she added. "I got quite the earful from him, but I'm used to that. Your people need to do a better job in your absence, Mark. I don't know if my sphere of influence extends much beyond the Area 6 office."

"Mrs. Robreno, I've established a rapport with Dr. Barton. I'm going to call her and try to make this right," he offered.

"You're a grown man," she conceded. "You do what you feel is right under the circumstances, but be prepared. You're entering another arena." She said an abrupt good-bye and then pressed out an extension.

"Alice, come to my office, please." The mother bear then rose from her desk to look out over US 1 where a freshly-smashed armadillo was being tended to by buzzards.

"You obviously have no clue about what or whom you're dealing with, Mark!" Tonya Barton's voiced boomed, forcing him to hold the phone a foot away from his face and well within earshot of Bryan Reinhold, who had arrived in just enough time to witness his making the call. "Those poor children at your school! How dare you allow people like the two I saw to teach in your school! This now becomes about you. This can be a career-ending episode, and I couldn't in good conscience defend you on the basis of what I saw! Shame on you!"

Mark felt like a dog getting the newspaper to the nose for dipping into the Pepperidge Farm Milanos. This woman a few weeks prior had been an understanding and nurturing soul to balance Roger Traynor's call for casualties along the way. She embodied empathy the same way Lady Liberty has carried her torch. Who was this person on the other end of the line? Was this the way the cookie crumbles? She wasn't done.

"Now you listen to me," she continued her tirade. "That man you have as an English teacher needs to be written up," she said, referring to Van Slyke, "and that older woman in the math class I visited obviously needed to retire a long time ago. I certainly hope that they're not representative of your entire faculty. You need to meet with your teachers immediately. Call an emergency meeting this afternoon and read them the riot act! Do you hear me?" she yelled. "Good-bye then."

Short of an occasional "yes" that he could utter when Dr. Barton needed to come up for air, the conversation was one-sided and the singularly most deflating experience of his twenty-two-year career in education. He looked at Bryan Reinhold and asked, "How may I fuck things up for you?"

"I had a question, but I've totally forgotten what it was," he revealed. "Oh yeah! Now I remember. Who the fuck was that bitch on the other line?"

"That bitch, Bryan, is the deputy superintendent of curriculum, and I used to be the principal."

"I've detained you this afternoon because the three-legged dog has resurfaced and needs our help." Mark started the faculty meeting with the metaphor he had created at the beginning of the year. "Some of you are aware that we had some visitors on our campus this morning, and frankly, they weren't impressed with what they saw in a couple of classes. Now, I recognize that grades are due and that has meant giving busy work to meet the deadline, but I've got to tell you, those days are gone. We've entered a whole new era of accountability, and the norms, the rules of the game are changing as I speak." Everyone's eyes were on him as he spoke, and he sensed their indignation at South Demming being called on the carpet for what had been a typical practice across the county.

"You know," Rex Hoffman seized the opportunity, "if they would have walked into my class, they wouldn't have seen much going on. What do they expect when grades are due?" This comment elicited a few nods and the obligatory "Dat's right!" from Larry Jefferson.

Joe Carrera, who had stood to the right of the podium, stepped forward and whispered in Mark's ear, "Magic, it could've been worse. They could've walked into Hoffman's class. It's bad enough that he's a clown, but how do you explain Moe, Larry, and Curly?"

"Look, people," Mark continued, "I'm asking all of you, if you're not already, to plan your instructional blocks to take up the entire period. I'm asking the assistant principals to dedicate more time in classrooms every day, and I'm asking the department chairs to assist anyone who needs help with time management."

At this point, Bryan Reinhold stood up and spoke. "I had the dubious distinction of being in the room when our principal was being chewed on, and it was ugly. He doesn't deserve to be in this situation. We don't deserve to be in this situation. I've been at South Demming all my life, and I'm not going to have us dragged through the mud."

This meeting lasted less than fifteen minutes, but it sufficed to stir the pot and get the room buzzing. Mark watched as they filed out, and he accepted handshakes and shaking heads from his loyalists, including Ron Shipman, David Canales, and the Iceman.

Dr. C waited until everyone left. "Hey, man, what did Barton say to you?" he asked.

"She told me that this might be a career-ending event for me, David." He watched as David contemplated this revelation, and his eyebrows formed an upside down V.

"They're trying to intimidate you, Marko," he said. "Who are they going to get in your place? South Demming would blow up if they tried anything that stupid."

"South Demming could blow up at any moment, David. It's a ticking time bomb!"

On his way home, Mark called Sylvia to prepare her.

"I already heard, and what they're doing is completely unfair," Sylvia began after he shared the debacle. "Beachwood High got a visit, and apparently theirs was a disaster. I can't begin to tell you how disappointed I am in all of them, especially Tonya."

"I got to tell you, Sylvia, that I think my days are numbered here."

"There you go expecting the worst," she countered. "Don't jump to conclusions. I'll talk to Dr. Kreinfeldt tomorrow morning. He's not in his office now. I'm sure he'll put in a good word for you. Mark, you've received no help since you've been there, and look at the cultural change you've made already. Those kids adore and respect you, and the community loves and respects you, and you've done that in such a short amount of time. Hang in there, babe. I'm on my way out the door now."

At seven o'clock the next morning, Dick Van Slyke's haggard face reflected back at him from his old computer screen. He moved about his room and scooped up a few of his belongings like his coffeemaker, his Maxwell House can, a box of coffee filters, and his coffee cup. He packed these in a large paper grocery bag and took them to his car. Going back to his room, he grabbed his briefcase, shut the light switch, and headed toward the main office where he found Mark at his desk going over the first wave of e-mail.

"Well, boss man, I've been doing some soul searching, and I'm kind of glad that yesterday happened."

"If you're trying to cheer me up, you're failing miserably," Mark said as he fantasized about ripping off Van Slyke's head. "Do you care to tell me why you're glad?"

Van Slyke studied him momentarily, and the slight showing of his brown teeth suggested a grin forming. As he began to speak, he alluded to his sticker-decorated briefcase. "You know, I've done a lot of traveling around the world, and I figure, I've got a few more spots on this briefcase reserved for places I haven't seen." He negotiated the 225 combination, turned the briefcase Mark's way so when it popped open, it would serve up his keys and his letter of resignation.

"What's this?" Mark asked.

"It's my going-away present, boss man. I've had it. I'm sixty-three, and I'm too old to work in a shithole like this and for a fucking backstabber like you!" He slammed his keys on the desk and tossed his letter at Mark like a Frisbee. "Whatever time I have left is my time," he said as he walked out of the office and passed Joe Carrera and the Buccaneer statue for the last time.

"Well, Magic, I got to tell you," Carrera started, "Hef tried to get rid of that motherfucker for years, and here you are in a little over a year making it happen. It was worth it hearing him call you a fucking backstabber, but I take extreme exception to the shithole remark. I like this shithole, and I have for years."

"Good riddance to that asshole." Ray Devereaux limped in, also apparently having overheard the key parts of Van Slyke's farewell speech.

"Hey, boss," Bryan Reinhold started before Mark interrupted him.

"Jesus Christ, is there a fucking audience out there?"

"Well, there was," Reinhold confessed, "but we're all in here now, and I was going to say if you need coverage for Dickhead's classes, take me off hallway patrol, and maybe those kids'll learn something for a change."

These were his people validating him in their strange and unique way. Mark smiled for the first time in a while, but he felt like a terminal patient with his intimates lining up to pay their last respects.

The STARS Committee members aligned to form the galaxy defined by Roger Traynor's conference table. Deputies, chiefs, and associates provided their crowded version of the Last Supper as they gnawed on doughnuts, sipped coffee, and laid low in their swivel chairs. Suddenly, above their slouched figures, Roger Traynor entered the room, and his voice straightened their postures in unison as though they were tied to puppeteers' strings.

"Good afternoon, ladies and gentlemen," he began. "We have some very urgent matters to discuss. All of you have been spending quality time in our neediest schools and gathering impressions. I have been made privy to certain situations that would appear to command immediate attention. I'm not about wasting time, so let's get down to business. Magda, what can you tell me about the principal and what the hell is going on at South Demming?"

As she prepared to respond, the mother bear noticed her reflection in the office window behind Traynor. "Well," she started, "the school was five points away from being an F grade last year and has been a D for most of its history. Mr. Mahovlic is very new; he's just completed his first year there, and it's a very high-maintenance place. Attendance and behavior are issues as well."

Roger Traynor's fingers on his right hand did their dance once again, and he stopped them by tucking the last three into his palm, wrapping his thumb tightly over them, and pointing at Robreno with his index finger. "Now, Magda," he began, "let me add the caveat that your ass also is on the line here. It seems as though what you're telling me is we need to make a change in leadership at South Demming."

The mother bear took one more glance at her reflection before speaking. "I believe that we need to give him some more time." She bit her lower lip as she awaited his response.

Eighty percent of the way closed to a fist anyway, Roger Traynor finished the job and pounded on the conference table. The STARS contingent straightened out their postures even more by tightening their asses. "Time? What do you mean by time? We don't have time! Get the paperwork going to get him the hell out of there!" he exploded.

Chief of Testing and Accountability Archibald Kreinfeldt, sitting next to the mother bear, also stole a glance at his reflection, and his neutrality matched his gray suit.

Chief of School Police Harold Starling adjusted his cufflinks and cleared his throat to release some phlegm.

Tonya Barton remained stoic. She already had gotten her earful by not immediately reporting her South Demming visit.

Nick Agnello wore a smirk. An action on his part made it to center stage at the meeting.

As Robreno sighed in acquiescence, Pamela Gratton, the associate superintendent of Area 1, took a sip from her coffee cup and made a proposal. "I'll take him in a heartbeat," she said enthusiastically. All the heads turned toward the end of the table where Gratton sat.

This caught Roger Traynor's attention. "And why is that?" he asked. Again, the heads turned to the opposite end as the tennis game continued.

"Look," Gratton began, "I'm the one who brought him to South Demming in the first place. Most of you know that the principal at Oak Park Elementary is battling cancer. She has taken a leave of absence. We've been expecting the AP over there to handle this alone, and it's not fair to him or the school. I can't spare a director to assume the role. I need someone with experience."

Traynor looked back to Robreno and asked, "Magda, can he run an elementary school?"

Becoming the mother bear once again, she responded. "He can run an elementary school blindfolded."

"Oh, I'm glad I caught you," Archibald Kreinfeldt said to Sylvia, as she was set to call it a day even though night had fallen nearly an hour earlier. "I'm afraid I've gotten some bad news at this meeting." Kreinfeldt recounted the events of the meeting, confirming her worst fears.

"This is absolutely unfair. You know the kind of obstacles he faces," Sylvia began unloading on her boss. "He's gotten no support since he's been there, and he's still making a difference."

"I know. I know," Kreinfeldt acknowledged her sentiments while glancing at his watch.

"So that's it! Nobody can do anything about this! Can you speak to Dr. Traynor?" Sylvia asked.

"I'll tell you what. They ain't no talkin' to him now," Kreinfeldt lapsed. "I'll wait until he calms down and bend his ear."

"Somebody has to do something," Sylvia continued. "How can she be allowed to get away with this? No one can do the job he's done there. Where's the justice? Do they think that community is going to stand for this?"

Kreinfeldt had no answers for these questions, and up until this moment, he had relied heavily on Sylvia to answer most of his questions. He did his best crossover dribble and managed to dodge the trap.

For several minutes, Sylvia sat back in her office chair, collected herself and her purse, and began to head out the door when a visitor arrived.

Noticing the tears in Sylvia's eyes, Pamela Gratton opened appropriately. "I guess you've already heard," she began, "but I promise you we're going to take good care of him in Area 1. We will see to it that he's successful."

"Pam, I appreciate everything you've done, but you need to know that he was building something special at South Demming. Who only gets fifteen months to turn around a school? The sacrifices that man has made and the sleep he has lost. He's poured his heart and soul into that school and its kids. All this is unbelievable! How can this happen? You were at that meeting. Please, I'll keep it confidential, but please tell me who said and did what. I have to know for my sanity."

"Sylvia, I will tell you this much. I had a similar situation—no, a worse situation with Jeannie, the principal at Beachwood High. Their visit was horrendous. When they brought this up, I explained to the group that visiting the day grades are due is counterproductive. I told them that I insisted they come back to see how the school functions on a normal day. In essence, I went to bat for my principal," Gratton explained. "Magda, in my opinion, didn't do enough for your husband, and I have to leave it at that."

Chapter 30

A NEW LEASE

Magda Robreno brushed the dyed black hair from her eyes as she slumped over the paperwork detailing Mark Mahovlic's transfer to Oak Park Elementary School. The accordion-like folds between her eyebrows faced downward and ran parallel to the downward-turned corners of her mouth, which worked in unison with the row of lines between her nose and upper lip. She etched her signature in the requisite spaces, striking as if the pen were a chisel.

Mark sat across from her that Friday and realized that her swivel chair had to be set at the maximum height because she actually looked down at him from her vantage point. Indeed her feet only grazed the floor from this perch she had set.

"Now, Mark, I want you to think of this as a second chance for you, a fresh start," the mother bear began. "I had to pull some strings to get this to happen. Dr. Traynor was ready to put you back in a classroom."

"Mrs. Robreno, I am a professional and will go where I'm needed, but I'll reserve my thoughts with respect to this situation," he answered her abruptly, not letting her know that he was aware she was lying.

"Your wife, on numerous occasions, has let it be known that you were not being supported at South Demming," she started. "I believe that I have provided you with every opportunity to succeed. I selected the best possible mentor for you, and you never took advantage of this.

I, too, have many thoughts regarding this situation, but for the sake of the years we've known each other, I'll bite my tongue."

"Mrs. Robreno, with all due respect, I think if you have an issue with Sylvia, you should address it with her. I'm sure she would be happy to discuss all this with you," Mark answered. This got no reaction from her as she chiseled off the final line and handed him the transfer packet, complete with post-it arrows for his signatures sentencing him to the northernmost portion of the county, some forty miles from his home.

As he read and signed, she spoke of the succession plan. "Jane Rosinski is an excellent veteran principal whom we coaxed out of retirement. She has a record of success in moving schools in a positive direction on the state exam. She also will get tough with teachers who are lax in their performance."

Mark let her talk. What he knew of Jane Rosinski was that her track record began and ended with being an elementary school principal. She was diminutive in stature and completely inexperienced in high school in any capacity. Part of him was glad they chose her because he believed she would fail miserably. The other part of him was very sad for his school. There were no winners on any side or corner of this situation.

"Your last day at South Demming will be Monday, and how it goes will depend upon your professionalism," Robreno continued. "I expect you to introduce her to the staff in an emergency faculty meeting first thing in the morning. I expect you to show her around during the day and be amiable. I expect you to place a positive spin on this. No one is to know about any of this until then. As for the students, I'm advising you to tell them that this move was your choice, that you did this as a decision for your family."

"Mrs. Robreno, some word of this already is out, and you need look no further than your own staff for this. Secretaries know one another, and they talk," Mark revealed. "For the previous two days, people from all over the school and this county have asked me if I'm leaving. I've dodged answering that question, and you can't hold me responsible for that. As for the kids, I will not lie to them. I have been nothing but upfront and straight with them since my arrival; my departure will follow that same path. How can being forty miles from my home be a family move? I'll put a spin on this that will work to some extent, but none of this was my choice, and I believe all this is a huge mistake."

"Nevertheless," she said as she slid off her high chair and stood up to look outside her window, "if anything goes wrong, it will be an indictment against your leadership."

"Unfuckingbelievable, Magic. So the rumors are true? What the hell are they thinking?" Joe Carrera said when he became the first to be informed formally. "There's got to be something we can do."

"I just got back from having to sign the paperwork to be transferred to Oak Park somewhere a day north from here," Mark informed him. "They've got their minds made up that this place needs someone else to steer it."

"So who are we going to get here, Magic? We don't have a say?"

"Don't know her," Mark answered. "It's somebody named Jane Rosinski."

"Who?" Carrera quizzed him.

"They dug up some retired principal from an elementary school who's supposed to take this place to the promised land."

Carrera blew his nose, shook his head, and said, "Please fucking tell me you're shitting me. First of all, Magic, and I apologize to all the women out there, this ain't the stomping ground for a female principal. Now you're telling me she's an elementary school person. Holy shit, Magic, have they lost their minds?"

They sat speechless in the office for a couple of minutes like monks abiding by a vow of silence. They had so much to say to each other and chose to spare the words. The second block bell rang for class change, so Mark excused himself and reached for his radio. "David, meet me on the track. Bring the golf cart."

Scouring the campus, South Demming Park, and the immediate neighborhood during class changes was their ritual together. They often debriefed in the open air and sometimes found solutions or brought rationality to problems. There was no solution to this, their final ride together. David pulled up. Mark got in and said, "Take me to the park; I've got something to tell you."

"Oh no, Marko," David cried out when Mark shared his news. "What is wrong with Robreno? It's like they're trying to make an example out of you and intimidate everyone else," he continued. "They don't care about this place. They don't care about the kids. I am so sorry, man. You don't deserve this. Hell, I don't deserve this. I'm here because you're here."

They pulled into the agriculture field and the dirt road leading back to campus. Behind them they could hear the hum of a tractor pulling a wagonload of watermelons down 165th Avenue. The migrant workers were picking beans, and it was a grand early fall morning. They stirred up some dust from the road that quickly trailed off on a light, cool breeze, and the sun's beams poked their way through the tall oaks to grasp them in warmth.

They parked under one and sat for a moment until David spoke. "It's like a painting out here, man," David offered his spiritual side. "This is probably one of the worst days of your life, yet this might be the most beautiful morning of the year. That's God telling you that everything is going to be okay, my friend. He has a plan for you."

For the last time, he watched as the football soared end over end; this time the old and the new, the familiar and the unknown, and the reason and the rhyme exchanged places as they tumbled downward through a crisp September night. This time the kick was too deep, and there was no return.

"The kids are planning to protest on Monday," Kim Bennett told Sylvia on the sideline.

"Kim, no one is supposed to know about this even though it appears everyone already does," Sylvia revealed. "Mark, I'm sure, appreciates the support, but I know he won't approve of any protest."

"They've made up some signs, and they're going to be all over the campus Monday morning," Bennett continued. "They've arranged for a sign-hanging party late Sunday night to make this happen."

When Sylvia informed him of this conversation, Mark went to Bennett and said, "Look, Kim. The sign thing isn't a good idea. The region office will think it's something I've orchestrated, and it's got the potential to arouse some strong emotions and create a safety issue, which is my biggest concern."

Bennett looked at him benevolently as her round eyes welled up and released tears. She wiped these off with both palms, her hands ending in a prayer pose, which she held pointed in his direction, and she said, "Well, you're not my boss anymore, so you can't tell me what to do." She ran off to her cheerleaders before he could react.

"You know what? Good for her!" Sylvia exclaimed. "At this point, why should you give a shit what the region thinks? Let them do whatever they want out of their love and respect for you. Hell, let the fucking news people come out for all I care! Let them see the fight that they've started."

Football took a backseat this night as South Demming disposed of Eastridge High 27–7. Mark needed to get out of Harnett Field, so Sylvia and he left early. They barely talked on the way home until she asked him, "So, what are you thinking?"

"I'm thinking that I'm tired, and I want to drink myself to sleep," he started. "In the long run, Robreno and all the other pieces of shit that got dirty with this have probably done me a favor. South Demming already has taken years off my life. The place will remain broken as long as it's viewed as being broken, and nobody, including me, at this point, gives a shit."

"You don't mean that," Sylvia said. "You make sure you keep your head held high and do what you feel is right come Monday."

"You're right. I don't mean that," he agreed. "I'm just numb to all this now."

Moments later, the train saw to it that their early departure would be evened out by its untimely arrival. They discontinued their conversation and went about the business of counting the cars as though they were rosary beads.

Looking like a stretch of highway just before the exit to some little town, the South Demming fence lines served as billboards, but their ads weren't about where to sleep, where to eat, or where to get gas. They were about loyalty, justice, and the intangibles that can't be put in writing but can be put into practice. At six in the morning, Mark walked with Joe Carrera, who brought a flashlight so they could do some reading.

"Leave our Principal alone!" "Mr. M Rocks my Socks!" "No M, No Uniforms." "Did Anyone Think to Ask Us?" These were a few of the sentiments that unlike highway billboards didn't bring together strangers; they brought together a community of different colors, different languages, and different socioeconomic circumstances that found a sameness that transcended barriers. Mark never had felt more powerful, and he never had felt so weak.

"The people have spoken, Magic!" Carrera exclaimed. "This doesn't have to be over. The students are staging a walkout this afternoon, and Ron Shipman needs to talk to you. He is putting together a town hall meeting for this Friday, and I've spoken to Mayor Warren, and he's reserved Hanford City Hall for us. All you got to do, Magic, is give it your blessings."

"At this point, Joe," Mark answered, "I don't like the idea of a walkout for safety reasons, but I'm starting to feel a little selfish with respect to a town hall meeting. I don't think it will do a damn bit of good, but if it makes certain people squirm, then I'm all for it. I just can't attend it."

"That's all I needed to hear," Carrera explained. "Shipman is going to arrange the format, and I'm going to see to it that Hanford City Hall has standing room only, ha ha!"

"Joe, I got to go to my office and figure out what I'm going to say, and all this shit has got to come down," he said, pointing to the signs, which included some that dangled from the highest point of the auditorium. "Could you get with Larry and Don when they get in and have them get the custodial staff to take them down?"

"I'll do that, Magic, but why?" Carrera gave out his best pained look that included his bushy eyebrows forming a V and his mouth shaping an anguished expression.

"Because when whomever the area sends to accompany my replacement gets here, I'll get blamed for giving her an unwelcomed arrival. That's just how it is, but tell them to save the signs. They're still appreciated."

At 7:35 a.m., Mark took the PA mike and addressed South Demming. "Good morning, Bucs. By now, many of you have heard that I'm being transferred to another school in the county. Please know that this was not my choice, and I can't begin to tell you how much I will miss all of you, but that being said, principals work at the discretion of the superintendent. There's a school north of us that needs me, and I'm being called into duty there. Change is never easy, but it is part of life. I've been hearing that some of you are planning on staging a walkout. This is not how I want you to show your respect for me. Please stay in your classes today. I expect each of you to welcome your new principal, Ms. Rosinski, just as you welcomed me last year. Everyone deserves a chance to prove their worth. Today is my last day. I'll be showing Ms. Rosinski around; I'll be out in the lunch pavilion. Please say hello to her, but don't forget to say good-bye to me."

"Well done, Mr. M," Alice Chandler-Lopez said as he concluded. Like ill-fitting handcuffs, she attached herself to him just as she did when he gave a similar speech to his faculty and staff a half hour earlier.

Jane Rosinski was as pleasant as she was misguided. She quizzed Mark about procedural things such as their exceptional student education (ESE) and English for speakers of other languages (ESOL) files, and if he wouldn't mind showing her the year's school-based budget system (SBBS) and a copy of their personnel allocation report (PAR). It became clear to him that she was a manager of systems and was more comfortable surrounding herself with acronyms than she was surrounded by people. She never asked him about the students and how they were and what they needed. He had to force her out of the office for a couple of hours to go visit some classes and mingle during class changes. There she got to see the spontaneous outpouring of warmth and affection for him as he shook hands, accepted hugs, and witnessed the tears that poured out from the weak and strong, black and white, young and old, and all the other traits, hues, and stages that characterized his belief in South Demming.

"These students absolutely adore you," Rosinski said to him as lunchtime approached. "From what I've heard of this place, I didn't think it could be this way. Why in the hell are they replacing you?

There's no way I'll be able to be you." Within this sincerity hid her fear, and while Mark appreciated her commentary, he pitied what he perceived to be her cowardice.

Lunchtime came, and accompanied by Rosinski and a skulking Chandler-Lopez who found some shade under one of the trees perpendicular to Mark's post, he presided over the pavilion for the last time.

"Hey, boss"—the Iceman came up to shake his hand—"who is that mean-looking lady over there?" Ice was referring to Chandler-Lopez, whose squinting in the daylight deepened her forehead exclamation point to the extent that it resembled a butt crack hovering over eyebrows.

"That's my boss. She's here to see to it that everything runs smoothly and that I don't do something to fuck up the master plan."

"Well, she's one nasty-looking lady," Ice continued, "and she's shit out of luck because you need to know that after last lunch and the bell for third block, the whole fucking student body is walking out in your honor."

Mark pondered the Iceman's revelation and weighed it against Robreno's caveat that the day's unraveling would be testimony to his leadership, and he shook his head and smiled. "Ice, see if Hey You can part with his megaphone; we're only ten minutes from D-Day here. Get the golf cart and bring it to the track." Mark then gave his last directive via the radio. "All radio holders, please be sure to be at your posts. We may have some reluctance to go to class. You may need to follow the students."

Chandler-Lopez, who had helped herself to a spare radio, approached him. "Mark, is there something going on that I need to know about?"

"Well, I'm hearing that the kids might be staging a walkout despite what I said this morning," Mark said as he stared at her awful forehead that now resembled a canal with its rivulets of sweat.

"And what do you intend to do about this?" she raised her voice and held her free hand at her hips.

Enjoying her discomfort, he replied, "I'm going to watch."

"And that's your answer? Do you realize how dangerous this can be?" She kept feeding him material.

"Did anyone from the area office realize the can of worms they might be opening up?" he questioned her question. "I certainly didn't plan any of this. I didn't ask for this. This is all bullshit, and you know that better than anyone! Apparently, I can't stop them from walking out, but I bet I'm the only one who can get them to go back."

Chandler-Lopez followed him but stayed in the social studies wing as he ventured out to the golf cart. He stood by it with his arms folded atop its roof and watched as several hundred kids took the risk of not going to class to spend a little more time with their principal. They carried the signs that they made. Joe Carrera had given them to Kim Bennett, who returned them to their creators. His personal favorite was "No M; No Uniforms." Now probably five to six hundred strong, they began clapping loudly, looking in their principal's direction, looking for him to give them something beyond good-bye.

Before addressing them, Mark took stock of the adults in his proximity. Lou Cruz came up to him, shook his hand, and gave him a hug. This was the gesture from an officer of the peace and drew applause from the students. The Iceman, Joe Carrera, and David Canales took turns patting him on the back and vicariously taking in his view. Mike Dale from the *Hanford News Leader* shook his hand and asked him if he could get some pictures. Chandler-Lopez kept her distance and was busily engaged on her cell phone, no doubt reporting chaos.

Taking the megaphone, Mark began, "First of all, let me get all of you who are kind of spread out to come over here by me." He watched as Lou, Bryan Reinhold, Ray Devereaux, Ron Shipman, and Nate Judson managed to herd the students into a surprisingly efficient oval by the golf cart. Within a minute, Mark began to speak, and his audience gave him their total attention.

"First of all, I can't begin to tell you how much I am awed and touched by your outpouring of love for me." Their cheers had him pacing his words like a political candidate addressing his constituents, only he wasn't running for office; he was being run out of office. "I'll never forget our short time together and how much it has meant to me to have the honor of being your principal at South Demming." Riding out another gust of affection, he said, "The folks who are my bosses believe how this day ends up will be a mark on what kind of leader I am, so I need one last favor from you. Please continue to do your best, stay peaceful and violence free, come to school every day, and I'm asking you, out of respect for me, to please now go back to your classes. You guys are the best!"

He watched as they rose as one and branched out in tributaries toward their classrooms. He accepted a few handshakes, a few hugs, acknowledged a few tears, and continued watching. He glanced at Chandler-Lopez, who again was on her phone, and wondered if the mother bear was taking a shit on the other end.

Mark enjoyed seeing her helpless and panicky, but his self-indulgence was interrupted by one final gesture. A clean-cut young black man clad in khaki pants and a neatly tucked-in white polo shirt tapped him on his shoulder, held out his arms with palms up, and began smiling and circling him, smugly nodding his head. At first, he didn't quite recognize him because his smile was minus a gold grille that was his trademark, and he had allowed the razor-cut hair designs to grow out and become indistinguishable. The uniform also was a new twist for him. He just stared and smiled.

"If this is what it takes to keep you here, then you can count me in!" He then rushed toward Mark as if to tackle him and placed his head into the middle of his chest as he gave him a quick, tight hug and ran away. Mark looked down at his shirt where the young man had placed his head and saw two tiny wet spots where his eyes had been. David St. Jean remained the architect of the unexpected.

Mark went back to his office with the hope of being left alone for his final two hours at South Demming. Instead he was greeted by David Canales, Joe Carrera, Ron Shipman, Cathy Acker, Ken Ferguson, and Bryan Reinhold. Reinhold sat at his desk with his feet up and was the first to speak.

"Sorry, boss. I'm just keeping the seat warm for you," he said. As he got up, he let loose an audible fart. "And trying to let in some fresh air as well."

"Well, my flatulent fat friend," Mark started, "you won't be doing that for me anymore. I guess you guys are here to help me pack my shit and take it to the truck, right?"

David was quick to respond to that idea. "Marko, leave everything here. Why should you go out with your tail tucked between your legs carrying your stuff? I've got boxes. I'll pack it up tonight, take it home, and bring it to your house over the next weekend. I won't let you be seen carrying your stuff out. They've tried to rob you of your dignity, and they couldn't succeed. Don't let them see you in any other light."

"They're already long gone, David. I guess Rosinski probably has to be sworn in at the area office and sign some shit as well."

Reinhold gave Mark a hug and said, "I'm going to miss you, big man," and he handed him a large plastic bag.

"What's this for?"

"Look inside. I already know what it is, so I won't be surprised," Bryan said.

Mark pulled out a jersey from the bag. It had "South Demming Buccaneers" on the front, and on the back where a name might be it had, "The Big Man." Underneath that was the number one.

Looking at all of them, Mark said, "I'm never going to forget you guys and everything you've done for me while I've been here. I'm going to find a frame for this."

"That'll be seventy-five dollars," Reinhold said. "We don't take personal checks." He walked out laughing, followed by everybody but Carrera and Shipman, who had on their game faces.

"Magic," Carrera began as he had thousands of conversations before, "we've got some unfinished business. You're a gentleman with a lot of class, and I know you don't want to bring any more attention to yourself and your family, but your fading off into the sunset is for cowboys, and you're a Buccaneer. Somebody has to take a sword up the ass for this."

"This has something to do with that town hall meeting you mentioned this morning?" Mark asked.

"Yes, it does, and I'm going to let Ron talk to you about it. I don't do good-byes, Magic, and we'll be seeing plenty of each other, so I'm just leaving now. I'll call you tomorrow." Carrera walked out wiping his eyes.

"Mark, what I've got planned only will happen with your okay, your blessing."

"Ron, I appreciate the gesture, and while I won't be there, you can count on me in spirit. Tell me what you have planned."

As Shipman laid out the plan, Mark thought it fitting that he, a bastion of free speech, the right to assemble, and the right to bear arms, be at least his last line of defense. He thought of his willingness to put all this together as he counted rail cars one more time, taking sharp notice this time of the ones that had graffiti on them. When this phenomenon became an epidemic two decades earlier, a young offender whom he had caught spray-painting a bathroom stall told him that fame was his driving force, and now Mark wondered to what extent that young man had evolved, and what, if anything, had he done since to leave an impression that could not be painted over.

With its very white pillars, steep concrete-step approach, and proudly waving American flag, Hanford City Hall remained the showpiece building among a handful of historically preserved edifices in the Old Town section. The eight pillars stood tall and plain, beginning and ending in bowls of concrete. Great care had been taken over the years to see to it that its façade remained pristine and, above all, white. Not until this unprecedented mid-September evening fifty-five years in the making did it begin to show its age as its auditorium swelled to the three-hundred-seat capacity, forcing another two hundred or so people to stand along the aisles or spill into the lobby or, worse yet, to wait outside where a closed-circuit television would deliver the happenings within. City hall had been a trusted venue for more than half a century, but the occasion on this night rendered it more dated than venerable.

Vicki Brown stood outside in the spill-out area. Fifty years ago, that's as far as her people would have gotten, but time had progressed even as it stood still in the black-and-white photos of city hall that decorated its lobby. Prior to the start of the town hall meeting, Brown was looking for some angle to complement the main story, and she struck up an off-camera conversation with an old man. Well into his eighties, he was hunched over a cane that had a dog leash wrapped around its handle, and at its end was a male retriever that was white in the muzzle and missing its right rear leg. "Excuse me, sir, but what brings you to this town hall meeting tonight?" Brown began.

The old man took off a weather-worn baseball cap, righted his posture as much as his aged spine would allow, and began scratching his full head of white hair. He fixed his crinkly eyes on Brown and said, "A good man brings me here, I know. Lived in this community all my life, so I figured I'd show him my support."

"And who's this?" Brown asked about the dog while bending down to pet him.

"Why, this is the only friend I got left in this world," the old man revealed. "Used to chase garbage trucks until one took his back leg a while back. Vet told me then I should put him down, but I wasn't about to do that. The two of us get along just fine, but whatever you do, don't ask him to shake your hand. He falls for that every time. Get it? Falls." The old man broke into a wheezing laughter that provoked a coughing fit.

"I'm looking to interview some people here as part of the news story," Brown shared once the old man caught his breath. "Would you mind if I brought my camera man here and we talked live? You'd be on TV!"

"Young lady, talking live beats the alternative. Why don't you do that?" the old man suggested.

Brown took a few minutes to negotiate the maze created by the crowd and reach her film crew. They followed her to where the old man had been, but he was gone and nowhere to be seen among the masses. "I don't get it," Brown told her cameraman after looking for him a few minutes. "He couldn't have gotten too far given his condition, but I don't see him anywhere. Damn!"

The lobby area was congested with teenagers and adults, some of whom were displaying homemade signs on poster board. Larry Jefferson and Joe Carrera shared the step up to the double-door entry and balanced a sign on their laps that said, "We Love Our Principal." There was a time when city hall wouldn't have them share the same water fountain, let alone the same sentiments. Another sign resting against a lobby table read, "Who gets only one year to fix decades of neglect?"

Outside again, the crowd suddenly parted like rows of dominoes pushed in opposite directions, making a path for the arrival of Roger Traynor, who on this evening was accompanied by Tonya Barton, Magda Robreno, and Alice Chandler-Lopez. All were dressed in business attire accessorized with irritation. Traynor's tie rested atop his prosperous midsection that jiggled when he used both of his arms to fling open the double-door entry and didn't bother to hold it open for the women in his tow. The trio of middle-aged ladies wore single-color dresses in burgundy, olive, and yellow, respectively, and as they followed one another in close proximity, they resembled a traffic light. This group went down the aisle separating the two sections of seating, negotiated the three steps to get on stage, and sat on the right side of a podium occupied by Ron Shipman, whose blue blazer was accented with a gray shirt, blue tie, and gray pants. The color choices were conscious arrangements for how he viewed the polarity of the occasion. He peered over his reading glasses to acknowledge the district personnel's arrival.

Already seated on the opposite side of the podium was Jane Rosinski in a black-and-white striped dress, Alana Tavares sporting a pin-striped charcoal pantsuit, and David Canales, whose seated position placed great strain on the stitching of his black two-piece.

"Ladies and gentlemen, please be seated," Shipman said from the comfort of his podium. "Thank you for taking the time to show and voice your support." Looking at the contingent to his left, he added, "Thank you for agreeing to hear our concerns."

This acknowledgment drew some boos from the audience, causing Shipman to exercise his tact as a moderator and set the ground rules for the evening. "Ladies and gentlemen, while we may not be in agreement with the school district folks on my left, please remember that they've agreed to hear us out, and for that, they deserve our respect. The rules of engagement are quite simple. Audience members are invited to share their sentiments regarding this decision and its impact. They each will be given a maximum of three minutes. We will do this for thirty minutes or until all those wishing to speak have been heard, whichever comes first. After their voices are heard, the district personnel will respond, and we'll open the floor for questions."

"I feel like we're being used as human shields," David Canales whispered to Alana Tavares, who was seated to his left and closest to the podium. Referencing Jane Rosinski, he added, "Why bring her here?"

Tavares nodded her head but provided a "Shush. They're getting ready to start."

"Will those who have indicated they will speak please come to the front of the stage," Shipman requested. Seven people made their way forward to represent the gathering's sentiments. Several among these were handpicked days ago by Shipman.

Dressed in maid's garb, a middle-aged and charcoal-gray-haired black woman was the first to speak. "Mr. Superintendent, this man that you sent away was the first principal that my son ever respected. He used to skip school and get failing grades. This man was the first to encourage my boy, and now that he ain't here, my son don't want to go to school. He's a special-needs child, but for the first time in his life, he was made to feel special. Test scores won't matter to my boy, and they can't measure what this man has meant to this school." This drew applause from the audience and provided segue for the next speaker.

Her dress swayed as she walked and settled into place over her taut body when she reached the dais located at the foot of the stage. Her strawberry-blonde hair was the perfect complement to her smooth, light complexion. Her appearance commanded attention, but her words demanded it. "Dr. Traynor, my name is Joy Mathews, and I am a graduate of South Demming, class of 1985. My son Matt played football and graduated from South Demming last year. I have been actively involved as the president of the Quarterback Club and have twin boys who are scheduled to attend South Demming next year, and I'm seriously considering sending them to a private school." She went on to characterize the school's past as one of violence and racial discord and briefly outlined the events that led up to an on-campus riot during her senior year. "The man you've dismissed as principal brought spirit to the school," she continued. "He made it a safer place; he truly cared about all the students, and respect for his leadership brought our diverse population together. You've made a tremendous mistake, and I'm asking you to reconsider." Again the crowd applauded and began clapping in unison until the next speaker was invited to step forward.

The young, clean-cut black man dressed conservatively in khaki pants and a polo shirt, but as he approached the dais, his gait revealed a semblance of arrogance and nonconformity. David St. Jean could shed an image but not an essence. He spoke fluidly and naturally. "My name's David, and I'm on track to graduate this year. I've even got a shot to get a scholarship for my academics. Mr. M—that's what everybody calls him—put up with a lot of garbage from me because he believed in me. I did a lot of things to disrespect him and this school, but he saw something in me that nobody before him did. I believe he saved me; now I'm asking you to save him, please!" About fifty students sitting in the back stood up and applauded loudly, and there was more.

Jose "Pep" Garces came to Hanford in 1963, a time when city hall was white within and without and a time when his people were permitted no voice in either of the two languages that he now commanded. He had walked up the steep steps, two at a time, determined to be heard. "My name is Jose Garces," he began, "and I'm a graduate, South Demming class of 1973." Knowing that there were those standing outside who did not speak English, he took a political moment to outline the circumstances of their families and characterize their struggle. He went on to read from a prepared statement. "I'm the executive director of the Migrant Education Program for this county and a proud Mexican American. You haven't exiled a principal, my friends; you've dismissed an ambassador. He came here under the most trying of circumstances, having to repair a relationship between the Mexican migrant community and the school system, thanks to the unconscionable actions of your school police toward our children. He presided over a walkout protesting US immigration policies and made all the right decisions before and after to guard students' rights to assemble peacefully. To you, he is disposable; to the Mexican community of Hanford, he is a hero! Everybody is here for the same reason. I hope you're listening. Reverse this decision. You can do it! Si, se puede!"

From the more comfortable open spaces outside the Hanford City Hall, a chant arose among those who understood the meaning. "Si, se puede. Si, se puede. Si, se puede."

It was loud enough to be heard by those within the auditorium, particularly the superintendent of schools whose temper was beginning to flare. After a few more heartfelt offerings that further inflamed the gathering's heated psyche, Roger Traynor could stand no more and succumbed to his torturers. "Magda, Goddamn it!" he said in the ear of the Area 6 associate superintendent. "You clearly don't know your people or the community you serve. This is a nightmare!"

"Ladies and gentlemen," Ron Shipman interjected. "I believe your time is up, and at this point, I'm inviting our guests from the district to respond."

Magda Robreno swallowed hard and felt a bead of sweat trickle down her back. "While I respect all your sentiments," she started, carefully enunciating each syllable, "we are a results-oriented organization, and South Demming was five points away from becoming an F school. Action needed to be taken."

Tugging at his tie and undoing the first top button of his shirt, Ron Shipman interrupted, "Mrs. Robreno, hasn't South Demming been a D school for every year that the state exam has existed?"

"Why, yes, but—" Robreno tried to get in a word edgewise to no avail as Shipman was just warming up.

"Let me ask you this, then. Do you know what percentage of students at South Demming goes to college?"

"No, I do not."

Shipman continued, "Are you aware of how many academic scholarships were awarded just this past year to South Demming students?"

"I do not have those statistics with me, sir," Robreno conceded. The crowd now was becoming more derisive with each succeeding question, with some resorting to laughter.

"Were you aware that the school's mock trial team has won two state championships in the past three years?"

Roger Traynor had heard enough and walked to the podium where Shipman stood and spoke into the microphone, "Mr. Shipman, I thought this was a public forum and not a debate. I thought that you were the moderator; instead you're presiding over a lynching." This comment drew boos from the crowd.

"With all due respect, Dr. Traynor, it is our former principal who has been lynched," Shipman said, and the crowd stood to applaud.

"Well, I can see that there is no possibility for constructive dialogue here," Traynor stated. "Bottom line is that the paperwork is in, and the man has been transferred to another school. He had his chances here. He had his time." He then motioned for the other members of his party to rise and said over the din, "Let's get the hell out of here. I'm going to need to see all of you in my office, 8:00 a.m. tomorrow."

The domino effect again came into play as the people arranged their makeshift passage, and the superintendent and his contingent weeded their way through the crowd.

Vicki Brown had some film editing to do if this was to make it to the eleven o'clock edition. She got her backdrop shots, she recorded her opening and ending, and she could provide the vignettes. All packed and ready to go, she and her crew were among the last few left in the old building. As they exited, she noticed the old man and his dog one more time. They were out of earshot walking down the old cobblestone street until they entered the tunnel formed by adjoining oak trees on opposite sides and were absorbed by the night.

Massive oak trees, well-used picnic tables, and a large green pond represented the comforts of Oak Park, a little haven untouched by time but witness to great change on its periphery. Once serving a prosperous middle-class Anglo and Jewish community, the neighborhood's sixties style ranch homes were trendy, and for those of conservative ambition, they were emblematic of the American dream. But even the oak trees in their strength and splendor couldn't forestall the winds that blew in a migration of people aboard primitive vessels who arrived upon the shores seeking political asylum. With a pioneer spirit, they began to carve out a niche as has been typical with most immigration patterns. In the eighties, Oak Park became a neighborhood in transition. By the nineties, a burgeoning Haitian community helped create a new real estate market that turned single-family homes into multiple-family dwellings supported by combined incomes brought in from busing tables in restaurants, cleaning hotel rooms, and driving yellow cabs. The Haitians were incredibly hardworking people, and their children represented their hopes and dreams. Most came with respect and humility, but as characterized in Ron Shipman's class, they were viewed quite differently from their Cuban counterparts, and like the trees that framed this enclave, their roots could only spread so far. Oak Park became one of several predominantly Haitian communities, all located on the northernmost tip of the county, Magda Robreno's Siberia.

The click-clack of oblong blocks pounding picnic tables provided a Caribbean beat, and the wind whooshing through the trees played accompanying music as Oak Park hosted its ritual 8:30 a.m. dominoes competition. The community elders enthusiastically slammed their dominoes into strategic positions and spoke loudly to one another in their native Creole. On this morning, two games were going on, and the participants seemed oblivious to the children beginning to line up in stations along a basketball court that constituted the back of the elementary school. A black fortyish adult female in gym shorts periodically blew a whistle to herd strays back into their groupings. The school bell supplanted the whistle, and the children rose in unison to meet their teachers lined up along the court's baseline. So began the ritual that led the captives to any one of three continuums that housed multiple classrooms, and this efficient and sterile arrangement was resuscitated in this manner on a daily basis.

The hallways were brightened by the excited faces of little black and brown children who revered their new principal unconditionally as they breathlessly arrived at their classroom doors. Having run just beyond the reigns of their instructors as if his appearance gave them permission to do so, they smiled, they waved, and the older ones gave him high fives. Mark fancied himself as the first person in recorded history to have been exiled to a place that provided him with instant celebrity status. Still, he hated being at Oak Park Elementary more than he hated anything in his life, and he didn't want or deserve to be loved.

So many people had told him that everything happens for a reason and that there is a master plan laid out for all of us. He believed that his disenchantment even in the face of this warm welcome was a telling emotion. He believed it was his time to get out of Demming and not hurt these children and their teachers. They deserved better. Mark prepared to walk away and never return, but as he moved his way toward the main office, he felt a little hand slip into his. He turned to see a doe-eyed, beautiful little five-year-old girl holding his hand and smiling up at him. He felt like Frankenstein's monster as she raised his hand and held it tightly to her cheek.

"She usually is afraid of anyone new," her teacher told him as she gently took the little girl by the other hand and led her to class. The teacher began walking the girl a few steps toward the classroom, and remembering something, she stopped, turned around, and said, "She doesn't have a father anymore; he left."

As Mark absorbed this revelation, another child, perhaps a six-year-old male, broke free from his teacher's grasp and ran toward him, almost losing his balance in the process. He was in a state of hysteria with a face flooded by tears and a pool of mucus running into his mouth and down his chin. He wailed as if he had a severed limb.

"I'm so sorry," his teacher apologized in advance of Mark's detective work. "He's still adjusting," she said.

"What's wrong?" Mark asked him, thinking that something horrible must have occurred.

The boy grabbed his hand with both of his and attempted to drag him in the direction of another boy toward whom he now pointed. "Dat, dat, boy," he stuttered, "he, he, he told me nah-nee, nah-nee, boo-boo."

He broke out into another hysterical cry that was so loud Mark felt like giving him a slap. Instead, he just looked down at him and said, "Kid, you think you've got problems?"

Chapter 31

HOPES AND DREAMS

The sun rose brilliantly but could not eclipse the darkness. Instead, it served as a spotlight. It settled first on the grassy area framing the canal. There were four blue-eyed, blond-haired children, two boys and two girls, sitting on blankets, pointing and laughing. Probably no more than five years old and dressed completely in white, they took great joy in seeing Nelson Taylor grab Leisy Pinto's arm and force her to jump with him into the canal. They resurfaced with T-shirts and blue jeans soaked and their hair plastered to their heads. The spotlight framed their perfect faces as they splashed each other and stole just one more kiss. Now panning away to the left of the couple, the spotlight captured Alexis Sanchez, who did her best cannonball to splash them, and when she reemerged, it illuminated her arms, which were free of scars and raised triumphantly. Now it followed the path of a Frisbee that led a splendid and athletic golden retriever to an inevitable soaking. The dog swam with the Frisbee in its mouth and emerged on the grass to shake its matted fur and make a delivery at the foot of a middle-aged gentleman wearing a baseball cap. He, too, laughed heartily as he acknowledged the animal. "That was one heck of a fetch, boy," he said. "I've got to shake your hand for that one!" With that, the dog gave him his paw, causing the man to laugh so hard that he nearly choked on his joy.

As if to improve the vista, a large cloth suddenly began wiping away the darkness, thus releasing sunlight everywhere. Peering from the outside of the windshield, the window washer sprayed a final layer of cleansing mist and said, "There are two sides to every story, boss. This is the other side, but for you, it's just a wake-up call."

For three more nights, Mark had the same dream, and with each succession a greater calm and clarity enveloped him. For Saturday morning, he awakened with a single purpose and picked up the phone to make a breakfast date with Manny Hernandez.

With a hearty breakfast fueling their musings, Mark and Manny talked about the less-troubled days of being teachers and about the obstacles they faced as administrators, deftly avoiding the singular subject of him until the agony was so great that Manny had to come out with it.

"Marko," he said, "what the hell happened with you over there?"

"Manny, that's a long, long story, and I'll probably write a book about it one day, but this isn't the place to talk about it. I've got an idea."

They went to Mark's car, and he drove them two miles to a strip mall that ran perpendicular to the set of railroad tracks that Manny had wondered about five years earlier. At first, he seemed baffled that Mark stopped there until they got out, and he followed him across the street to the tracks. From this vantage point, they extended so far that they appeared to meet the sky.

"You remember the question you asked me about these tracks?" Mark asked Manny as he pointed at them and continued raising his hand until it pointed toward the horizon.

"Yeah, actually I do remember," he answered.

"You got a little time left this morning?" Mark asked.

"Let's go," he said. "I've got to break in these shoes anyway."

For the next hour, Mark shared his story with Manny as they walked along the tracks. On that morning, they never discovered where the tracks went because the horizon continued to stretch, always out of their reach, like the sultry summer mirage of water resting atop an asphalt highway. The funny thing about it was they knew that going in.

Printed in the United States
By Bookmasters